Eric took his f   set of arpeggios.

Kayla grinned. "I knew you'd think of something, Eric! What are you going to do, fly us over the gate or something?"

"Better than that," he muttered. "I'm calling the cavalry."

. . . He knew exactly the tune to play: *Danse Macabre*. The first notes were deceptively soft, the calm before the storm. . . . Then the violin solo, the notes hammering down like nails in a coffin, followed by the melody, faster and harsher. . . .

He could feel it starting around him, the gathering of tension in the air, whispers of sound beyond normal human hearing. The shadows on the grass, visibly darkening as he played, slowly rising from the ground. Fingers of cold ran down his back, but he ignored them, concentrating on the music.

"Eric, what in the hell are you doing?" Kayla looked around in alarm at the thickening shadows around them.

He wanted to say something to calm her, but he could feel his Nightflyers testing his power over them, tugging at their leashes, and he knew what would happen if they escaped his control, even for a moment.

No choice. He was in it; he'd have to finish it. There were only two ways to get out of this one. A winner, or Nightflyer-chow. He stood up, and started toward the front gate. "*Now* we're going to rescue them," he said, with *far* more confidence than he felt, his shadow-troops adrift behind him.

SUMMONED TO TOURNEY

MERCEDES LACKEY

ELLEN GUON

AN URBAN FANTASY

BAEN
FANTASY

A Baen Books Original

Baen Publishing Enterprises
P.O. Box 1403
Riverdale, NY 10471

ISBN: 0-671-72122-4

Cover art by Larry Dixon

First Printing, June 1992

Printed in the United States of America

Distributed by Simon & Schuster
1230 Avenue of the Americas
New York, NY 10020

*Dedicated to the memory
of the victims of the Loma
Prieta earthquake, October, 1989,
and other victims of natural
disasters around the world*

● CHAPTER ONE

The Mountain Top

Leaves whispered in a breath of breeze, as the early morning sun crept across the hills of San Francisco. A starling perched on the eaves of a four-story townhouse chirped in blissful appreciation of the sun on his back, the gentle breeze, the perfect Northern California morning. This house on a hill had a wonderful view of the Bay and the famous Bridge which was not being sufficiently appreciated by the two-legged being below him. There was still fog on the Bay, though it had crept down the hill just before dawn; the towers of the Bridge rose above the downy sea of fog like the towers of lost Ys. Sun shone out of a near-cloudless sky, making the pearlescent fog glow faintly.

Clank.

"Sonuva*BITCH.*"

The starling fluttered its wings in startlement and gazed warily down through the green leaves at the odd, blond-haired, pointy-eared creature that had made both noises. Korendil, Knight of Elfhame Sun-Descending, Magus Minor, Envoy to Elfhame Mist-Hold, and firstborn Child of Danaan beyond the Sundering Sea, let out another paint-blistering oath that frightened the starling above him into flight.

Korendil, Knight of Elfhame Sun-Descending, was not communicating well with the hot tub.

He considered kicking it, remembered that he was barefooted, and thought better of the idea. He leveled an angry glance at the recalcitrant object instead.

"I primed your pump," he said to it, resentfully. "Thomas *swore* to me that your motor is repaired. I saw to it that the heater was working myself. *So why will you not perform?*"

It would all be so much easier if Beth and Eric would permit him to attend to these things by magic — there would be no need for pumps or heaters or other-arcane mysteries of Cold Iron and electricity. The ancient (as these things were reckoned in California) cedar hot tub would be even now bubbling merrily away, heating for the house-warming/Faire Opening party tonight. But no, they had flatly forbidden any such thing, even so simple an act as kenning and reproducing a paltry few fifty-dollar bills to ease their way.

"We have to keep a low profile, Kory," Beth kept saying. "The Feds are looking for us. There are things we can do, and things we can't do — passing fifty-dollar bills with the same serial numbers and having appliances that work without being plugged in are a couple of things we can't do. It wouldn't surprise me to know that the Feds have caught on to the elven trick of money-kenning. If the Feds found L.A. bills up here, or heard about some strange people who don't seem to need electricity, they'll be on us like fleas on a hound."

"But I do not understand why these Feds should be looking for us — " he had said, puzzled. "There was nothing for them to find in Griffith Park."

"They don't have an explanation for what happened to — to Phil," Beth had replied, her voice breaking a little, as it always did when she spoke of the old animator who had been her friend. "They don't have one for what happened to my apartment, either — or to Eric's. They don't like things they can't explain. Eric and I are the common links to all three places, and right now they'd like nothing better than to trump up some kind of charge that all three of us were involved in a drug ring or something, just to get the mystery off the books."

"And you know they were looking for Beth when the fight at the park was over," Eric had put in, mildly. "I doubt they've given up on that. Especially if they have a warrant."

Kory had shaken his head, unable to understand such blind thinking — but he had been forced to agree to abide by his friends' rules. It had been hard, though, especially this past winter when it had become so hard to earn money, and Beth and Eric had gone about with long faces, sometimes quarreling out of worry. He had feared for all of them, then, and not from these "Feds." He had feared that love would turn bitter in their hearts, that they must regret ever seeing him. It had been hard to keep from working magic then, and he had only refrained because he had known they *must* feel it was necessary, since they had gone to such elaborate lengths to keep their names from appearing in any official records.

Take this house, for instance. Officially, it belonged to Greg Johnson, a friend of Eric's, and inherited from Greg's maiden aunt who had lived here most of her seventy-two years. But Greg was something Beth called a "computer wizard," although Kory had never once seen the glow of magic about him, and he was so wealthy by mortal standards that he already *had* a dwelling he much favored. This townhouse, although it had been lovely in its day, full of glowing woodwork, with a garden even an elven lady would have been charmed by, had become neglected over the years. Greg had kept it locked and boarded up — until a friend of a friend of a friend had directed Eric to him with their tale of woe, and their acute need for housing they need not furnish references for.

They lived here rent-free — the bargain they had struck being that they would restore the place to its former glory. And there were many, many things that Kory could do there that Beth and Eric had not frowned upon. Though why it should be a bad thing to reproduce a bill of paper money, and a good thing to reproduce a sheet of walnut paneling, he was not certain.

He had only to stroke a piece of the woodwork with his magic, whispering to it, instructing it to recall its beauty — and gouges or insect-holes would vanish, carving reappear, forty years of paint peel away, and the wonderful carved moldings of seventy years ago would shine forth as if newly oiled and newly hewn.

Only. Hmm. Well, Eric understands that it is a strain for me, if Beth does not. Since he was not a major mage, the cost to him in terms of exhaustion, personal energy and stress was high, especially when working alone. But he was no longer working alone; Eric could use his Bardic magery to tap into deeper sources of energy, and feed them to Kory, and the toll was not as high as it would otherwise have been.

Beth didn't understand what he was doing; Eric, in whom the magics of Bards ran deeply and strongly, saw it, but could not yet replicate it. That would come, in time, Kory had assured him. Eric had laughed, and retorted that he was in no hurry — what he could do already scared him enough!

It was simple enough, really. Every made thing held within it the memory of what it had been like when it was first created. Learning that was part of kenning, the means by which the elves (or Great Bards) studied a thing to replicate it. Once Kory had kenned something, he could not only reproduce it, he could repair it, by building upon that memory. That was how he had restored Eric's boots after the Battle of Griffith Park — the boots that Prince Terenil had created for him—

Now it was Kory's turn to swallow grief; Terenil had been more than liege, he had been that rarest of things among elvenkind, who chose their bonds carefully, for they would bind for centuries. Terenil had been a friend.

Well, none of this was making the hot tub function.

He stared at the dark wooden tub with resentment. He had repaired the wood magically, after Beth had salvaged it from someone else's discard heap. Thomas Crawford, who repaired appliances when he was not busking at Faires, had fixed the motor in return for a pair of magically-made boots like Eric's. Kory had traded many pairs of boots and leather pants and bodices for other work done on the house — for Faire folk were an eclectic lot, and many of them, like Thomas, worked at the kind of odd jobs that would have been the lot of a tinker in the old days. And *all* of them coveted Eric's boots and leather trousers. Kory himself had seen to the heater, since it was of ceramic and glass, copper and aluminum, and not made of deadly Cold Iron. So *why* would it not work?

He was more than half tempted to turn his magic loose on it anyway, and Beth's tender sensibilities be hanged. But he knew what she would say if she saw it. She'd already given him the lecture once.

"People are curious at housewarming parties. They prowl, they poke, they look into things and ooh and ahh. And if they see something that's working without being plugged in — they're going to talk. And when they talk, the Feds will hear about it."

Well, perhaps if he made it look as if it were operating in a normal fashion . . . leaving it plugged in and not functioning correctly was dangerous. But if he plugged it into a socket that wasn't working and *then* magicked everything, no one would know the difference. Not even Beth.

He found the end of the cord, and picked it up, intending to pull it loose and plug it into one of the out-

door sockets he and Thomas had determined was dead
and not worth the reviving —

And it came up loose in his hand, the plug plainly
lying in the middle of the path.

He flushed with embarrassment, glad beyond words
that there was no one here to have witnessed his
humiliation. The episode with the microwave popcorn
had been bad enough; the encounter with the vacuum
cleaner that he had mistaken for an Unseleighe
monster was worse. He would never have been able to
live *this* down.

Still blushing, he took the cord to a socket he knew very
well was live, and plugged it in — and was rewarded
immediately by the Feel of electric power flowing
through the cord under his hand, and the hum of heater
and pump beyond the screening evergreen bushes.
When he returned to the tub, the eddies in the water told
him that all was well, and the water would be ready for
soaking when they returned from the Fairesite. He stood
up, then, and basked in a little glow of self-congratula-
tion. He was no Great Bard, but he had, by Danaa, done
his share to make the house — and especially the gardens
— into wonderful places. He had not restored the gardens to their former manicured state. He had, instead,
created a miniature version of the kind of wilderness-
garden often found Underhill; a place full of hidden
bowers, little moss-lined nooks, home to flowers and
birds in all seasons, and green in all seasons too. One
could travel from the house to the hot tub without ever
once coming under the neighbors' curious eyes —
which, given that Beth had insisted that this be a "clothing optional" tub, was no small feat.

Kory himself was looking forward to his first soak
in this marvelous piece of human ingenuity. Beth had
introduced him to the wonders of hot tubs at an odd
meditation-place just south of here, in the city called
"Santa Cruz," and he had been an instant convert.

Wonderful stuff, hot water . . . that marvelous invention, the shower, for instance —

A shriek from the windows above made him jump, as startled as the starling had been earlier. The shriek was feminine, and followed by a curse as paint-blistering as his own had been.

"Korendil!"

He looked up, guiltily; Beth leaned out of the bathroom window, head covered in soapsuds. "How many times do I have to tell you?" she not-quite-shouted, *"The hot water runs out!"*

He blushed as scarlet as he had earlier. Like Beth's other maxim, "It works better when you plug it in," he kept forgetting that. It was easy enough to forget, when he was always the first one awake because he needed so little sleep, and the hot water tank usually recharged long before either of the other two was awake enough to even think about showering. He shrugged and grimaced elaborately, then sent a tiny surge of power to the reservoir of cold water in the half-basement. Fortunately, the new hot-water tank (traded by a contractor for three pairs of boots) was not Cold Iron either.

A cloud of steam gushed from behind Beth, out through the open window, like a bit of fog that had escaped the rest down in the Bay. Beth's head disappeared with a muffled exclamation; Kory waited a few moments to allow her to complete her shower, warm her body, and cool her temper. Then he returned to the house, following the tunnel he had created by asking the evergreens to interlace their branches above the path that ended at the lower entrance.

The townhouse was four stories in height, which had made Beth a little nervous in light of the recent earthquake. Kory had done his best to make the place as flexible as he could, given that he was working with materials and a plan that had been built nearly a century ago. He and Eric had removed every vestige of load-bearing brick and plaster, and had replaced them with conjured wooden siding on the exterior, and conjured wooden paneling within. He had worked on the supporting joists until they were supple but incredibly tough, gradually transforming them into something very like ancient briar; the whole dwelling *should* flex in a quake, but should not tumble down.

He really did *not* want to test that, however. With luck, they never would have to.

The bottom story was little more than a workshop and laundry-room. The workshop was new; he and Eric had added it. Kory smiled, recalling all the hours he and Eric had spent here, readying the house. They had strengthened the bonds between them, working together silently, sometimes with magery, and sometimes only with their hands. *Nesting,* Kory thought fondly. Domesticity suited the formerly footloose Bard. Not that he'd ever admit it.

The second story was public rooms, entered from below by the interior stair, and from the main street by a staircase to the front door. First from the front of the house was a huge room that Beth referred to as "the living-room," which had been the single change they had made to the interior layout. They had knocked down walls between what had been a room Greg called "the parlor" used only to entertain guests, and a dining room, to make one huge room. It was a place Kory found very comfortable, full of light and air, and overstuffed futon-chairs and sofas. Behind that room was the kitchen, which Beth had pronounced "hopelessly outdated." It too had been remodeled. The only things he had not been able to ken and reproduce had been the appliances. Fortunately, after he had seen all the work they had done up until that point, Greg had willingly bought those. Opposite the living room, on the opposite side of the entrance-hall, was the "media room," with the overflow of Greg's electronic toys: two televisions, a stereo, three kinds of tape players and a VCR machine. In back of the "media room" was a storeroom, still packed with wood, aluminum nails and wooden pegs, and the rest of their building supplies.

The third story was all living quarters; four bedrooms, including one master bedroom; two bathrooms. The fourth story had been servants' quarters in the days when the house had been built; once again he and Eric had removed walls to make bigger rooms, four of them. One was a library, with floor-to-ceiling bookcases. One held their music and musical instruments. One was Eric's retreat from the world, and one was Beth's. When Kory felt the need for peace, he generally went out into the garden. Rain, fog, chill — these things meant very little to one of elven-blood. More important was being able to Feel the power-flows, to tap into the magic welling up from the nexus-points into Underhill.

Those here in the north had never been walled away, as they had in the south, in the place the mortals called Los Angeles. But they were not as strong, either. The elves who had settled Elfhame Mist-Hold were a different sort; less used to wielding powerful magic and much more used to blending in with the human world. Kory's cousin for instance — Arvindel — he who had been second-born to the elves who had settled here on this western coastline — *he* actually worked among the humans, and no one the wiser. He was a dancer in the Castro District, and many were the humans who yearned after him when seeing him dance.

And Arvindel — he of the varied and capricious appetites — often indulged those yearnings. And just as capriciously dropped his conquests, afterwards.

"Fickle," Kory had teased him.

"Overfond fool," Arvin had replied, and half serious, more so than Kory. There were no few of his own kind who looked askance at this close liaison with short-lived

humans, may-flies, who would fade and die in the blink of an elven eye. . . .

Kory shuddered away from the thought. *This is no day to worry about trifles like the future,* he told himself. *Particularly when a year ago you thought you had no future, and a scant few months before that you were spell-locked and Dreaming.*

Time, which normally had no meaning for elvenkind, had set its seal on him, if he was thinking in terms of "months" and "the future." Well, a pox upon Arvin, and upon anyone else who thought ill of him because of it!

He ascended the staircase, to emerge in the kitchen just as Beth, head wrapped in towels and body enveloped in an enormous white terrycloth bathrobe, descended from the bathroom above. She shot him a look, he spread his hands in apology. "I crave your pardon, my lady," he said, bowing a little to her, as he would to a lady of his own kind, "I fear I am but an airhead."

Her mouth quirked in a smile, despite her attempts to keep that same smile from emerging. Finally, she laughed. "Elves," she said to the air above her head. "Can't live with 'em, and there's no resale value."

Seeing that he had been forgiven, he shamelessly collected a kiss; a long, slow, sensuously deep kiss. She pushed him off — regretfully — a moment later, however. "No, you don't," she half-scolded. "We'll never get to the Fairesite at this rate. Have you eaten?"

He nodded, then added, with a wistful expression, "But that was before dawn. I fear I may waste of famine e'er we reach the site — "

What he really *wanted* was to watch her work the microwave; an arcane creation that fascinated him endlessly — and which he had been forbidden to touch after popping all of their twenty-five packets of microwave popcorn in a single evening.

She raised an auburn eyebrow at him. "Where are you *putting* it all?" she asked, incredulously. "If I ate as much as you do, I'd look like the Goodyear blimp!"

Having no answer to that, he simply shrugged. She busied herself for a moment at the refrigerator, then put a plateful of frozen sausage-biscuits into the microwave. She set the machine, then stepped aside to towel her hair dry while they heated. Kory leaned back in his chair, admiring her. He liked her very much as a redhead; it was a good color for her. A pity that the change had been mandated by their attempts to fool those "Feds" that were haunting their footsteps. A pity too that she could no longer sport those "cutting-edge" hairstyles she had favored, as well. In an attempt to change her silhouette completely, Kory had told her hair to become auburn and curly, and had instructed it to grow — very fast. She now had a mass of red curls that reached to the middle of her back (which she complained about constantly), and she made him think of tales the older Sidhe told of Ireland and the fabled mortal beauties of old. He'd made a new Faire costume for her which included an embroidered leather bodice and boots to match, in black and silver, with a pure linen skirt and loose-woven silk blouse of lovely forest green. Since she had been well known in Faire circles for only making the briefest of concessions to the dress-code, this should throw off hunters as well.

He had made Eric's hair into a mane of raven black; for the rest, the changes the young Bard had wrought in himself were enough to confuse pursuers. He no longer indulged in drugs or overindulged in alcohol, and he had added muscle in rebuilding this house. The result was something quite unlike the vague-eyed, skinny, sickly-looking creature Kory had first encountered. And in *his* new Faire costume, which matched Beth's except that the colors were burgundy and silver, instead of black, he was quite an elegant sight. Kory's own garb was of a piece with theirs, in scarlet and gold. The embroidered patterns matched, as did the placement, making it very clear to anyone who saw them together that they were an ensemble. Since neither Beth nor Eric had ever worked in a formal group at the Faires, that, too, should help to confuse things.

When they went out street-busking — which was how they had been paying for items like food and other necessities — they all wore their Faire boots and shirts, with jeans. The effect was striking, and caught quite a bit of attention for them down on the Wharf. Kory was quite proud that he had contributed in a material way to their success as buskers.

Danaa knew that his playing certainly wasn't outstanding enough to do so. He was competent with drum and bones, but nothing more. And his singing voice, while pleasant, was not going to win any prizes either. Beth and Eric outshone him completely in both areas.

And when Eric exerted his full power as a Bard — coins and bills leapt into their hat.

Eric, however, was inclined not to use his power in that way unless it were direst emergency — as it had been during the first month of their escape from Los Angeles. He felt that it was a cheat, that people were not rewarding his skill as a musician, they were being hypnotized into giving him largesse. Kory silently applauded such a decision; it said a great deal for Eric's growing sense of ethics. Beth sometimes seemed exasperated when he said things like that, but she also seemed to be pleased, if in a grudging way. Kory wondered often about Beth — how she could be so honorable, and then turn to and display an equally high ethical callousness. Eric just said that it was her television background, as if that explained it all.

Beth shook back her wild mane of curls with a grimace. "I can't get used to this," she complained. "It's just so weird, having all this hair — " The microwave *beeped* then, and she pulled an oven mitt over her hand and took out the plate of biscuits.

Kory grinned. " 'Tis that, my lady, or be recognized. Wigs, they might expect — and hair-dye and curls. But not such a length, and obviously yours. True?"

"True," she sighed, and put the plate down on the table, snatching a biscuit for herself and biting into it. "Very true. And I'm the one who keeps harping on the fact that we have to be underground. I just wish I knew another way of making a buck without coming out of hiding besides busking — everybody in L.A. *knows* I'm a musician, and somebody is bound to have let it leak."

"But they aren't lookin' for a trio," Eric yawned, shuffling sleepily through the door, and enveloped in a robe even larger than Beth's. "And they're a lot more likely to look for you with a rock-group than with a busker." With all his newly-acquired muscle hidden beneath the bulky cloth, he looked as frail as he used to actually be. He kissed Beth between yawns, and gingerly picked up one of the biscuits, juggling it from hand to hand until it cooled off.

"That's true," Beth acknowledged, hugging him, and then pushing him into a chair. Eric was not a morning person in any sense of the word, and had been known to wander into furniture until he actually woke up. He smiled sleepily at Kory, who mimed a punch at him.

"Are you going to be awake enough to ride?" the elf asked him as he ate half the biscuit.

Eric nodded, and reached for the cup of coffee Beth was handing him. "With enough of this in me, I will be," he said, after a swallow. Kory sniffed the tantalizing aroma wistfully; one mouthful would have put *him* in a stupor; one cupful might actually kill him — but it smelled so good.

Beth handed him a mug of cinnamon-hibiscus tea, which smelled nearly as good, and did not contain any of the caffeine that was so deadly to his kind. "He'll be fine, Kory," she said cheerfully. "He's ridden up behind me plenty of times, you know that. You'd be amazed at what a good grip he has when we're going sixty-five."

"I still wish those things had seatbelts," Eric muttered, but Kory suspected that Beth hadn't heard him. He took another biscuit. "Are we changing here, or at the site?" the Bard asked.

"The site," she replied, trying to get a comb through her hair. "I've got passes for us through the Celts as 'Banysh Mysfortune,' the name we auditioned under. So don't tell anyone your real names unless they're somebody I already cleared, okay? Even if you think it's one of your best friends and they think they recognize you."

Eric shook his head, and knuckled an eye. "I think you're being overly paranoid, Bethy, but if that's the way you want it . . . " He shrugged. "I don't have any best friends but you guys anyway — and if any of my old girlfriends showed up, I'd just as soon have an excuse not to recognize them. Are we doing the Celtic shows?"

Beth nodded; one of the first people she had contacted after their initial flight had been the head of the Celt Clan, a very resourceful gentleman, as Kory had seen when he'd met them at a Berkeley hamburger place. Evidently people in San Francisco — some of them, anyway — took the appearance of fugitives from the law on their doorstep in stride. He had been their chiefest help — had "networked," was the word Beth used — gotten them in touch with others, and within a few days they had been settled into this townhouse and began putting new lives together.

At first, transportation had not been a problem; the BART system ran everywhere they wanted to play, and Kory could ride in the metal trains and buses, even though it was sometimes less than comfortable. He had rather enjoyed walking home from the stores with his arms loaded down with bags. It had been an entirely new experience. And, at first, things had been too precarious for them even to think about doing Northern Faire — making the house livable was taking up all the time they had to spare from street-busking. But as Faire-season loomed nearer for the second year of their tenure here, and Beth had realized that they could make a substantial amount of money if only they could *get* there, she had become increasingly anxious to find some sort of transportation that could take them outside BART's magic circle.

Oddly enough, it was Kory who had provided that. He had reminded her that most autos were too painful for him to ride in. Then he had mentioned, wistfully, that it was too bad that horses were no longer common — he could have called up a pair of elvensteeds for them in a trice.

Beth had narrowed her eyes in sudden speculation, but it had been Eric who had said, as if a memory had suddenly surfaced, "Elvensteeds? But what about that white Corvette I saw Val driving? The one that was a horse, except it wasn't a horse — "

"Elvensteeds can counterfeit anything," Kory had said without thinking. "They will not stand up to much of an examination, but they can counterfeit the appearance." Then he had hit himself on the side of the head, in a gesture unconsciously borrowed from Eric. "But of course! I can call us elvensteeds, and ask them to counterfeit us cars — "

Beth had shaken her head. "Too conspicuous — and there's always the chance that somebody would try to mess with them in the parking lot, and then what?" She'd bitten her knuckle in frustration. "No, what I wish is that we had some way to get a pair of bikes."

"Bikes?" Kory had said, as Eric blanched. "You mean, motorcycles? But the elvensteeds can counterfeit those, as well!"

"The parking lot — " Beth had protested.

"Well," Eric had put in reluctantly, "we could leave them and get off and walk and they could go hide themselves. People would think we'd gotten rides or hitched, and the ones who saw us ride in would just think we'd put the bikes inside one of the Admin buildings or something. Then when we needed them, Kory could call them in again. And it wouldn't be that conspicuous for us to have bikes around here, not like a car, anyway; I know lots of buskers that have bikes." He'd gulped. "There's just one thing; I can't ride."

Beth had shrugged. "So, ride behind me. Kory? You think you can pull this off?"

He had nodded. "I can copy enough of Thomas's Ninja to make ours pass, I think. I know a way to keep them from being meddled with in public places. And I can conjure us leathers, easily enough." Beth had rolled her eyes at that, but had agreed, taking safety as a prime consideration. Kory had taken advantage of the situation to conjure leathers in "their" colors: burgundy and silver for Eric, scarlet and gold for himself, and black and silver for Beth. She had made a face and muttered something about the leathers being anything but inconspicuous, but she wore them anyway.

So their problem had been solved; and if they always arrived dry even when it rained, that could be chalked up to the San Francisco weather patterns, that would have one side of the street drenched and the other bone-dry.

"Then let us wear leathers," Kory said with relish. He loved the outfits; loved the way they felt as if he was donning armor for a joust, or hunting garb for a wild ride. Eric sighed, ate another biscuit, and headed back up the stairs to change.

Beth took the time for another large cup of coffee; Kory finished his tea, reached for a bit more Power, and clad himself in his leathers between one sip and the next, planting his helmet on the table next to him with a muffled *thud*.

Beth shook her head. "I can never get used to you doing that," she complained.

"Hazard of living with elves, lovely lady," he said, standing up, and tucking the helmet under his arm. "If you'll excuse me, I'll go fetch the steeds from the garage."

"Thanks, love," she said, blowing him a kiss as she turned to run up the stairs. "For that, I forgive you for running out the hot water."

He grinned, and trotted back down the kitchen stairs, taking another path than the one that led to the hot tub. This one wound around the edge of the privacy fence and ended at the tiny garage occupying an otherwise useless odd-shaped corner of the garden.

It wasn't much of a garage; it would have been barely big enough for a sub-compact car. It held the two elvensteeds quite comfortably, with plenty of room for them to transform into their normal forms if they chose. Kory's steed matched his colors of scarlet and gold; Beth's twinned her black and silver. Kory had based them loosely on the Ninja models of what Beth called "murder-cycles," but he had made up a style-name — "Merlin" — and a company — "Toshiro." That way, if people thought there was something wrong with the way the bikes "should" look, they could blame it on the fact that they'd never heard either of the company or the model. The names were private jokes; a merlin was both a small falcon, and the use-name of one of the greatest of Bardic Mages, although few humans these days seemed to realize that Bardic connection. And "Toshiro" was for the human who had created many great movies of Japanese culture, movies that Kory had often watched in the long hours of the night when Beth and Eric still slept.

He wheeled them out one at a time, setting them up in the street in front of the street-side door, and waited for Beth and Eric. They came out quicker than he'd had any right to expect; Beth on the run, stuffing her hair down into the back of her jacket, with the bags containing her costume, his, and their instruments slung over her shoulder. Eric followed more slowly, locking the door behind himself and, as always, settled himself behind Beth rather gingerly. Although Kory couldn't see his face, he had the feeling that Eric wore a look of grim and patient determination.

Poor Eric; he never felt safe on these pseudo-metal beasts. Kory wondered if he'd have felt any better if they had been in their proper horse-shape.

Probably not.

He looked over at Beth, her face hidden behind the dark windscreen of her helmet, and nodded. She handed him his bags; he stowed them safely in the saddlebags on the "flanks" of his steed. Although these elvensteeds needed no kick-starting at all, they always kept up the pretense that they were real bikes by going through the motions of starting them.

Of course, with an elvensteed, there was never any nonsense of struggling with a motor that wouldn't quite catch. . . . The bikes roared to life with twin bellows of power; Beth let out a whoop of exuberance, and shot off into the lead. Kory followed, grinning happily. Beth had needed this for some time; to get back into the Faire circuit, to see old friends without worrying if the mysterious "Feds" were going to catch them — and she especially needed the party tonight.

For that matter, so did he. He hadn't had a celebratory party in —

Danaa, is it that long?

High time then.

An odd humming reached his inner ears, a musical sound that accompanied a trace of magic energy; he leaned over the handlebars of his bike and smiled as he traced it forward. Eric was humming —

So was Beth.

He laughed aloud, and popped a wheelie.

It was going to be a most excellent day.

● CHAPTER TWO

As I Walked Through the Fair

Eric Banyon kept his eyes shut tightly through most of the ride, his stomach lurching with every turn. He joked with Beth and Kory about his fear of riding; he never let them know how real that fear was. At one point in his life he had actually envied some motorcycle maniacs who had stunted their way past a bus he'd been riding; now that memory seemed to belong to another person entirely.

I was high, he told himself, *or drunk. Or both.* There were drawbacks to going clean and sober.

Or maybe it was so simple a thing as the fact that something that looked easy when you had no prospect of engaging in it — well, relatively; as opposed to, say, piloting a 747 — became something else entirely when you *had* to do it.

And the simple truth was that Eric had been terribly sheltered in this one aspect of his life. He had never once owned a vehicle of any kind. As a child, he'd been driven from place to place by his parents; as an adult he'd cadged rides or used public transportation. He *did* have a driver's license, which he'd taken care to keep updated, but he'd obtained it by taking the test on a dare, when high on a combination of grass and mescaline. He had no memory of the test, or even whose car he had taken it in. Like many things that he'd done back then, it had seemed a good idea at the time.

Kory had a license—kenned from his, with Kory's picture substituted for his own. So long as no one ever asked him to produce his at the same time, there should be no trouble. Kory *could* drive; he could probably drive anything, Eric suspected. Or ride wild mustangs or pilot a 747. In all likelihood, no one would ever even think of stopping Kory, he was just that competent.

Or even if they did, he or Kory could probably play head-games with the officer to make him give them warnings and ignore the licenses. The "Obi-Wan-Kenobi Gambit," they called it. "These are not the elves you're looking for—"

Eric had never once driven anything that he remembered. He may have driven any number of times that he didn't remember; there was a great deal of his life that was lost in an alcoholic or drug-enhanced fog. But now that he was sober and staying that way, he had no intention of being at the helm of *any* vehicle when Beth and Kory were around to drive it. Hell, he wasn't even certain he knew how to start these things! Let them deal with the motorcycles—even if Beth did drive like a graduate of the Evel Knievel School of Combat Driving. He'd stay a passenger, unless, of course, it was a dire emergency and both of them were incapacitated.

Not bloody likely— *I hope,* he thought, and clung a little tighter to Beth's waist as she rounded a curve and the bike began to lean. The elvensteeds weren't metal; Beth had learned with great glee that they wouldn't reflect radar-guns. So she only gave speed-limit signs any weight when it was obvious that the limit was there for reasons of safety. At any other time—well, he'd learned his lesson on the first ride. Now he no longer watched anything, not even the passing landscape; he just closed his eyes and listened to the music in his head. There was always music in his head these days; he was only now starting to learn what it meant, instead of flying on instinct.

His stomach lurched. *Better not think about flying.*

The advantage to Bethy's driving, as he had learned when they showed up for pre-Faire auditions and rehearsals, was that they got to the Fairesite in a reasonable length of time. Beth must have really been pouring on the gas this morning, though, because he felt her slowing down much sooner than he had expected to, and he cracked open one eye to see that she was about to turn down the gravel "back road" to the campgrounds. He relaxed, and flexed his fingers a little, one hand at a time, as she pulled onto the road, gravel crunching under the bike tires.

Kory pulled up beside them, and Eric felt the gentle touch of inquiry, mind-to-mind, the elf sent to him. *I'm okay,* he thought back. *Just a little stiff from the ride.* Now that they weren't racing along at ninety-per, he could enjoy what there was left of the drive, despite the jouncing. It was going to be a beautiful day, that much was certain. Not too surprising, really; some of Kory's kin were coming to the house-warming party, and Kory had hinted they might Do Something to ensure cooperative weather.

Convenient. Wonder if maybe I'll be able to do something like that someday. . . . With Southern California in the grip of a five-year drought with no end in sight, he'd be real tempted to tamper. . . .

But would that be right? If he mucked around with the Southern California weather, what would that do up here? Would it have consequences that would reach even farther than that? What if he inadvertently created another Dust Bowl?

He mentally shook his head. There had been a time when he wouldn't have thought about consequences, he'd have just done what he wanted to. Was this a result of being sober for more than a year, or was it something more than that?

Jesus, I'm getting responsible in my old age. Maybe it was watching Ria Llewellyn, seeing what she did to people and things by running over the top of them to get what she wanted. Strange. He loved Bethy — but there was something about Ria . . . the memories concerned with Ria, half-elven child of the renegade Perenor, were the sharpest of all of his recollections of the battle to save the elves of Elfhame Sun-Descending. There was just something about her —

He shook the persistent memory of blue eyes away, with just a faint hint of regret. In the end, ironically enough, it had been Ria who had saved them all. She had fought her father, when it became obvious that Perenor was mad, stark, staring bonkers — and that had given Terenil and Kory their chances to strike. And it had bought Eric and Beth time to move the magic nexus of the Sun-Descending Grove from the old, destroyed Fairesite, to a new Grove in the heart of Griffith Park, a place central to every elven Grove and a place that would — at least in the foreseeable future — never fear the destructive hand of humans. *That* had freed, Awakened, and empowered the elves of the L.A. basin, who were slowly taking their lives out of holding patterns they'd been in for more than ten years.

Yeah, well, Ria's at the Happy Home at the moment, with pineapple yogurt instead of brains. That Healer-chick thinks some day she may be able to bring her out of it, but frankly, I doubt it. Not being a fan of necrophilia, I doubt there's much of Ria Llewellyn in my future.

Some of Beth's hair escaped from inside her jacket to tickle his nose, and he brushed it away with a grin. Now *that* was a distinctly odd circumstance: Beth with a full mop of dark red hair. The girl he'd broken up with just before his involvement with elves and magic started had red hair. Maureen — who, he'd heard from the grapevine, had really abysmal taste in boyfriends since. One had ordered her around and made like he was her agent until her real agent threw him out; the next one had sponged off her for six months, then disappeared; and he'd heard that the current one was a borderline psycho and leaving bruises on her, occasionally.

Yeah, well, I was no prize, either.

He'd expected the color-change on Beth to make him feel really uneasy — but it didn't. She was still Beth Kentraine, only now instead of black hair in a punk tail, she had the most glorious mane of deep red curls he'd seen outside of a movie. Like the chick in *The Abyss*, and not like Maureen at all. It was lots of fun to play with, too — though he could sure understand why she didn't want to camp out on site with it to worry about. Hard to keep a mane like that clean and unsnarled without magic helping. And Beth Kentraine was not at all happy about using magic in ordinary life.

They'd decided to go ahead and bring the bikes into the parking lot, after quite a bit of discussion, and park them in the middle of a lot of other bikes. Then Kory would work something like the "Obi-Wan" thing on them, only it would make people ignore the fact that they were there. So even if the Feds were on to them, it was unlikely that they'd try to meddle with the bikes, even if they were looking for them. Eric hadn't quite believed in the "spell," if that was what it was, until Kory had proved it to him — parking his bike in the *worst* area in Chinatown, throwing the spell on it, and walking away. They'd come back five hours later, and there wasn't even a fingerprint on the bike.

Kory's learned a lot from his kin up here. A couple of the other elves had been taking the Southerner under their wings, so to speak; teaching him little things that didn't take a lot of magical energy, but were very effective. And they had helped him out by kenning and replicating a lot of the raw materials they'd used in restoring the house, letting him save his energy for harder things, like restoring the wood and brickwork. Eric had gathered that this lot was in contact with more

elves — and even humans — out on the East Coast; a
set of elves that wanted to integrate as much as possible
into human society. They even had something to do
with — of all things — racecar driving.

More power to them. There was a hefty faction — from
what Eric had been able to make out — that were dead-
set against that. And it seemed that Perenor wasn't the
only renegade in the world, either, though fortunately
there didn't seem to be any more like him on *this* Coast.
"Sheebeg, Sheemore" all over again — only it turned
out there was a *name* for these renegades and they even
had their own organization of sorts. "The Unseleighe
Court," that was what Kory's cousin called it. But they
seemed to keep themselves concentrated away from
Cold Iron and in areas as isolated as possible — which
meant they weren't real fond of the West Coast. North
Dakota, now, maybe. . . .

Eric shook himself out of his daydreams; the parking
lot was just ahead, and it was time to stop worrying
about the problems of the world and start thinking
about the day ahead. They still had to make some
money — "the old-fashioned way" — because they'd
pretty much drained the cookie-jar dry setting up for
the party tonight. It was gonna be slim pickings unless
the hat filled well this weekend and next week.

*Don't think I can handle any more miso soup and ramen
noodles for a while.*

There was a cluster of bikes of all sorts off to one side,
huddled together like musk-oxen; Beth brought the
bike to a halt just behind Kory and all three of them got
off. Eric took the bags from both of them, Beth and
Kory walked the bikes over to the herd and parked
them; Kory passed his hand over both.

That was it; no fireworks, no flashes of light. But as
the three of them moved off, a couple of other riders
came up and parked their bikes right behind the
steeds, blocking their egress — something that would

never have happened if they'd "noticed" the bikes were in place. Eric grinned, and slung his bags over his shoulder. All was as it should be.

Including Kory; when Kory took his helmet off, there was no way of telling him from any ordinary human.

Well, any ordinary, incredibly blond, six-foot-six, hunk-of-all-time, rad babe of a human, anyway.

Pointy ears and cat-pupiled eyes had been effectively camouflaged by another tiny little spell. Kory stood out, all right — and that was a good thing. He was the most striking of the three, visually; if there was anyone still looking for them, they *wouldn't* be looking for someone that looked like Kory. That in itself should throw confusion into the pursuit. And anyone who was looking for "Beth" and "Eric" would spot Kory first; since he was a stranger to the Faire-circuit, no one would connect him to any of the regulars. Because of that, the existence of "Tom and Janice Lynn" — who just happened to bear a superficial resemblance to "Eric Banyon and Beth Kentraine" — would be more plausible. And they would all be accepted as new-comers without too much question.

Some of their old friends, most notably a few of the Celts, folks who knew how to keep their mouths shut, were in on the ruse, but most of the Faire regulars weren't.

Beth got the passes at the Admin building with no problems and no questions asked; from there they went off to Celtic Camp (or as Eric liked to tease Ian, Keltic Kamp) to borrow a tent for a quick change. About thirty other Celts and Celt hangers-on had the same idea; the competition for space was fierce. But Beth and Eric were old hands at this; they managed to wiggle out of their leathers and into their costumes using no more than about two square feet of space. Kory undressed with sublime unselfconsciousness —

but Eric did not miss the stunned expressions of those around him and the covert glances out of eyes, male and female. Clothed, Kory was a hunk. Stripped to the skivvies Beth insisted he wear in public, and he was causing a lot of people to reach for their drool-catchers.

Yeah, I don't think there's going to be too many problems with people recognizing us. He grinned as he wriggled into his leather Faire pants. *Nobody's gonna be looking at us. This is gonna be fun.*

The bike leathers and helmets went into the costume-bags; the bags went to Admin to be locked up. Beth wasn't taking any chances on someone making a try at their expensive-looking riding leathers, even if Kory *could* magic up new sets right away. For one thing, producing identical leathers within an hour of their loss would cause some serious questions to be raised, even if only the thief knew the leathers had been taken. Anybody who'd snitch someone's personal property could be low enough to try and peddle the information of the miraculous reproducing clothing to some other interested party. And if it was the Feds who snitched the suits — the cat would definitely be out of the bag.

Not a good idea.

He laced up his leather vest over the front of his silk shirt, transferred the flute to his embroidered gig-bag, and slipped outside the tent to wait for the others. Funny, the bag used to be the classiest part of his costume; now it was the shabbiest. He'd have to ask Kory if the elf had the energy to make him one to match the rest of the costume. Beth followed a moment later, trailing Kory. As they conferred for a moment, getting their bearings, one of the ultra-period Elizabethan types sashayed by, in all her black-velvet, pearl-embroidered majesty, a galleon in full sail. She paused for a moment, one eyebrow lifted.

Eric waited for the usual comment — or, more scathing, the eyebrow to lift just a bit higher, followed by a slight sniff, before the galleon sailed on. *Authenticity Nazis,* he called them, and not entirely in jest. He'd gotten used to them over the years. They'd given him no end of grief because of his careless approach to costuming; he usually shrugged and ignored them. She probably wouldn't care for the light leather breeches, or maybe the silk shirts — or even the appliqued leather vests that matched their boots. Granted, it did look a lot more like Hollywood's idea of Elizabethan than was accurate, though Kory swore he hadn't made that many changes; simply given them an older version of breeches than the silly little puff-pants that were correct. But he hoped Kory wouldn't be upset when she gave them the inevitable thumbs-down. . . .

The eyebrow remained where it was. "Quite — striking," the galleon pronounced. "Really, quite elegant." Her eyes lingered on Kory's legs, and Eric did his best not to snicker. He should have known. She was a sucker for a hunk in tight leather pants. For that, she'd probably have forgiven them if they'd worn their biker leathers. "You must be professionals," she continued. "I don't remember seeing you here last year."

"Not as a group, milady," Kory said, bowing so gracefully that the galleon flushed with pleasure. "We've been rather busy getting settled in the area. We've had some jobs Outside, but this is our first year at the Faire together."

"I'm looking forward to hearing you." The great black construction picked up her skirts and sailed majestically on to her next appointment — Opening Parade, no doubt. Eric checked Beth out of the corner of his eye. Her mouth was twitching.

"Was that a queen?" Kory asked, politely. Beth fell apart, laughing. Fortunately, the galleon was out of sight and hearing range.

Kory looked sorely puzzled, but Eric managed enough of an explanation to satisfy him as they dropped their bags at Admin — where Caitlin gave them a cheerful if harried "thumbs-up" as a welcome for them. Just Caitlin's little way of encouraging the newcomers, who were, by her very different standards, a class act. Caitlin was *not* in on the secret; Eric had wanted to tell her, but Beth voted him down. In the end, he'd had to agree, reluctantly. Caitlin knew too many people, and she might let something slip without meaning any harm.

They hit the "streets" and headed for their chosen busking-site near the tavern, hoping to get it before anyone else staked it out.

Their luck held; they reached the shelter of the trees and got themselves arranged *just* as another group arrived: a lutanist, a harpist and a mandolin player. The dark-haired harpist sighed; Beth shrugged. "Try back in a couple of hours," she said. "We'll be doing the Celtic show, and if you get here before we leave, we'll just wrap up and turn it over to you."

The harpist brightened. "Thanks!" she called, as they headed off at a brisk walk to whatever had been their second choice.

They won't be trotting like that in a couple of hours, Eric noted. He hadn't recognized any of the three players — there was a certain amount of turnover among "Rennies," and these three didn't have quite the same casual saunter of seasoned hands. Although the morning had begun cool, by noon it was probably going to be pretty warm, and most Renfaire costumes got very hot quite quickly. Heat exhaustion was a constant problem, especially among those who were new at the game. That was why he and Beth had agreed on several particular shady sites for busking, if they could get them, even though *their* costumes were a lot cooler than they looked.

He was fitting the pieces of his flute together when he was startled by a familiar voice calling his name.

"Eric? Eric Banyon?"

He came within a hair of turning; he certainly jumped a little, nervously. Then — *:Gently, Bard,:* came another voice, this one deep inside his mind, steadying him as if Kory held a comforting hand on his shoulder. *:Remember who you are. Do not react. She is coming up behind you — she is going to touch you.:*

"Eric?" A real hand touched his elbow, and he turned, carefully schooling his face into a mask of surprise and puzzlement, mixed with a bit of annoyance at familiarity from a stranger. "Jesus, Eric, did you dye your hair or some — "

She stopped and stared at him when he didn't respond. It was Kathie, of course. Kathie, who had driven him out of Texas Faire and contributed in no small way to his drinking problem. Dressed, not in one of her carefully embroidered Faire shirts and bodice-skirt combinations, but as a "traveler," one of the paying customers, in designer jeans and a halter-top.

"Like, excuse me?" he said, in a deep Valley accent. "I think you've got, like, someone else in mind, I mean, y'know?"

She looks terrible, he observed, dispassionately. She'd lost at least twenty, maybe thirty pounds; her complexion was pasty, and from the harshness of her speaking voice she'd been doing way too much grass. She had that vague, not-quite-focused look of someone who's been smoking dope for so long it's gotten to be a permanent part of her system. *Stoned and anorexic.* She stared at him with her mouth a little agape; not a pretty sight.

And I used to be in love with her. Like his reflections on the days when he'd taken that driver's test stoned, it seemed worlds away, as if it had been someone else entirely who thought he'd lost the universe and all reason for living when this woman threw him over for a chance to sleep her way into a pro band.

:It was another person, Bard,: Kory said solemnly, as

Beth kept her own expression icily aloof. *:You were another person entirely. You met misfortune and grew; she met with fortune and diminished.:*

She looked prosperous enough; at least her clothing was expensive. Kathie collected herself as Eric moved enough away that her hand was no longer in contact with his arm. "Come *on*, Eric!" she said — or rather, whined. "Quit the BS! I know it's you! Y'still have the bag I gave you!"

"What?" he said, thinking quickly. "Like, this?" He pulled the embroidered gig-bag around and looked at it. "Oh, man, listen babe, I mean, I hate t'like, y'know, thrash out yer day, but like, I got this'n the flute in a pawnshop down in Pasadena." He wrinkled his lip a little, in simulated disdain for the bag and its contents. "I didn' wanna, y'know, take a really good instrument out here in the boonies." He scratched his head in an utterly *un*Eric-like gesture, and shrugged in a good imitation of the moneyed youngsters he'd watched on Rodeo drive, when they weren't impressed with someone. Indifferent to any distress they might cause, but going through the motions. "You're like, about the fifth person t'think I was, y'know, this Eric dude. I mean, sorry babe." He shook his head. "Name's like, Tom, okay? This's, like, our first gig out here, right Jan?"

He turned to Beth, who nodded confirmation. "We're, like, twins," she lied smoothly, and smiled. It was a very cool smile, and Eric hoped she wasn't really as angry as she looked. "We've been like, a duet forever, but it's always been like, conservatory gigs, y'know? Kory like told us we oughta like try the Faire this year, when we like got him to make it a trio, you know?"

:She's not angry,: Kory chuckled mentally. *:Or rather, she was very angry with this woman a long time ago, but now she is enjoying her discomfiture.:*

And if I know my Bethy, the fact that Kath looks like hell is pretty entertaining too, he thought wryly.

Kathie looked from one to the other of them, now totally confused. "If you're thinking of, like, Eric Banyon," Beth continued, in the same drawling Valley accent as Eric, "Somebody with the Celts told me he'd like had a major accident or something—"

"No—" Kory put in, in a voice completely without accent—very Midwestern. "His apartment blew up, and he disappeared. Somebody said he might have gotten in trouble with a drug ring or something. That's what Ian told me, anyway." He shrugged, insincerely. "Sorry. You could go talk to Ian if you can find him. He should be over with the Celts."

"Oh." Kathie backed away, slowly, her face crumpling. For one moment Eric was tempted to stop her—

:*If you do, Beth* will *be angry at you*.:

I feel sorry for her, Eric thought, as she turned and plodded away. *I mean, look at her, she isn't even doing the Faire, she's a "traveler." I don't know what happened to her, but it must have been pretty awful.*

:*I think she came here to try and find you,*: Kory warned, :*And if that is true, she could be either a plant, or someone else's unwitting stalking-horse. In either case, she is dangerous to us. I begin to believe now in the wisdom of Beth's plans*.:

"Stick to the script, Banyon," Beth muttered under her breath, leaning forward to adjust his collar.

"No problem, love," he replied, with a grin. "Hey, all I have to do is remember the kind of rat she was back when, and it gets kind of hard to feel too sorry for her."

"That's my boy." She smiled back. "Now, let's make some pretty music for the travelers, hmm?"

"Okay." The travelers were starting to fill the streets between the booths; Opening Parade must be over. Kory already had his bodhran out and ready; Bethy was tuning the last string on her mandolin. Pity they wouldn't allow guitars out here, but the mando had a surprisingly loud "voice," and Beth would be giving it all she had. Between the three of them, they ought to give the travelers some spirit for their money.

"Signature tune?" he suggested. Beth flashed him a smile, and Kory nodded. "Okay, Kory, lead off; Beth, in on four."

Kory got the attention of anyone within hearing distance with a rousing four-count on the hand-drum, then he and Beth jumped in with the tune that had given them their name — "Banysh Mysfortune."

They ran it through twice, but the crowd didn't look to be in quite a giving mood, so as they rounded up the "B" part on the second pass, Beth called out "Drowsy Maggie!" and Eric followed her change.

He half-closed his eyes in pleasure. *This* was the way it should be; this was what he'd missed for the past year and a half. Not that they hadn't been busking; in fact, they'd gone out to Fisherman's Wharf most days when there was any chance of catching a crowd. But this was different — the crowds in the mundane world were harder to catch and hold. Ordinary people were off on little trips of their own, and they weren't planning on taking the time to stop and listen. They didn't necessarily want to hear folk music, either. Faire-goers were ready to be entertained; they wanted to hear something they wouldn't get on the radio. That made all the difference.

There were toes tapping out there in the crowd, and heads nodding. The boothies around them were paying attention too, and that meant they were doing just fine. The galleon sailed by, on the arm of another black-clad fellow whose surfer-tan contrasted oddly with his hose and doublet. She stopped to listen, too.

"Rutland Reel!" Beth called out as they finished up "Drowsy Maggie." If Eric hadn't been playing he'd have grinned. It was really a fiddler's tune, and the fingerings were a stone bitch, but he loved it, and the supersonic pace was bound to charm some cash from the crowd. Besides, they'd arranged it so that Kory had a place for a bodhran solo in the middle, to give him and Beth a rest, and they were going to need it.

They hit the change — and exploded.

The crowd loved it. When they finished, with a flourish, and swept immediately into a bow, change rained into the hat, and one of the boothies popped out of the tavern long enough to salt the hat with a fiver. Eric raised a surprised eyebrow at her; she just grinned from under her little dried-flower wreath. "Lunch is on us, and don't you dare go anywhere else," she said. "Just do some more Fairport Convention stuff," and then she scampered back to work.

Eric looked at Beth, who chuckled. "The request line is open," she responded. " 'Riverhead' into 'Gladys' Leap' into 'Wise Maid,' right off the record, just keep it trad-sounding, or the Authenticity Nazis will get us."

"Can do," he agreed, and they were off again.

By the time they were ready to break, the hat was heavy, and it wasn't all change by any means. The folk running the tavern offered beer or lemonade; Eric thought about the beer, then chose the latter. No point in spoiling a spotless record by getting drunk on his butt by accident, just because the day was hot. He hadn't been drunk since the night of despair —

That night, after Beth had told him Kory'd vanished, had been the worst night of his life. And it hadn't ended with that; he had watched his apartment going up in flames on the evening news, and had realized from a clue on the news that Perenor had been systematically killing all the potential Bards in the L.A. basin. He had grabbed for the whiskey, and something had made him stop.

That was the night he'd decided that help wasn't ever going to be found in the bottom of a bottle.

Besides, Eric Banyon had an established reputation for getting plastered at Faires. Tom Lynn should be different; another way of confusing the Feds and the Kathies.

By the time the Celtic show rolled around at 11:30, there was no doubt that they'd done the right thing, coming out here. There was more in the hat than he'd made in the best day of his life at Faire, and the day wasn't even half over yet. Beth emptied the take into the pouch she kept *under* her skirt — wise lady, she knew very well that cutpurses of the traditional kind were alive and well at Faire, though they probably wore "Motley Crüe" t-shirts. Eric had lost his own pouch that way the morning after he'd awakened Kory with his music. Though he hadn't known what he'd done at the time.

They turned the spot over to the harpist and her friends, and promised the tavern people to return after the show for the lunch they'd offered. They hurried to "catch the Celtic bus" before it left without them, running hand-in-hand like three kids, laughing all the way there.

They formed up with the other musicians in a loosely-organized mob; the chief gave the signal, and they were off.

The show was more of the same, but this time there were dancers to play for, and the show-mistress was the one calling the tunes. And there were more musicians to play with, which came very near to sending Eric into a full Bardic display of his power. He pulled himself back from the brink at the very last moment, exhilarated, but a little frightened by how easy it had been to call up the magic. He held himself in, then, just a bit; keeping his power under careful rein, like a restive horse. He exerted it only twice; once to throw power to Kory, who could never have enough with all the work he had to do, and once to grab a faltering dancer and save her from throwing out her knee.

That was something he hadn't even thought of doing until he somehow sensed the accident coming, a moment before it did, and let the power run free for that brief measure of time. She never even noticed that anything was different.

But Kory did, and the warm look of approval the elf cast him made him glow inside. Magic — the important magic — wasn't all big battles, the building of palaces. Just as important was keeping things around you running smoothly. He hadn't understood that when Kory and Arvin told him, but he did now.

The show finished, and thoroughly exhausted, they headed back to the tavern for that promised meal and a chance to listen to someone else. The trio that had replaced them were good, and it was a pleasure to sit and hear music instead of producing it, at least for a little bit. Once again, Eric opted for lemonade, and this time was rewarded with Beth's glance of approval.

That sobered him. Had she been watching him, waiting for him to revert to his old, bad habits? Probably.

I wish she'd said something, he thought, a little bitterly. *But — then again, maybe I haven't had a chance to prove myself out yet, at least not in the places where all the temptation is.*

But before his mood could sour, Beth got his attention. The trio by the tavern fence was playing "Sheebeg, Sheemore," and Kory's face wore an expression of wistful sadness. Eric had a pretty good idea why. Although it was a lovely tune, Banysh Mysfortune never played it, because it always reminded Kory of how many friends he'd lost to Perenor. . . .

"Where are we going to set up next?" Eric asked, touching Kory's hand for a moment, and trying to give him something of the same support the elf had given him when he'd confronted Kathie.

Kory shook himself loose from his mood, and turned his attention to them. "Indeed," he said, "that is a good question. I'm loathe to deprive those three of such a location. We are, frankly, louder than they, and it is quiet here. I do think we could afford to go elsewhere." He looked sideways at Beth. "Could we not?"

"We certainly could," she replied, an impish grin on her face. "And I have a very choice spot in mind. After all, we've had lunch; now is time for desert!"

Eric laughed. "I might have known!" he said, and pointed an admonishing finger at her. "It's all going on your hips, and you're never gonna be able to get back in those leather pants!"

"What?" Kory asked, bewildered, looking from Beth to Eric and back again. "What? What is this about?"

"The chocolate truffle booth by the Kissing Bridge," Eric replied, shaking his head. "Beth's a closet chocoholic."

She hung her head in mock shame. "Mea culpa. But I still think we should see if the venue's free, and grab it if it is. And I promise not to overindulge. But I've earned *one*, surely?"

"All right," Eric conceded. "One. But there'd better be something there *Kory* can eat." He raised an eyebrow at the elf. "Don't forget for a second that chocolate has caffeine in it. *I* haven't."

"There is," she said confidently. "White chocolate amaretto truffles. No real chocolate at all, I checked. Or white-chocolate-dipped strawberries. Or peanut-butter fudge. Or—"

"Enough! So, we play for dessert, and then?" Kory asked.

"Then we take a break. Go back to the camp and have something with salt in it to drink." Eric was adamant on that. "We can let the newbies wear themselves out, and we can catch the dinner crowd. We've done all right, we can afford the break."

"I think you should sing a bit, Beth," Kory added reproachfully. "You haven't yet." He gave her the look Eric called "lost puppy eyes," and she made a face. But when Eric gave her a dose of his own version, she capitulated.

They left the tavern and wandered down to the Kissing Bridge. A fiddler and bodhran-player — Eric recognized Ian and one of the girls from this area he knew by sight, though not by name — were just wrapping up and glad enough to relinquish the place and claim their rewards. Evidently the other two put in a good word at the booth as they collected their goodies; the boothies nodded before Beth could even approach them and gave her the high-sign.

"So what are we up to?" Eric asked, putting out his hat.

"If I'm going to have to sing, so are you two," Beth said, with a look that told them she'd take no argument to the contrary.

Eric sighed. "Do I get to pick?" he asked plaintively.

"One," she said.

"All right." He grinned. " 'The Ups and Downs.' "

"Oh no — " she protested, but it was too late. She was stuck with a song about a girl who should have known better — and she couldn't even cry off, because the man's part was longer than hers. All *she* had to sing was the part where she complains about how he's taken advantage of her, and tricked her into thinking he'd given her his name when he hadn't.

"Be grateful I didn't pick 'Ball of Yarn,' " he said, grinning even harder. "Or worse."

She only groaned, and nodded to Kory to lead off again.

The rest of the afternoon was even better; with no money worries for the day, they joined several others whose "take" hadn't been as good, to give them a boost. Kory was even persuaded by the step-dancers to join them in an impromptu table-dance. It paid off handsomely for the girls; Kory fairly charmed the coins out of the hands of the ladies, and Eric thought once that one yuppie-type was going to stuff a bill into the waistband of his breeches, but she evidently remembered that she was at the Faire and not a Chips revue at the last moment, and put the fiver in the hat.

By the time the Faire security chased everyone out, Beth had gone to boothies three times to get the change they'd collected converted to bills, and every time she came back, her smile was broader.

When they were in another tent, changing back into their riding leathers, she whispered the total to Eric, who whistled. Even allowing for the fact that it was a three-way split, it was worlds away better than *he'd* ever done alone. Today alone was going to cover the utility bills for the month. Tomorrow might well take care of groceries for the month as well —

— and the Faire would run for the next seven weeks! That meant their take at the Wharf could be put aside, saved for leaner times, like the winter.

Last winter had been very lean; too many days of cheap noodles, too many arguments with Kory about the advisability of using magic to conjure up better food. Too many weeks wondering if they were going to be able to pay the electric bill; too many nights huddling together to save on heat. Too many times wondering if their odd menage was going to work — if Beth was going to storm out, if Kory was going to flee Underhill, or if he himself was going to give in to his temper and bludgeon one or both of them. Faire season was going to make the difference.

Faire season was going to keep them together.

Eric donned his helmet and mounted up behind Beth, his heart completely light for the first time in months. It was going to work. *They* were going to work.

And now was truly time to party!

● CHAPTER THREE

My Feet Are Set for Dancing

Eric's elation lasted as long as it took them to get to the highway; then it turned into terror. He'd forgotten that the three of them were going to have to make some serious time to beat the others back to the Bay — and that Beth and Kory knew very well that all the cops were going to be babysitting the crowd pouring out of the Faire and would have no one free to see to the back roads.

He wasn't afraid they were going to break the posted limit; he *knew* they were going to shatter it. *He* was afraid they were going to break the speed of light.

He just kept his head tucked down, his legs tucked in, and held onto Beth's waist. And kept his eyes closed.

To distract himself, he replayed the Celt show in his head, trying to figure out why it was he had so nearly gone into full Bard-magic mode.

It wasn't the other musicians; that just helped after I got there. It wasn't the songs themselves; we've done them a million times. Was it the crowd?

That had something to do with it, he decided. But why *this* crowd, when they'd played for crowds just as big on the Wharf and he'd never had that happen before?

What was different about a Faire audience?

Finally, he decided there was only one thing it could be. Attitude. The crowds on the Wharf were not looking for anything, they had no expectations, and they were not ready for the unusual. The travelers at the Faire were *expecting* things; expecting to be surprised, to be entertained, expecting to enjoy themselves with something entirely new and different. They were even willing to suspend their disbelief and pretend they had been magically transported back in time.

They were ready to believe in magic.

And that readiness to believe had helped him give them magic. He could have done all kinds of things by accident if he hadn't recognized what was happening and put a lid on it.

Christ, that's what happens with a classical audience too; they sort of put everything mundane on hold and let their imaginations go. It's just that I haven't done a concert gig in so long, I'd forgotten it. That must be why I was able to bring up those nightmare things when I was a kid.

It made him wonder what would happen if the travelers ever got wrapped up enough in something that they *did* flip over into full belief. The idea was a little frightening; he'd had trouble hanging onto the tiger's tail as it was.

But if there ever came a time that he would need that belief, and the power that came with it, well, it was a good idea to know what it could do.

They can't work magic themselves, but they can give me the power to do it. Wonder if that was why Perenor was trying to get them and the nexus under his thumb, to harness all that creative energy for his own use. . . .

That sent him back to thoughts of Ria Llewellyn. She was *not* a good person to be around if you were weaker than she was, that was for sure. She'd drain you dry, and throw away the husk with a little shrug of regret. Eric suppressed a shiver; he'd come darn close to becoming one of those used-up husks. When he'd stomped off to Ria, mad because Kory and Beth had — well — done what was natural, she'd taken him into her home. *Now* he wasn't so sure that where she'd taken him hadn't also been partly Underhill; like the old ballads where someone goes Underhill for a day, and when he comes back a year has passed, he didn't think he'd spent more than a couple of days with Ria, but it had been *months* in the real world. Time enough for the Fairesite to be bulldozed, for the nexus there to begin to fade, and for Kory to give up in despair and go off by himself to die.

And when Ria had taken him Underhill, he'd been different. He hadn't been able to compose; he'd barely been able to play, and when he did, it was with none of the "juice" he'd become accustomed to having.

Ria had been draining him; of that he was certain. No, she was not a good person to be around when you were something less than she was.

But if you were her equal —

He played with that notion a while. It was dangerous, but intriguing. She was a very sexy, very capable lady. And there was a soft side to her that he was pretty certain she hadn't let anyone see but him: a vulnerable Ria who had been hurt over and over by an indifferent mother and a manipulative father.

What if they *could* meet again as equals?

Hell, and what if a boat could fly? One is about as likely as the other. Her brain's fried, and that's the bottom line. Hopefully whatever Happy Home Elizabet has her in is careful not to hire abusive attendants. Otherwise they'd have themselves a sure-enough sex doll, 'cause she wouldn't know or care what was happening to her.

He cracked an eyelid open and took a peek; sighed with relief. They were just coming down off the mountain and San Francisco lay before them, like a jeweled crescent pin around the Bay. Kory and Beth would have to cut the speed now; they were about to hit traffic.

The lights were on when they pulled up to the house; Eric felt Beth's muscles tense under his hand, but Kory brought his steed to a halt and pulled off his helmet, shaking his hair loose. As Beth pulled up beside them, he grinned.

" 'Tis Arvin, Pelindar, Treviniel, and some of the others. They have hasted ahead to help us. Oh, and Greg is here as well, but they have chased him from the kitchen —"

"My microwave!" Beth bleated, and abandoned the bike, leaving Eric to balance it precariously from the passenger's seat. It hovered for a moment, until he could get control, fortunately. He managed to keep it from falling over, scooted forward to grab the handlebars, and got off. Kory shook his head, and led the way to the garage.

Funny how that bike kind of balanced itself for a minute. I guess my luck-factor has really kicked in today. They walked the bikes to the garage, locked them in, and came up through the gardens.

There were two elves — Eric could see their pointed ears if he looked really closely, the way he did if he suspected illusion — already in the hot tub. They waved indolently at Eric and Kory as they passed, but didn't move. By the stature and the fact that they looked like adolescents, Eric guessed that they were Low Court elves, the kind that were tied to specific oak groves and couldn't leave them without a lot of magical help from their High Court relatives. The Low Court kids — he always thought of them as kids, even though they were usually hundreds of years old, since that was what they looked like and often acted like — tended to hang out in shopping malls a lot. They'd use their magics to copy or snitch whatever hot fashion items took their fancy, replicate just enough cash to buy themselves endless meals of junk food, sneak into the movie theaters, and play video games that lasted for days. No one ever noticed them, since they looked just like all the other kids in the malls. The kids — the real, human kids — seemed to instinctively know the difference, though, and they tended to keep away from the elves.

The sole exceptions were the occasional misfits — usually girls, nerdy, bookish, and usually very lonely — who would be taken up by one or more of the elves over the course of a summer. At the end of that summer, the girl would return to school, transformed by her brief fling with magic and by the subtle touches of the elves. Sometimes they stayed misfits, sometimes they became very popular — but the end result was that they had usually found out what magic there was that lurked within them, and were much happier than they had been before.

They would never remember anything more than a summer romance with someone really incredible that centered around the mall. The elves took care that any memories more than that never stayed, and the one who had chosen the human lover would change his or her face so that it would never be recognized again.

Eric often wondered if that was what Kory had originally intended to do with him and Beth. If so, he had changed his mind at some point. And Eric got the feeling that some of his kin did not approve.

Yeah, these mixed-species marriages never work. . . .

Oh well, if they didn't approve, at least they were being civilized about it. They weren't shunning Kory or his human friends. Which was more than you could say for — oh — the average Italian-Catholic getting involved with a Lebanese-Arab.

Much less two, though the elves seemed a lot less hung up on the mathematics of sex than humans. He'd seen them going around by twos, threes, and mobs. Hell, Arvin usually had a whole harem.

He followed Kory up the stairs, into the kitchen. Beth was nowhere to be seen. Arvin was in charge of plates of little somethings that looked incredibly fattening. He was idly filling tiny cups of pastry with something from a big bowl — not touching either, of course. Eric liked Arvin, a lot. The elf looked like a dark blond version of Tim Curry, and had a wicked sense of humor. One of the Low Court elves, a gorgeous girl in full punk gear, except it was pink, was doing something with the microwave. Evidently *she* knew what she was doing; she was setting the time, putting trays of sausages in, and nuking them until they sizzled, then dropping them into a warming-pan to stay hot. She grinned saucily at Kory, who only sighed. There were two other elves Eric didn't recognize; one, a real fairy-tale princess type who looked like she wouldn't know how to file her own nails was cutting up veggies with brisk efficiency and arranging them on dip plates. A vast set of trays of cold cuts and cheese already completed bore mute testimony to her expertise. A second, another Low-Court, this one a surfer-duuuuude complete with tan, glaring Hawaiian shirt and baggies, was running the trays out to various locations in the living and entertainment rooms.

Arvin looked up from his work. "We have things well in hand," he said mildly. "Revendel and Lorilyn cleaned e'er we arrived, so there is nothing of that for you to do. I sent them to soak in yon human boiling-pot. Greg is below also, making certain the outdoor speakers function still."

Eric looked around. "I can't see anything else for anyone to do," he said, gratefully, as Kory nodded agreement. "Look, I don't know how to thank you guys —"

"A trifle." Arvin dismissed his thanks with a wave of his hand. "Enough that you have built us a trysting and dancing ground below." His eyes glittered wickedly. "And we *shall* be using it, take heed."

"Just don't take it into the street and scare the neighbors' kids," Eric advised. "Okay? Kory, we might as well get a quick shower and change."

"Aye. The mob will be here soon." Kory tossed his helmet into the air, where it promptly disappeared, and ran up the stairs. Eric put his away more mundanely, and followed.

Beth was already out of her clothes and into the shower; they joined her. It was a tight squeeze for three, but they'd done it before. There wasn't as much horseplay as they usually indulged in, but they were still breathless with laughter when they tumbled out, now clean, to scramble into clothes.

Kory and Eric opted for comfortable versions of their Faire outfits: soft, baggy cotton pants instead of the tight leather, and bare feet instead of boots. Beth was doing something she had seldom done before the hair-change; she was wearing a dress Kory had made for her. Soft black and silver, silky and floor-length, it looked vaguely period, but Eric couldn't pin it down to a particular style. Kory had one of those peculiar smiles when she twirled around in it, though, so Eric suspected that it was a copy of an elven design. Whatever, she looked terrific, straight out of the Kevin Costner *Robin Hood*.

The master-bedroom overlooked the front steps; the window was open to the glorious breeze coming in, and there were voices right below. Beth blew both of them a kiss and flew down the stairs to open the door as the doorbell rang.

After that, the guests began arriving in herds, and someone was always answering the door. At least half of the guests were elves, who had chosen, to keep from revealing themselves to the humans, Eric suspected, to enter the normal way rather than just popping into the garden. Most of the rest were the Faire folks who were in on the secret identities of Tom Lynn, Janice Lynn, and Kory Dell — or at least, they knew Kory Dell was a friend of theirs. No one knew about the elves' existence except Beth and Eric — even the former members of

Beth's old rock-group Spiral Dance seemed to have put the Battle of Griffith Park out of their minds. There *were* other humans who knew about elves, like the bunch over on the East Coast Arvin referred to now and again — but the elves themselves had not seen fit to introduce Eric and Beth to them. Maybe they would, someday.

There were more of their Faire buddies than Eric had realized. The Celts alone filled a room. Of course, *one* Celt was perfectly capable of filling a room all by him/herself. . . .

In no time at all, the party was in full swing. There was a group in the entertainment room, laughing, talking, and munching away while cutting-edge rock played in the background. There was a second group in the living-room, watching a videotape someone had made of the Celtic show today, commenting sarcastically and making jokes. A spillover group of costumers in the kitchen were trading project rehashes, to the fascination of the punk-elf in pink. And Greg might just as well not have bothered about the ground-speakers; no one was using them. The clear spot in the garden, just big enough for dancing, held a tiny band of buskers who hadn't gotten their fill of playing during the day — and dancers who hadn't gotten their fill of dancing.

Oh — the buskers are dancing, and the dancers are busking. That explains it.

The hot tub was as full of people as it could be. Eric had a notion that the little nooks and corners made for privacy were full too, but he wasn't crass enough to check them out.

He spent the evening wandering, too restless to settle down, too full of nervous energy to stay in one place for very long. He spent some time with the crowd in the entertainment room when Arvin gave them a free show to the *Rocky Horror Picture Show* soundtrack. Small wonder Arvin didn't have to ken and replicate money! Even *here* he had people stuffing bills in his waistband. And Arvin finished the set with an even bigger harem than usual. . . .

Eric grinned and wandered off. He danced a little, played a little, talked a lot — ate quite a bit. And drank almost nothing, which surprised him. It was as if he'd lost his taste for it.

Funny, he thought, lounging back on the grass and watching Beth dance with Ian, *I never used to think it was a real party unless I'd gotten stoned, drunk, or both.* It wasn't as if there was any lack of opportunity; wine was more plentiful than soft drinks tonight, though there was nothing whatsoever with caffeine in it, as a safeguard against one of Kory's folk accidentally getting a dose. Plenty of people had brought stronger stuff, and he'd had lots of those bottles offered to him. And he knew he'd smelled the green-sweet smoke of weed from the secluded areas of the garden.

I guess I'm having too much fun. I'd hate to miss any of this by being flat on my back — or flat on my stomach; I've done that, too.

Gradually the crowd thinned; he found himself escorting people to the door and looked at his watch. He could hardly believe it when it read one a.m. But the kitchen clock agreed with it — and when he looked around, he realized that the only guests left had pointy ears and looked nowhere near ready to retire.

As if he had read Eric's mind, Arvin turned away from the pink-punk elf-girl. "Anyone not in a condition to drive has been found a driver or has been put to bed upstairs. Beth I sent up to bed not five minutes ago. Kory needs but an hour or so of sleep — but *you*, mortal, will feel the effect on the morrow if you do not seek yon waterbed."

Eric nodded reluctantly. "But — " he said, feeling as if he ought to at least make the motions of being a host.

"Go!" Arvin scolded. "Kory is host enough for us!"

He left, gratefully. Beth was already asleep, in her usual place in the middle of the king-sized waterbed. He stripped off everything but the cotton pants and took his usual place, on the right.

The sounds of the party — much quieter now — drifted up through the hall and the windows. He listened to the music for a moment, puzzled, trying to determine what record it was, when a sudden change in key and tempo made him smile. It wasn't a record, of course, it was elves making music in the garden, blessing it and the house in their own peculiar way.

He fell asleep, still smiling.

Something awakened him, though he couldn't remember what. A whisper of sound, like someone calling to him very quietly, from very far away.

:Bard, do you hear me?:

"No, I don't," he muttered to himself, trying to bury his head beneath a pillow. "Go away."

He blinked once, looking around the dimly-lit room. Beth was still asleep, one arm flung out towards him, her hair in a wild tumble on the pillows. From downstairs, he could hear quiet elven voices . . . Kory and his friends, talking in the kitchen. Eric glanced at the clock, and winced, closing his eyes again. *Three a.m.!*

:Bard, do you hear me?:

He sat up abruptly, the waterbed shifting underneath him at the sudden movement. *:Yes, I hear you. Where are you?:*

:Outside.:

He moved carefully off the waterbed, trying not to awaken Beth, and to the window. Outside, the street was shrouded in fog. Someone was standing outside on the sidewalk, barely visible through the mists, looking up at the house.

Several moments later, after pulling on the black silk robe that Kory had conjured for him, Eric was padding quietly down the stairs. He slipped past the elves in the kitchen and out the front door, still not certain why he didn't want to tell anyone else about the unexpected visitor. The concrete was cold and damp against his bare feet.

And the stranger was nowhere in sight.

Great, he thought. *Just what in the hell is . . .*

He noticed it then, the strange, unnatural silence that had settled over the sleeping city. Like the world was holding its breath, waiting for something to begin.

In the distance, a dog barked. And another. A flight of birds, nesting in the oak tree next to the front door, suddenly took wing, wheeling overhead and scream-ing shrilly.

Something . . . something's wrong . . .

He could feel it then, a low, rumbling noise that seemed to be growing louder. The ground rippled beneath his feet, rising gently like a wave, then falling. The front door began to rattle in its frame, at first quiet-ly, then more insistently. Eric turned back to the house, took a step forward, and . . .

The earthquake hit in full force, hurling him to his knees. Everything was moving, panes of glass shattering like gunshots, the sidewalk cracking beneath his hands. Eric covered his head with his hands, trying to protect himself from a spray of flying glass as a pickup truck was shoved hard against the streetlight. With a rending crash, the house across the street ripped away from its neighbor, tilting slowly before collapsing into the next building.

As suddenly as it had begun, the rumbling ended. He could hear the wail of dozens of car alarms, but no other sound. A small aftershock rippled beneath him, then was gone.

He stood up unsteadily, and stared at the ruin of the street. Two of the houses had collapsed completely, while several others were canted at strange angles.

Something struck him in the small of his back, and

he looked up to see plaster and wood falling from the fourth floor of his house into the street. The house began to fold in on itself, like a stack of cards in slow motion. He stared, too terrified to scream. Then someone shoved past him, climbing the wreckage of the house, screaming curses and prayers incoherently.

Himself.

The other Eric disappeared through a ruined window. He still stood on the street, frozen in shock. The streetlights flickered once, then went out, leaving everything in foggy shadows. A moment later, his duplicate climbed through the window, carrying an unconscious Beth. He set her down gently on the broken concrete, and immediately began mouth-to-mouth resuscitation. Blood was mixed with her long red hair, pooling on the sidewalk.

He stood there, unable to move. The other Eric slowly looked up at him, tears mixed with blood on his face. "You didn't stop it, you bastard," his other self whispered. "Kory's dead in there, a Cold Iron nail through his face, and Beth's dying . . . and you didn't do anything to stop this!" Something fluttered past the other Eric, a half-glimpsed shadow. Another, a touch of darkness, flitting past them.

He could see them now, the shadows in the fog. Nightflyers. Hundreds of them, moving down the silent street. They moved past him as though they couldn't see him, circling around the other Eric, Beth still cradled in his arms. His double yelled in pain as one of the creatures brushed against him, and swung at it, not connecting with the lithe shadow. Another slipped by, with a delicate touch to his back, his exposed face. Others gathered at the edge of sight, drifting with the fog.

I can't move — can't do anything — He tried to call a warding, something that would protect himself and the other, but the magic eluded him, just out of reach. *Dammit, Beth always told me to practice doing magic without*

*using the flute, and I never did, and now we — and I — are
going to die for it!*

The night brightened with a burst of light as the
other Eric summoned a Ward, his Bard magic blossom-
ing before him. The creatures recoiled for a moment,
silhouetted by the bright light, then closed in. The light
flickered once, then vanished. The shadow monsters
flitted aside; for a brief moment, he could see his own
dead face, blankly staring. Then the Nightflyers turned
to face him, radiating malevolence, their shadow-claws
reaching . . .

"Eric! Wake up! Eric, please, wake up!"

He blinked, looking up into a pair of concerned
green eyes. Kory moved back so Eric could sit up, and
he realized that Beth was watching him, too. "Guys,
I'm okay, it was just a bad dream."

There was a frightened look in Beth's eyes, something Eric rarely ever saw. "It's the same bad dream,
right?" she asked. "The same nightmare you've been
having once a week for the past month." She glanced at
Kory, then back at him. "Want to talk about it, Eric?"

*Houses collapsing down the street, Beth's blood on his hands,
the nightmare creatures closing in around him —* "No, I
don't want to talk about it. C'mon, it's not a big deal.
Just a nightmare." He managed a laugh. "I should
probably stop eating lunch at that burrito place near
the Park. Their food would give anybody nightmares."

"This isn't funny, Eric!" He recognized that look in
her eyes now . . . it had nothing to do with fear, it was
that tough-as-nails Beth Kentraine that he knew and
loved. "I'll call a doctor tomorrow. Somebody has to figure what's going on inside your head, love."

"Of what value is a human physician?" Kory asked.
"Eric is a Bard, not a normal person. There should be
nothing wrong with him that he cannot cure himself."

"We're talking about something wrong up here,
Kory — " Beth tapped the side of her head. "Humans

have special doctors for that kind of thing. Psychiatrists. And even magic isn't good for that kind of stuff . . . remember Perenor? He was crazy-psycho, a real nut case. His magic didn't help him there."

Kory's eyes widened in horror. "Eric isn't like Perenor! He could never be like Perenor!"

"I didn't mean he was like Perenor, just that it's the same kind of thing."

"I don't want to talk to a shrink," Eric protested. "Beth, it's just a bad dream!"

"A bad dream that you've had for over a month!"

"Look, I've talked to enough shrinks in my life, okay? I don't want to see another one, ever."

"Eric, I love you. I don't want you to have to go to a psych. But something's wrong, and you have to do something about it."

"No shrinks," Eric repeated stubbornly.

"We'll talk about this in the morning," Beth said, matching his stubbornness.

"Beth . . . " Kory began hesitantly. "You say this is a human thing, but could this have something to do with Eric's magic? Some Bards have the ability to look into the future, or to call to others from the past . . . "

His own eyes, staring and lifeless — "Kory. It's only a dream. Maybe Beth's got the right idea, maybe I'm nutso, but it's still only a dream."

"But Kory could be right." Beth sat up suddenly. "Eric, have you ever used your Bardic magic to look into the future?"

"Bethy, I've only been a Bard for a year! Give me a break!"

She gave him a look. "Well, you could give it a try," she said. "Take a look into next week and see if it turns out like your dream."

Oh God, I hope not. "Okay, okay, I'll try it, if only so you won't sign me up at the local psycho ward. Now, I think we all could use some more sleep, right?"

He lay there in the darkness, listening to Beth's quiet breathing, the waterbed shifting as Kory turned over onto his side.

I can't be seeing the future, he thought. *That can't be what's going to happen to us. San Francisco destroyed, Nightflyers everywhere, all of us dead . . .*

I won't let that happen.

In his mind, he thought about a particular melody, light and airy: "Southwind." A gentle tune, one that had always reminded him of quiet pleasures and warm evenings with friends. Good memories. That was the tune he would use to look into the future.

He could hear the lilt of the melody, adding just a touch of ornamentation at the end of the B part, a little trill to wind back into the melody. He imagined the way his fingers would press on the flute keys, the exact timing of his breath.

"Oh, what the hell," he muttered, moving carefully so he wouldn't wake Beth or Kory. "I'll never be able get back to sleep tonight anyhow."

● CHAPTER FOUR

A Moonlight Ramble

Once upstairs, he retrieved his flute from its stand, then moved quietly down the stairs and out into the garden. There was one place that he loved most in Kory's garden, a small stand of birch trees that circled a grassy area in a ring.

Eric sat down under the leafy trees, which had been scrawny saplings until two months ago, when Kory had "convinced" them to grow more quickly.

As always, he had the same sense that he had felt that night, years back, in the old oak grove at the destroyed Southern Fairesite, that feeling of magic lying just beneath the surface, woven into everything around him.

Just enough moonlight shone through the night fog to reflect off the flute as he brought it to his lips. It was his favorite kind of San Francisco night, the city finally quiet and sleeping as the fog swirled through it. Little tendrils of fog moved around the trees; he could taste the fog, thick and damp, as he breathed in the night air. And over all of it was the sense of belonging; this place was his, this was his home.

He'd never felt that before, not during his childhood or all the years of traveling. Now, in the perfect still-ness, he played for himself and for the sleeping city.

He frowned at the first note he played: flat, and very thin. He adjusted the flute accordingly, and played another note, clear and vibrant, followed by the first few notes of "Southwind."

The tune unfolded before him, lilting notes fading into each other. He concentrated on the tune, on the coldness of the flute's metal against his fingers, on the way his lips shaped each note. After a few moments, the world faded from around him, and he was alone with the music, playing out his soul to the birch trees that bent closer to hear him.

All right, he thought, *now let's take a look Elsewhere.*

He began weaving that into the tune, the future that he wanted to see, letting the dancing notes build it out of moonlight and fog. Suddenly, it was there, shimmering before him.

Ria Llewellyn?

She stared at him, an image of mist and fog. Behind her, he could see the outline of a motel room, neon signs flickering beyond the window. Her eyes were bright with astonishment, and more than a little fear. He followed her look to the other side of the room, where he saw . . . himself, wearing a pair of silk pajamas and looking more than a little bewildered.

Eric was surprised, too. Too surprised to keep playing, he missed a note, then another. The image of Ria vanished instantly as he lost the thread of the melody, swirling back into the fog.

He sat back, his fingers clenched tightly around the flute. Then, hesitantly, he brought up the flute again and began to play.

This time, he didn't blindly reach out for whatever image would appear. Note by note, he built the idea, gathering in the moonlight as a canvas. Then he sat back and looked at what he had created.

A hospital room. Seated by the window, an elderly woman in a red silk dressing gown, staring out through the darkened glass. No, not an elderly woman; a blond woman in her thirties, her face drawn and pale, motionless, giving the impression of great age. Her eyes never moving, she gazed intently through the glass — at nothing. An empty courtyard.

The blue eyes never wavered, only blinking occasionally. He could hear someone moving through the room, the sounds of someone walking closer. "Time to be in bed, Miz Llewellyn," an older man's voice said, and then the orderly was helping her stand, walking with her back to the bed. He tucked her under the blanket, then moved out of sight. A moment later, the click of a door closing. And the blond woman was now staring at the ceiling, her eyes never moving, the expression on her face never changing.

Eric drew back from the image, horrified. *It isn't fair! She was cruel and manipulative, but she never deserved this!*

But if the other image was also a Far-Seeing, then maybe eventually she'll be okay. Maybe eventually she'll get past what happened to her at Griffith Park.

But if that was a True Seeing, and she does recover —

— then what in the hell am I doing in a motel room with Ria Llewellyn?

Okay, okay. Better not worry about that right now. Concentrate on what I saw in the bad dream . . . let's see if you have any basis in reality, little nightmare . . .

The images of Ria faded back into the mists, as Eric began playing the tune again. Slowly, focusing all his concentration on the image, he called out into the night, trying to reach the future he'd seen in his dreams, over and over again. Then, suddenly, he saw it, the images spread out before him.

A desolate landscape of San Francisco, the streets dark and deserted, buildings half-collapsed, shattered. He stood at the corner of Market and Castro, near the entrance to the subway station. It was a part of the city that he'd walked through many times, especially with Kory . . . Korendil loved to walk through the Castro District. Kory's cousin Arvin, the dancer, lived only a few blocks away.

Now, the streets were empty of any sign of life . . . not a human being, or a bird, or stray cats, or even insects. Only broken glass, and wrecked cars, and the occasional shadow flickering in the moonlight.

No, not shadows, he thought. *Nightflyers.* Quietly, trying not to draw any attention to himself, Eric moved down the street, past the movie theater and the bookstores, wondering what else he could find here. There was nothing, no sign of life, no clue as to why this had happened.

He stepped over the corpse of a young blond child, lying on the sidewalk, and towards a newsstand. He looked around for a newspaper, wanting to see the date printed on it, and then stopped short. He turned, very slowly, and looked back at the corpse.

Tiny shadows were flickering over it, barely visible against the boy's pale skin. Eric reached down and lifted one of the shadows, the nearly-insubstantial creature feeling like damp tissue paper against his skin. It was tiny, not quite the size of his palm, but already he could see the distinctive billowing-cloak form of a Nightflyer.

Jesus, these things can breed!

He dropped it quickly, brushing off his hand. The shadow bounced against the concrete, then drifted back to the corpse, hovering over the dead boy's eyes. Shivering, Eric turned away.

A Nightflyer was floating directly in front of him.

Eric brought his flute up to his lips, desperately thinking of anything he could use against the creature. He was about to launch into the first notes of "Banysh Mysfortune," when the shadow-monster stepped back several paces. In a strange, almost courtly gesture, it bowed to him, then faded from sight. Eric stared at where the creature had stood, and blinked in astonishment.

In the next moment, he was seated in the garden again, the fog coiling around the trees beside him. Eric buried his face in his hands, trying to think.

It's going to happen. Something is going to destroy the city, and these things are going to take over, and all of us are going to die, and my future self yelled at me for not preventing it, and one of those monsters bowed to me! Dammit, none of this makes any sense!

Kory was waiting at the back door as he trudged back through the garden. "I could not sleep," the elf said. "Your magic awakened me."

"Sorry about that," Eric muttered, heading towards the doorway. Kory caught his hand as he walked past. "Eric, what is wrong? Why won't you tell us what you have dreamed?"

I can't tell him that it's just a dream. Not anymore. "Kory, do you believe that a mage can see the future? Not just imagine it, but really see it?"

Kory nodded. "Of course. It is a very difficult spell, but I have known several elven lords who could look into the future."

"And if you see it, does that mean it's going to happen?"

"I don't know. I don't think so. Lord Terenil . . ." Kory's voice caught slightly on the name of his former lord and mentor, killed two years ago. "Terenil said that he could see the different paths that lie ahead, that there were always several futures before him. That the future was like the wind, but something that could change without warning. He said that it was dangerous to look too often into the future, because that might make one future, the one that you perceived, more likely than the others."

"That makes sense," Eric said, sitting down on the porch stairs. "Kory, I — I don't know what to do. I think I've seen the future, and it's awful. Really bad. I don't know what I can do about it."

"Do you wish to tell me about it?"

Beth, lying dead in his arms . . . "No, not really. Let's just say that it's really awful, and I sure don't want to see it turn into reality. What can we do to change it?"

Kory gave him a troubled look. "Perhaps we should talk with someone else, another mage, to find out whether or not this was a True Seeing. We could cross over to the Faerie Court of Mist-Hold, and talk with the Queen. Or talk with some of Beth's friends, the human witches and healers. Beth said that Elizabet and her apprentice, Kayla, would be in the city this weekend. We could skip the Faire today, call them and ask their advice."

"That's a better idea than calling a shrink, that's for sure. Especially if this is magic-related." Beth plunked herself down on the steps next to them.

"You too, huh?" Eric grimaced.

"Yeah, it's tough to sleep when neither of you are in the waterbed. Even tougher than when you snore, Eric."

"Thanks a lot!"

"Well, it's four a.m., and I certainly won't be able to go back to sleep. What do you guys want to do for a few hours until sunrise?"

They all smiled at each other.

"Hot tub!"

The three musicians walked into the cafe, musical instruments slung on straps and in hand. One of the waiters gave them a peculiar look, probably wondering why three scruffy street musicians were walking into his restaurant. Elizabet and Kayla were waiting for them, already seated at one of the window tables.

Eric slid into the seat next to Kayla. "A new pair of safety pins, kid?" he asked, looking at the pair she wore instead of earrings. They matched perfectly with her torn t-shirt, black leather jacket, and studded armbands.

The girl favored him with a wicked look. "It's my way of getting Elizabet to buy me a new pair of earrings."

The older healer laughed, ruffling Kayla's short brown punked-out hair. "This girl is a never-ending source of joy to me. I'm very glad you crossed my path that night, child." She looked at Kory, Beth, and Eric. "Perhaps you would want to order breakfast? Everything at this cafe is quite good. We've been eating here every morning during the conference."

"How's the conference going?" Beth asked.

"Reasonably well. Any time you gather more than a hundred Wiccans together into one building, there will undoubtedly be chaos. But I believe we are accomplishing something. Just yesterday, we worked on a formal contract of apprenticeship, so that the other witches won't necessarily have to adopt their students, as I have with Kayla."

A waiter took their order, then hurried away. Beth waited until he was out of earshot, then leaned forward, her elbows on the table. "Liz, I mentioned this over the phone . . . we're here because of a problem. Eric has been having a lot of nightmares lately."

Elizabet stirred her coffee. "Both Kayla and I are experienced at healing traumas and emotional problems, though Kayla's turning out to be better at that than I am. She's done very well with Ria Llewellyn in these last few months."

"How is Ria?" Eric asked neutrally.

"Some days, she's better than others," Kayla replied. "Sometimes she's almost lucid. A few weeks ago, she gave me this." She lifted a small amulet from where it rested on her t-shirt, tugging the necklace over her head and handing it to Eric.

He looked at it closely, wondering where he had seen something like this before. It was a small circle carved out of some kind of translucent rock, maybe a geode, with the outline of a shadowy mountain drawn out of the colors of the rock.

"I'm not certain what it is, but it's unusual," Eric said. "It might be magical, I can't tell."

Kory leaned over to look at it, puzzled. "It looks like one of the mountains in the Faerie Realm," he said thoughtfully. "One of the distant mountains, near the edge of the Lands Underhill."

Eric handed it back to Kayla. "It's probably harmless, but I'd be careful with it, anyhow. Why did Ria give it to you?"

"I don't know. She was nearly catatonic for days afterwards, and then couldn't remember it when I asked her about it. Sometimes I feel like she'll never get better . . . "

"You're doing fine, child." Elizabeth smiled reassuringly at her protégé. "Some healings just take longer than others." She glanced at Eric. "Tell us more about these nightmares, Eric. Are they all the same dream?"

He nodded. "Mostly the same. They're mostly about earthquakes." *And Nightflyers, those shadow-demons that I summoned accidentally several years ago. First at that concert, and then at Ria's, and now in my dreams . . . why do those damn things keep turning up in my life? It's like I have some weird affinity for them, somehow.*

The Nightflyer, bowing to him . . .

"And last night, after we talked about how this could be a precognitive dream, I tried to look into the future. And I saw the same thing as in my dreams, except this time I was awake." He stared down into his cup of coffee. "I'm afraid that I might be seeing the real future, that this is what's going to happen to us."

"What can we do about this?" Kory asked. "If this is a true future that Eric is seeing, we will want to do everything we can to prevent it from becoming reality."

Elizabet thought about it for a minute. "Kayla's very sensitive. If Eric looked into the future again, while she was near him, she might be able to determine if this is a fantasy that Eric is creating in his own mind, or something real."

Eric glanced at the young healer, wondering if he really wanted the punkette kid in his mind.

The girl grinned, showing teeth. "Don't worry, Bard. I'll be gentle."

"Thanks a lot," he muttered.

"We should try this as soon as possible," Elizabet continued. "Maybe tonight."

"There's something else wrong, isn't there?" Beth asked.

Elizabet grimaced, just a little. "Yes, unfortunately. Eric isn't the only one who's had problems with nightmares lately. Several of the Wiccans at the conference have had the same problem. Not dreams about earthquakes, but other things. Kat and Lisa had a similar nightmare, about being hunted by some kind of shadow-creature."

Eric's fingers tightened around his coffee mug.

Beth was quiet for a long moment. "Eric, how soon do you want to do this? We really need to get some rest so we can hit the Embarcadero, or we'll miss the business lunch crowd."

"Okay." He sat back in his chair. "Tomorrow night."

Monday, they were standing in the Embarcadero plaza across from the Italian fast-food place where two dozen gray-wool "suits" were busily chowing down on pizza slices.

Beth scanned the crowd, and pointed to a corner with some benches next to it. "How 'bout that one, guys?"

Kory began unpacking the instruments. Eric just stood there for a moment, looking very tired, before he opened his flute case and began to fit the pieces together. Beth couldn't blame him for being tired, considering what had been happening lately. She just hoped that Kayla and Elizabet could do something for him. Maybe some caffeine would help. "Guys, I'm in desperate need of coffee. You too, Eric?"

He nodded blearily.

"Sparkling water for me," Kory said, looking up from where he was seated on the bench, rubbing the bodhran to tighten the drumhead. "The French brand, please."

Elves, she thought. *If we're not careful, Kory'll be the first yuppie elf in history.*

She headed over to the closest food stand, glancing around at the crowd as she stood in line. A shiny new Mercedes, pale blue and with dark-tinted windows, was parked on the street nearby. A blond man in a blue business suit — *the expensive kind,* Beth thought — stood with another man, staring down at a map spread out over the hood of the car. He looked up and saw her watching him. A moment later, he walked up to her, smiling shyly.

"Excuse me, miss?" the man asked. "Could you show me the best way to get to the Japan Center from here? I have a map in my car, but the one-way streets are so confusing. . . ."

"Sure, not a problem." She walked to the curb, where the man's friend was puzzling over a map spread out on the hood of their Mercedes. "Probably the best way is to go straight up to Van Ness, then over to Geary —"

Something hit her hard, in the small of her back, and she fell into the open car door, landing on the back seat. A split-second later she heard the door slam shut, and the sound of the car's engine starting. The interior of the car was very dark, and smelled of new leather and strange chemicals. Something cold and metallic pressed against the back of her neck, and she froze, not daring the breathe. Very slowly, she turned to stare down the barrel of a small pistol, only inches from her face.

The blond man shook the pistol at her like a teacher admonishing a naughty child. "Please, don't bother screaming. No one will hear you outside the car. Now, if you'll just sit back and relax, everything will be fine."

They're right, the barrel of a gun looks awfully huge when you're staring down into it. "If you guys think you're kidnapping me to get a ransom," Beth whispered, "you are in for a big surprise. Why are you doing this?"

"We're not interested in money," the blond man said, and Beth felt the car lurch out into traffic. "Please, don't ask any more questions." He sat back, the pistol resting in his hands.

Beth edged away from him, until her back was pressed against the car door. She glanced down at her watch, noting the time. *Think like a hostage, Kentraine. Be smart. Figure out everything you can about these bastards. Knowledge is power.*

Power. . . .

She tried to calm herself, to concentrate, imagining that long-haired too-handsome face, imagining him seated on the plaza bench, probably already wondering why it was taking her so long to get two cups of coffee and Perrier. . . .

Eric, hear me. Eric, I'm in trouble, I don't know what's going on, but I need your help, you and Kory. Come on, Eric, listen to me. . . .

"Son of a bitch!" The pistol cracked against the side of her face. Everything went white for a moment, and she tasted blood. "You're going to sit there and do nothing and think nothing, girl," the man warned her. "Or I'll kill you."

"Bastard," she muttered, covering her face with her hands, trying not to tremble too much. The tears were harder to fight, but somehow she managed to keep from crying or shaking too much by staring down at her clenched fists in her lap, only occasionally reaching up to wipe away the blood from her mouth.

It was a small room, bare concrete walls painted white, at the end of a series of concrete corridors that led out from the silent underground parking garage. The dark-haired man in front of her was also white, wearing some kind of white laboratory coat. He frowned at her when he saw the blood on her face, and gestured for her to sit down in one of the two wooden chairs in the room. He took the other chair, sitting in front of the plain table with the laptop computer set up upon it. The blond man and his driver took up positions next to the door.

Her jaw still ached, but the pain was nothing as hot as the fury in her brain. *I don't know what in the hell is going on here, but I'm going to kill someone,* she thought. "So, schmuck, why did you bring me here?"

He smiled. "Call this a recruitment drive. We have a form here that you can sign, which'll allow us to treat you as one of the team, defining your legal rights in this situation."

She hardly believed she had heard him say that. "Team of what? Psychopaths? No thanks, slimeball."

"Or we can work out some other arrangement," he continued, as if she hadn't spoken. "But it would be much easier for us if you volunteered. Much easier for you, too."

"Or there's a third option: you can let me go, and maybe I won't send the cops and the mother of all lawsuits against you, mister," Beth said angrily.

"You won't file a lawsuit against us." The man gave her a cold, patronizing smile. "You don't even know where you are, or who I am. If we toss you back out on the street, all you'll be able to do is spin some ridiculous story about being kidnapped by government officials. And no one will believe you, of course."

"So you're a government agency?" *Christ, none of this is making any sense!*

"What is your name?" he asked, glancing down at the laptop computer on the table in front of him.

"Up yours," she replied tightly.

He shook his head. "Not a very original answer. So, tell me about yourself. What are you afraid of?"

Bastards like you. What kind of place is this, anyhow? She didn't bother to answer his question, studying the

blank white concrete walls. It looked too solid to be an
office building. She remembered the thin plaster walls
of the television studio, and how you could hear people
yelling through them at every hour of the day and
night. This was more like a bunker than an office building . . . who built in concrete slabs, anyhow?

"What are you afraid of?" he repeated.

*Police, handcuffs, the blood staining the walls of Phil's
house like a surrealist painting . . . run away, before the Feds
catch you and lock you up forever in a dark, airless cell. . . .*

"You know," she said in a conversational voice, "I bet I
could break your nose before your goons could stop
me. That would be an interesting experiment,
wouldn't it?"

The man made a note on his computer, then looked
up at the blond man. "Bill, please turn off that fan by
the door. Yes, thank you."

She glanced at the fan, then at him. "Why did you do
that?"

"It felt a little chilly in here, don't you agree? Don't
worry, there's plenty of air circulation in the building."
He glanced back down at his computer screen, wrote
several more words.

"So, is there anything you're afraid of?" he asked again.

"Damn, it's getting stuffy in here," she muttered,
glancing at the fan again. The room seemed smaller,
the air already heavier, harder to breathe. . . . "Nothing. Nothing scares me. Especially not an asshole like
you. Do you really think you're going to get anything
out of me?"

He smiled.

"I think we're finished here, boys. We'll need to go to
level 4-A next . . . call ahead to clear the hallways, I'd
rather not run into another misguided Berkeley intern
who doesn't understand the situation."

"But that's the Aerodynamics level, sir." One of the
young thugs had a puzzled expression on his face.

So did Beth, she was sure. *Government . . . Berkeley intern . . . aerodynamics . . . it felt like we were driving for no more than an hour and a half . . . am I in the Dublin Laboratories?* She shuddered involuntarily at the thought of hundreds or thousands of nuclear weapons, possibly only hundreds of feet away from her. *Armageddon at my fingertips. But that's not all they do at the Dublin Labs. Other kinds of research, too. So why am I here? And why in the hell did these idiots kidnap me?*

She stood up slowly, wondering whether she should try to make a run for it, maybe risking getting a bullet in the back. Or maybe she should just wait and see what happened next . . . *they need me for something, hell if I know what. That's what this whole song-and-dance is about. So maybe I wait and see what they want, and then use that against them?*

It seemed like a good idea, as they walked through the empty corridors and down several flights of stairs. Until she saw their destination, the huge metal sphere crouched in a corner of a lab, covered with dials and pressure gauges.

"You're not —" she said whitely, and turned to run. Blondie caught her and she screamed, kicking him hard. He cursed and dropped her, staggering back into a table covered with glass beakers and notebooks. The other thug grabbed her before she could bolt for the door, and shoved her through the narrow metal opening. The tiny chamber reverberated as he slammed the door, spinning the bolts shut tightly. Beth screamed and pounded on the glass window until her hands ached.

All light vanished suddenly as the room outside went dark. Beth slid down the cold metal wall, huddling on the floor of the chamber.

This is insane, they can't do this to me, they can't — A low rumble and hiss of machinery began, and she could feel the air pressure increasing. She swallowed, feeling her ears pop suddenly, and closed her eyes, trying to calm herself.

This can't be happening to me. What kind of lunatic locks someone in a decompression chamber? Especially someone who's ... claustrophobic ... like me....

Stay calm, stay calm. Don't let this get to you. They're doing this deliberately, you can't let them win....

She pressed her fists against her face to stop her hands from shaking. She could feel the screams building against her tightly-closed lips. The darkness seemed to close in around her, thickening, too heavy to breathe. An invisible hand tightened around her throat, cutting off her air —

Hyperventilating. I'm hyperventilating. Have to slow down my breathing. Think, Kentraine, there's plenty of air in here, you're not going to suffocate, that's all just in your mind....

Breathe. In, out. In, out. Slowly, calmly, you can do it, just concentrate on your breathing....

Her breath was very loud in the tiny room, gasping for air. She was too hot, it was too hot in here; she ripped open the front of her blouse, just as the room's temperature seemed to plunge by fifty degrees. She wrapped her arms around her knees, and shivered. Nausea hit her like a wave, and she choked, losing the rhythm of her breathing.

God, please, please.... She gulped for air, and the panic hit her, overwhelmed her ... she heard screaming, and recognized it as her own voice. Her stomach emptied itself suddenly, and left her choking on the taste of coffee and bile. She couldn't breathe; the darkness brightened to a checkerboard of glittering black and white, as she shook and trembled and wanted to die.

A creak of metal an eternity later, as the door opened slowly. She tried to get up, but she couldn't stand. The blond man lifted her to her feet, but her legs were trembling too much, and as he let go of her she crumpled back to the metal floor. She couldn't stop crying; she couldn't speak or scream, only cry, deep wrenching sobs that hurt her aching chest.

The dark-haired man shoved a piece of paper and a pen in front of her; she tried to pick up the pen, and dropped it, her fingers too numb to hold anything. "I'm sorry, I'm sorry," she managed between sobs, as they hauled her back to her feet and toward the door.

She couldn't remember how long she walked, gasping and sobbing and unable to feel the floor beneath her feet. They let her fall down onto a plastic mat, in a small concrete room without a window, but it was cooler, she could feel the chilled air against her skin, not the insane darkness that had clenched her throat and ripped the air from her lungs. She lay there and cried, feeling like something was broken inside, something wrong with her heart and her head. She couldn't think, everything was too blurry and bright and terrifying. She cried and cried, huddled on the plastic, until someone turned off the light overhead, and then she began to scream again.

● CHAPTER FIVE

Nonesuch

"No, I didn't see where she went, no, I don't see her anywhere, and will you stop asking me that!" Eric snapped in frustration, "The answer doesn't change by asking the same thing over and over!" He walked as quickly as he could on the crowded sidewalk, craning his neck in vain for a glimpse of Beth. Kory followed him several feet behind, looking uncertainly at the pedestrians on the street.

"But why would Beth leave us here?" the elf asked plaintively.

Eric couldn't help himself; he exploded. "Jesus, Kory, I don't know! *Stop asking these stupid questions, okay?*" People glanced at him in startlement at his outburst, then away, quickly. Kory's eyes darkened with anger for a moment — but the moment passed, and Eric tried to put a leash on his temper, feeling ashamed of himself, but too upset to admit it. Something was wrong, something was very wrong, but he didn't know what or why, and that *wrongness*, coupled with Beth's disappearance, had him at a breaking-point.

"Look," he said tightly, after affronted silence from Kory, "why don't you see if *you* can figure out which way she went? You're the one with all the experience at — uh — hunting. Don't you have some kind of tracking ability or something?"

More silence for a moment, and he turned to see

Kory staring vaguely off into space. "I think she went that way," Kory said, and pointed east.

"How did you figure that out?" Eric said, trying very hard not to snarl. If the elf knew *that*, why couldn't he figure out where she was exactly?

Kory shrugged helplessly. "Just an intuition. I think she's over there somewhere." Kory waved in the general direction of Oakland, Berkeley, and Alameda.

"Only two million people live in that direction, Kory!" he growled. "Can't you narrow it down a little?"

"We should start searching over there," Korendil replied, his eyes focused on the far distance. "We should search until we find her. That is what any good hunter would do."

Eric couldn't help it; Kory's simplistic "solution" brought out the sarcastic side of him with a vengeance. "Right. You want to start walking through Berkeley and Oakland? You want to go ask two million people if they've seen her? Be my guest. It should only take you about fifty years or so."

Kory gave him a level look. "Have you a better plan?"

Eric's mouth tightened. "I'm going to retrace our route and figure out where she might've gone, whether anybody saw her leave, all of that. If you want to go off on a wild goose chase across half of the Bay Area, then do it! I'm going to do this scientifically, like the cops do . . . damn shame we can't call any of them in for this."

He thought about it for another minute. "Besides," he continued, half to himself, "maybe Beth just decided to go home." But the mere idea had a false ring to it. *Without telling us. When she'd just gone to get coffee. Sure.* "You can do what you want. But *I* think the first thing we should do is check around here some more, then check back at the house in case she left a message, and then make a plan of action if we still haven't gotten anywhere."

Kory nodded, as if Eric had answered him, then

picked up his and Beth's instrument cases and began walking away.

Eric stared at the moving crowd of business-people, wondering where to start. *She went for coffee and mineral water. That means it was one of these places here . . . maybe the donut place, or the Italian food stand . . .*

A flash of something colorful and familiar caught his eye; he looked up just in time to see Kory walk aboard a Metro bus, not fifteen feet away from him, and the door closed behind him.

"Goddammit, Kory!" Eric ran to the bus, nearly falling into the path of a speeding BMW as the bus pulled away into traffic. "Dammit, Kory, I didn't mean it!"

The bus pulled away, Kory still on it, doubtless headed for Berkeley. He gave chase for another futile minute, then gave it up as he avoided death by Beemer for a second time.

He sat down on the curb, winded, and wondered what in the hell he was going to do next. Beth missing, and Kory vanishing off to search the East Bay house by house. . . .

For one selfish moment, Eric seriously considered burying his face in his hands and crying, but that wouldn't exactly be constructive. Kory knew where he was; he knew how to get around on his own. And he could have magical resources he hadn't told either of his human partners about, maybe things he couldn't do while they were around. Maybe he would be able to kick something up if he went off on a lone hunt. And if he didn't, well, he knew Eric would be going home if he came up dry. So if Kory had gone off to hunt the way an elf could, playing a magical MacGyver, Eric had better go play Spenser Junior, boy detective.

First stop, the donut shop.

He pushed the door open, and the bell over it jangled as shrilly as his nerves. "Excuse me, miss?" he asked the young woman behind the counter. "I'm looking for someone. . . . "

"Well, you've found someone," the woman looked like she'd come straight out of a James Dean movie, pink waitress uniform and bleached, teased hair and all; she glanced at him from across a tray of fresh donuts, and smiled flirtatiously. "What can I do for you, handsome?"

He didn't answer the smile. "A friend of mine is missing. Tall gal, long red hair, very pretty . . . "

"Sorry, I don't notice the women very much. Want a donut?" Her continuing smile suggested that he might want to try something else instead of a donut. Eric felt the blush beginning at his ears, and fought it, somewhat unsuccessfully.

"You haven't seen anyone like that?" he persisted.

The smile faded. "No, can't say I have." She turned away from him, plainly dismissing him as a lost cause. He spoke to her back as he pushed the door open again.

"All right. Thanks." She ignored him.

He quickly retreated from the donut shop, looking around for other likely places. The sushi stand probably didn't sell coffee, or the Thai shop, but the Italian place. . . .

The portly, elderly man behind the stand nodded with recognition as Eric described Beth. "Pretty gal, long red hair? Stacked?"

At last! "Yeah," he said eagerly, "that's her."

The old man rubbed the top of his bald head, and smiled at him the way you'd smile at a slightly stupid child. "I don't think you need to worry about her. She left with some friends. I saw her talking with them on the curb, then they all left in their car."

Friends? A car? Why wouldn't she have come back for us? "What kind of car?" He couldn't believe she'd just *leave* like that if it really *was* friends. So it had to be something else altogether. Cops? Maybe the Feds had caught up with her? But that didn't match the feeling of *wrongness*. . . .

"A nice car," the old man replied vaguely. "A really nice car. It was blue."

Eric tried to imagine just how many "nice blue" cars existed in the Bay Area. "Great. Thanks. You've been a real help." *Shit.*

He turned away from the stand to ponder his next move. *All right, think this through. Beth wouldn't just leave without telling us where she was going. Those guys weren't friends, no way. Besides, we don't know anybody with "nice" cars; everybody we know drives wrecks. Maybe they were Feds, or something worse. But what could be worse than Feds?*

He didn't want to think about that.

Four hours later, he didn't want to think about anything. No sign of Beth, and no new clues other than the old man's comments about her "leaving with friends." Eric sat heavily on a bench, wondering what he was supposed to do next. Go home? But that wouldn't accomplish anything either, and it would take him *away* from one end of the "trail," such as it was.

At five p.m., the Embarcadero Plaza was like a sea of human beings, waves of people headed toward the parking lots, Metro, and BART stations. He lay on his back on the bench at the edge of the stream of humanity, looking up at the four tall skyscrapers and a glimpse of blue sky, and tried to come up with some tactic he hadn't tried yet.

"Excuse me, can you help me?"

He jumped in startlement. "What?"

Eric looked up to see a young, blond man in a blue suit smiling at him. Blond, handsome, but not as cute as Kory. He smiled back, without any real feeling.

The young man took a step closer. "I'm a little lost. I've got a map over here, but I don't know where I am on it exactly. Do you know how to get to — " The man gestured at his car, parked in a red zone a few feet away, with a city map spread out over the hood.

Eric froze.

A blue car. A Mercedes.

A nice blue car. Just like the one that drove away with Beth —

Eric tried to jump away and fell off the bench, landing on his hands and knees. Before the man could react, he vaulted to his feet, and took off like a sprinter towards the plaza. The blond man cursed and grabbed for him; Eric felt his hand catch and slip off the fabric of Eric's jacket.

If there had been any doubts as to the man's intentions, that move had canceled them.

Eric leaped over another bench, dodging around a trio of businesswomen and a young man selling flowers. He clutched his flute case to his chest as he ran across the plaza, trying to spot a place to hide. In the Embarcadero, there weren't very many options.

He tripped over the curb, dashing across the street as the traffic light changed to green. Drivers honked at him, then a squeal of brakes behind him caught his attention. He glanced back to see a car skid to a stop inches from the blond man, who was only a few seconds behind Eric.

He turned the corner, and then another, hearing the man's running feet close behind him . . . and stopped short, confronted by a blank wall.

A dead-end alley. Dead, just like he was going to be, if that blond guy caught up with him.

He glanced back, trying not to panic. No time to get the flute out of its case. No time for anything, in fact. Except maybe to yell for help and hope somebody paid attention.

Or to try magic-music without the flute.

He puckered up, took a deep breath, and began to whistle the first thing that came to his mind, thinking *very* hard about being invisible. His mind had no sense of priorities; it chose a jaunty Irish tune, "The Rakes of Mallow." He nearly lost the melody as the blond man

dashed around the corner, slipping on some of the
scattered garbage. The stranger quickly regained his
footing, and looked around the alley.

Frowning.

His glance slid over Eric as though he wasn't there.

I'm not, really. Just part of the garbage in the alley, m'friend.
Managing to calm down a little, since the trick was
working, Eric whistled the B part, willing the man to
give up, turn away; willing the man to see nothing.

It was a long, tense moment.

Finally the blond man obliged, a snarl of frustration
on his face, walking back toward the plaza.

It was tempting to run off. Even more tempting to
stay where he was —

Beth. If those men have her —

Still whistling, Eric strolled after him, simultaneously
thinking about being invisible while rooting in his
pocket for the stub of pencil he usually kept there. He
snatched up a bit of litter as the man reached his car,
then jotted down the number of the Mercedes' license
plate on the scrap of sandwich-paper he'd caught up.
The blond man conferred with another business-
suited type standing by the car, then they both got into
their vehicle and drove away.

Eric didn't stop whistling until the car turned the
corner onto Market Street and disappeared into traffic.

Then he sat down on the curb and thought, very
hard. Harder than he ever had in his life. About kid-
nappers in fancy cars. Kory, who was still gone after
several hours. And Bardic music, which had saved
them once, back in Los Angeles, and was probably the
only thing which could save them this time.

*God knows, I sure can't go to the San Francisco cops over
this! And where in the hell is Kory?*

Korendil, Knight of Elfhame Sun-Descending and
Elfhame Mist-Hold, squire of the High Court, Magus

Minor, and Child of Danaan, stood with his arms crossed, trying to understand the forces behind an electrical fence.

He had sensed the danger from it, and noted the way that the grass had been carefully cleared away from it. Then, trying to understand what was so alarming about a plain metal fence strung with wires, he was treated to the spectacular sight of what happened when a hapless sparrow had the bad sense to try landing on the fence.

Just as dazzling as his battle with Perenor, in a small way . . . and with the same result for the sparrow.

It would seem that climbing this fence is not a good idea, he thought, considering the scorched bird lying dead at his feet. *Even if Beth is here, somewhere under the ground ahead of me.* She was there; he was sure of it. It had been intensely frustrating to try to make the Bard understand that his ability to track Beth depended not so much on spell-born magic as on the spiritual bond that the three of them had forged. Tracing her had been like playing the child's game of "warm — getting warmer." That was as close as he could come.

Perhaps it was just as well that Eric had remained behind to try human means of tracking. Without the Bard nearby to confuse the vague tuggings in his heart, it was easier to pinpoint Beth. He walked back toward the road and the place where the bus driver had stopped to let him out, and then to the guard gate. Beyond the gate, he saw that the road led into a large parking lot, surrounded by several block-like gray buildings. "Excuse me?" he asked politely, knocking on the glass panel of the guardhouse at the gate.

The panel slid open, and a woman peered belligerently out at him. She wore a uniform that Kory liked immediately, a dark blue jumpsuit with different badges pinned on it. It was very attractive. The woman would have been, too, if she had not been frowning. He wondered what he could possibly have done that would so raise her ire.

"Go away, kid. Your peacenik friends aren't doing their annual blockade of the Labs until next month." Her teeth bared in something less like a smile than a snarl. "Unless you want to start early. You could spend the next month in jail, until the rest of them arrive."

He shook his head, not understanding the woman's strange speech. "No, I am not wanting to go to jail. I'm here looking for a friend of mine. I believe she is inside this place."

"Hmmmph. Should have said so." The woman gave him an odd look, but softened her frown a little. "You look so much like one of those hippie-activists, I figured you were here to make trouble."

"No, no trouble," Kory said earnestly. "I just want to find my friend."

"What's your friend's name?" she asked, consulting a printed list.

Now he was getting somewhere. "Beth. Bethany Margaret Kentraine."

The woman shook her head. "Sorry, she's not on the cleared list. Maybe she's working back at the University? A lot of the interns get switched back and forth between the various labs . . . "

The sense of *Bethness* was even stronger now. Why was this woman claiming that Beth was not there? "I know she is here," he protested. "Down there — " he pointed off in the distance.

The woman's expression hardened. "Sorry. If she's not on my list, she's not here. You'd better move along, now."

"But I have to find Beth," he told her stubbornly. He turned away from her and began walking through the tall metal gates.

"Hey, kid!" The woman called from behind him. He

heard the sound of sirens going off, a shrill wailing noise. Kory kept walking.

The next sound he couldn't ignore, a loud blast of noise from directly behind him. He turned. . . .

. . . . and found that he was looking down the twin barrels of a shotgun.

"Back through the gate, kid," the security guard gestured with the shotgun. "No one goes into the Labs without clearance. You seem like a nice boy, but you can't go any further."

He looked over the gun into the woman's eyes, pleadingly, trying to trap her gaze. "Please, I have to find Beth. I promise I won't damage anything here —" He caught her eyes; held them with his own. Touched her mind.

:Please . . . just let me walk through.:

The woman nodded, slowly, her eyes blank and unseeing, and Kory turned away, satisfied that she would no longer impede him. He continued down the road toward one of the square, squat buildings. Several people with drawn guns ran past him, heading for the gate-house. Movies and television he had seen suggested that they were answering the alarms the woman had triggered — but the same shows also told him that if he acted as if he belonged here, rather than as an intruder, they would ignore him without the intervention of magic.

He let himself in through the double glass doors of the largest building, looking around curiously. Another human in a similar uniform to the woman was seated behind a large desk. Before the man could respond to the door opening, Kory touched *his* mind as well; he glanced at Kory, then back at a screen on the table, ignoring the presence of a stranger. A bright red light was flashing on his desk; he paid no more attention to it than he did to Kory.

Kory crossed the sterile, white-painted entry-hall,

stopped in front of a large row of elevators, and pressed the button. He looked up as another team of blue-jumpsuited humans ran to the double glass doors, taking up odd positions near the glass. It reminded him of another one of the movies he and Eric had watched on the television, with the policemen moving in pretty, dance-like patterns through rooms and stair-ways, hunting for an enemy. These humans seemed to be running in the same patterns, one dashing forward and then stopping behind a desk or a potted plant, and then another running past the first one, to stop at another desk or potted plant. It would probably be a good idea to leave the area as quickly as he could. The humans would not be inclined to ignore him for much longer, and he wasn't certain he could hold *all* of their minds at once.

The elevator arrived with a happy DING! sound, and the doors opened. Kory stepped inside, and stopped, freezing as a primal fear chilled him through all of his veins.

Iron. Cold Iron, all around him. Not touching him, but close enough that he could feel the chill on his skin, the whisper of death in the silent metal.

He wanted to turn and run, to get as far away from this place as possible. He'd been in elevators before . . . Eric and Beth had taken him up in the elevator to the top floor of a place called The Hyatt, so they could drink wine in a restaurant and watch the sunset from a vista of windows overlooking the city. But this elevator was different, built of more solid metals, more deadly metals.

He took a deep breath, and reached for the button panel inside the elevator. He couldn't retreat; not with a lobby full of wary, angry humans behind him. And besides, all of his instincts told him he had followed the right path. *Beth is down there. I cannot leave her here. The iron will not harm me, it is hidden behind layers of plastic and other metals. I can ignore it. I can do this. I can.*

The elevator doors closed. Kory kept a tight hold on himself, fought down his fear, and considered the array of buttons, each one with a peculiar slot next to it.

He tried to decide which one to try first. He knew Beth was on one of the lower levels, but how deep? He could spend days in this place, trying each button.

Just to get started, he pressed one button. The elevator did not move.

Odd. Elevators move to the floor you press. So why wasn't this one moving? Kory chewed his lip, and again noticed the strange slots, next to each button.

The slots were roughly the size of one of Beth's old credit cards . . . he remembered how impressed he had been by the idea of giving someone a piece of plastic and in return they would give you all kinds of clothing, boots, even food. But Beth said they couldn't use her cards anymore, the police could track them that way.

In any case, he didn't have any of Beth's credit cards with him, not now. If he needed one of those cards to make the elevator work, this might turn out to be more difficult than he thought.

Perhaps there was an easier way. . . .

He knelt and pressed his hand against the elevator floor, twitching slightly at the feel of plastic against his palm. *But not Cold Iron. I can touch this, it won't hurt me.*

He pressed harder, a magical push against the elevator floor, forcing it downward.

The elevator descended silently, and Kory closed his eyes, trying to imagine where Beth might be, trying to "reach out and touch someone," as Eric always joked, trying to find . . .

There! The elevator chimed and the doors slid open for him.

It was another featureless hallway, with a young man seated behind another desk. Kory looked at the man's badges and insignia, and decided that he did want a badge with his own picture on it. Perhaps after he and

Beth left this place, they could go find someone who made those badges. . . .

"Hey, how did you get down here? Where's your security badge?" the young man blurted, as Kory approached.

The sign over the young man's desk was interesting: Psychic Research Wing. Q Clearance Required.

Psychic . . . Kory knew he'd heard that word somewhere before. Perhaps Beth, talking with one of her Wiccan friends. Clearance, now that was a word he understood . . . that was when everything was half-price at Macy's, and Beth had to go buy clothes for herself. Together, though, the sentences did not make much sense to him.

As Kory considered this, the youth reached under his desk, and when his hand emerged, he held a small pistol, aimed directly at Kory with an assurance that told the elf that the human knew how to use this thing, and use it well.

:Please. You should not threaten someone, especially a warrior like myself. I do not intend you any harm. I am seeking my friend Beth Kentraine. I know she is here, somewhere . . . have you seen her?:

The young man stared at him, his hand dropping, his mouth and mind both opening like poppies in the sun. An image appeared in Kory's mind, of a woman walking down a hallway . . . no, barely able to walk, a stranger supporting her on either side. A door closing, and the sign 13-A Room 12 on the wall outside it.

"Thank you," Kory said gravely, and started down the corridor. Behind him, he heard the clatter of the pistol falling to the ground, followed shortly by the sound of a body landing on the plastic floor.

He carefully followed the row of signs, each labeling a closed door. From behind one door, he could hear someone crying, as if from a very far distance. Someone was calling out hoarsely from behind another door, the words too faint to understand. He stopped in front of "13-A Room 12," and tried the doorknob. It refused to open. Kory frowned, and considered the lock for a moment, then closed his eyes, gathering his will.

Korendil was not a Great Mage, not as innately talented as the Bard, but Terenil had taught him a few tricks, in the years before caffeine and depression had claimed the elven prince. Such as how to escape from a locked cell, if necessary. But a trick for breaking out from a cell ought to work for breaking into a cell . . . He touched a fingertip to the lock, and willed the door to open, the bolts to slide back. A soft click, and he turned the knob, opening the door to look within.

It was quiet, and dark. He stepped into the small room, allowing his eyes to adjust to the darkness. Someone was huddled on the floor against the far wall, not moving.

"Beth?" he called quietly.

The figure did not move. Kory held out his hand, calling light, and a soft glow filled the room.

"Beth?"

Kory.
He was staring at her, those leaf-green eyes reflecting the light in his hand. He was so handsome . . . and so far away, outside of her skin, too far for her to touch.

She was cut off from everything, everyone, smothered in fear and darkness. Just like when she was two and she'd followed her folks out into the dig, and the trench they'd abandoned had collapsed, burying her. Dirt had filled her mouth, like this thick darkness — suffocated her, just like the darkness was doing now. One of the grad students had seen her hand and dug her out; he'd known CPR. . . .

But there was no friendly grad student here, and Kory didn't know CPR, and anyway this darkness was thicker and more treacherous than dirt.

She wanted to say something to him, but the silence

within her head was too loud, drowning out everything, her thoughts, her words. Somehow he didn't seem to see it, the thick darkness pressing in all around them, closing her in, pinning her against the wall. Even with the light in his hand, she could see that the light itself was being eaten by the darkness, becoming part of the screaming in her mind that wouldn't stop, couldn't stop. She felt the tears welling up again, and wrapped her arms more tightly around her knees, trying not to cry.

He knelt next to her, touching her face. With another surge of horror, she realized that she couldn't feel his hand, couldn't feel anything. All of her body was numb, lifeless. She was dead, only her heart hadn't figured that out yet; it was still beating somehow, a wild, erratic rhythm.

I need to tell him about the darkness, Beth thought, desperately. *I need to tell him about how the room is pressing against my skin, that there's no air to breathe, no way to escape.*

She opened her mouth to tell him, and the voice screaming in her mind filled the room with sound, and it wouldn't stop, it wouldn't let her go. . . .

"Beth?"

She was staring at him, not saying anything. Something was wrong. He didn't understand. She should be glad to see him; he'd come to take her away. Why was she looking at him that way, and not speaking? She recognized him, he knew that, but why wouldn't she say anything?

She was sitting strangely, too, all curled up against the wall. He'd never seen Beth sit like that . . . usually she sprawled out on a couch, or draped herself over a chair like one of the stray cats he occasionally brought into the house for milk and conversation. He saw that she was trembling as she tightened her arms around her knees.

Hesitantly, he reached to touch her face, a gentle caress. Her eyes stared at him, unblinking. She didn't smile or laugh the way she usually did, when his fingers brushed against the ticklish spot on her neck.

Something was very, very wrong.

Then she began to say something, and Kory smiled in relief. If she would just tell him what was wrong, then he could do something —

She screamed.

The shriek pierced Kory like a knife. Panic closed his throat as he tried to calm her and got no reaction, not even recognition in her eyes. He didn't know what to do, if there was anything he could do . . . the sound seemed wrenched out of Beth's throat, ending in deep sobs that shook her entire body.

He did the only thing he could think of. He sat down on the cold plastic floor beside her, and held her until her body stopped shaking, and she closed her eyes.

He thought she might be asleep. At least she wasn't screaming. But if she woke again, with that animal-like fear filling her eyes — what was he going to do?

He wished desperately that Eric was with him, to help him understand what was happening to Beth, to help him figure out how to help her.

One thing was certain . . . Beth was sick. This wasn't like the other human sicknesses he had seen, with Eric lying in bed for several days, his nose very red, and coughing frequently. Or the time that Beth had lost her voice; she'd only been able to speak in a funny hoarse voice that made all of them laugh. He knew those sicknesses; even elves were touched with Winter Sickness, though very rarely.

This was something different. He'd never seen one of the Folk with this kind of sickness, unable to talk or move. Even the friends that he'd lost to Dreaming, they had just slipped away into a last sleep, never to awaken. Beth's sickness was something he didn't understand, something he'd never seen before. She needed a healer, like Elizabet or Kayla —

But the first thing he had to do was take her from this strange place with their clearances and too many guns, and back to San Francisco. Once back at home, with Eric, the Bard might be able to help her — or they could go fetch the healers.

A good plan of action.

But before he could move, the door slammed shut. Kory looked up, then stood up carefully, trying not to awaken Beth. He crossed to the door, trying the lock.

It wouldn't open. He glanced down at the orb of light in his hand, and sent it into the lock, to open the door for him again.

Nothing happened.

"Damn, that's impressive," a voice on the other side of the door said thoughtfully.

Kory glared at the door and the unseen person behind it. Without eye-contact, he would not be able to get the human on the other side to help him. Rage burned in his heart as he realized that this must be the person who had put her here in the first place — perhaps even the person who had given her this illness. *I must to get out of here, now! Beth is hurt, sick, and no one is going to keep us locked up!*

He hurled his will at the door, a magical blast that should've broken the door in two.

Nothing happened.

Beyond furious, Kory flung himself at the door, pounding on it with both hands. After several seconds of futile effort, he stepped back, considering the situation.

A sound from Beth, and he turned. She was lying on her side, crying again, and hitting her fist against the floor. He knelt swiftly beside her and caught her hand, afraid that she would injure herself, and pulled her gently into his lap. He tightened his arms around her, truly afraid for the first time since they had left Los Angeles. For the first time since he had awakened in the Grove, he was alone and helpless.

Eric, something is very wrong with Beth, and we cannot leave this room, and I do not know what to do. . . .

Warden Blair hid a smile and listened to Smythe babble. The security guard was sweating, now, and Blair enjoyed making people sweat. "No, sir, I can't explain what happened. Yes, you're correct, he didn't hit me physically, but something knocked me out. I don't know whether he had a gas canister concealed on his person, or it was some new kind of weapon, or . . . "

"Enough with the excuses, Smythe," Blair said tersely. "So, this is the sequence of events . . . Wildmann at the gate reports a caucasian male intruder, long blond hair and green eyes, roughly age twenty-five. She says that he is polite to her, but tries to walk into the installation. She hits the red button, fires a warning shot, pulls the shotgun on him, and he vanishes, right in front of her eyes. Just disappears into thin air. Somehow he gets into this building, lobby security reports nothing, and he gets past the elevator security system as well. Then the guy waltzes in here, you can't stop him, he breaks into one of the rooms . . . which sets off the alarm, something *you* weren't capable of doing . . . " Smythe flinched visibly. " . . . and then Harris locks him in there, with one of our patients, using the new security system."

"Well, if he pulled some kind of trick on Wildmann, then maybe that's what he did to me," Smythe said faintly.

"Or maybe you and Wildmann are both equally incompetent." Blair pointed at his office door. "Get out of here, Smythe. Go find something useful to do, like collect unemployment."

The young man's eyes widened. "You can't fire me!"

"I just did." He touched his intercom button. "Harris, please come to my office immediately."

The young man clenched his jaw and spoke through his teeth. "If you fire me, Blair, I'll go to the newspapers. I have a friend at the *Chronicle*, they'd love to hear about this project. I know that not all of the patients are here voluntarily, I know that you tricked some of them into signing the consent forms, some of these people aren't mentally competent enough to *sign* a consent form—"

"Don't bother," Blair said, cutting off the torrent of threats. "If you talk to the press, you'll be in more trouble than you can possibly imagine." Blair leaned forward, elbows on his desk, narrowed his eyes, and smiled. "Keep this in mind, Smythe. I can find you. Anywhere. You know that's the truth. If you try and sabotage this project, I'll find you. And I'll bring Mabel with me, or one of the others. You remember what Mabel did to Dr. Richardson, right? You were the one to find him, as I remember."

Smythe's face was as pale as the whitewashed concrete walls of Blair's office. "All that blood from his nose and mouth . . . she didn't just kill him, I could see his brains oozing out through his ears . . . you wouldn't do that to someone, sir!"

Blair's smile widened.

A knock on the door interrupted them. "Come in," Blair said, enjoying the sight of the young man's bloodless face. Harris walked in, glancing curiously at Smythe.

"Escort Mr. Smythe out of the complex," Blair said quietly. "He is no longer employed with Project Cassandra."

"Of course, sir."

Smythe swallowed awkwardly, and spoke. "I'm not scared of you, Blair. You — you wouldn't do that deliberately to someone."

Blair met his eyes and held them. "Do you really want to find out?" he said softly.

After a moment, the young man broke eye-contact and shook his head. Blair noticed with satisfaction that his hands were shaking as well. Harris walked him out, closing the office door behind him.

Blair leaned back in his chair, propping his feet on his desk. *Idiots,* he thought. *I'm surrounded by incompetent idiots. Even Harris, who lost that kid today in San Francisco. He still can't explain how the kid got out of a dead-end alley. Fools.*

Then he smiled, thinking about his latest . . . patient. *Someone who can get through our top security systems, show up thirteen levels underground in a complex that's supposed to be impervious to the best terrorists and foreign agents in the world . . . I want to take this one apart. I want to find out what he can do, find out how to use him.*

I'll need a good leash on this one, though. Probably the girl; that seems to be what brought him in here in the first place. She's useless to me right now, anyhow. And she may be ruined completely — I underestimated the effects of her claustrophobia.

And then there's the other boy. He registered even higher, a bright light shining in the darkness of San Francisco. We'll get him, too.

I'll prove to those bastards at DoD that we can do it. All of them that said I was a crackpot, that this could never work . . . they'll see. When I show them someone who can walk through security systems like they don't exist, or someone can ditch a top military agent like Harris in less than ten seconds, they'll believe me then . . . they'll have to believe me.

Still smiling, Blair shoved his chair away from the desk and left his office, walking down the corridor to meet his newest acquisition.

● CHAPTER SIX

The Hanged Man's Reel

"Kory? Beth?"

Eric stood in the front hallway, burdened with two
armfuls of musical instruments, hoping against hope
that the next thing he'd hear would be a resounding
"Eric, you're home!" from Beth, followed by a hug
from Kory and a kiss from Beth. Then they'd all laugh
about the weird events of the day, and probably still be
laughing as they piled into the bubbling hot tub. . . .

Only silence greeted him.

He walked down the hallway and into the kitchen,
sitting down at the table and burying his face in his
hands. He looked up longingly at the bottle of Black
Bush on the counter, then away.

No. No whiskey. I've got to think, to figure this out —

It had gone so bad, so quickly. Now he didn't know
what to do. He'd envisioned disasters, figuring that
their good luck was too good to last, but they'd always
been things like . . . Kory falling off a ladder while
fixing the roof. Beth, slipping on the wet deck near the
hot tub. Himself, setting the kitchen on fire while
trying to make pancakes. But not this, never this.

His first impulse was to run. They'd kept a small
amount of cash in the house for just that reason, in case
the cops came knocking at their door one afternoon
and they had to run fast. He could catch the night bus
out of town with that money, be out of California and

into Oregon by daybreak, and he'd be out of reach of the local cops. Except that blond man hadn't acted like a cop — a local cop would've flashed a badge and slapped a pair of handcuffs on him before he could blink, and hauled him away in a black-and-white . . .

That expensive blue car. Policemen don't drive Mercedes. In any case, he couldn't leave Beth and Kory behind. Two years ago, sure, not a problem, but not now. They were the closest damn thing he had for family, and he wouldn't abandon them.

The lyrics from a Faire song drifted across his thoughts: "No, nay, never . . . no, nay, never, no more, will I play the Wild Rover, no, never, no more . . ."

And I won't, Eric thought. *They're depending on me. I won't let them down.*

Except how in the hell am I supposed to help them? I don't know where they are, what could've happened to them . . .

What can I do?

He wanted to scream, or cry.

Instead, he set his flute case on the table, and opened it.

The flute lay there quietly against the crushed velvet, no hint of anything that had happened before reflected in the silvery metal. No sign of dragons, or elven sorcerers, or shadow-demons called up from the darkness . . . no hint of anything, in fact, just a simple musical instrument waiting to be played upon. Eric quickly fitted the pieces together, and played a quiet note, a long A tone. He slid down a mournful minor scale, then into a run of arpeggios. It was hard to concentrate, when his mind kept slipping back to Beth and Kory, and the dark fears that he kept suppressing, holding at bay — *I'll find them. They're out there, somewhere. I'm a Bard, I can use the magic, I can do it. I'll find them.*

Then he began to play "Planxty Powers," an old O'Carolan tune, one that the Irish bard had composed in honor of Fanny Powers, perhaps his lover, certainly his friend. The tune brought back a rush of memories to Eric, of sitting around on haybales at the Renaissance Faire, drinking mulled wine and playing music with friends. Of the first time he'd met Beth; how she'd flashed her ankles at him while dancing a strathspey in the Scottish show, then asked him to teach her that strathspey tune, so she could play along on her ocarina.

And Kory . . . how he'd come home late from the Southern Faire, to find an elf living in his apartment . . . those earnest green eyes, asking him to help. . . .

I won't fail you, pal. I'll find you . . . I'll find you. . . .

The music wove itself into strands of light around him, bright sparkles reflecting off the kitchen windows. He called it closer, and the light danced around him. Within it, he searched for them, calling up images of Kory and Beth, casting his vision out further and further into the city around him . . .

The light became a glow, with him encased at the heart. A softly glowing sphere, that showed him flitting images of the life of the city beyond; places they had been, places they had touched. The park, dark and mostly deserted now, shadows filling the space below the trees. The BART station near the house, as bright as the park was dark, trains pulling up to the platform in uncanny silence. The wharf, bustling with tourists. The Castro district, bustling with . . . a different kind of life. The Embarcadero, the Pig and Whistle where they sometimes played, the Opera House. . . .

All of the scenes, flitting silently in, then out of focus, as his heart searched the city below for the people he loved.

Now the scenes were unfamiliar, and a little less focused; streets, houses, lawns. . . .

Buildings, tall ones, like offices, but with a more closed-in look.

A corridor —

He caught a glimpse of Beth, and concentrated, trying to see exactly where she was. It was difficult, holding the melody and the magic, delicately reaching. . . .

"Beth! Bethy, can you hear me?"

Blair smiled at the young boy seated next to the closed door to Room 12. Harris stood next to the door, an intense blue-eyed watchdog. "How are you doing, Timothy?" he asked.

"Just fine, Mr. Blair," the boy replied. "The bad man inside, he's stopped trying to get out. I guess he's figured out that I won't let him."

"Good work, Timothy." Blair nodded to Harris, who gently moved the boy away from the door. "Now let's talk with this new fellow. Timothy, don't open the door unless you hear my voice, okay?"

"You bet, Mr. Blair."

Harris checked his handgun in its shoulder holster, and opened the door quickly, scanning the room before stepping aside to let Blair enter the room.

The newest acquisition to the Project was seated on the floor next to the red-haired woman. The woman seemed to be asleep, but even across the room, Blair could still sense the turmoil in her mind. The blond man looked up at Blair with eyes burning with fury.

That's right, little fellow, Blair thought. *Hate me. Give me a handle to use on you, a window into your thoughts. Let's see what you're afraid of. . . .*

:You think to imprison me, a Knight of the Seleighe Court? And now you try to entrap my mind! I'll kill you first, bastard!:

Blair couldn't understand all of that . . . *what in the hell is a Seelie Court?* . . . but he certainly understood the way the young man launched himself from the floor, hands reaching for Blair's throat.

Harris intercepted easily, hurling the kid against the wall. Harris always made it look so easy. *Years of practice,*

Blair thought, a little enviously. Harris was used to the difficult ones, the ones that tried to fight before they settled down to become a useful part of the Project.

Harris crossed to where the woman was slumped against the wall. Grabbing her long hair with one hand, he drew his handgun with the other, pressing it lightly against her temple. The woman flinched once at the touch of the metal against her face, but otherwise was completely unaware of anything happening around her.

The young man moved painfully from where he had fallen onto the concrete floor. A trickle of blood slid from his mouth; he ignored it, looking up at Blair and Harris with eyes filled with hatred.

"Now, let's talk," Blair said calmly, sitting down on the bare concrete floor. "I don't think I need to explain Harris' role in this, do I? Behave yourself and be a good boy, and tell me what I want to know, and nothing will happen to your friend. Understand?"

:Never, Unseleighe scum. I will kill you and leave your bodies lying for the forest creatures to feed upon, I will curse your names for a thousand years, I will laugh as your blood pools at my feet, I will do anything to kill you, even brave the touch of Cold Iron itself.:

Blair blinked, astonished at the clarity of the young man's thoughts. "I don't think you understand your situation," he said slowly. "You aren't in any position to—"

He stopped short. The key — the kid had given him the key without even realizing it! Admittedly, it was the strangest phobia he'd ever heard of in his life, but it was a lock-hold he could use. . . .

"I'll be back in a minute, Harris," he said thoughtfully, and left the room.

At the end of the hallway, in the new construction area, he found what he was looking for. It took a little improvisation with a pair of handcuffs and some wire, but then he had what he needed.

Of course, he didn't understand why the kid was so afraid of certain kinds of metal, but that didn't matter. The fears themselves were unimportant; it was the effect of the fears upon the subject that was so valuable. He walked back into Room 12, and held out the contraption with a smile. The kid's eyes widened.

Blair moved cautiously toward the young man, handcuffs ready in one hand. Suddenly everything happened very fast; the kid knocked the handcuffs out of Blair's hand, making a dash for the door; Harris dropped the handgun and tackled him from behind, wrestling with him until Blair could snap the modified handcuffs onto his wrists.

The kid screamed, a long gut-wrenching wail of despair, as the wire wrapped around the handcuffs touched his bare wrists. Then he fainted.

Well, it wasn't exactly the response Blair had wanted, but it was a good start. He'd never seen such an immediate physiological reaction to a mental aberration, but that didn't matter. It just meant that it would be easier to work with the kid, later.

Then he saw the pistol, lying on the floor next to the woman. She was staring at it, uncomprehending. Her hand twitched, moved toward the handgun. . . .

"STOP!" Blair shouted at the top of his voice.

The woman jerked her hand back, clutching her hands to her mouth. She began to cry again.

Harris, breathing hard, reached down to pick up the pistol. "Sorry, boss," he said. "Next time, I'll be more careful."

"You'd better be," Blair said tersely. "We can't afford any more mistakes." He glanced at the unconscious blond boy. "We'll start with him in the morning."

The image faded. He reached out his hand, through the layers of light, as Beth's face disappeared into the shadows.

Eric set down the flute. *So much for magic,* he thought. *After all's said and done, it can't help me find my friends.*

He tried to think of another plan of action . . . maybe calling the cops? It would mean some awkward questions to answer, and possibly a lot of trouble over Phil's death, but the more he thought about that, he decided it was worth the risk. Sure, they might have found some physical evidence that he and Beth were at Phil's house after he was killed, but the odds that they could conjure up some proof that he and Beth were the killers . . . *not too damn likely,* he thought. *It's worth the risk.*

His hand was reaching for the phone, and it hit him a split-second later.

Fire and ice, burning upward from his wrists, an unbelievable pain that knocked him out of the chair. He didn't feel the impact against the floor, but lay there, gasping for breath. Then Kory's voice, screaming in his mind —

:Eric, help me!:

A flurry of images, too fast for Eric to recognize. The pain ripped through him, an agony that went on and on, not stopping. . . .

Darkness.

Eric curled into a ball on the floor, tasting blood where he'd bitten his tongue. For several long seconds, all he could do was lie there and breathe. Then the realization hit him.

Kory. That was Kory. Somehow he made me feel what he was feeling, somehow he . . .

Oh, Christ, is he dead? Could someone have gone through . . . whatever that was . . . and survived? He could be dying right now!

He took several deep breaths, closing his eyes and concentrating on the images that had flashed through his mind.

Beth, huddled in the corner of a room, illuminated by witchlight . . . what is wrong with her, why won't she speak to me?

A pair of handcuffs, wrapped with some kind of wire. . . .

A woman at a gate, refusing to let him pass. A sign on the gate, black words printed on white . . . Dublin Laboratories. Authorized personnel only.

Eric sat up abruptly, his fists clenched. "Kory, what in the hell were you doing in the Dublin Labs?"

He remembered joining some Faire friends for the yearly protest, sitting in the street in front of the gate until the cops showed up to take them away. The armed guards, the electric fence, the ground beyond the fence was probably filled with land mines, for all he knew. . . .

He thought about the impossibility of breaking into the Labs to rescue them . . . *for God's sake, they build nuclear bombs there! The place has the best security in the world, millions of armed guards! How am I supposed to get them out of a place like that?*

What in the hell are Kory and Beth doing in a place like that?

He sat there, breathing unsteadily, wondering what he was supposed to do next. A single-handed assault on the Dublin Labs just didn't seem like a good plan. If he had a personal army, maybe he'd have a chance. But alone . . .

No. He wasn't alone. They had friends in San Francisco, good friends who would help them out. Especially when he told them what Kory had told him, just before their "connection" had been cut. The Mist-Hold Elves, sure, they'd help in a second.

If Kory was still alive. . . .

He forced himself to relax. Panicking wouldn't solve anything. He began dialing.

Five minutes later, he'd listened to eight answering machine messages, two unanswered ringing phones, and one "This number is out of service, and there is no new number" message.

What a great night for this, he thought sourly. *Everyone's out at the Forty-Niners game. Terrific. Couldn't the Bad Guys have picked something other than a Monday night for their kidnapping and attempted murder?*

He dialed the last number on his list, the Holiday Inn near Pier 39. After two rings, someone picked up the phone.

"Elizabet?" Kayla asked. Even across the phone lines, Eric could tell instantly that she was crying.

"Kayla, this is Eric. What's wrong?"

The girl spoke all in a rush. "Elizabet went downstairs to buy a stupid newspaper, she didn't come back, it's been over two hours, the stupid local cops say that's too soon to file a missing person report, I'm all alone in this stupid city and I know something's wrong, I *know* it—"

"Whoa, slow down!" Eric tried to kick his mind into overdrive. *Three disappearances in one day? A coincidence? Not bloody likely.* "Elizabet's not the only one who's disappeared today." He quickly described the events of the day, and the images Kory had sent to him, and the unbelievable pain he'd felt at the same time.

"That sounds bad," Kayla said seriously, gulping down her tears, and getting herself under tight control. "I don't know too much about elven physiology, just what Elizabet and I learned after that fight at Griffith Park . . . I don't think Cold Iron is immediately fatal, not unless it breaks the skin. I'm not certain about that. Elves are so weird, it's hard to say. One of the L.A. elves told us about how long-term exposure to Cold Iron is deadly, but I think he said it took a couple days to kill someone."

Eric realized he had been holding his breath, and reminded himself to keep breathing. "Thank God. So Kory's probably still alive."

"Yeah, but he must be in a world of hurt." Kayla's voice was tight. "Cold Iron apparently triggers all of the nerve synapses continuously during the time of exposure. It's like having your hand stuck permanently in an electrical socket. Really weird. Elizabet has always wanted to know more about it, since we're doing a lot of work with the L.A. elven community now, but we can't exactly do experiments with it, y'know? All of our information is secondhand, and usually hundreds of years old."

"You'd better start at the beginning, Kayla. When exactly did Elizabet disappear? And did you see anyone suspicious around Elizabet today?" *Like two guys in suits, driving a pale blue Mercedes?*

"Okay, okay." He heard the sound of her blowing her nose on the other end of the phone line. "Elizabet and I spent all day at the conference. It was great, I met this priestess from Mendocino who loves Oingo Boingo's latest album as much as I do . . . anyhow, we came directly back to the hotel after the last discussion ended. I didn't see anyone following us or anything like that when we were walking back."

"Anyone suspicious at the conference?" he asked, waiting for the payoff.

"Well . . . yes. These three guys showed up right as we were about to break for the night. They were wearing business suits, so they stood out like sore thumbs against all of us."

Bingo.

"Did you see their car? Was it a blue Mercedes?" he asked, breathlessly.

"No, they were still hanging around the conference when we left, asking questions of various people." Kayla's voice took on a harder tone. "So, Eric, what's your plan? What are we going to do?"

Plan? You mean, I'm supposed to have a plan? Eric suppressed an impulse to blither insanely and spoke quietly instead. "We'll get them back, of course."

"How?"

"First, I'm coming over to your hotel to get you. Don't open the door for *anyone*," he said, wondering if Kayla was on their list, whoever *they* were. "I'll be over there as soon as I can."

He hung up the phone, thinking fast. Bus service in San Francisco was one of the best in the world, but the buses would stop running in another couple hours.

If only he had a car. . . .

But he did have transportation. Two motorcycles. In the garage.

Except he didn't know how to ride a motorcycle.

Except these motorcycles were really elvensteeds, old friends of Kory's that had agreed to live with them and pretend to be motorcycles. They were Faerie horses, they just looked like motorcycles. At least, that was what Kory said.

He slung his flute case under one arm, grabbed two helmets from the hall closet, and headed to the garage. Inside, the two motorcycles sat tamely. Kory had sent the two bikes — horses — back over to the Faerie Court that morning (since they didn't like Earth-style horse feed, or so they said), so at least they were well-fed. Or fully fueled, depending on how you thought about it.

"Listen, horses," Eric said awkwardly. "I have to ask a favor of you. Kory and Beth are missing, and I need to find them. I don't know how to ride either horses *or* motorcycles, so you'll have to get me there. I gotta get over to the Holiday Inn at Pier 39 and get Kayla, 'cause they have Elizabet too. Are you willing?"

For an answer, the bright red and gold motorcycle's engine coughed into life, revving loudly. A moment later, the other bike followed suit.

"Uh, thanks. I appreciate it." He lifted the garage door, then sat gingerly on the red bike, stuffing the flute case into the tank bag and fastening the spare helmet onto the seat clip. "Hey, you," he called to the black and silver bike, "You'll just have to follow us, okay? We need to get Kayla before anything else. She may be in danger too, I don't know."

The black bike's headlight flashed once. Eric assumed that meant an affirmative, but he wasn't certain.

"All right, then," he muttered. "Time for the cavalry to come to the rescue."

The bike sat motionless for a long second, and Eric began to wonder whether or not this was going to work. Then the bike kicked itself into gear, popped the clutch, and vaulted out of the garage so fast that Eric nearly fell off. A split-second later, the black bike followed them into the street.

It's just a horse, Eric thought dizzily, as the bike weaved through the cars, heading straight down Geary toward the Pier. *It's just a horse. And it's only doing . . . eighty-five miles an hour. In a thirty-five zone. Oh my God.*

Eric tried to look calm, tried to look like he was actually controlling the bike and knew what he was doing, but after the third high-velocity skidding turn around a corner, he gave up and wrapped his arms around the tank bag, holding on for dear life. The bike made a noise between an engine cough and a chuckle, and accelerated through a red light and into another high-speed left turn. Eric closed his eyes and refused to open them.

The wail of a police siren forced him to look up. One of San Fran's finest was right on their tail. The two bikes swerved through another right turn, heading due west off Van Ness up into one of the hilltop residential areas. *We're going in the wrong direction!* Eric thought, glancing back as the police car followed them up the hill. The bikes zigzagged through a small series of streets, then turned north again. Eric's heart and stomach both leaped into his throat as he realized they were heading straight for a large stone stairway leading back down into the city below.

With all lights off. As if that made any difference.

"No, don't!" he yelled involuntarily as the bike leaped up onto the sidewalk and then down the stairs. The police car screamed to a stop at the sidewalk behind them. The bike bounced down the stairs, jolting Eric with every one, and skidded to a stop at the bottom of the stairway. It revved its engine, waiting for the black bike to reach the street beside it.

The rest of the ride to Pier 39, thank God, was totally uneventful.

Eric left the bikes parked on the street near the hotel's back entrance, and hurried up the stairs to Kayla's room. He knocked on the door, then knocked again. "Hey, Kayla!" he called, suddenly afraid that he might not have gotten there in time.

The door opened suddenly, and a small hand reached out, grabbed him by the wrist, and yanked him into the room. Kayla quickly shut and locked the door.

"They're out there," the girl said quietly, her back against the door. "Three guys in business suits. They don't have a warrant, so I wouldn't open the door for them."

"Smart thinking, Kayla. Was one of them a young, blond, muscular guy?" Eric asked.

"No. All older men, in their forties or fifties. They weren't the same guys I saw earlier today at the conference."

"We'd better assume they all work for the same company." Eric walked to the window, looking down. "It's a big drop, do you think you can do it? Or do you want to risk going through the hotel?"

She bit her lip, but looked not only determined, but eager. "Of course I can do it. How are we going to get away, though? Did you bring a car?"

Eric thought about the two motorcycles, now parked sedately in the motel lot. "Uh, no, not exactly."

She shrugged. "Well, let's get moving, Bard. Hallway or window?"

"Let's try the hallway first," he said. He opened the hotel room door, glancing down the corridor.

Three men in business suits. Not ten feet away from his nose. Eric slammed the door shut.

"Then again, the window is probably a better idea." He picked up a chair, advancing on the window. "Stand back, kid, this'll probably make a real mess."

"No shit, Sherlock." Kayla stood next to the door, and visibly flinched as someone pounded on it hard from the other side.

Eric swung the chair hard against the glass. It shattered loudly, almost loud enough to hide the sound of two someones slamming themselves against the hotel room door. The door buckled, but held.

"Come on, kid!" Kayla ran toward him, as a gunshot echoed from the corridor outside. One of the three men kicked the door open, just as Eric grabbed Kayla and dived through the window.

They fell haphazardly toward the street below. Somehow he had managed to pucker up and begin to whistle a descending melodic minor scale as they exited — in the final quarter second, their tumble slowed to a high deceleration, but impact-less landing.

The motorcycles rolled up beside them a moment later, engines rumbling.

Kayla blinked and stared at the riderless bikes.

"It's okay, they're friends." Eric climbed onto the red bike. "Just hang on real tight, okay? They don't slow down for turns."

"Hey, I've never fallen off a bike in my life," Kayla said, seating herself on the black bike. "Except maybe if you count that time up in Wrightwood . . . SHIT!" The black motorcycle made a strange noise, something that sounded vaguely like a horse's whinny, as it accelerated out of the parking lot. Eric glanced once at the speedometer as the bikes headed toward the Bay Bridge, and wished he hadn't. *Can't they wait to do ninety miles an hour until we're at least on the freeway?*

"What now?" Kayla whispered, staring at the huge floodlight-illuminated area beyond the guard gate.

"I don't know," Eric replied. *What we need is an army,* he thought. *The U.S. Cavalry coming over the hill.*

It never works out like this in the movies. You never see the hero crouching in the dirt, trying to figure out a plan that won't get him killed. Usually the hero just walks right in, guns blazing, and rescues everyone. Wish I could do that.

Dammit, I'm a Bard! I should be able to do something! Everyone always treats me like I can do anything; all the elves are so sickeningly respectful toward me, even a lot of Beth's Wiccan friends. They all think I'm hot stuff. He remembered meeting Kory's cousin, the exotic dancer, and how the elf had bowed so courteously to him when Kory introduced him as "Eric, the Bard —"

Another flash of memory: standing amid the ruins of Castro Street, and the shadow-creature bowing to him —

It hit him like flash of light, the sudden realization of what he could do.

I need an army. So I'll call an army.

I can do it, he thought. *I've done it before, it's so easy. And they'll answer me, they always have. I can summon an army of them and make them obey me. Nothing can stand against them, nothing can kill them, no guns or explosives or anything. I can bring them here, control them, and use them against my enemies.*

But my dream, with the Nightflyers taking over the city . . . is it because of me, because of what I'm thinking of doing right now?

No. I can control them, keep them from killing anyone. I kept that one from hurting Ria, right?

I'll have to risk it. I don't have any choice.

He took his flute from the case, and played a quiet set of arpeggios, warming up.

Kayla grinned. "I knew you'd think of something, Eric!" she crowed. "What are you going to do, fly us over the gate or something?"

"Better than that," he muttered. "I'm calling the cavalry."

There was no Irish tune that he could use for this. But he knew exactly the tune to play. "Danse Macabre."

The first notes were deceptively soft, the calm before the storm. Then the violin solo, the notes hammering down like nails in a coffin, followed by the melody, faster and harsher . . .

He could feel it starting around him, the gathering of tension in the air, whispers of sound beyond normal human hearing. The shadows on the grass, visibly darkening as he played, slowly rising from the ground. Fingers of cold ran down his back, but he ignored them, concentrating on the music.

"Eric, what in the hell are you doing?" Kayla looked around in alarm at the thickening shadows around them.

A wild flurry of notes, and they encircled him, drifting shapes that danced with the wind. He called to them, and they answered, laughing silently as he brought them to him, one by one. When he finally let the flute fall away from his lips, they floated before him, a huge shadow-army awaiting his command.

While he was caught up in the music, he'd been fearless; now he saw them, and he was terrified.

Chills ran down his spine — a cold born of fear that he'd gotten himself into something he could not get out of again. He'd had trouble controlling *one* Nightflyer — whatever had made him think he could control an army?

Did he control them? Or were they controlling him? Had they used him to bring them here?

Kayla crouched beside him, visibly pale and

trembling. He wanted to say something to calm her, but he could feel his Nightflyers testing his power over them, tugging at their leashes, and he knew what would happen if they escaped his control, even for a moment.

No choice. He was in it; he'd have to finish it. There were only two ways to get out of this one. A winner, or Nightflyer-dessert. He stood up, and started toward the front gate. "*Now* we're going to rescue them," he said, with *far* more confidence than he felt, his shadow-troops adrift behind him.

• CHAPTER SEVEN

A Maid in Bedlam

"W-wait a minute," Kayla stammered, pulling at his sleeve. "Wh-what if they get away from you?" Her eyes were big and round and her face pale in the faint light that reached them from the lab parking lots.

He started to brush her off, a little drunk with sheer power, with the intoxication of controlling so many of the creatures —

But doubt set in immediately; did he *really* control them? Sure, they came when he called, but was that control? Could he really keep them from doing something they wanted and he didn't? And what would happen when they were out of his sight? He recalled the Nightflyer of his vision bowing to him with a shudder. Was that what had happened in that glimpse of the future? Would he lose control of his army?

Would they somehow destroy the city? A chill ran up his back and he shivered at the memory of the dream — and that waking-dream of his vision.

He surveyed the horde of Nightflyers, shadows against the shadows. There was nothing to suggest he was not the one in control, at least for now. He swallowed once, and told himself that he wouldn't lose control of them — because he didn't dare.

But that meant that there was no more time for hesitation. Right now, this moment, they were his completely. If he waited a moment longer, they might not be. But he needed time to think!

Very well, he'd buy himself some time.

He was operating on pure instinct here, but the elves had told him, time and time again, that he could trust those instincts. He followed his impulse and froze them in their places with a brief, chilling run, pitched a little sharp with his nervousness. The notes bit like acid, but they did the job; the Nightflyers stopped moving, completely, giving him the unsettling impression that he was watching a movie on freeze-frame.

Now what?

He stared at them, while he made up his mind exactly what he wanted from these creatures. One of the themes that occurred over and over in the stories of encounters with the supernatural was "be careful what you ask for." There should be no "loopholes" in what he demanded of the monsters, no way that they could obey his orders and still follow their own wishes. He needed them to create as much havoc in there as possible. But only within the confines of the labs; he couldn't afford to let even one escape, not if that vision was true and the things could breed.

A fence; that was what he needed. A way to confine them to the grounds of the labs. But something like that would take more magic than he had by himself. He needed some help, and time was trickling away: time that Kory couldn't afford. By himself, he was a battery, and his charge was running out; he needed a wall-socket, or better yet, a generator —

The nexus!

Every elven community on this side of Underhill centered about a nexus, a place where the fabric between the worlds had been pierced, and the result stabilized to permit magical energy to pass into the human world. Sometimes a nexus had been created, often it occurred naturally. All of the greatest, most populous communities centered on a correspondingly powerful nexus. Elfhame Mist-Hold in San Francisco was no exception.

The magical forces the elves used could also be used, with varying success, by humans with the proper talents.

Humans such as Bards, for instance.

No sooner thought of than tapped; he'd *created* a nexus once, with the help of Spiral Dance. He certainly knew how that wellspring of magical energy looked and felt like, how it acted. Though he'd never actually been there, he knew where the major nexus here in the San Francisco area was; he couldn't *not* know, such things were magnets to him. He had only to remember what the magic felt like and *reach* —

The energy responded to his touch before he was ready for it.

He lost the world for a moment, engulfed in a tidal wave of power; it surged up around him in a flood of golden light and sweet music, capturing him and spinning him around like a bit of cork in a whirlpool.

Dizzy and disoriented, he fought his way back to himself only by concentrating on the metal flute still clenched in his hands. His eyes weren't working properly; instead of seeing his real surroundings, he Saw the power, swirling around him, gold and amber, lemon and umber. After a moment he blinked, and found himself back on the hillside above the labs, still facing the army of shadowy Nightflyers. They hadn't moved, so however shaken he'd been, his momentary lapse of control hadn't affected the hold he had on them.

And Kayla still stared at him, her hand clutching his sleeve, so although it felt as if hours had passed, it couldn't have been more than a few seconds. The only songs he could think of on the spur of the moment that involved fences were all cowboy ballads —

Well, whatever worked.

Although the Nightflyers had been immobilized, he

sensed that they were aware of what was going on. Now that he had tapped into the nexus-magic, he felt their excitement — and their hunger — centered on him. Suddenly he had gone from "commander" to "prime rib special." It was not the most comfortable feeling in the world. Hurriedly, he called up the first "fence" tune that came to mind, spinning the power into a boundary around the lab complex, following the fence and roofing it over as well.

They were not pleased with that — he felt a sullen glow of dull anger emanating from them; a sickly heat that irritated rather than comforted. But before they reacted further, he directed their attention to the complex, creating a dazzling little bubble of energy, moving it to dance for a moment just above the gatehouse, then popping it.

Their reaction was not what he had expected. He lost their interest entirely. Except for the control he still held over them, he might just as well be one of the rocks on the hillside. There was something down there that he couldn't sense — something that the Nightflyers wanted, badly. If they had been hungry when they felt him tap the power of the elves' nexus, they were ravenous now. And he had been demoted from "prime rib" to "leftover veggies."

Well, whatever it was, if it occupied their attention, that was fine with him. The less attractive he looked to them, the better. And if it was a "who," rather than a "what" —

Conscience twinged for a moment, but he thought of the brief glimpse he'd had of Beth, the pain he'd felt from Kory. And he told himself that anybody who worked in a place that would kidnap and torture people, damn well deserved what he was going to get when the Nightflyers found him! They tugged at their restraints, eager to be off; he checked the barriers between the lab and the outside world one more time and found them solid.

Time for one last precaution. He emitted a burst of power, and they turned back to him, like so many dark rags snapping in a high wind.

"There's some people down there," he said, slowly, thinking the words as he said them and hoping they would get the sense of them. "They look like this —"

He pictured Beth, Kory, and Elizabet, spinning images of them out of the dusk and fog and faint starlight. Beside him, Kayla relaxed marginally. The Nightflyers stirred, impatiently. They cared nothing for these images; not when there was something waiting for them that they found much more intriguing.

He called their wandering attention back to the images. *"Don't touch them,"* he said forcefully, impressing his will on them —

— or trying, anyway.

"Don't touch them," he said again. "Don't hurt them, don't frighten them. Leave them alone. Or else —" He didn't know what to threaten them with, so he left it at that. Evidently they didn't realize that, or they didn't care, for he felt their preoccupied assent. They strained to get at whatever it was that was so attracting them, and after a moment to let their tension build, he released them.

They streamed towards the labs, and he and Kayla trailed in their wake. Kayla clung to his arm, silent — Eric kept his apprehension and doubts to himself. Sure, he and Kayla saw the Nightflyers — but what about ordinary people? Could the monsters affect them as well? Would they be able to get rid of the guards, like the muscle-bound gorilla in the little glass-enclosed booth at the gate?

He got his answer immediately, as a pair of them swarmed the lighted gatehouse, flowing into it and filling it with an impenetrable darkness. When they flowed out again, there was no sign of the man who had been inside. Eric averted his eyes as he and Kayla passed; guilty, and not sure whether or not he should be. God only knew what the Nightflyers had done to the guard, a man who hadn't done Eric any harm, who might not have any connection with what had been done to Beth and Kory. He couldn't even remember if Dublin Labs used rent-a-cops on their gates, or real company employees. . . .

"What — what did they do?" Kayla whispered, nervously, staying right with him, glancing at the silent gatehouse out of the corner of her eye. There was nothing moving in there. Whatever the Nightflyers had done, it had been permanent.

His fault.

"I don't know," he admitted, as his feeling of guilt and sickness increased. He wished that there had been another choice, something else he could have done. Now he knew what the "sorcerer's apprentice" felt like, unleashing a power he didn't really understand and wasn't entirely certain he controlled. A power that just might turn on him if it wasn't satisfied.

Kind of like riding the tiger. Don't get thrown off, and don't get off if it's hungry. And try not to look when it eats someone else, someone who never did you any harm. Eric, you're a real louse, you know that?

Kayla shivered, and he hugged her shoulders, glad of the human warmth of her. They went about a hundred yards further in, then Kayla tugged him to a stop. "I th-think we'd better stay here," she stammered. "Th-the others have to come this way to get out. If-if we k-keep going, w-we might miss them."

If we keep going, we're going to have to look at what the monsters are doing in there, he thought — but nodded, and let her tug him off the sidewalk, into the shelter of a crescent of bushes and trees. Ahead of them, inside those formidable buildings, the Nightflyers were looking for something. Whether or not they found it, they would be encountering more people in those halls and buildings; people who would probably meet the same fate as the guard. Death? Worse than death? He was beginning to hate himself, beginning to wish he had *thought* before he'd done anything. People were always telling him that — " Eric, why don't you think before you jump in?" Well, this time he'd jumped in, like always, only people were going to die.

Yeah, but they're people who grabbed Beth and Kory and tortured them! They've probably done things like that to lots of people! I mean, God only knows what they do in there — maybe they're testing nerve gas on street people, grabbing winos for drug testing —

But did that give him the right to act the way they did?

Fiercely he told his conscience to *shut up*, and followed his army.

There would be no walls and barriers to hide the Nightflyers' victims in there. And he didn't want to see them.

Maybe it was wrong of him to avoid witnessing the results of his work. Certainly it was cowardly. He wasn't going to rationalize that fact away, but he also wasn't going to watch what they were doing. And if he didn't have to see the victims afterwards, he wasn't going to. What was the point? It wouldn't make him feel worse than he did now, just sicker, at a time when he couldn't afford any weakness.

What he *was* going to do, however, was to stand here with Kayla, keep tapping into that nexus of elven power, and keep those walls standing tall and strong between his personal horrors and the outside world. No matter how many or few innocents there were inside this complex, the ones outside it were all innocent, at least of doing anything to him.

One by one, the lights shining from the windows of the buildings began to dim, and he and Kayla shivered together, avoiding the shadows beneath the trees.

Elizabet sat quietly in the corner of her cell, ignoring

the outside world — which at the moment was a generous ten foot by ten foot cube. She kept her concentration turned completely inward, carefully regulating her heart-rate and brain-wave patterns so that it would appear that she was semi-conscious, terrified into near-catatonia as her captors seemed to want.

Be fair, now, she chided herself. There was only one of her captors that wanted her prostrate with fear. That repellent man, the one calling himself Warden Blair, who was clearly the one in charge. She had seen his type before.

Forty going on nine. Nasty little man. This was the first time she'd been in the power of someone of that type, but she had a fair idea of what to expect. Brilliant, ruthless, sociopathic.

Leader of a group of those like him, he would carefully collect them; he would cultivate them, set himself up as a substitute father-figure, and collect blackmail material on them so that if they actually began to think for themselves, they could be threatened and would never dare leave his employ. Elizabet had most often encountered these little pods of psychopaths in the sciences. They were usually involved in the hard sciences: physics, computer sciences, and math. But they occurred in the "softer" sciences too, as Warden Blair's little cabal proved.

They had been nasty little children, no doubt of it; the kind that tortured and tormented other kids' pets and hid in books and laboratories. Later, they joined Mensa in college and went into psychology not to discover themselves but to find out how best to stick knives into the souls of those they considered inferior to themselves. They tended to be mostly boys; girls in general were more connected to society than boys, even when abused. That was certainly the case here; in fact, she hadn't seen any women here in anything but strictly subordinate roles. This "project" of Blair's was a kind

of boy's club in many ways, where females were still
"icky," still "the enemy" — for there wasn't a one of
these men that had grown emotionally beyond the age
of nine. That was probably why the little-boy psychics
that backed up the guards here worked for Warden
Blair so readily. He was one of them; their pack-leader,
their Peter Pan. And it explained why he was so eager
to destroy her mental stability. A man like Blair would
not tolerate a strong, independent woman anywhere
about him. Any woman in his "project" would have to
be reduced to the status of non-person.

Well, none of that got her free of this place. And thinking about him made her angry. Anger disturbed her
equilibrium, and if she wasn't careful, that would give
her away to the monitors. She was certain that there *were*
monitors. They hadn't attached any wires to her, but she
had no doubt that every bodily and mental function that
could be monitored was being watched. In this ultra-
secret complex there must be a great many technological
breakthroughs available to the scientists that the general
public wouldn't see for a decade or more.

Being duped into captivity had been her first and last
mistake. After the initial shock and the drug they'd used
on her had worn off — which was long before the car she
was in reached the lab complex — she was ready and
wary, feigning a fear and confusion she did not feel.

She suspected they had been relying heavily on the
drug to keep her disoriented. They must not have ever
had a healer with as high a drug tolerance as she had,
and she had no intention of letting them know how
quickly their narcotics wore off, how little they affected
her. If they did, they'd drug her again, and she
intended to retain her advantage.

Warden Blair had revealed more to her about himself
than he dreamed, and certainly she had given very little
away to him. His open questions about what frightened
her, for instance — so clumsy even a CIA operative would

have been ashamed. Even if he'd had someone with telepathic skills monitoring her, the chances that a telepath could penetrate her mind to read more than she allowed him to see were slim to none. She let him think that she was afraid of the dark; a simple phobia, and being left in total darkness was no hardship to her. And it was pitifully obvious from Blair's clumsy threats that he had no notion just how extensive her personal contacts were — nor how high up they reached. She had favors owed to her by some fairly high-powered lawyers and private investigators — not to mention Ria Llewellyn's still-loyal second-in-command — and when she failed to return from this conference, there were going to be several people asking awkward questions. People it would be difficult to shut up. People with money, political influence, or both.

Warden Blair was going to discover he'd taken the wrong "holdover hippie" — that was one of the kindest things he'd called her when she failed to give him any real answers to his questions. Interesting that his intelligence was so poor; either he wasn't relying on government sources, or someone was withholding information from him. Was that happening at the source, or in his own organization? She rather hoped it was the former; attempts to probe her files should set off alarms that would alert some of her friends — and her friends' friends — to the fact that Warden Blair was showing an unhealthy interest in her. Add that to her turning up missing, and the FBI might come calling, asking Dr. Blair some very awkward questions.

With luck, they'd demand to inspect the premises. There were others here besides herself; she'd sensed them as she cautiously explored the confines of her prison. She didn't dare go further than that; her telepathy was not all that strong, and she could not know if who she touched was a friend and fellow prisoner or one of Blair's tame psychics.

Of course, waiting for official help was going to take time, and time was critical for some of her patients. If she could manage it, she should try for an escape on her own. She knew that she must be in a sub-basement of some kind; that was frustrating, since it meant that even if she won free of her cell, getting to the outside was going to be very difficult. On the other hand, she was middle-aged, female, and black — and if she could find a cleaning-woman's smock, she could probably scrub her way to freedom. *No one ever looks at janitors. Particularly not black women janitors.*

The more she thought about it, the more appeal that idea had. The only problem with it was that left the others she had sensed still locked away.

Could she walk away and leave them there? They didn't have influential friends; it was just a matter of accident that she did. Her own influential friends would be unlikely to move very energetically on behalf of other nebulous captives on her word alone — they would be unlikely to move if their own interests weren't involved. She didn't know names, faces — if she couldn't actually cite the names of people known to be missing, Blair could say she was crazy, deny that there was any such thing going on here. It couldn't be that hard to hide a few dozen people; not with all the government facilities that must be available to him.

Miserable little lizard, she thought bitterly. How soon would it be before Blair's flunkies caught Kayla? That was a thought that truly chilled her. If this were Los Angeles, she wouldn't have worried; Kayla's extensive street-side connections made her impossible to catch on her home turf. But this wasn't Los Angeles, and Kayla hadn't had the time to make those connections here. She was essentially trapped in her hotel room, unless she had the wits to call Beth Kentraine for help—

She was also a minor, whose guardian had vanished. She could be charged with anything and "arrested," taken into "protective custody," and no one would make any complaints.

Except Kayla herself. Which wouldn't change a thing.

But even as she thought of Kayla — Kayla in Blair's hands — *something* changed. As real as a storm-front, as full of potential, and as difficult to pin down without the proper instruments, the passing of this "change-front" raised gooseflesh on her arms and brought all of her senses to alert. Elizabet wasn't a precognitive, but she was at least a little sensitive in every extrasensory area.

Something had just happened, out there, outside the walls of this lab. Something that changed everything, that negated every calculation, every plan. And unless she was very much mistaken, all hell was about to break loose. Her Gram used to say, "When devil walk, people should hide."

It certainly felt like devils were walking.

Be damned to Blair's monitors. If this was as big as it felt, it wouldn't matter what the monitors recorded. Blair was about to have a surprise. Fire, flood, earthquake, or something she couldn't even guess at — these labs were going to experience catastrophe. If there was enough confusion, she would be able to walk right out. She gave up her pretense of catatonia in favor of the tightest barriers she could raise, and sheltered behind them. Waiting.

Something told her that the wait wasn't going to be long.

Dr. Susan Sheffield watched the needle of the seismograph with one eye, and the rest of instruments with the other. One of her techs followed the countdown silently, lips moving. When he reached zero, he clutched involuntarily at the edge of the desk, even though the probability of them actually *feeling* anything, even if this run was successful, was less than half a percent.

Unless, of course, by pure coincidence, they had chosen the moment Mother Nature had picked for a shake to run Poseidon.

Nothing happened of course. It would take several minutes for Poseidon to vibrate this little faultlet loose, even under the best of circumstances. They'd only picked it because it ran directly under the Dublin Labs property, one of hundreds of little cracks coming from the San Andreas.

"Ia, Shub-Niggurath," muttered Frank Rogers, her partner.

"Say what?" she replied, without removing her attention from the instruments. Oh, they'd record whatever happened, but *if* it happened, she wanted to see it.

"Lovecraft," he told her. "Howard Phillips. Horror writer. Shub-Niggurath was one of his Elder Gods — the 'Black Goat of the Woods With a Thousand Young.' I was thinking the San Andreas is like that — Big Mama Nasty with a thousand little nasties spawned from her. The little nasties wouldn't matter squat if Mama wasn't there to back them up."

"Yeah, well if Poseidon works today, we'll have a way to lasso Mama," she said. "And we'll have the data to prove it."

Just at that moment, the needle jumped — tracking the course of a quakelet on the scrolling paper. "Shut it off!" she yelled, as she sprinted over to the bank of other geological instruments. The tech threw the switch and shut Poseidon down as she and Frank frantically took sight-readings in case any of the recording monitors might possibly have failed. Every reading Sue took made her feel like cheering more. Finally Frank let out a whoop. "Hot *damn!*" he yelled, waving his clipboard. "Come look at this one!"

The rack of crude sensors was entirely dead. As it should be; they measured nothing — only registered electrical flow across pairs of contacts set all along the faultline at varying depths. That they were all dead meant that the contacts were no longer touching.

Which meant the fault had moved, easing stress. Quietly, infinitesimally, without so much as a beaker shaking. And along the *entire* faultline.

Poseidon was an array of devices that were the sonic equivalent of a laser: coherent sound. What Frank and Susan had proposed was that if a Poseidon line could be set up along a fault under stress — like the San Andreas — low-frequency, coherent soundwaves could trigger tiny quakelets along the entire length, for as long and as often as it took to ease stress along the faultline. So far it had worked well enough to warrant a bigger proposal, taking the project out of the stage of pure research and into the stage of attempted application. The Big One everyone dreaded might never happen now. . . .

And the pinheaded holdover hippies that picketed every month might be persuaded that there was *legitimate* research going on here. Susan was getting damned tired of running a gauntlet once a month, and wondering if this time *she* would be the one who'd have to spend hours getting red paint off her car.

Not that there wasn't a military application to Poseidon — but Frank had agreed with her to destroy the figures and any reference to their other finding. That one single Poseidon CSAA (coherent sound amplification array) placed at a point of maximum stress *could* trigger a "Big One." *She* was far more right-wing than Frank, and she didn't want that information in the hands of the military. All it took was one nut . . . and unlike radioactives, CSAAs didn't require any equipment that couldn't be bought on the open market — nor did they need bombers or ICBMs to deliver them. Just a good power-source.

And earthquakes didn't discriminate between civilian and military targets. In fact, civilians were far more likely to be the victims; the technology that made military structures hardened against nuclear attacks also made them earthquake-resistant.

No — the military didn't need to know about Poseidon.

"You know, I just had a horrible thought," Frank said, turning toward her with a look of stark terror on his face.

"What?" she asked, alarmed.

"Remember when they put through that law about fault-line disclosure, and all those scumbag real-estate scammers couldn't sell their fault-line property?" he moaned. "You realize we're about to make those parasites *rich?*"

She sighed and started to make a snappy comeback — when the hair on the back of her neck started to rise.

Warden Blair rarely left his lab complex between seven in the morning and midnight; about the only thing that could lure him outside the walls was the prospect of another pickup.

The walls of his office were studded with television monitors, one for every cell in the complex. Most of them were uninteresting; the occupants were asleep or drugged unconscious. One of the catches from today, a black woman, was one of those — the only thing that made her interesting was that she had passed out in the corner of her cell, wedged into a sitting position. *Stubborn bitch.*

She'd been worse than that red-haired piece; she hadn't been anything less than polite, but she'd been just as adamant in refusing to give him any information at all and in refusing to sign up on the project. She'd stared at him and answered — when she answered at all — in words of one syllable, as if she was speaking to a particularly dense child. When he refused to answer any of her questions, she gave him a look of disgust and disdain — exactly like the one his ninth-grade teacher had given him when she discovered the frog he was dissecting was still alive.

Bitch. The word applied both to Mrs. Bucher and this hag. They both made him feel like a naughty little boy without saying a word. Well, it was too late to do anything about Mrs. Bucher, but this old bag was going to find out she was sneering at the wrong man. Maybe he'd turn Bobbie loose on her . . . when Bobbie got done, she'd be a lot more cooperative.

The other new catches, now — they were much more interesting. The man was, anyway. They'd finally had to take the cuffs off him a half an hour ago; all the devices they had monitoring vital signs went into red-alert. Heart rate was way above the safe line, brain-scan showed seizure conditions and unbearable pain. Blair had never seen so severe a psychosomatic reaction — especially not to something as nonsensical as physical contact with metal.

Now the young man huddled in the corner, head sheltered in his arms. The attendants reported that there were burn marks two inches wide circling each wrist.

So, he not only had a new type of psychic, he had someone who could reproduce stigmata-type marks. He'd been wanting to get his hands on a stigmatic for some time — the problem was every single genuine stigmatic was protected by a horde of Catholic stooges.

Once he got his hand on the third member of that little gypsy trio, and the kid who'd been with the old bat, he'd have *quite* a little stable. More than enough to impress —

The monitors went blank. All of them, at the same time.

For a moment, he stared at them, unable to believe

that his state-of-the-art, triply redundant equipment had just failed on him.

No — it *couldn't* have failed on him. Someone out there had pulled the plug on his office.

He surged to his feet, suffused with rage. Whoever that someone was, he was going to pay—

He headed for the door, but before he took more than two steps, something came through it.

Through the *closed* door.

Something dark, shadowy. And very big. But transparent, and his mind dismissed it as a projection or an illusion. One or two of his stable were quite adept at creating projections, and if something had gone wrong with the equipment, the electronic fields that kept them from sending their creations outside their cells might also have malfunctioned.

He was quite certain it was harmless. Until he touched it.

Then he screamed with pain and shock — screamed even louder as it enveloped him, sure that one of his men would break down the door and save him. But his men had troubles of their own. . . .

He continued to scream for a very long time.

● CHAPTER EIGHT

Hame, Hame, Hame

Kory huddled for a long time in the shelter of his folded arms, waiting for the pain to ebb, waiting for his body to recover from the shock of prolonged contact with the Death Metal. Physical shock was not the only thing he had to recover from; his mental processes had undergone similar damage. He did not understand these humans, the ones who had imprisoned him. Oh, abstractly he had known that there were humans who were sick, mentally unbalanced — but he had never encountered any himself. Until now. Until he had touched the thoughts of the man called Warden Blair.

In some ways, he was as shaken by his encounter with Warden Blair's mind as he was by what had been done to him. Never before had he encountered a person who so desired the pain and degradation of others; who thrived on it as anyone else would thrive on love and praise.

Even Perenor was not so twisted — he was ruthless, and he thought of humans as no better than animals, but he would never have done to them what this man has done. He used people, but he did not go out of his way to hurt any save those he felt had hurt him. Even me, he only set to sleep in the Grove. Even Terenil, he sought only to kill. This man is like the Unseleighe, and I do not understand them either.

Blair devoted himself to inflicting pain, humiliation, specialized in reducing his fellow humans to groveling, weeping nonentities. And then, he would take every opportunity to reinforce what he had done to them, keeping them ground beneath his foot.

He hated everyone; he hated and despised those beneath him, he hated and feared those above him, and he hated and wanted to dispose of his equals. If there was anything that Warden Blair cared for besides himself, Kory had not seen it.

What he was doing to those in his power was only a pale shadow of what he *wanted* to do to them. What he had already done — sometimes with the aid of his former captives — was horrifying. And not only did he feel no remorse, he regretted that he dared not take his activities as far as he would like.

What he had done to Beth — that was typical of him. It was by no means representative of the depths to which he had already gone. Warden Blair had killed, both directly and indirectly, although he himself had never dirtied his hands with anything so direct as a blade or one of the humans' guns.

That he left to men he had hired for the purpose. This was something else Kory could not understand: to hire someone for the purposes of assassination. But then, he had never understood humans or Unseleighe who made that their practice.

Once or twice, Warden Blair had found it necessary to deal death personally — but when he did, it was assassination of another sort, through the intermediary of poison. As a scientist, he had access to many poisons, several that mimicked perfectly ordinary illnesses.

And his only regret was that he had not been there to witness and enjoy the death, when it came. He routinely dispatched in this way those he had captured who proved to be too much trouble. He was already considering such an end for Beth, should she continue to resist him.

Beth — Despite his own weakness and pain, he crawled to her on his hands and knees, to gather her up in his arms and hold her. Now that he knew what Blair was like, and what the human had done to Beth, he knew that there was only one way to reach her. She would not trust anything coming from outside her — but she might trust a mind-to-mind link. She had erected shields to hold others out, but she would not have held them against him.

He held her close, shut out the pain of his body, the cold of the cell, and focused himself inward. Inward to seek outward. Inward for control, so that he might have the stability to forget himself and look into Beth's mind and heart.

He sent out a questing tendril of thought; encountered her shields, and called softly to her. *:Beth — Bethy, my lady, my friend, my love — :*

The shields softened a little. He touched the surface of her thoughts, and did not recoil from what he found there — a chaos of fear — and old memories, more potent for being early ones. *Can't breathe — choking — strangling — the air going, the walls falling in —*

Her shields softened further and he passed them by. He countered her illusions with nothing more than his presence, knowing now what fear it was that held her prisoner. *:Your lungs are filled, the air is fresh and pure. I am with you, and I will not let the walls close in. Bethy, you are not alone.:*

She finally sensed his presence in her mind, and grasped for him with the frantic strength of one who was drowning. He stood firm, holding against her tugging, vaguely aware that she confused him with someone else, some other rescuer. That was fine. If she had been rescued before, she would be the readier to believe that she was being rescued again.

:I am here. I will help you to safety, my love. Do not let yourself despair.:

She clung to him, mentally and physically. He felt her thoughts calming; found the place where her fear originated and fed back upon itself. That gave *him* something to work on; he caught the fear and held it, sensed that she was listening to him now, and knew who he was.

:There is air to breathe,: he told her silently, calmly. *:This is only a room. If the blackguard stops the air, I will start it again. If he changes it, I will protect you. I have sent word to the Bard; he is working to free us.:* That last, he was unsure of. He knew that he had briefly touched Eric, and that Eric knew what kind of danger they were in, but whether or not Eric knew where they were, and could do anything about it — that was another question altogether. He was only one man. He had the magic of the greatest Bards at his beck and call, but could that magic prevail against one such as Blair? He had imprisoned an elven warrior, even though he did not seem to know what it was he had captured. Could Bardic magic be strong enough to counter what this man could do when elven magic could not?

But the elf pushed his own doubts into the background. He must keep his thoughts positive. Beth needed them, needed him to be strong and with no doubts.

Just as she had been strong and without doubts for him, when he had despaired of saving his people, his Elfhame, himself.

How long he held her, he was not certain. Only that after a timeless moment, she reached up and touched his cheek with a shaking hand.

"K-Kory?" she whispered hoarsely. "Kory — I — "

He raised his head — and something in the quality of the atmosphere told him that there was something very different about the place, something that had changed in the past few moments. Something was very wrong.

"Kory?" Her own arms tightened about him, and he felt her shivering. "Kory, something's wrong — there's something out there —"

"I know," he whispered. He sought to identify what he sensed as he held her. It wasn't Unseleighe; it wasn't anything from Underhill at all, either from the ordered Seleighe side, or the chaos of the Unseleighe lands. It wasn't human spirits . . . or human magic. But it was somehow connected with humanity.

Its evil was human evil, that same evil that lived in Warden Blair. It was that shadowy horror that Beth sensed, that made her shiver and forget her fear of being buried alive. There were things worse than death, and in the darkness of their cell, Kory knew that he and Beth sensed one of those things brushing them with its regard.

It examined them, minutely, as he held his breath.

And passed them by.

Kory let out the breath he had been holding in. Then he realized something else that was not as it had been: the silence. While the room they were in was supposedly soundproof, elven senses were sharper than human, and the sounds of footsteps, conversation, and other noises leaked across the threshold of the door. There had been sound out there in the corridor; there no longer was.

Cautiously, he created a mage-light; it lit Beth's face with a faint blueish glow from the palm of his hand. Her eyes were round and wide with fear, her face drawn and bloodless. Whatever he sensed from the being outside their door, she was more sensitive to it. He had hesitated to create the light, for fear it would attract the attention of the thing that had examined them, but nothing happened.

He considered his options, and the continuing silence in the hallway beyond. And he considered his own strength, which was nearly spent.

This would be the last attempt at magic he could make without a great deal of rest and recuperation.

Once he had finished a final attempt on the lock, their only recourses at escape would have to be purely physical. On the other hand, what did he have to lose? If what he and Beth sensed was truly out there, prowling the corridors of Warden Blair's stronghold, the human had a great deal more to worry about than keeping his victims penned. Whatever magery had countered his own, it might be gone now.

He sent the ball of light into the mechanism of the lock, as he had before; exerting his will upon the stubborn mechanism to make it yield. This time, however, he was rewarded by the faint clicking of the tumblers. And no one on the other side of the door relocked it.

He freed himself from Beth's clutching hands, stood up shakily. She started to protest, stopped herself as he moved carefully across the darkened room to the door. He waited for a moment with his hand on the handle, extending his weary senses out beyond the metal of the heavy portal, feeling nothing in the immediate vicinity. He turned the handle, carefully; the door opened smoothly and quietly.

The hallway beyond was deserted — and curiously ill-lit, as if some of the lights had failed. Beth joined him at the door, hunched over, as if by making herself smaller, she could elude the attention of whatever was out there, human or nonhuman. Kory looked cautiously around the doorframe; there was still nothing to be seen in the hall; there wasn't even a human behind the desk-console at the end of it. He frowned; surely that was wrong. Shouldn't there be one of those uniformed humans with badges there at all times?

He stepped out into the corridor and motioned Beth to follow. She was still crouched by the wall, staring up at him. "Beth, we must leave here now. That creature could return."

"I can't," she whispered. "I can't move, I can't feel my legs."

He moved back to her, helping her to stand. She leaned against his shoulder. He could feel her trembling, and tightened his arm around her waist. "Can you walk?" he asked.

"I think I can," she said faintly, then spoke stronger. "Of course I can walk. No twisted little government shithead is going to get that victory over me. I'm walking out of here *right now.*"

Kory couldn't keep the smile off his face. This was the Beth that he knew, the human woman that he loved.

They slipped into the hallway, backs flat to the wall. Still, there was nothing to be seen anywhere in the hall, and nothing to be heard. Only an empty, echoing silence.

When they reached the desk-console, Kory stopped and peered over the edge of it. He was half-afraid that he would find a body there; that was the way it always worked in the human television shows. But to his immense relief, there was no body; there was nothing, in fact. Only a half-eaten sandwich and a can of cola, beneath row after row of darkened squares of glass, which he recognized, after a moment, as small television sets.

Beth peeked over the edge and frowned at those. Before he could stop her, she poked at some of the buttons beneath the nearest, but nothing changed.

"Are those supposed to do something?" he ventured.

"The ready-light is on. These should be working." Beth touched another button, with no visible result. "These video screens should show the insides of the cells, but they're not working at all."

"You understand these things?" he asked, amazed. This console was more complicated than the most intricate sorcery he had ever attempted. Something that could allow you to Farsee into the cells . . . *In the cells.* . . .

"Beth, my lady," he said urgently. "Other cells — think you that we were the only captives here?"

Her head snapped up; her eyes met his. "No," she replied, slowly. "No, we couldn't have been. That creep knew how to break people too well — he *had* to have had practice." She began searching among the buttons and switches for something, cursing softly to herself when she could not find it, then snapped her fingers and pulled out a drawer. There was another, smaller bank of labeled buttons there, as well, besides pencils, sticks of gum, erasers, loose bullets.

"Got it," she said in satisfaction. She pushed two buttons in succession; one marked "Emergency Override," the second under a piece of masking tape with the words "cell doors" written on it, labeled "Mass Unlock."

She hesitated for another moment, then looked up at Kory. "If this system is anything like the one on the psych ward that I worked on, the unlock key won't work unless there's a real emergency — like a fire. And we're just lucky that there *is* a manual override to the computer-driven system. We're gonna have to manufacture an emergency."

Her words meant very little to him; he seized on the ones he did understand. "If we wish to release other prisoners, there must be a fire?" he asked. She nodded. "Very well then. There will be a fire."

Even exhausted, fire-making was a child's skill for any of the Folk. He stepped back along the corridor to their empty cell and considered the contents. There was bedding on the bunk, padding on the walls, all flammable. It would do.

He closed his eyes, and sent power into the cell. The bedding ignited with a *whoosh;* the padding took a moment longer, but within a heartbeat, it too was in flames.

Alarms sounded immediately; the lights in the corridor flickered and failed, and new, red lights came on. In the cell itself, water began to spray from the ceiling.

Since it did not suit Beth's plans to have the fire extinguished, he gave the copper pipe leading to the fixture a brief mental twist, blocking it. The spray of water died, and the fire continued to blaze merrily.

Far down the corridor, now, he heard people screaming, pounding on doors, and the sounds of some of those doors slamming open. He trotted back to the console, very pleased with himself.

"Will that suit — " he began, when Beth grabbed his hand and began sprinting down the hall, towards a sign over which blazed the words "Emergency Exit."

The feeling of something very old and very evil passing outside her door made every hair on Elizabet's body stand straight on end. She wasn't sure what to make of it; whatever was out there, it didn't match any horror she had ever encountered. But then, she hadn't encountered many really nasty things in her life; she had spent her time on the magics of life, not death.

Whatever it was, it passed her by as she held her breath, waiting for it to sense her and attack.

When she was certain it wasn't going to come back again, she let her breath out in a long sigh.

But what was that — thing? Another of Blair's little friends? Or was it something that Blair had attracted without knowing what he was doing? If so, he was in for a shock, especially if it was looking for him.

She decided that she was better off not moving for a while. No telling what the thing was hunting — and she was certain that it was a hunter; had an unmistakably predatory feeling about it. No telling how it hunted, either. If by sound, then her best bet was to stay quiet. Let Blair and his flunkies make all the noise and attract it.

But it was very hard to remain motionless, silent, sitting in the gloom of her cell, wondering if the thing was going to come back.

Another thought occurred to her after a moment: was this another of Blair's little ideas, something designed to make her more cooperative?

That almost seemed more likely than that it was something Blair had attracted.

If it is, I'm not going to let one haunt spook me into playing footsie with that creep, she told herself, a little angrily. *It's going to take more than a bogeyman to frighten me!*

An earthquake or a fire, now — trapped down here in a locked room in a sub-basement —

As if someone was reading her mind, fire alarms screamed out into the darkness all up and down the corridor — red emergency lights came on in her cell, startling her as much as the alarms.

She got herself to her feet, cursing middle age and the slowing of her reflexes. She ran for her door, praying that there was an emergency override on the locks in case of catastrophe — and that someone had been compassionate enough to use it. Which, given the kind of people who worked for Blair, was not a "given."

She emerged into the corridor with a half-dozen others, equally frightened, equally bewildered. She sniffed the air; no smoke on this level, but that didn't mean there wasn't a fire somewhere above or below.

One thing was obvious: there wasn't a single uniformed guard or one of Blair's suited goons among the milling, frightened people in the corridor. Whatever had happened — they'd been presented with an opportunity to escape.

"Get the rest of the doors open!" she shouted, taking charge. "Then let's get out of here!"

A woman with aggressively butch-cut hair whirled and stared at her, while the others stopped and gaped — perhaps wondering if she was one of them, or one of the enemy. The woman sized her up, then nodded, and began flinging doors open along the left-hand side of the corridor. Elizabet did the same on the right, until they were all open, the occupants either joining the rest in flight, or remaining huddled in the red-lit interior of the cells. Half of Elizabet wanted to run in there and coax them out as a few of the others were trying to do—

But the sensible half said that their window of escape might be closing at any moment. She had patients to care for, and a ward out there, waiting, probably frantic with fear.

She turned and ran for the emergency stairs.

The Nightflyer directed the steps of her host's body downwards, as the lights went to red and strange howling noises split the air. She — or it; Nightflyers were all hermaphroditic females, neuter until breeding conditions were encountered. Sometimes she thought of herself as both. One level down was something very important; something so important that her host hated the people who worked upon it with a passion undimmed by the fact that he was dead.

The Nightflyer sensed that this thing had something to do with whether or not the Breakthrough would be made. The music-maker was part of it, of course, and she was the ForeRunner, who would breach the barrier between the Waking and Nightmare Realms, but the Breakthrough itself would not occur unless some great outpouring of Waking fear gave her the energy needed to cast the bridge across the barrier and hold it open.

She was not precognitive in the sense that humans understood the word; she sensed the future in a myriad of pathways. That *this* object had the potential to make something happen, and *that* human knew the key to an event.

As now. The music-maker had the potential to bring the Breakthrough, even though it meant that the Nightflyers who answered the call would be forced to

obey him. Potential future pathway; one Nightflyer
would find a host. Potential future pathway; that host
might lead her to something instrumental to the
Breakthrough. At the moment, it appeared that
Nightflyer would be her.

Down. That was the direction of the highest potential
futurepath — and she followed the potential as a
compass-needle follows a magnet.

There were a half-dozen white-coated humans coming up, fleeing in panic; she ignored them. They had
nothing to do with her, or the potentials of the
moment. At the bottom of the steps, she paused and
tried the door. It opened to her touch, but not on a corridor of rooms, as she had found on the level above.
This door opened on a single large room, filled with a
maze of complicated devices. Blair's memory told her
that this had been a storage area, until "Project
Poseidon" came and did something, and found it perfect for their needs. What those needs were, Blair did
not know. He only knew — the memories dimming as
the body cooled — that he hated these people for
taking even an unused part of "his" building, and for
using money that could also have been "his."

Sounds from the other side of a wall of machines told
the Nightflyer that there was still someone here. This
might be a complication, or it might be another
advantage. While it was in a host body, it could not kill
quickly and efficiently, as it could when it was in its
natural form — though to take a host, as only it could
do, it did not kill quickly *or* quietly.

But while it was in a host, it also could not be com-
pelled to return by the music-maker. Therefore it was
remaining in the host, however uncomfortable and
inconvenient that might be.

She moved, slowly, into a hiding place among the
machines. She was not used to the way this body
worked as yet, but she sensed a possibility with the

as-yet unseen human, and it would require stealth to
make use of the new potential that was unfolding. The
human must not guess that she was there.

She wedged the body between two machines and
beneath a table, in a way that would have been painful
for the original occupant. Once there, she concentrated on reaching outward to that other human's
mind. There was something that the human was doing
that was important. . . .

The human, a male, had remained behind to perform a task of securing machines, despite a danger that
he perceived. The Nightflyer sensed something
beneath the surface of his concerns, and probed
deeper.

There was relief there, that the machines could not
be used as weapons, for only he and one other knew of
that capability.

The potentials flowered, powerful and clear. This
was the information she sought.

Quickly, she absorbed it all; the machines, how they
worked, and how a single one of them could be used to
trigger a massive earthquake. It took the Nightflyer a
moment to comprehend just how massive an
earthquake — and precisely what that meant to her.

At that moment, it took great control to keep from
bolting from her hiding place, and taking one of the
machines then and there. But she did not have the
means to power or control one. She watched the
human's thoughts as he locked down the equipment,
then fled like the others; and she contemplated what
she had learned.

One of the machines was directed very near one of
the points that would trigger a major quake. Near
enough, in fact, that the humans here had hesitated to
use it for this experiment, and in the end, took a chance
that the experiment would fail rather than take the
greater risk.

She could go out now, and manually re-aim the machine. The fire and the escape of her host's captives would cause a great stir — she could use that and her host's high status to order this building sealed before the humans learned of her meddling. Then she could return to this level, and use the re-aimed machine.

And then, all she need do would be to wait.

Potential crystalized. This was a good plan, with high probability of success.

She squeezed her host's body out of its hiding place, and set to work.

Kory supported Beth as she stumbled and nearly fell; there was something very odd about the absence of guards and Warden Blair's men. Was that strangeness connected with the evil creature he had sensed outside their door?

Suddenly, without warning, a shape out of nightmare loomed up in front of them, blocking their path. Kory knew it the moment it appeared, although he could not put a name to the thing. It was the creature — or one like it — that he had sensed outside their door.

And it loomed above the body of one of the guards, mantling shadowy wings over it, as if it were a great bird of prey.

Beth stifled a gasp; Kory backed carefully away from the thing. It did not move, apparently intent over its victim. After a few seconds, it drifted away, sliding through a half-opened doorway.

Well, now they knew where the guards had gone.

He glanced at Beth, and saw that she was standing motionless, her back pressed against the wall, still staring at the spot where the guard had lain. "Beth, we must leave here — " he whispered urgently to her.

"Can't you feel it?" she whispered back to him. "They're all around us, hidden in the shadows.

They're so close, I can feel them brushing against my skin, stealing the air we're breathing. We'll suffocate here, as the walls fall in around us, and the shadows will eat our souls . . . "

"No!" He gathered witchlight in his hand, casting light into every corner of the corridor. "There's nothing around us, Beth. We're close to the exit, just another doorway and some stairs. I know Eric is out there, I can feel he's close to us" — *And so can anyone else within five hundred leagues, my friend the Bard is shining like a torch tonight* — "Lean on me, love, and we'll walk out of here together."

Her hand tightened on his, and he half-carried her past the place where the guard had died. He saw another Emergency Exit sign with a feeling of relief, and herded Beth toward it. As they reached it, a flood of people appeared coming from the other direction, and crowded into the door with them. There were a great many more people in this building than he would have judged, and it seemed as if all of them had chosen to bolt into the staircase he and Beth had taken.

That was not so bad — many people would provide confusion and cover, in which they could escape.

And more victims for that — creature?

Was *that* something Eric had called, in an effort to free them? If so — could the Bard control something like that? Or had he taken on more than he knew?

Kory could only hope that the Bard knew what he was doing, as he and Beth let the press of humans carry them up the stairs and into the free night air.

Eric and Kayla waited as patiently as they could for something to happen. There didn't seem to be much going on out there, though, and Eric began to wonder if he'd made a really bad choice of weapons. Maybe he should have gone to the police after all — or the media —

The Nightflyers had all headed towards one building;

he and Kayla watched them drift inside, not all of them by means of doors or windows. A few of them seemed to be able to pass right through solid walls if they wanted to; something that did not bode well for his sleeping habits for a while. From the look on Kayla's face, he had the feeling the same was true for her.

But since they had entered the building, it looked like business as usual from the outside. Those shadows drifting across lighted windows — they could just as easily be late workers as his otherworldly creatures. No one came running out of there, screaming or otherwise —

Alarms sounded, shattering the silence, startling both of them into shrieks, which fortunately were drowned in the klaxon-horns. He grabbed Kayla and hauled her back, deeper into the shadows, as she tried to bolt for the building.

She couldn't have heard him unless he yelled, but his meaning was plain enough: they needed to stay where they were.

As armed security guards appeared from other parts of the lab complex, racing towards the building in question, Eric noticed that the lights in the windows had all turned red. *Is that some kind of emergency lighting? Did the Nightflyers finally do something that triggered an alarm?*

The front doors burst open as guards took up defensive positions — and were promptly overwhelmed by the rush of frantic people streaming out of the building. Some wore white lab coats, but only about half; the rest were in ordinary street clothes. Some looked injured; there were groups of two and three helping each other along. There were a lot more of them than Eric would have expected; evidently there was a lot of work going on at night. He peered through the confusion, hoping, fearing —

And spotted a pair of familiar heads as a knot of people passed under a sodium-vapor light, ignoring the guard who tried to stop them. One blond — one red —

"Elizabet!" Kayla squirmed out of his grip and sprinted away, and he didn't even try to stop her this time, assuming that the confusion would cover her. He made a dash of his own for *his* two targets; brushed aside a guard whose bewildered expression told him there was something odd about the situation, and threw his arms around the two who were supporting each other.

There was no time for greetings, though; he swept them from an embrace into a stumbling trot, heading for the gate. No one moved to stop them — no one made a move to stop *anyone* who was trying to leave.

At some point between the place where he caught Kory and Beth, and the entrance, Kayla and Elizabet joined them, making a group too formidable for anyone to trifle with. At the entrance, Eric guided them all off to the side, shoving Kory and Beth ahead of him. "I've got transportation," he said to Elizabet, "but there's something I have to take care of back there. You guys go back to the house — I think it's safe, I don't think those goons knew where we live. I'll catch BART back home."

Elizabet looked as if she wanted to object, but finally nodded, tersely. "Neither Beth not Kory look as if they're in a fit state to be left alone," she said. "And knowing what happened to me — we'll stay with them. Kayla, I think Beth may need you the more. I'll stay with Kory."

Eric nodded his thanks, and left them heading in the direction of the bikes. He turned, and went back to the edge of the fence.

Now to put the genie back into the bottle. If I can. . . .

• CHAPTER NINE

Beauty in Tears

The creature glided slowly in her direction. Dr. Susan Sheffield crouched further into the corner, watching as *something* slid past the tall yellow barrels.

The scientist in her noted calmly that the creature seemed to be comprised of different light intensities, which shifted as it moved. No, not variable light intensities, but rather the absence of light. As it floated through the air, it — absorbed? deflected? — light waves, creating the shadowy framework. It also seemed to be slightly confused by the heavy metals disposal canisters. Possibly the contained radioactivity, or maybe the metals themselves? No way to know, not without some extensive testing. . . .

The other part of her mind was too numb to think, too horrified to consider anything but screaming. But she knew that making a single noise would be fatal. She'd seen one of these *things* kill Frank, and the new lab tech, the boy whose name she could never remember. At least, she hoped they were dead.

The creature inched closer, blotting out the last of the light. She was too terrified to scream; she closed her eyes, wishing she could at least *know* what had killed her. . . .

A faint sound pierced her terror, a sound that she felt resonating beneath her skin, even though the room was completely silent. A melody, strange and alluring, calling to her, calling. . . .

She opened her eyes again, to see the creature still floating in the air before her. It began to move away, drifting toward the stairway. Without thinking about it, she moved after it, following it up the stairs. The music seemed to be saying something to her, something too important to ignore, even with the shadows of death moving through the hallways around her.

She followed the creature up the long flights of stairs, through the emergency exit and toward the main lobby. Other shadow-monsters joined them in this strange trek, drifting past her through the white metal railings.

Something stopped her by the door, though; a silhouetted human figure, standing near the doorway, staring at something beyond. A moment later, she recognized him — Warden Blair, the project manager of the team down on Level 13, one of the "sealed" floors. He stood very close to the doorway, his fingers clenched white on the lintel, as though trying to hold himself back from a force that was pulling him through the door.

She stood there for a moment, as the creatures drifted past her, coiling around her ankles and swirling her skirt around her knees. Beyond, she could see the floodlit area beyond the glass doors. Standing beyond the doors was a young man with long dark hair, playing a flute. As she watched, the shadow-monsters drifted toward the young man, gathering before him, a shifting dark cloud.

Blair turned and saw her. She recoiled at the look in his eyes . . . *there's nothing human there, a corpse has more emotion in its eyes* . . . and stepped back, though the music still tugged her forward.

Those inhuman eyes fixed on her face, lit with a strange hunger. Blair let go of the doorjamb, and reached out a clawlike hand toward her.

Susan dove past him, into the dimly-lit lobby. Her

hand slapped the door release knob by the side of the glass doors, and she slammed into the doors shoulder-first, falling through to the concrete steps outside. She glanced back; there was no sign of Blair in the shadowy lobby. Now she didn't have to worry about a homicidal maniac . . . instead, she had two hundred of those deadly creatures gathered on the asphalt not quite fifteen feet in front of her.

No problem, she thought crazily, and fainted.

All right, Eric. You get one try at this; don't screw it up. He took a deep breath, and looked out at the gathered assemblage of Nightflyers on the pavement. *I can handle this. It's just like conducting the high school orchestra back home.*

Except that the kids in the school orchestra weren't going to eat me alive if I made a mistake. . . .

The Nightflyers waited patiently. Eric could sense that they were watching him, waiting for . . . something.

For me. They're waiting for me to make a decision, to lead them. The image of the Nightflyer in the ruined city flashed through Eric's mind, the creature bowing to him as if to a great lord, a leader.

That's what I could be to these guys. A leader. He imagined himself at the head of the unliving army, sweeping through the countryside and righting all wrongs . . . no more wars, not when there wasn't a conventional army on the planet that could fight against his troops. No more crime, no drug-wars in the streets of the city . . . no one dying of violence, no one at all, ever again.

Except when these Nightflyers get hungry and need to find a dinner somewhere.

Then again, maybe all of that wouldn't be such a good idea after all. . . .

Eric shuddered, bringing himself back to the present. He saw that the crowd of Nightflyers had moved closer to him while he'd been daydreaming, and now were hovering only a few feet away, almost close enough to touch. *Get your act together, Eric, and get rid of these guys before you end up as the Blue Plate Special yourself.*

He brought his flute up to his lips, and began playing a slow slipjig, "The Boys of Ballysadare" — a tribute to fallen soldiers, young boys killed in a battle nearly forgotten in the mists of history — one by one, the Nightflyers faded from view, like shadows touched by bright sunlight. Eric felt sweat running down his skin, as he realized just how many of the creatures he had summoned, and still had left to banish.

One of the Nightflyers drifted very close to him as it faded away, the shadow-wings brushing against his skin, a touch colder than ice. He held onto his concentration like a shield, willing the monsters to go away, return to that strange place from which he'd called them. Only a few left, he saw as he began playing the A part of the tune again, only a few . . . one of his fingers, damp with sweat, slipped on the smooth metal key of the flute, and the remaining Nightflyers surged forward toward him. He caught up the thread of the melody again, holding them at bay until the last one was gone, and he was alone in the parking lot.

Eric slid down to his knees on the asphalt, the flute clutched in his nerveless hands. The adrenaline charge hit him a split-second later, his heart pounding too fast, hands shaking with the realization of how close he'd been to death.

Next time, maybe I'll just call in the Marines instead.

He managed to stand up somehow. Fortunately, he was still alone . . . no, he wasn't. He saw an older woman, dark-haired and wearing a laboratory coat over her clothes, slumped on the pavement a split-second later, and hurried to her. Eric knelt beside her, checking her throat for a pulse.

At his touch, the dark-haired woman opened her

eyes and blinked at him. "It's okay," he said quickly. "It's all over."

She sat up slowly, looking around the parking lot. In her eyes, Eric recognized the same look of total shock that he'd seen in the eyes of the Los Angeles elves, after the battle in the park.

"Do you have a car?" he asked. "I'll help you get home."

She nodded, not speaking.

He helped her to her feet. She leaned against his shoulder, walking unsteadily. As they approached a blue Suzuki jeep, parked alone beneath one of the floodlights, she silently handed the car keys to Eric. Well, he knew in theory what to do. As Eric drove the jeep out of the Dublin Labs parking lot, weaving like a drunkard, the woman looked back once at the brightly-lit laboratory complex and began to cry.

Beth held tightly to Kory as the motorcycle banked through the turn from Van Ness onto Geary Street, accelerating through the pools of light and shadows cast by the streetlights. Something bothered her about the moving shadows, the way they glided past the motorcycle and disappeared behind them.

The faerie motorcycle braked delicately into a right turn, heading up their street and toward the only lit house . . . *of course Eric forgot to turn off the lights in the garage when he left the house,* she thought and smiled. *Figures. I just hope he remembered to lock the front door —*

They pulled up into the driveway, the bike courteously switching off its own headlight. She slid off the motorcycle and nearly lost her balance, grabbing onto Kory for support.

"I'm okay," she muttered, then repeated the words louder for Kory's benefit. A moment later, the second motorcycle pulled into the driveway, and Elizabet and Kayla followed them to the front door.

Inside, the house was warm and dark. Beth felt her way carefully through the darkness, turning on lights as she went. She continued into the kitchen and the living-room, making sure that all the lights were switched on. She caught the curious looks from Elizabet and Kayla as she went into the dining room to turn on the light in that room. When all of the first floor of the house was brightly lit, she rejoined them in the living-room, slumping into her favorite chair, a Papa-san with a fat pillow-seat.

"Do you want something to drink?" she asked, remembering to be a good hostess. "Some tea or coffee?"

Kayla shook her head. Beth noticed that Elizabet was giving her apprentice a different kind of odd look.

"Is anything wrong, Beth?" the older woman asked, watching her intently.

"No, not at all. I'm just glad we're home. Are you sure you wouldn't like anything to drink?" She stood up, walking to the wooden cabinet by the fireplace. "Well, if no one else wants anything, I think I'd like something." She reached for the bottle of Stolichnaya, and realized for the first time that her hands were shaking.

Elizabet stood up, and took the bottle from Beth's hand. "I don't think that would be a good idea, Beth," the healer said firmly.

Without even thinking about it, Beth slapped her across the face.

She brought her hand up to her mouth, suddenly horrified by what her hands had done. "I'm sorry, I didn't mean to . . . I . . . " To her horror, she burst into tears.

Beyond Elizabet, she could see Kory, staring at her. "I'm okay, I'm okay," she said, angrily wiping the tears from her eyes.

"I think you need some rest," Elizabet said, taking

her by the arm. Something about that touch, it seemed too familiar to her . . . she glanced at Elizabet's face, and saw her handsome dark features melt, changing into something else . . . a man's face, a man wearing a business suit, smiling at her with that look of a little boy with a new toy, he was going to take her apart like a clock and toss all of her gears and wheels across the floor. . . .

She shoved Blair away from her, sending him falling back against the cabinet, and turned to run. Kayla was blocking her path, though . . . why was the little healer kid trying to help Warden Blair? Kayla said something that Beth couldn't hear, and then the world went very bright, the white light blotting out everything else. *Very strange*, she thought as the light washed over her and carried her away.

Susan stretched, not wanting to open her eyes. *What an awful dream*, she thought, remembering her nightmare. *Wish I'd gotten more sleep. It's going to be hell, trying to run the computer data on that test run, if I'm half-asleep and can't think straight. . . .*

She switched on the light on the nightstand, and heard a strange noise from the kitchen. She sat up abruptly.

Burglars!

She reached for her bathrobe, then suddenly realized that she was still wearing her clothes from the day before, the lab coat and skirt and blouse and pantyhose, sans her lab shoes. Quietly, she moved through the hallway, pausing to pick up a heavy marble bookend from the table near the window.

She took a deep breath, hefted the reassuring weight of the bookend in her hand, and looked into the kitchen.

A handsome dark-haired young man stood in her kitchen, staring in perplexity at her espresso machine, which was currently spraying hot water into the air.

The man from my nightmare last night. . . .

"I'm really sorry," the young man said, gesturing at the hot water on the countertop and floor. "I didn't mean to wake you up or make all this mess, I just wanted some coffee before I went home."

"This machine is very temperamental," she said, recovering enough from her surprise to grab a potholder and use it to twist the machine's spigot several times. The flow of hot water ceased, and a stream of fresh coffee began to pour sedately into the waiting pot. "Give it a few seconds, and it'll be ready."

"I'm sorry if I startled you," he said after an awkward silence. "I would've left last night, but by the time we got to your place, I'd already missed the last BART home. I slept on your couch . . . I hope you don't mind."

No, not at all, I love having figments of my imagination stay over for breakfast.

Not imagination. That wasn't a dream last night. It was real, all of it was real. . . .

Either that, or I've gone mad.

He took down a mug from the shelf above the espresso machine, and poured himself a cup of coffee, as Susan stared at him.

"Okay, kid," she said in her best lab manager's voice, the one that worked so well on the obnoxious young interns from Cal Berkeley. "I want some answers, right now. What happened last night at the labs?"

"It was . . . it was a mistake," he said, staring at his coffee mug. "I shouldn't have done it, I know that now, but I couldn't think of anything else to do, and I thought Kory was dying . . . I could've lost control of them, and not banished them all . . . Christ knows what those things would've done if that had happened."

Her voice sharpened. "*What* did you do?"

He looked up at her, an odd expression in his eyes. "I called them. You saw them, you were right there on the lawn. I brought them there, and let them go. What happened in there?"

This kid . . . he thinks he caused what happened last night, whatever that force . . . those creatures . . . were, that came into the Labs. And maybe he's right, because I saw them gathering around him in the parking lot, as though he was calling them back.

She heard herself describing what she had seen in a calm, detached voice, the one she used to read papers at conferences. "Those things . . . killed a lot of people in the Labs. I don't know how many. But Frank is dead, and that boy, and God knows how many other people."

"Excuse me, please," he said faintly, and made a dash for the bathroom down the hall. Through the open door, she could hear him being quickly and violently ill.

She stood there alone, trying to gather her thoughts. She felt unnaturally calm, distant from this insanity that had suddenly engulfed her life. *It's called shock, Susan,* she thought.

Several minutes later, he returned to the kitchen, and took a quick swallow of coffee. There was a different look in his eyes, something she couldn't identify.

"Who are you? What's your name?" she asked.

He glanced up at her, a wary expression in his eyes. "Maybe . . . maybe I'd better leave now."

She stood between him and the only door out. "Not until you answer my questions, kid."

He looked as if he was going to say something else, then shook his head, pursed his lips, and whistled a brief sequence of notes, something she recognized as the beginnings of an Irish tune called "Whiskey Before Breakfast," and . . .

. . . and she blinked at the sudden bright sunlight pouring through the kitchen window. Her back was aching, as though she'd been standing on her feet too long; she looked over at the clock above the espresso machine, and blinked again.

Ten a.m.? I've been standing here like this for two hours?

And she realized something else: she was alone in the kitchen. There was no sign of the strange young man, or where he'd gone, only a half-filled coffee mug left on the kitchen counter.

The choice was to go home or call home; he only had change for one. Eric sat on the BART bench, staring at his clenched hands in his lap. He could see it now, in his mind's eye . . . the Nightflyers gliding into the building, leaving nothing alive behind them. He knew he could've seen it before it had happened, if he'd bothered to think about the consequences of his actions.

What did they do? How many people did they kill, when I let them into that complex?

Something small and shadowy whispered in the back of his mind: *We will tell you, if you let us come back . . . Bring us back, bring us back . . .*

"No!" he said violently, loudly enough that the other passengers on the subway looked up at him. He leaned his head against the glass, closing his eyes to shut out the rest of the world.

No, I won't bring you back, he silently said in the direction of that shadowy voice. *No dice. I know what you are now, and I'll never do that again, never.*

The image of the Nightflyer bowing to him in the ruined streets of San Francisco hit him like a fist, a mental sending that was as clear and sharp as a memory.

You have/will/are helping us, the voice continued. *Help us again. Lead us, bring us back . . .*

With a sudden clarity, Eric saw the Nightflyers, poised around him, but just beyond reach . . . just beyond a veil, thin and shimmering, that was all that stood between the waking world and the realm of nightmares. He understood their way of thinking in all times at once, past/future/present, and how they hungered for all things human and living. And how they needed him, needed someone or something to break through that thin veil and bring them into the real world. He could feel their slow and patient thoughts, simmering evil that was completely inhuman, and how they had watched him — since he was a child, they'd known he would be a Bard someday (if he lived that long) and would be able to aid them . . . waiting for a moment, a Breakthrough, when the Special Ones could get through.

Well, you're going to be waiting a hell of a lot longer than that! he thought to the waiting throng. *Because I'm not doing it!*

Not evil, not us, the voice said quietly across the void between the two worlds. *But different, and in need of your masses of humanity to survive . . . we need you, as you needed us. . . .*

Eric reached out blindly with his thoughts and shoved, hard, until he no longer heard the voice, and he was alone again in his own head, with no whispering evil by his side. Like a sleepwalker, he left the BART train at the Powell Street Station to change to a Metro bus, and then to step down from the bus and walk up the hill to their house. Even from the end of the street, he saw the two motorcycles parked in the driveway, and felt a weight, that he hadn't known he was carrying, lift away from him. Knowing that Beth and Kory were home, knowing that they were all right, he couldn't keep a smile from his face. Until he remembered again what he had done to bring them home.

The front door was unlocked, and he let himself in, hanging his jacket from one of the hooks near the door. He heard someone in the kitchen, and his nose filled with the smell of fresh sausage and eggs frying. The smell awoke the sour taste in his mouth again, and the twisting sensation in his stomach. He decided that maybe he'd skip breakfast, just for today.

Kayla walked quickly out of the kitchen, carrying a plate of food and a glass of milk — she stopped short at seeing Eric in the hallway, a strange expression on her face. After a split-second, Eric recognized it as fear.

She gave him a lopsided smile. "Hey, Bard! Glad to see you made it home all right. You sure look terrible."

He swallowed hard. "Kayla, is everyone okay? Where are Beth and Kory?"

"Kory's fine," Kayla said. "But you'd better talk to my boss about Bethany. Everyone's upstairs right now."

She looked fine last night . . . well, maybe not fine, but okay. Not bleeding or anything. What could've happened after they left for San Francisco?

The exhaustion finally hit him, as Eric started up the stairs. An accumulation of terror, too much magic, too little sleep, and no food . . . the world began to turn white around him, and he grabbed the bannister for support. Kayla caught him and helped him sit down; everything was too blurry, moving too fast around him.

"You're not in very great shape, either," the young healer observed clinically.

"It's been one hell of a night," Eric said, hoping that he wasn't going to be physically sick again. That would've been the perfect ending to a thoroughly awful night. And it had started out with such an adrenaline rush as he'd realized just how much power he had as a Bard, how he could summon his own personal army of demons and rescue his friends, and no one could stop him. . . .

And God knows how many people I killed last night, it's my fault, it's all my fault. . . .

Kayla's hand rested on his shoulder, and he felt the dizziness pass, and a wave of . . . something . . . wash over him instead. Suddenly he felt a little better, as the nausea faded away. "Thanks," he said.

"Not a problem," the kid replied. "That's what

Elizabet calls the Kayla Patented Jump-start, perfect for those bad magical hangover mornings. You kind of overdid it last night, Bard."

"Don't you think I know it," he muttered, his face in his hands.

"Eric!"

He looked up quickly, to see Kory vaulting down the stairs towards him. The blond elf caught him up in a bearhug, then held him at arm's length, his eyes searching Eric's face. "You look terrible, my friend."

"I know, I know. Nothing that some sleep won't cure." He stood up slowly, and glanced upstairs. "Is Beth okay?"

Kory's face fell. "I do not understand this at all. This must be a human thing, because I have never seen an elf suffer from this illness."

"Is she awake? Is she — " Eric moved past Kory, heading for the bedroom door. He stopped in the open doorway.

Beth was sitting up in bed, wearing her usual sweatshirt, her dark red hair falling loose over her shoulders. Even from the doorway, he could see that something was different, though he couldn't tell exactly what. It wasn't just the way she was sitting so quietly, or the tired look in her eyes . . . it was in the tilt of her head, the way she sat . . . something was different, and Eric already knew that he didn't like it.

She looked up and saw him, and her eyes brightened. "You look terrible," she said softly, smiling at him.

"I know, love." He sat down on the bed next to her, caught her hand and brought it to his lips. "You look kinda awful yourself."

"I'm glad to see you back, Eric," Elizabet's warm voice spoke from across the room. Eric saw the older woman for the first time, seated in the warm sunlight in the window seat. "We were all worried about you."

"Nothing I couldn't handle," he said, trying to sound nonchalant. *Nothing I couldn't handle . . . badly,* he thought. *Nothing I couldn't handle without getting a lot of people killed.*

"Will you be all right without me for a few minutes, Beth?" the healer asked. "I need to talk to Eric."

"Yeah, sure." Beth waved away any concerns.

"I'll send Kayla in to keep you company," she said, and called downstairs to her apprentice, who ran up the stairs a couple seconds later, giving her mentor a pseudo-military salute before sitting down in the window seat that Elizabet had just vacated.

Eric followed Elizabet out of the room, out into the garden. The woman sat down wearily on the grass. "How are you doing, Eric? You look tired and stressed out, but not too much worse than that."

"I'm okay," he said cautiously, sitting down next to her. "What's going on with Beth?"

Elizabet hesitated. "It's a little difficult to explain. What do you know about mental illness, Eric?"

"Not much." *Not much more than three years with the expensive shrinks my mother hired could teach me. That I wasn't nuts, but I had to give them the answers they wanted to hear.*

"Well, without knowing exactly what happened to Beth last night, all I can guess is that she's suffering from an affective disorder of some kind — possibly a variation of post-traumatic stress disorder. In layman's terms, I'd call it extreme shock and the beginnings of a nervous breakdown. Definitely that . . . she cried for three hours last night without stopping. But she won't talk about it — without adequate information, there's no way to know what's really going on." She stretched, rubbing her eyes. "I'll need to get some sleep soon, or I won't be much use to anyone." She sat up, giving Eric a curious look. "Kory said something about how Beth thought she couldn't breathe, last night in the labs. Do you know anything about that?"

He thought about that for a minute. "No, not really. But . . . Beth's claustrophobic. And they were underground; I'm guessing there weren't any windows down there. Could that have caused this?"

"A normal claustrophobia attack wouldn't cause anything this severe. I'd expect to see high anxiety levels, possibly some fairly serious psychosomatic reactions, but not anything like this. It could've caused the elevated metabolic levels she was showing last night, but not any of these continuing effects."

"What about physical damage?" He had to ask. He had to. "Was she raped?"

The healer shook her head. "No, definitely not. Any damage is completely mental and emotional. But something happened to her in those labs which she won't talk about yet, and that something is what triggered all of this. And it happened before all of those . . . creatures . . . showed up at the labs. By the way, I'd like to talk to you about that," she added, giving him a very penetrating look.

He flushed. "Later," he said.

"All right." She accepted that, as she accepted most things, from elves to frightened runaways. "Listen, I need to get some sleep soon. Will you sit with Beth for the next few hours? I don't want to leave her alone for too long."

"Is there any particular reason why?" he asked, concerned.

"I'd — I'd rather not say. Just keep an eye on her, all right?"

Without even thinking about it, Eric reached out to touch the woman's thoughts. Genuine fear for Beth hit him for the first time, reading the thought that was uppermost in the healer's mind. "Do you think Beth is suicidal?"

Elizabet nodded slowly. "It's possible. That's why we're not going to leave her alone right now. I'd rather not take the risk."

He felt an icy touch inside, a cold ball of fear that wouldn't go away. "I'll stay with her."

They walked back inside the house. Upstairs, Beth was asleep, the lines of tension no longer visible in her face. He took over Kayla's place in the window seat, settling down on the pillows. He leaned back against the sun-warmed wood, feeling the terrors from last night washing away, being replaced by new terrors.

He had never expected this, never thought this could happen. Beth had always been the strongest of them all, the most determined, the one who refused to turn away from a fight. He couldn't imagine a Beth that wasn't strong-willed and outspoken, vibrant and always laughing. The concept of a Beth who was so quiet and pale, who cried for three hours without stopping; he couldn't believe that this had happened, that this was real.

He had been so afraid for Kory, knowing that something awful was happening to him, that he might've been dying, that he hadn't even thought that something worse could be happening to Beth. Now Kory was fine, and Beth was the one who had been badly hurt, and hurt in a way that he didn't understand.

And himself . . . the only word that he could think of to label himself was *monster*. Without even thinking of the consequences, he'd summoned the Nightflyers and turned them loose, killing God knows how many people in those labs. He was a monster, as much as any Nightflyer — and they knew it, those strange intelligent shadow-creatures from across the veil of dreams, and they saw him as their leader, one of their demonic horde. . . .

And somewhere in the back of his mind was a strange feeling telling him that now, when there should be nothing left to do but heal, this wasn't the end of it, a little prescient touch that things were only going to get worse. . . .

• CHAPTER TEN

Off She Goes

"I'm not insane, I'm not expendable, and I'm not going." Susan sat back with her arms folded, glaring at her boss. "The Poseidon Project is at a critical stage right now, and there's no way in hell that I'm going off to some FBI summer camp to be grilled by psychiatrists for six weeks. If I go now, with Frank and Dave missing, we'll lose weeks. If you cart me off, we'll lose months. Maybe more. With all the cuts going on, we might even lose the budget for the project, and that's insane." As an afterthought, and with a glance at the tape recorder on the table, she added, "Sir."

Colonel Steve O'Neill had an uncharacteristically exasperated look on his face. "Your opinion is noted, Susan," he said dryly. "But I'm up against a wall right now. The boys Upstairs want to know what happened here last night, and so far you're the only living witness who can still speak in complete sentences."

"What about Warden Blair?" she asked, remembering her strange encounter with the scientist in the stairwell. "*He* was there. I think the cause of it was on his floor. What's more, he's just as sane as I am. However sane that is. Why not get him to speak his piece?"

"I've been told to keep my hands off of Dr. Blair," the colonel said grimly. "But if this goes on much longer without any rational reasons for what happened, they won't have any choice." He sat down across from her.

"Susan, can't you just give me a better explanation of what happened here? This story of floating shadow-monsters just isn't going to fly in Washington, and you know that."

She grimaced. "What rationale are they giving right now, colonel?" "Rationale" was not the first word that came to her mind. She wanted to say "fairy tale," but the tape was still running.

He shrugged. "So far, the only explanations are mass hysteria and some kind of mass hallucination, combined with the kidnapping, defection, or mislaying of fourteen Lab employees. Once the alarms went off, everyone headed down their safe routes to leave the building. The ones who didn't are either completely *non compos mentis* or missing. I think the Agency boys are still searching the lower levels, in the hopes of finding more of those people." He shook his head. "The current theory is that some kind of toxin might've escaped from one of the sealed rooms and gotten into the air vents, though we all know that can't happen, because of the security design."

She refrained from snorting. *Nerve gas, you mean. Or an air-born hallucinogen. And sealed-room protocol doesn't mean squat when you're dealing with people who might have been hit with it themselves and have just gone off on their own private trip to Oz. And sealed-room protocol won't work with something so new the filters can't catch it. A micromolecule, or a virus, maybe. But you can't say that, because of the tape.*

The colonel continued, blithely unaware of what she was thinking. "So they're saying it could've been deliberate, but there are only ten or fifteen people with security access to all levels, and they're all accounted for. Another theory is mass food poisoning, but that really doesn't hold water, either. So far no one is talking about the Japanese, or terrorists, but that can't be far behind. This whole thing is giving me an awful headache," he concluded, rubbing his temples.

"At least you weren't here last night," Susan said quietly. "I keep wishing I'd kept to an earlier plan of going to the San Francisco Opera with some friends last night, instead of running the data correlation tests." She allowed herself a single outburst of anger — in part, to help cover her grief. "Why can't you just put down what *I* saw to a mass hallucination, if you won't believe me?"

The colonel wasn't going to be sidetracked, even though she had given him a decent out. "All right, Susan. Let's go over it one more time, just to see if there's anything we missed. You were in your office, waiting for the computer to run the comparison tests on the last experiment . . . "

She nodded, wearily. "It was our first verified successful run. We recorded an energy release with a Richter equivalent of zero point nine, just enough to tap the needles on the seismograph. If all hell hadn't broken loose afterward, I would've been at your office door at eight a.m. this morning, waving test result printouts at you and screaming wildly. Happily, but wildly." *Why didn't I go watch Tosca fling herself off a bloody building? Why couldn't we have run the tests this morning?* But she knew why: because she'd been too excited, too impatient . . . nothing could've convinced her to leave the lab at that point. Finding the exact resonant frequency for that rock stratum and pinpointing the fault . . . no, leaving the lab at that point would've been inconceivable.

The colonel nodded. "After the test, what happened?"

She continued her recitation. Same words, for the benefit of those who would be listening to the tape, hunting for discrepancies. "Frank started to power down all the machines, and that new lab tech, Dave, was helping him with that. That's when the alarms went off. I knew we couldn't leave, not until all the equipment was secured, so I told them to keep working, that we'd still have time to clear the building." She could feel her hands trembling, and fought back tears. "I wish I could go back in time and tell them to get the hell out, screw the equipment. So we were still in there when that first *thing* came through the doorway, oozing right around a closed door. It opened up in front of us, going from a thin shadow to a huge billowing shape. I don't think Frank even had time to blink, it just fell over him and he screamed, and then he was gone. The kid and I were standing there in shock, and it drifted toward him next, moving slower. I threw something heavy at it, I can't remember what — probably an oscilloscope or something. That fell right through it, but it paused long enough for both of us to get to the door."

If I'd gone to listen to an aging diva play an hysterical diva, they'd still be alive.

She heard a rising note of hysteria in her voice and quelled it. "In the hallway, I saw Mira Osaka from Dr. Siegel's team, just sitting on the floor and staring at her hands, like something was wrong with them. I tripped over her — that's when the creature killed Dave, it just slid over him like a wave. He was screaming, and I was trying to get free from Mira, because she'd grabbed onto my wrists. I think I hit her, trying to get away, and then the thing was coming after me. It seemed to ignore Mira. I made it into a storeroom, and it followed me in, but couldn't find me in there. I don't know why. Then it suddenly turned and left, and I followed it out, and that's where I saw the guy with long dark hair, the one who was in my apartment this morning."

Colonel O'Neill reached over and switched off the tape recorder. "We have to talk, off the record. You know what'll happen if I give this tape to the FBI, don't you? They'll listen to it for five minutes, and then cancel your clearance. I don't want that to happen." He glanced down at the tape recorder. "All right, this is what we're going to do. Susan, you're going to tell me that story again, and it isn't going to include anything about shadow-monsters or people disappearing into thin air. Or a hippie in your apartment. I'll rewind the tape, as a friend and someone who wants you *on* that damn project, and you give me the edited version three times. Here's what happened. The alarms went on. You tried to get out of there, Mira was in the hallway, you didn't see what happened to Frank and Dave. They just never came out of the lab." He paused for a moment, as if in thought. "And while the Feds are going over this report, I'll send someone over to your apartment to dust for fingerprints. If we get any that aren't yours, I have private accesses to the national print banks. People who owe me favors. Maybe we can find this mysterious long-haired boy, and when we do, we can get some better answers to all of this out of him instead of you."

She was stunned. "Steve . . . that's *illegal.*"

"I know, I know." He shrugged. "Call it a command decision. I'm not going to let this sink your career, not when you're so close to doing something meaningful on this project. You're a good scientist, Susan. In all senses of the word."

She slumped a little, relief making her want to cry again. "Have I ever told you how glad I am that you were assigned to helm this project? I've been so afraid of the military applications of this, but you've always had the view that we could use this to help people, not kill them. Thank you for that, Steve. Thank you for having ethics."

"Not a problem." He smiled. "When we're done here, take the rest of the day off, Susan. Medical leave. Go shopping, go into the city, do anything you want. Just don't go home for a few hours, okay? Now, go to the lady's room. Have a cry. Come back here and we'll do the tape, then you take the day off."

"Okay. Thanks, Bossman." She stood up to leave, and impulsively hugged him.

Colonel O'Neill smiled at Susan as she left the room,

then his face went flat and impassive as the door closed, as though he was only a puppet, with no puppeteer to animate his movements. That was how he felt, when he thought about it . . . when he was given the license to think about it. Like he was watching a puppet show from within his own mind, seeing himself move across a stage. All he could feel was that strange feeling of distance, of emptiness, as though all of this was happening to someone else. He thought he ought to be terrified, but he couldn't be, because the emptiness left no room for anything else in his mind, even fear.

A few moments later, he glanced at his watch, then rose from his chair and walked briskly down the hallway. Beyond another door, Warden Blair sat silently at a computer console, not even bothering to look up as O'Neill entered the room.

"Did she believe you?" Blair asked.

"I think so," the Colonel replied woodenly. "At least, she said she wouldn't go back to her apartment, so I shouldn't have any problems sending a team over there to scout for prints and fibers. Maybe we'll find her mystery boy, maybe not."

Blair shook his head. "The boy doesn't matter — my people can follow him like a lighthouse beacon, anywhere in the city. What matters is that there is no interference with this project, at least for several days. And that no harm comes to your Dr. Susan Sheffield for those several days. After that, she won't matter at all. In fact, you'll probably need to kill her. Do you understand?"

"Of course." Something shifted in the emptiness of his thoughts, at the idea of harming Susan. *I . . . I don't want to do that,* he realized.

Blair continued, coldly, with calculation. "I can't control her, not without damaging her ability to complete the project. We'll need her technical expertise to complete the Breakthrough, the work that she hasn't completed yet." Blair seemed to be speaking more to himself than to O'Neill.

For a moment, O'Neill felt that strange emptiness lifting from his mind, the fog clearing slightly. His fingers strained, touched the flap of the holster at his belt, the .45 automatic nestled within. It was so difficult, harder than anything he'd ever done . . . he unsnapped the flap, wrapped his fingers around the grip, tensing. . . .

"Don't do that," Blair said absently, and Colonel O'Neill screamed inside, in fury and hopelessness, as his disobedient fingers rebuttoned the holster flap, then clenched into a fist in his lap. "I still need your services, Colonel," the thing that had been Warden Blair said in a serious tone. "I can't let you kill yourself yet. And as far as killing me . . . if this body dies, I'll simply take yours instead. Keep that thought in mind, if you think you might be able to break free."

"I'll . . . kill you," O'Neill said in a strained voice. "Don't know . . . what you are, but I'll kill you."

He felt Blair's attention focus on him, pressing down upon him like a great weight. It was more difficult to think, more difficult to focus on a single thought — he clutched desperately at the hatred, the last emotion being slowly stripped away from him.

But he couldn't fight it; it was like fighting the tide, or the turning of the planet. When it was over, there was only a small part of him left, locked deep beneath the waves of emptiness. A tiny scrap, able only to watch and weep, without acting.

Something like a smile passed over Blair's lips. "Much better. Now, your next assignment . . . I need competent laboratory personnel to replace the lost Poseidon Project team members, so we can reschedule the project. Despite the presence of the Federal officers, we should be able to resume work sometime tomorrow."

"I'll take care of it," O'Neill heard his own voice say, and he rose to leave the room.

"I'm sure you will, Colonel," Blair said, smiling.

I've seen that kid before, I know I have, Susan thought, walking past the opulent displays at Macy's and into the women's shoes department. *That handsome face, the long dark hair . . . I know him, I know that I know him. . . .*

She paused in front of a display of sequined shoes, momentarily distracted by the thought of finding shoes to match her favorite black sequin dress. *Attack sequins. Guaranteed to stop traffic.* Shopping was excellent trauma therapy, a new idea for medical treatment, she thought, eying the sequined shoes and then deciding to pass on them, at least for now.

In the next department, she considered a new British trenchcoat, perfect for foggy San Francisco mornings. It looked like a good buy, especially with the matching scarf; a warm and comfortable coat, as comfortable as an old friend.

Hands in the pockets of her old coat, listening to flute music, surprisingly lovely and unexpected. . . .

And connected with that boy, somehow.

Susan shook her head, trying to remember. A concert . . . no, she would've been wearing better clothes, probably her black wool wrap over a dress, not the old worn jacket with holes in the pockets. But if it wasn't a concert, where would she have heard him play music before . . . where?

She paid for the new coat, and left with the package under her arm, back toward the parking lot. The wind had picked up, swirling leaves around her feet as she crossed the street. Near the parking lot attendant's booth, a gray-haired man with his cap on the ground was singing Gershwin to the street, mostly ignored by the pedestrians. And that was when it came to her.

A street musician! That boy is a street musician!

Elation hit her in an adrenaline rush; she laughed out loud, and began to think back of all the times she'd seen street musicians in San Francisco, the different corners and tourist areas and business districts . . . down near the Pier, maybe? Or Ghiradelli Square? Maybe at the cable car station, where the crowds of tourists waited in endless lines to ride the cable cars? Fog, cold, wind . . . where would she find those at an hour when she wouldn't be at the lab?

"Now the quest begins," she said under her breath. Unlocking her car, she sat down in the driver's seat and reached for the stack of maps in the glove compartment. With a map of San Francisco spread out in front of her, she plotted out the best approach to the Pier area, then folded up the map and started her car, carefully backing out of the parking lot and into the late morning traffic.

Maybe this is crazy. Maybe I'm searching for someone who's nothing more than a hallucination . . . maybe we all really were poisoned by the cafeteria meatloaf last night at the labs, and I only imagined the guy. Then again, maybe he's real . . . and if he's real, he's the answer to all of this. If I can find him, the bastard who's responsible for what happened to Frank and Dave and all those others, then maybe I won't be afraid to go back to the Labs anymore, afraid to go home to a silent apartment and afraid of trying to sleep tonight . . . afraid those things are going to come back for the one that got away.

At first, her quest seemed hopeless — on a chilly San Francisco morning, very few street musicians were at the Square or Pier 39. She asked at the Pier management office whether they might have a list of the musicians who regularly played there, and had to listen to a serious-eyed woman take ten minutes to explain that except for the performers who did shows on the small stage at the center of the Pier, they had no way of tracking the street musicians.

She stopped at Pier 45 for a quick lunch, then went back to Ghiradelli Square for another attempt. This time she hit paydirt: a quartet of musicians playing wild Celtic music for a small crowd. She waited until a lull in the music, then asked them about her mysterious musician.

"Sounds like someone I've seen at the Renaissance Faire, last few weekends," the male guitar-player said. "He's not a regular, but I've seen him there with some friends."

"You were just watching the red-haired girl," one of his female companions teased him. "He was with a woman with bright red hair," the musician informed Susan. "And another man, a blond hunk of a guy. I'd bet they'll be back at the Faire on Saturday."

Saturday . . . too many days away, by Susan's reckoning. "Do you have any idea where I could find him before the weekend?"

"Try the Embarcadero," the man suggested. "I think I saw him there once, playing for the business lunch crowd."

Susan thanked them politely, and headed back to her car. She drove back to the Embarcadero, within walking distance of where she'd started this odd trek, parked and walked to the open plaza.

Too late for the lunch crowd, she realized as she walked up the concrete steps. The plaza was mostly deserted except for businessmen apparently hurrying to meetings and such stuff, and the food stands were obviously shutting down for the afternoon.

She asked the proprietor of a hot dog stand about the street musician, and was rewarded with the man's big smile. "Oh, yes. Beth and Eric and Kory. They're going to play for my daughter's wedding next month." The man fished in his wallet, and pulled out a ragged business card with a number scribbled on the back. "This is their phone number. They live somewhere off Geary Street, maybe on the top of the hill near Broderick? Anyhow, here's the number."

If they take my clearance away, maybe I have a future as a detective, she thought, smiling. "Thank you," she said, writing down the phone number and the street information. *Anyhow, that's enough detective work for one day,* she decided. *Now it's time for combat shopping. . . .*

She made it home before the afternoon traffic began, the long slow trek of cars going across the Bay from the city, in time to see the last of O'Neill's cleanup crew leaving her apartment.

"Find anything interesting, boys?" she asked.

The youngest of the Colonel's agents gave her a shy grin, and his superior chivvied him out of the apartment, nodding once to Susan.

She sat down on the couch and thought about the impossible, and what had happened last night. Suddenly she was consumed with the desire to know more, to find out what O'Neill and the other honchos had discovered while she was merrily spending money at Macy's.

Five minutes later, she was on her way back to the office. The gate guard checked her I.D. more carefully than she usually did, but let her pass in without any problems. She was on her way to O'Neill's office when two business-suited Federal agents caught her by the elbows and escorted her in another direction.

"Gentlemen, please!" she said, extracting her elbows.

"Sorry, ma'am, but it's very urgent," one of them said, as they escorted her down to one of the lowest levels in the building, and left her at an office door.

She shrugged, knocked, and walked inside.

And stopped short, seeing her boss and Warden Blair seated in front of her. Together.

"Ah, Dr. Sheffield," Blair said, looking up from a stack of papers. "We weren't expecting you until tomorrow morning. Good, we can talk now."

"We're making some changes in the project," O'Neill said awkwardly. "Because we're so shorthanded now as a result of last night's . . . incident, Dr. Blair is going to be supervising the project, as well as bringing some of his own personnel onto our team."

She was speechless for a moment, then found her voice again. "He's *what*? You can't do that, Bossman!"

"I don't think you understand, Dr. Sheffield." Blair gave her a cold smile. "I'm your boss now. I will be supervising this project, with Colonel O'Neill's assistance."

She frowned, and decided to dig her heels in. "Like hell you are. There's no paperwork on this, no clearance from DoD, nothing. I'm not handing anything over to you, mister, not without the correct paperwork."

"Susan." That was Steve, in the conciliatory tone she remembered from too many late night arguments. "The paperwork will follow in a few days. But since we're so close to getting some genuine results on the project, I thought it best to bring Dr. Blair in immediately."

"We *have* genuine results already, Steve! We don't need this idiot to help us!" She leaned forward, speaking earnestly. "Steve, don't do this to me, please. It's been our project, ever since Day One. This — whatever else he is — he's *not* a geologist or a geophysicist, he's a *psychiatrist*. He not only doesn't have the authority, he doesn't know the Richter scale from a musical scale! Why don't you just bring in Jane Goodall to supervise us, while you're at it?"

"I don't have any control over this situation," Steve said, not meeting her eyes.

Who's jerking your chain, Colonel? she thought bitterly. "I won't be a part of this, Steve. I'll quit. And I'm not bluffing, you know I'll do it." She looked up into Blair's eyes, wanting nothing more than to slap that contemptuous look on his face, and suddenly remembered . . .

. . . recoiling at the look in his eyes, knowing there was nothing human there, a corpse without emotion . . . stepping back, though the music still tugged her forward. Those inhuman eyes, lit with a strange hunger . . .

This is insane, she thought. *He's just a scientist, not a demon. There are no such things as demons, and I'm not sitting across from one.*

But inside, deep down in her gut, she *knew.* "You're one of them," she whispered, more to herself than out loud.

"One of what, doctor?" Blair's eyes followed her intently.

"Excuse me," she said, hoping she could get out of the room without being physically ill. Now she could see it clearly, the shadow behind his eyes, the emptiness where a human being's mind should have been. She made it to the door, but Blair's voice stopped her.

"Think about your job security," he said. "Think about your clearance. Think about that story the colonel taped about the floating shadow-monsters, Dr. Sheffield. I found that story of yours to be absolutely fascinating, and I'm sure the State Board of Mental Health will, too. If you quit this project, I'll make sure they hear of it."

"Go screw yourself," she said with dignity, so angry that she was fighting back tears, and slammed the door behind her.

Two cups of coffee later, the problem wasn't any easier to solve. She had considered assault and battery, intent to cause grevious bodily harm, aggravated assault, assault with a deadly weapon, and various other physical options. She'd also considered exorcism, remembering the emptiness looking back at her from within Warden Blair's eyes. She'd also considered just saying the hell with it and running away, so far that they couldn't find her, and never coming back. Or just leaving, period. She dismissed the threat of siccing the Mental Health Board on her; they didn't have time to chase after one middle-aged scientist, no matter *who* Blair thought he knew. They were too busy with child-abusers and serial killers. With her credentials, she could be back in work in a European lab within days. Or better yet, the Japanese; *they* had a vested interest in this, and they had lots and lots of lovely multicolored yen to spend on it. If she wanted to run away.

But I don't want to run. I want someone to explain what in the hell happened last night at the labs, and I want someone to pay for it, whoever caused the deaths of all of those people. I don't believe in mass hallucination, or the food poisoning theory. I want to know that those creatures can't exist, and that there's a logical explanation for all of this, so I can go home and fall asleep without being terrified of dreaming.

And I want to know why Blair's eyes make my skin crawl. . . .

She took the scrap of paper out of her purse, with the few words written on it: "Eric, Beth, Kory. Geary and Broderick." And a phone number with it. She considered the piece of paper, and also considered a third cup of coffee, but decided that it was too much of a good thing.

"I could find them," she said out loud. "I could."

She thought about it, and wondered whether she was just going to escape from the tigers by leaping off the cliff. Blair terrified her, but at least he hadn't killed anyone, at least not in front of her. The long-haired boy, he'd *controlled* those creatures. At least, he said he controlled them.

But then she remembered his shy awkwardness in her apartment that morning, and thought: *A mass murderer shouldn't blush because he's spilling hot water on a counter.*

Maybe he could explain all of this to her, help her find the answers. She wanted that more than anything — to know, to understand.

To find out for certain that she wasn't insane.

And she thought about San Francisco, and the layout of the streets. On Geary and Broderick, there wouldn't be that many houses to check. She could find them, just by walking the area.

She left a dollar on the counter for the coffee, and headed back to her car. During that hour-long drive, she contemplated the insanity that had taken over her life. And beneath it all was the tiny doubt . . . what if it really was just a hallucination? Or insanity?

Or what if it all was real?

It was early evening, and the last light was fading as the fog slowly rolled in over the city. Eric had been up in the window seat, trying to read a book, or at least had stared at the first ten pages for the last several hours, but without any success. It was too difficult to push the dark thoughts from his mind.

It had all happened too fast, much too fast. One day he'd just been Eric Banyon, comfortable in his old life, and then all of this Bard insanity had begun. Suddenly he was a Bard, and had more magic at his disposal than he ever could have imagined in his dreams. A *lot* of magic — sometimes he could sense it within him, a waiting pool of pure light, and he knew that he'd only touched the edges of it, that there was so much further he could go. Summoning the Nightflyers had been so easy, he could've called thousands more of them without straining himself. He'd frozen that scientist lady in her tracks without even thinking about it, just a reflexive grab for magic with a quick whistled musical phrase.

It was too easy, and too powerful. He remembered how high he'd been, summoning his demon army, drunk on the raw power of it.

How am I supposed to live with this? He thought about the other example of overwhelming magical power he'd seen, the insane elven mage Perenor. And his sorceress daughter, Ria. No, Ria hadn't been insane — somehow she'd learned to live with her abilities, at least to the point of not being a physical menace to the city she lived in. He was sure she'd never lost control . . . *well, except for maybe that one argument we had, back at her house in Beverly Hills. But she was* really *angry at the time. . . .*

How had she managed that level of control? How did anyone manage it, when you had the raw power singing inside you, calling out to be used?

If that lady wasn't catatonic in a hospital in L.A., I might want to ask her about that, Eric thought. The idea of asking Ria Llewellyn for anything appalled him, but it made sense, in a strange way. In a way, she was the only one who could understand what was happening to him, this terror of the sheer magnitude of his magical abilities. *Absolute power corrupts absolutely, and I've got a damn near infinite supply of absolute power,* he thought grimly.

"Hey, Eric."

He looked up instantly, to see Beth smiling faintly at him from the waterbed. He was at her side a moment later. "How are you feeling?"

She had a kind of fragile look to her, and an odd expression in the back of her eyes he didn't like. "Okay, I guess. Kinda thirsty. Is there anything to drink around here?"

"I'll get you a glass of water." He was halfway to the door when a scream ripped through the air.

Beth was staring at her hands, then looked up wildly at him. "Eric, my hands, they bloody, they're covered with blood!"

"No, Beth — "

"Everything's moving . . . the walls are cracking . . . I can feel the floor giving way . . . Eric, we've got to get out of here!" She clutched at his hands. "No, they're waiting for you outside, they'll kill you! I can see them, you'll carry me out the window and they'll be waiting, waiting . . ."

Elizabet and Kayla burst into the room. "You're dead, you're all dead!" Beth wailed, and burst into tears. A split-second later, Kayla touched her very lightly on the temple. Eric could feel the burst of magic, an electrical crackle across his skin. Beth relaxed back onto the pillows, no longer screaming but still crying softly. Eric looked up as Kory leaped into the room, dripping wet from the hot tub or shower.

Eric wanted to scream himself, or cry. Instead, he moved away to let Elizabet and Kayla get closer to Beth. Kory was staring at Beth with horrified eyes, and Eric knew exactly how he felt.

At that exact moment, someone rang the doorbell downstairs. "I'll get it," Eric volunteered, and headed downstairs. He felt he couldn't take another second of that blank look in Beth's eyes. What nightmare had she just lived through, hallucinating it right in front of him?

It hit him suddenly, like a brick between the eyes — it was *his* nightmare that she'd just seen, the earthquake destroying the house . . .

His feet continued down the stairway, independent of the turmoil in his mind. The doorbell rang again, and he felt a momentary irritation for whoever it was on the other side of the door — didn't they know that his world was crashing down around him?

It has to be the door-to-door Bible salesmen. Only they have timing this bad.

Susan reached for the doorbell again. This was the fourteenth house she'd tried — she had been keeping count — and so far no one matched her descriptions. No one even knew anyone fitting the descriptions that was living on this street. She stepped back in surprise as the door opened suddenly.

The long-haired young man from her worst nightmare stood in front of her, blinking.

There was a long moment of total silence, as the young man stared at her.

"Well," she said at last, impatiently, "aren't you going to invite me in?"

● CHAPTER ELEVEN

Two Fair Maids

"Bard!" Kory came clattering down the stairs behind him before he could think to do anything, even to slam the door in the woman's face. "Eric, Elizabet wants — "

Eric turned to stop him, but it was too late. Kory jumped the last couple of steps, and skidded to a halt behind him. He stared at the woman from the labs with his eyes gone big and round with surprise.

Slit-pupiled, green cat-eyes. Situated between pointed ears.

Kory was not wearing his human guise. Of course he wasn't; he was tired, worried, and among friends on his home ground. He didn't have to think about keeping up an illusion.

Eric did not need to turn to know that the woman was staring at Kory with the same look of astonishment on her face as Kory was wearing.

Oh shit. As if things weren't bad enough. Before he could even move, however, *she* had forced the issue, pushing past him and closing the door. Then she leaned her back against it so that the only way to get her out would be to forcibly pry her off the door, get it open, and *then* throw her out. No doubt, with her kicking and screaming every step of the way.

He backed up a step. She stared defiantly into his eyes. "I want some answers," she said firmly, "And I want them now. *Who* are you, *what* are you, what did you do back at the labs, *why* did you do it, and *how*? And in God's name, what were those things you called up?" She moved her gaze slightly to meet Kory's for a moment. "Your type, I know, or at least I think I do. I grew up on Tolkien. I've read my Celtic myths. Provided I'm not currently hallucinating all of this, locked up in a little cell. You're either an elf, or I'm seriously ready for a jacket with extra-long sleeves. I don't know what the hell you're doing here, but if I can believe in shadow-monsters that kill people, I can believe in elves, no problem."

Kory drew himself up to his full height and put on all of his dignity. The loose shirt and jeans he wore somehow became the rainment of a prince, and Eric got the fleeting impression of a coronet encircling his head. "I am Korendil, Champion of Elfhame Sun-Descending, Knight of Elfhame Mist-Hold." He placed one long hand on Eric's shoulder. "This is my friend and brother, Bard Eric. If you have aught to challenge him with, you must also challenge me."

Eric didn't know whether to laugh or cry or both. Bethy was upstairs falling apart, this crazy woman had tracked him down and wanted to know what he had been doing at the labs — and now Kory was issuing formal challenges. It was just too much.

He blinked away dizziness. "I —" he began, and his throat closed up. Then his mind went blank.

All three of them stood there staring at each other like a cluster of dummies in a store window, until the sound of someone clearing her throat politely from above them made them all turn. Elizabet stood at the head of the stairs, with Kayla perched, a round-eyed gargoyle, at her feet. Both healers were watching all of three of them like Jane Goodall and Dianne Fosse examining a trio of strange primates with unexpected behavior patterns.

"Would someone like to tell me what is going on here?" Elizabet asked.

Before Eric could get his mind and mouth to work, or even his body unfrozen, the lab woman looked up and addressed the healer as the person in charge. "I am Dr. Susan Sheffield," she said, taking an aggressive stance, feet slightly apart, hands on hips. "I work at Dublin Labs — and last night — "

"All hell broke loose," Kayla offered brightly. The woman favored the kid with a glare that had even Kayla shrinking back.

"Last night," the woman repeated tightly, "I watched some kind of shadow thing kill my research assistant and my partner. They told me today that anyone else that didn't get out when the alarms went off is either dead or crazy." She half-turned to glare accusingly at Eric. "And *he* told me it was all *his* doing."

She stabbed a finger at Eric, who shrank away from her, wishing he could melt into the wall. Wishing he could undo everything and go back to the night of the party. Back when things were simpler.

Kayla had gone very pale and quiet; Elizabet looked from the woman to Eric and back again, then nodded, as if making up her mind.

"I think we need some tea," she said, decisively. She descended the stairs like the Queen of England, as Eric repressed the urge to giggle insanely. Instead he followed meekly in her wake, preceeded by the lab woman and trailed by Kory and Kayla.

His mind went blank again for a moment. Somehow he found himself sitting at the kitchen table with the rest, a cup of tea in his hands that he did not remember pouring. He sipped it. Chamomile. Just the thing for nerves. He wanted a drink . . . and he knew he didn't dare get one. One drink wouldn't be enough, and how many would it take before the Nightflyers started whispering to him again? And how many more before they started to sound like his best friends? Back when he'd been drinking, he'd thought a lot of rotten people were his best friends. . . .

"I think you should know, before you make any more accusations, that two of us were unwilling 'guests' in Dublin Labs last night," Elizabet said, watching Susan Sheffield over the rim of her teacup. The scientist narrowed her eyes, looking skeptical. "There is a third victim of detention asleep upstairs right now, suffering severe post-traumatic stress syndrome. If this were someplace like Iraq or South America, I would have said she'd been tortured." At the scientist's look of shock, she added smoothly, "But of course, this is the United States, and nothing like that ever happens here. Does it?"

Susan Sheffield opened her mouth as if to say something, then closed it. Elizabet followed up on her advantage. "And of course, since this is the United States, no one kidnaps middle-aged health professionals from conferences on the psychic, ties them up, shoots them full of sodium amatol, and drags them off to a sub-basement at Dublin Labs. Do they?" Elizabet didn't wait for Dr. Sheffield to answer. She rolled up one of her sleeves with clinical detachment, displaying rope burns around each wrist and a bruise the size of a golf ball on her bicep, a bruise with a needle-mark clearly in the center. "He really was awful, too," she remarked. "I'm surprised that he didn't break the needle off in my arm. But then, I wasn't cooperating."

"How did you — what did you — "

She rolled her sleeve down again. "I told you, I was a health professional; I'm a licensed psychiatric therapist. As it happens, I've gotten jabbed with a needle meant for someone else from time to time in the course of my job. I never thought that would turn out to have been such a good thing. Lucky for me, I've gotten accidental trank doses so many times that my tolerance is pretty high. Otherwise, when the alarms went off, I might have been one of the ones I had to leave behind in the cells."

"Others?" Susan said sharply. "Cells? What others? What cells?"

"The cells on the thirteenth floor below the ground," Kory put in, shaking back his hair. He leaned forward earnestly. "The cells where the evil man put Beth when he took her from us, and where he also put me and tortured me with Cold Iron. I swear to you upon my honor that he did this." He displayed his own wrists, which up until this moment had been hidden in the long cuffs of his soft silk shirt. Eric gulped and averted his eyes, and beside him he heard Susan Sheffield gasp. As well she might. It looked for all the world as if someone had been working Kory's wrists and lower arms over with red-hot wires.

Eric's hands tightened around his cup, as his own wrists burned and throbbed in sympathy. *That was what I Saw,* he realized, suddenly, *when I tried to reach him with the Bardic magic. That was what I felt. They were hurting him, and the Cold Iron might have killed him if the pain didn't turn him crazy.*

"Level thirteen?" the scientist asked, licking her lips nervously as Kory covered his wrists again. Her eyes had gone from skeptical to wary. Eric had the feeling that the reference to this thirteenth floor hadn't taken her entirely by surprise. "But thirteen is a sealed level, it's the one just above mine. That's — that's Warden Blair's labs, the Cassandra Project! How did you get in there? Nobody gets in there! I mean, I know he has about four times the number of lab people than anyone else, but — you aren't lab people — "

Both Kory and Elizabet nodded, but it was Elizabet who spoke. "We didn't 'get in,' we were brought in. Our charming host called himself Dr. Blair," she said calmly, outwardly unmoved by the display of Kory's burns. "And I would guess that when the alarm went off, there were about a dozen of us who got out of our cells — our *locked, monitored* cells — and escaped. There were at least as many who didn't, who were either too broken, too cowed, or too frightened to run. Or, possibly, too crazy."

"He said that there were fourteen lab people missing," the scientist said, as if to herself. Then her gaze sharpened as it fell on Eric. "But what about *him* and his pet monsters? What's he got to do with this?"

Eric's wits finally came back, and he straightened up, looking back at her with all the defiance he had left. "I knew that my friends were locked up in Dublin Labs, lady — high-tech, Fed stuff in there — and everything pointed to the Feds taking them. What was I supposed to do, call the cops and tell that to go arrest some Feds, or maybe write my representative in Congress? Was I supposed to just let them rot in there? Look what they did to Kory! I had to get them out!" He swallowed once, then continued. "So I used the only weapon I could think of. It wasn't a good choice, but I didn't know that then. I didn't know what they'd do, I didn't know that they'd manage anything worse than scaring people. I thought — I don't know what I thought. I know that I didn't think there'd be anyone innocent in there." He dropped his eyes, then, to stare at his hands and the cup in them. "I thought everybody in there would have to know what was going on, would have to be bad guys. *I* don't know what goes on in a place like that! I'm just a musician."

The scientist started laughing, a note of hysteria in her voice. "Just a musician. *Just* a musician! Playing Pied Piper to a bunch of man-killing monsters and you're *just* a musician!"

For a moment, Eric thought that Elizabet might slap the woman to bring her out of her hysterics — but when he looked up, the healer just pursed her lips at him and shook her head slightly.

Susan passed from hysterical laughter to soft weeping within a few moments; sobbing into her hands, crying with a peculiarly helpless tone to her voice. Elizabet left her alone for that, too, until she got herself under control, and wiped her eyes with a paper napkin. Then she looked up at Elizabet, and when she spoke, her voice was steady.

"I could believe just about anything of Warden Blair before today," she said steadily. "And now, after this afternoon — I *can* believe he'd do anything. The man was as cold as a snake, and had about as much moral sense."

"Do you have any idea what Warden Blair did there?" Elizabet asked urgently. "I have a very traumatized woman upstairs. If I have some idea what might have happened to her, I might be able to help her."

Susan Sheffield pursed her lips. "I know he had a lot of equipment," she said, finally. "He was supposed to be running some kind of psych project. That was what rumor said, anyway. But he had all kinds of equipment that he'd scrounged from all over the labs that no psych project would need. Colonel Steve likes to use mythological names for our projects, names that kind of have something to do with the project itself. Like, mine is 'Poseidon,' because it's got to do with earthquakes, and Poseidon was the god of the sea and earthquakes."

"Poseidon, the earth-shaker," Elizabet muttered. "But 'Cassandra' — that was the prophetess of Troy, the one doomed both to speak the truth of what would come and never be believed." She pondered a moment. "Could it be that he was attempting to collect psychics for some kind of *government work*? Seeing the future, perhaps?"

The scientist shrugged. "He was popularly thought of as a real nut-case; nobody who had ever met him wanted to work on his projects. As I said, I could believe about anything of him. And — " She paused and her face paled. "And some of the people who quit his project had — bad luck. Pretty bizarre bad luck, really. . . . I'd never thought about it before, I guess nobody did, but it was things like the intern kids getting kicked out of their grad programs or being forcibly transferred to other universities. I remember one kid in tears, because they'd told him to either quit or go to Anchorage. And we sure never saw them around the labs anymore."

Elizabet snapped her fingers in front of the woman's eyes, startling her. "You were going to tell me something about the equipment Blair has," she said firmly.

"Weird stuff," the scientist said faintly. "Oh, a decompression chamber, for one thing; that had been sitting in the corner of *my* space since I'd gotten my floor and I was just as glad to see it go upstairs — but what would a psych project need with something like that? And one day one of my grad students came back giggling that the dumpster from his floor was full of boxes from — " she blushed crimson " — from, ah, one of those — ah — 'adult toy stores.' You know — "

"Pornshops," Elizabet said crisply. The woman flushed again.

"Yes, well, this one is supposed to be really popular with the — ah — 'leatherboys.' The ones who like to tie each other up. Handcuffs, restraints, and gags, according to my lab kid." She rubbed her cheeks, and averted her gaze. "There were lots of boxes. So many that Charlie asked me if Blair was planning on holding a party. A 'black tie-down party for thirty,' he said."

"Hmm." Elizabet seemed lost in thought, and asked the next question absently. "What did you mean, earlier, when you said that you would believe just about anything of Blair before today?"

Susan's flush vanished, and her face went dead-white. "Today — today when I saw Warden Blair, he wasn't the same man at all. Oh, outwardly he looked the same, but — the snake that used to be on the thirteenth floor was someone I wouldn't have trusted without all the cards on my side of the table, but he was still someone I understood. I've seen his type before. But today — he's changed, and I can't read him at all. I think he *would* do anything."

Eric had a horrible, sinking feeling, the feeling as if

he *almost* knew something. And that when he found out what it was, he was going to be really afraid. Not that he wasn't afraid now, but—

Suddenly Susan Sheffield seemed to wake up, and she stared at Elizabet as if the healer had just sprouted horns and wings. "What am I doing, talking to you like this? You don't have clearances, you don't have any right to know *anything* about the labs. I came here to get you to answer *my* questions, not the other way around!" She shoved her chair back and stood up, angrily. Eric distinctly heard Kayla mutter *damn.* "I'm getting out of here, and when I do, I'm calling Colonel Steve and letting him know I found you."

But Kory was between her and the door, instantly. She looked up at him, surprised, probably wondering how he had gotten there so fast.

"We shall not imprison you, my lady," the elf said gravely, "but we cannot allow you to do that."

Susan's response to that was a quick knee to Kory's groin.

Eric heard something like a muffled *clank.* Then *she* bent over double, clutching her knee and moaning.

Kayla giggled. "All that and endurance too," she said with a grin. Elizabet glared at her, but she kept on grinning.

Kory remained in the doorway, shaking his head sorrowfully. "I am very sorry, my lady," he said over Kayla's snickering, "but I have seen those television programs also."

Elizabet rose, graceful and unhurried, and got the scientist back over to a chair. But instead of placing her hands on Susan's knee and doing something about the pain as Eric had expected, she sat back in her own chair.

:Why isn't she helping?: he asked Kory silently, forming the words carefully in his mind. This telepathy thing was still new to him and it didn't come easily. Nor was it of any use much outside of normal vocal range. A dif-

ferent kind of speech, was all, and if he wanted to talk to someone on the other side of town, he might as well use the telephone; it was a lot more reliable.

:I believe because she has no strength to waste and wishes to save it for Bethany,: Kory replied the same way.

"Gentlemen," Elizabet said after a moment, while the woman massaged her maltreated knee, "why don't you go into the other room for a moment. And Kayla, go sit with Beth. I think Susan and I should talk together a little. You can watch the door from there easily enough."

Kayla started to protest, but a look from Elizabet quelled her. She got up sulkily, and left with a look of disgust at being excluded. Eric and Kory followed.

Kayla clattered noisily up the staircase; so noisily that it had to be on purpose. Eric waited until Kayla was up the stairs before saying anything.

"Kory, Elizabet needs to know what happened to Beth, right?" he asked, flinging himself down into a chair. Kory seated himself on the couch, across from him. "Not just what *happened* to her, but what went on inside her head."

The elf nodded, slowly, his blond curls looking a lot more wilted than Eric was used to seeing. "I believe so."

This is taking a lot out of him. Me, too. "And *we* need some serious reinforcements." He scratched his head. "Look, I tried to get through to your relatives when you got caught, and I couldn't reach them. But I was using the phone — *you've* got to have some way of getting to them, you know, elvishly. Right?"

Kory glanced warily at the kitchen door as the voices on the other side of it rose for a moment. "I can contact my cousins, yes," he replied. "And at nearly any time or place. But — why need we reinforcements? Are we not safe again, and together? Have we not defeated the evil men? Once Bethany is well — "

"Is the guy that kidnapped you dead?" Eric

countered. "You just heard that woman say he's still around. As long as *he's* around, we aren't safe." He ran his hands through his hair distractedly, trying to think of all the angles. Plotting was not his forte. It should be Beth doing this, not him. "Shit, we aren't safe now, if he knows where we live. I'm only hoping that he doesn't, that the reason he took Beth in broad daylight was because he doesn't know who we really are and where we live. I dunno, he was picking up psychics, maybe he's got some kind of psychic sonar that zooms in on people like Elizabet and us. Maybe that's how he found us. I hope so. 'Cause if he knows where we live, we're in deep kimchee."

At Kory's look of bewilderment, he shook his head. "Let me see if I can explain this right. Remember — ah — *Die Hard 2*?" The elf was an insatiable consumer of action films, good, bad, and terrible, and with his magic, if they didn't have the cash, it was easy enough for him to sneak into theaters with his Low Court cousins, so it was a safe bet that he had seen the movie and he would recall it.

If the film industry had more fans as devoted as Kory, Hollywood would have nothing to worry about.

"Remember how the bad guys had friends in with the good guys?"

"The special army team; yes, I remember." Kory frowned. "I think I catch your meaning. While those who are honorable would condemn Warden Blair's actions, they are prevented from knowing about them by friends of Blair's who have been corrupted by him."

"Pretty close," Eric said, relieved. Fortunately for them all, Kory became less naive about the human world with every day, particularly where human failings were concerned.

Hooray for Hollywood.

"And these same corrupt men have the resources to find us again," the elf brooded. "This is an ill thing. I believe I must call the others. Arvin above all will know what to do."

"Good. Excellent. How soon do you think they can be here?"

Kory pondered for a moment. "Bard Eric, would you say this is an emergency?"

He gave a thought to what the elves might consider an "emergency." His peril and Beth's — not a chance. They were human, and important only to Kory. But Kory—

"Yeah, I'd say so," he replied. "Tell Arvin that the human had you captured and bound with Cold Iron — that he's going to come after you again — and that once he has you it would only be a matter of time before he figured out what you are. That means humans — *in the government* — would know all about elves. And *that* would mean that none of you would be safe outside of Underhill." He smiled a little to himself; Arvin might well be indifferent to the fates of Kory's pet humans, but he *adored* living in human society and he'd go mad from boredom in the carefully controlled world of Underhill. That would bring him around soon enough—

"You might tell him that given this set of humans, they might even figure a way for themselves to actually get into Underhill," he added. "They're scientists, and once a scientist knows that something is possible, they find ways to do it."

Put that in your little leprechaun pipe and smoke it, Arvin.

"I shall do that," Kory replied, a certain grim delight on his face. "I think I can have at least a dozen or two here within the hour, with that to fling at them."

That was good news. "Okay, you take care of that. I'm going upstairs. By the time they get here, I may have some idea what's going on with Bethy." He vaulted up out of his chair and sprinted for the stairs, noting absently as he passed the kitchen door that the murmur of voices sounded less angry and more — anxious.

And maybe Elizabet's getting through to the scientist-lady. I sure hope so. I don't want to have to wipe her mind clean of what happened at the labs and anything to do with us.

This Bardic magic stuff was getting messier all the time. Seemed as if every time he used it to fix something, he had to use it again to fix what the fix had messed up, and then fix the problems that the fix to the fix had brought up.

Why couldn't things be simple, like in one of those awful Role Adventure Escape books? Just find the Magic Talisman and poof, all the crayon-box dragons would roll over on their backs. . . .

He paused at the door to the bedroom and peeked inside. Beth was asleep, but he doubted it was anything other than magic-induced sleep. Kayla looked up as the door creaked, surveying him warily from her perch in the window.

And just find the Wand of Wizardly Wonder, wave it, and everyone is healed of everything. Including death. He shook his head a little unhappily. *I could do with one of those right now. And not just for Bethy.*

"Kayla?" he whispered, easing himself into the room. "You're gonna have to spot for me. Kory's calling in some kind of elven SWAT team to back us, and I'm going to try to find out what happened to Bethy, since she won't tell us."

The kid's expression sharpened with interest, until she looked like an alert little fox. "What are you gonna do, Bard?"

He grimaced ruefully. "Wish I knew. Oh, I have a plan — I'm gonna try and get inside her head. But once I'm in there, well, I dunno what's gonna happen. So you'll have to play it by ear. Sorta put a lifeline on me and haul me out if something goes wrong, okay? You're better at this than Elizabet is."

"Jeez, you don't ask for much, do you?" the kid muttered. Then, louder, "Okay, I'll do what I can. But —

shit, Bard, I don't know what I'm doing here. So don't sue me if I mess it up."

"If we both mess it up, kid, there isn't gonna be anything to sue." This was going to be dangerous for Kayla — not so dangerous as it was for him — but she could get hurt and he hoped the healer kid realized it. From the expression on her face, she did. From the expression on her face, she also had no plans to try and back out.

Kayla gritted her teeth. "I know," Kayla said grimly.

He settled himself on the bed next to Beth, one hand covering one of hers. What should he use to key on? There weren't any Celtic songs about mind-reading. . . .

Oh, of course. Gordon Lightfoot. Perfect. He closed his eyes, and hummed the first few bars — and Felt the power take hold of him.

"Okay," he muttered, "let's get this over with."

He came up out of his trance with a scream.

And he found himself the center of an audience. Kayla he had expected, and maybe Kory — but the tiny room was full of bodies, human and elven. His eyes went first to Elizabet — and, to his immense relief, he saw a pale-faced, round-eyed Susan Sheffield crowded in beside her. Kory stood on the other side of the scientist, and the rest were jammed in however.

He checked the elves first, and they were equipped for mayhem. Elegant, but definitely no one was going to mess with them. Knives long enough to qualify as swords hung at many sides; the elf he had last seen dressed in pink-punk style was still in pink, but it was a catsuit, and she had a bandolier of throwing knives across her chest. One end of a *bo* staff peeked over the heads of those on the right side, and were those arrows on the left?

So they'd taken the threat seriously. Good. They'd

better. The threat was a serious one. He hadn't been throwing bull when he'd told that stuff to Kory. Odds were nine-to-one it was true.

"Well?" Elizabet said, as he struggled into a sitting position — not an easy feat on a waterbed.

"Remember what you said about torture?" he asked the healer, who frowned and nodded. "Well, that's what he did. Somehow he figured out that Bethy's a claustrophobe; there's nothing in Beth's memory of how he did it, but I'm guessing maybe he used her reactions to questions and had a lie-detector on her. Then he locked her in that damn decompression chamber in the dark, and started increasing the pressure." He snarled as he spoke, and the scientist whitened a little further. "Real clever, too. Torture without leaving marks. Wonder what he'd have done to you, Elizabet?"

Kayla was livid, and holding her anger well; much better than he had expected she would. "That's probably what I was for, boss," she said to Elizabet, who nodded. "He was gonna snatch me, and tell you to cooperate or he'd take me apart and not be too careful about putting me back together. I almost wish that son of a bitch would let me get within a few feet of him, guards or no guards. . . ."

"There's more," he told them, "but right now, the only thing that's pertinent is that she's got the phobia mixed up with *my* precognitive dream about the Big One. The one we were kinda talking about. It's pretty clear, and there's Nightflyers mixed up in that one, too. That gonna give you enough to work on?"

"That should give me enough to break her out," Elizabet told him. "Once I've got her out of this hallucination-cycle she's in, and talking, the rest will come."

He heaved a sigh of relief, and rolled to the edge of the bed. Several sets of hands helped him up, and he staggered with fatigue as he got to his feet. Kory caught and held him, and he looked up into the friendly, worried, elven face he knew so well. "I have a nice nervous breakdown coming," he said conversationally. "I've earned it, and I'm by-God going to take it as soon as this mess is over. But right now — we've got things to take care of. Is Arvin in here, somewhere?"

"Here, Bard," said a voice at the back, somewhere near the *bo* staff.

"Okay, let's all of us get out of here and let Kayla and Elizabet do their thing. I've got something that involves all of the rest of us." He looked straight at Susan Sheffield. "You, especially."

"Me?" She looked confused and apprehensive, and probably would have backed away from him if there hadn't been so many people.

"Yeah, you, and that Home for Deranged Scientists you work at. Let's move it on out of here." He nodded at the door, and let the tide of the others carry him down the stairs and to the living-room.

Once there, the "audience" arranged itself around him in a semicircle; Arvin wordlessly handed him a glass of Gatorade, which he downed with gratitude. His head hurt, he was ready to drop, and he wanted to sleep for a week. He could have used one of Kayla's jump-starts, but she was busy with something more important.

Christ, I haven't felt this bad since my last hangover.

And yet, he was calm for the first time in weeks, maybe months, because now *he* had some answers. He wasn't crazy, his dream was a warning, not a hallucination. And he wasn't — entirely — to blame for what the Nightflyers had done. He *had* been their tool, and there was some blame there; he had allowed himself to be deceived and that was something he was never going to forget. But others had been their tools as well, and one of them was standing awkwardly beside the sofa.

"You said your project had something to do with earthquakes, right?" he said to Susan Sheffield. She nodded uncomfortably. "So what's it all about? And what's going on with it right now?"

"I can't tell you that — " she began. He interrupted her with a downward slash of his hand.

"Damn your clearance crap anyway!" he spat, and she winced away from him. Arvin looked impressed. "All right. *I'll* tell *you*."

His time in trance hadn't been spent entirely in Beth's mind. And it hadn't been at all under his conscious control. Someone, or something, had guided and impelled his vision. Maybe it had only been his subconscious, which had always been better at putting two and two together than he was. Maybe it had been his conscience, which had lately been pretty good at making him face up to the facts, no matter how unpleasant they were.

Whatever it was, once he'd seen in Bethy's memory what she had been put through, his trance had taken a different turn without him thinking about it. He had leapt into an omniscient point of reference right over Warden Blair's shoulder, and fast-forwarded to the Nightflyer invasion.

He knew a lot now. He knew that Warden Blair wasn't Warden Blair anymore — and hence, the change that Dr. Sheffield had noticed. And he knew what Project Poseidon was.

"You built yourself an earthquake machine down there, didn't you?" he said to Susan, whose eyes widened with shock. "Not one to *read* them; one to *make* them. I don't suppose you worried much about the implications of that."

"That's all I thought about! It's meant to trigger microquakes, to relieve stress along faultlines," she said defensively. "It's going to help people, to save lives — "

"Yeah, but your project's in Warden Blair's hands, lady," he countered as she blanched. "And by the way, I wouldn't go back to my apartment right now if I were you. He told that Colonel Steve of yours to send you a little reception committee after that unscheduled visit you made to the office this afternoon. He got worried, and he wants to make sure he has your services for as long as he needs them."

Her face went paper-white, then flushed. "You'd better be telling the truth," she said angrily, "because I have a way of checking that."

He spread his hands and arched his eyebrows. "Be my guest. Check on it. I'd rather you did that than walk into an enemy ambush."

"I need the phone." She changed her challenging gaze to Kory, who moved politely out of the way of the phone on the wall — but stayed within grabbing distance of her in case she tried anything.

She dialed a number, which must have been answered on the first ring. "Hi, Betty, it's Susan. Listen, I was supposed to have a cleaning crew over this afternoon, are they there yet?" She listened for a moment, and her angry flush paled to white again, though her voice remained steady. "Well, good, Betty, that's terrific. Yes, they certainly are handsome young men. Yes, they're bonded, that's why I let the firm have a key. No, they'll probably be there a while; they're cleaning everything. That project's coming to a head, and the place is a pig-pen. Thanks Betty, I just wanted to be sure they'd gotten there. No, thanks, I'll probably be working late. Bye."

She hung up, and when she turned to Eric, her hands were shaking. "A nosy, elderly neighbor can be a wonderful thing, sometimes," she said, with a false little laugh.

"Yeah," he replied.

She made her way carefully to the sofa, and sat down on it. *How much else do I tell her?* he wondered, watching her. For all the profound shocks she'd had, she was coping pretty well. Encountering Nightflyers, death, Bardic magic, elves, and betrayal all in forty-eight hours could put quite a strain on the brain. . . . But he needed her input.

Okay. He might as well go for the whole thing. "You said that you'd noticed something weird about Blair the last time you saw him?" he asked carefully. "I mean, weirder than usual."

"The lights were on, but nobody was home," she said without a second thought. "Or — no, somebody was home, all right, but it wasn't human — "

She stopped, suddenly, and he saw her putting all the facts together in the way her brow creased and her eyes widened. "One of those *things,*" she gasped. "One of those horrible shadow things took him over, like in *The Exorcist!* Didn't it?"

He nodded, while all of the elves except Kory looked puzzled. *Great. Kory didn't tell them how I sprung him. That's not going to make them real happy with me, even if it isn't a direct threat to them. Yet.*

"Right," he said wearily. "And *that* is what's in charge of your project. In charge of something that can trigger the Big One, instead of preventing it. And just what do you think it's going to do with something like that?"

He thought for a moment that she might faint, she grew so white, but she recovered.

"All right," she said, slowly. "All right. I believe you. For whatever I'm worth, you've got me on your side. Now what?"

"Now you sit there for a minute," he told her, and turned to the others, taking a deep breath.

Okay, kids, it's story-time with Uncle Eric. Got a lot of catching up to do, and a short time to do it in. "When you last saw our heroes, they were recovering from the big party," he began. "This is what happened when you all left them — "

● CHAPTER TWELVE

Tom O'Bedlam (Reprised)

Eric waited in sick suspense when he finished his narrative. He more than halfway expected the elves — Arvin in particular — to jump all over him for the way he'd handled the Nightflyers. And he definitely expected them to be on his case for bringing them across in the first place. But they weren't and they didn't. And in a way, their actual reaction surprised him more than anything else.

Silence for a moment, then thoughtful nods. Susan looked sick, though — and more than a little afraid of him. Well, he didn't blame her for either reaction. Kory laid a comforting hand on his shoulder, and he covered it with his. That was one thing he could count on, anyway. Kory would stand by him, no matter how boneheaded he'd been, and help him fix what he'd done wrong.

"Ye didna do too badly, Bard," one of the more stiff-necked, High Court types said grudgingly. "I canna say that any of us would have acted differently."

He couldn't have been more amazed if they'd handed him the Congressional Medal of Honor. "But—" he stammered, "but — I screwed up! I did everything wrong that you could think of! It's my fault there's one of them playing around in Blair's body right now!"

But it was Arvin, not Kory, who leapt to his defense.

"No one," Arvin said fiercely, "no one in all the history that we know, has ever brought more than one of the Nightflyers over from the chaos of the Primal Plane where nightmares are. *No one.* Not even the Unseleighe. How could you know what they would do? We don't!" He looked down at Eric broodingly, no longer the careless, light-minded, exotic dancer. That persona was gone, shed as easily as shedding a costume. Arvin was a Warrior now — capital "W" — and looked it. Lightweight armor, short sword, hair tied back in a businesslike braid.

He'd shown up on the doorstep ready for a fight. "Oh, there are some few things you might have done differently, had you not been so weary and so concerned for the others."

"Like?" he prompted.

Arvin shrugged. "You should have counted the evil beasties before you sent them out; if you had been a practiced sorcerer you would have known to control them with binding spells to harm no one who was not directly involved with the abductions. And yet — that might not have been enough; they might be clever enough to find loopholes in binding spells. There is some fault resting with us, even."

Arvin and Kory both glanced over at another High Court warrior — Eric finally recalled his name as "Dharinel," and that he was one of the Mist-Hold elves that did not approve of Kory's liaison with humans. He didn't much approve of humans in general, as far as that went; he avoided coming out from Underhill as much as he could. Eric had only met him once or twice, at the time when Kory had introduced them to the Mist-Hold court, and once at a gathering of Arvin's. And he had shown up on their doorstep only once: to lecture Kory on his duty, and to find himself escorted politely to the door.

Dharinel nodded sourly in agreement with Arvin's

last statement. "Korendil wished us to teach you, Bard," he said with obviously unhappiness. "Because he is only a Magus Minor, and knew nothing of the Bardic Powers or how strong you would or could become. I opposed that training. One Taliesen, I felt, was enough, especially in these days when no one believes in magic. If the humans had lost their magic, that was to the good. Or so I thought. Now, it seems, events have proved me wrong."

Well, don't apologize or anything.

"If we all survive this, Bard, we will see to your proper training," Arvin said firmly. "I will make certain that High Lord Dharinel takes care of that *personally.*" The veiled glance he threw at the other elf implied a whole lot more than Eric understood.

What am I, some kind of counter in a game of elven politics? was his first thought, and *what does he mean, "if we survive?"* was his second.

"If?" he said, swallowing. "What's with this 'if' stuff? You know something I don't?"

"The reason that you could not reach me when Kory was first taken," Arvin said, his expression grim, "was that we had Seers of our own who had experienced some disturbing visions of late. Visions of the earth shaking hereabouts; of terrible death of humans. And yes, of a horde of some shadowy creatures that we *thought* might be Nightflyers. Only we were not certain; in fact, it seemed far more likely that they were some creation of our Unseleighe kindred. And there were those of us — " he cast a resentful glance at Dharinel " — who were of the opinion that it did not matter if disaster overtook the humans here. But that was before this morning."

Dharinel did not — quite — snarl. "My own sister — who is a Seer — undertook to Foresee if this great disaster could have any impact upon those of us Underhill. We had no reason to think that it would, of

course, none whatsoever. But she is a cautious creature, and felt it might be worth the effort. That was
when she Saw that the energies of the quake would
close off the accesses here to the Elfhame, stranding
any who were here in your world, and isolating them
from the rest of us. Bad enough, that — but worse
would come. For the creatures we had seen were
Nightflyers in their dozens, but worse, they were
breeding on the misery and death following the quake,
breeding *in* the newly dead bodies. The breeding
Nightflyers, growing stronger and more cunning,
would find a way to prey upon the elvenkind so
stranded, taking Low Court first, then High. And then
— driven by hunger for the new prey — then they
would break across the barriers themselves, and pour
into Underhill."

Arvin nodded, and Eric whistled in mingled surprise
and dismay. He knew that Nightflyers could kill; he
hadn't known they could kill elves.

"That discovery is what had us isolated from you,"
Arvin said. "We were in conference, trying to discover
what we could do to prevent such a catastrophe. Now,
perhaps, we know."

"It's a quake that starts it all, right?" Susan Sheffield
asked in a quiet voice. Dharinel and Arvin turned as
one, as if they had forgotten she was there.

"That is what the visions seem to tell us," Arvin said
carefully. "Of course, as with all visions of the future,
the picture is unclear, often distorted. The future is
uncertain and many things can work to change it."

"You think Blair might go ahead and run your
machines without you?" Eric asked. "I mean, can he?
Don't you have to be there or something? Isn't everything, like, secret? You keep what you're doing in code
and in hidden notebooks?"

She smiled faintly. "Sorry kid," she said regretfully.
"This isn't the late-late show. These days, especially if

you're doing research on a government grant, you have to keep clear instructions and up-to-the-minute protocol, in case you get hit by a truck — or — or get 'compromised' as Steve likes to say — and somebody else has to pick up where you left off."

She shook her head, thinking of all the regs she had to follow — not for the sake of good science necessarily, but to keep her grants. She had never guessed how much of her life would be tied up in bureaucratic crap. "You've got to be ready for inspections, and be ready to prove you can do what you say you can. There's only so much grant money and lots of people want it. Especially Teller's boys, and he still has clout, the old bastard." She shrugged. "It wouldn't be easy for someone to crack my computer protections, but anybody with a higher access priority than mine — like Colonel Steve — is going to be able to bypass those." She smiled wanly. "I hope you've got a guest room. I think I'm going to need it."

"So as soon as they figure out that you aren't coming home to your apartment, we can bet on Blair having his hands on your stuff." Eric sighed and buried his face in his hands. "God, I wish we had Bethy in one piece. She's so much better at this real-world strategy stuff than I am. There's so many things to try and think of — "

"I think," Kory said, slowly, "that there are only two questions that should concern us at the moment. How soon will it take the Blair-creature to learn how to operate your mechanisms — and how long will it take for him to make the earthquake happen when he does?"

She was awake. And — not in a street full of bodies, nor a chamber with walls closing in on her. That was an improvement — at least for as long as it lasted.

Beth kept her eyes tightly closed, and took in the

evidence of her other senses. Was she hallucinating
again, or sane, however temporarily? Or worse — still a
captive? Sound — the murmur of voices from
downstairs, and the faint sounds of traffic from outside.
Scent — the green of the garden on a gentle breeze.
Touch — the crisp feel of sheets on her body, the soft
cotton of the quilt Karen had given them under her
hands, and the faintly undulating warmth of the
waterbed.

*I'm home. I'm safe. There's no earthquake, no monsters, and
no mad scientist. . . .*

She waited, holding her breath, for all of that to
change. It always had. Only this time she held her
breath until she couldn't stand it anymore — and it
didn't.

"You might as well open your eyes, Beth Kentraine,"
said a voice she knew. "Because I know very well that
you're awake."

"Elizabet!" Her lids flew open without any urging on
her part, and she sat straight up, making the waterbed
slosh. Elizabet sat on one padded railing, while Kayla
perched on the other. Both of them watching her.

Doesn't that kid ever just sit *somewhere? It's like she's only
there for a second before she decides to take off for somewhere
else.*

"What happened?" she asked, not sure what she
meant.

"Ah." Elizabet's dark brow arched upwards. "That is
what I wanted to ask you. What happened to you in the
lab complex? Every time I attempted to ask you — well,
you were most uncooperative."

"I'd — rather not talk about it," Beth faltered.

But Elizabet leaned over and seized her wrist, forcing her to look into the healer's eyes. "I do not really
care that you would rather not talk about it, girl," the
healer said fiercely, enunciating each word with care.
"You have work to do that you can't do as walking

wounded, and if you *don't* talk about what happened, I can't do anything for you!"

Beth wanted to deny that she needed any help — but the trembling, hollow place inside her told her that she did need it, and needed it badly. At any moment, she could find herself on that street, or in that tiny room. There would be no predicting it. She would never be able to sleep, waiting for nightmares; never be able to sit within four walls, waiting for them to crush her. The spells would return, throwing her back into horror with little or no warning. And she knew it.

What had been a simple phobia, easily dealt with, had become a mental cancer eating at her sanity.

She took a deep breath, and clenched her fists in the fabric of the quilt. "Some goons grabbed me on the street and shoved me into a car. I don't know where they took me, at least, I didn't until we broke out — Dublin Labs, right? All I knew was they got me into this place that was like some kind of prison."

Elizabet nodded. "Then what?"

"There was a man," she said, slowly. "Probably the same one who nabbed you. He — he wanted me to sign some papers, sort of check myself into whatever program he was running."

"He said the same to me. We think he was collecting psychics," Elizabet said, giving Beth a moment to steel herself against what she must deal with next.

"Well, I told him to go stuff it," she said. "He — didn't like that; I guess he likes people being afraid of him and it really pissed him off that I wasn't. He kept asking me questions, and he — he turned off the ventilation."

The mere memory was enough to make her sweat. But then Kayla touched her other hand —

And suddenly, it wasn't quite so bad. The feeling of edge-of-panic was still there, but not so bad. She licked her lips and continued.

"Then — I thought he might rough me up, but he

didn't. He had his goons drag me around and shove
me into a decompression chamber. And he — he
turned off the lights — and — "

I can't! she thought, panic rising to choke her throat
shut. *I can't, I can't talk about it, I —* The walls were closing in; they were going to collapse on her, she saw them
moving, leaning down, about to topple —

Kayla touched her wrist again, and Elizabet did the
same on the other side — hardly felt at all amid the
wave of fear and panic that had washed over her.

And then — the fear was gone. Mostly, anyway.
There was still sweat on her forehead, and running
coldly down her spine, and her stomach was full of
new-hatched butterflies, but the walls weren't moving,
and she could breathe again.

She blinked in amazement, then stared at the two
healers, knowing they had done something, but not
sure what it was that they had done to her. "How in *hell*
did you do that?" she demanded. "I was about to go
into a full-bore claustrophobia attack! How in hell did
you stop it?"

Kayla shrugged, and Elizabet simply smiled. "Half of
our work was done for us," the older woman said. "Eric
exercised some of his own powers to find out what had
happened to you — and when we went to work on you
while you were still unconscious, we discovered that he
had already half-healed you. Without even realizing it,
I suspect. That may be why the poor child looks like a
puppy's favorite rag right now."

She seemed to remember something — in the
depths of the worst of her nightmares — a strain of
melody. An old Shaker hymn, "Simple Gifts." And even
now, as she thought of the melody, she felt a calm descending over her, and new strength coming to her.

The same one she and Eric had used to heal Kory
when they thought that they had almost lost him.

A melody that she had followed out of nightmare

and into ordinary fear — out of madness and into sanity.

"Am I cured?" she asked, incredulously. "I mean, am I —"

Elizabet shook her head. "You're still claustrophobic, and the only way you're going to get over that is going to be through a few months of desensitization training. I'll put you in touch with a therapist who's also a Wiccan. But for now, Kayla and I have put a layer of mental floss between you and the memories, that *should* get you through the next few days or weeks."

"Now," Kayla said firmly, "about the *other* problem. The nightmare —"

The images rose up before her, terrifying and nauseating. Wrecked buildings. Bodies in the street. Her hands covered in blood — only they weren't her hands, because she was dead, on the ground in front of herself, and there were these horrible shadow-creatures everywhere —

"It's not a nightmare," Kayla said, again putting that insulating touch between her and the memory. "It's real, I mean, it *will* be real, unless we can do something."

Beth shook her head. "Huh?" she replied cleverly.

"What Kayla is trying to say is that it isn't a dream," Elizabet told her, with her dark face shadowed by even darker thoughts. "What you experienced just now — and what you were locked into — was Eric's vision of the future. Remember, that was the nightmare you all came to talk to me about. It wasn't something that came out of some kind of mental imbalance, it was a true glimpse of a possible future. But it's not just a vision only he has had; not anymore. There were some other folks at the conference that had dreams that sounded like his."

"Yeah, and that's not all," Kayla put in. "Here's a hot news flash; your friends with the pointed ears have seen the same thing, too."

"Which means?" she asked, her mouth drying with a different kind of fear altogether.

Elizabet folded her arms as if she felt a breath of chill not even the warmth of the room could dispel. "That it becomes more and more probable with every hour that the vision is soon to become the reality. *Soon.* Within days, maybe even hours." She nodded at the door to the bedroom. "There's a war council going on downstairs right now to try and figure out what — if anything — we can do."

She waited, watching Beth with the same kind of patient expectation that a top sergeant has when he calls for volunteers from a crack unit.

What the hell do I know about those shadow-things? Or about earthquakes, either? I wouldn't be any help —

Unless she knows something she isn't telling me. . . .

Ah hell. It's Eric and Kory down there, trying to play leader. Kory makes a great knight-errant, but he's not exactly a team player. And Eric can't even plan a grocery run.

God help us, the two of them together are worse. . . .

She recalled only too well the times she had sent them out after simple staples, flour, eggs, milk, and toilet paper — and they had come back with pretty candles, macadamia brittle ice-cream, and Brussels sprouts. Not a roll of toilet paper or an egg in sight.

Men. Can't live with 'em, and you can't get a new operating system.

"All right," she said, reluctantly. "I guess I'd better get downstairs before they start looking for someone to sell 'em magic beans."

Elizabet just smiled.

The creak of the stairs made Eric look up, expecting to see Elizabet or the punk. Instead —

"Bethy!" He leapt up from his seat on the couch, vaulted the elf in the pink cat-suit, and rushed for the stairs. Beth's red hair was straggly and damp with

sweat and tears; her face pale and thinner. But the smile on that face, though weak, was genuine. And the eyes held no fear, no ghost of insanity.

Kory was right behind him, but the elf had other ideas than his simple hug. He scooped Beth up in his arms, carried her the rest of the way down the stairs, and placed her gently in the chair he had vacated. Eric plodded back down to his own seat, feeling vaguely upstaged.

There was nothing wrong with Beth's mind, which further relieved him; they caught her up with what had been going on in less than a half an hour. She took it all in and asked two or three intelligent questions before sitting back with a frown of thought on her face.

"Shit. We are in a world of trouble." She shook her head and looked straight at Susan Sheffield. "You're taking this all very well."

The scientist sighed. "Either I'm crazy, in which case anything I say or do isn't going to matter squat, or I'm not crazy, in which case I'd damned well better do something to help, if I can." She smiled faintly. "I never was a political activist; I figured on trying to make things better by actually doing something instead of going out and getting my face on TV and my name on somebody's shit-list. Looks like it's time to ante up, doesn't it?"

"You will," Beth said grimly, "as soon as I figure out where you can be useful. But I have to admit, I'm really kind of surprised that you aren't freaking out over this Tolkien-fan's wet-dream, here." She waved her hand at the elves; Eric nodded. That was one question *he* wanted an answer to.

Susan Sheffield blushed. "I — ah — oh, shit, this isn't going to sound any crazier than anything else. I've seen you elves before. And not in a fantasy book either."

She glanced over at the one in pink. "I've seen — I

remember seeing — her, in particular. And a really good-looking kid that isn't in this room, a kid right out of a beach movie. Except, of course, that he had those eyes and ears."

There was a chorus of *"What?"* Arvin looked amazed; Dharinel outraged.

Dharinel was the first to recover. He did not turn on Susan but rather on the young elven girl. "You!" he thundered, his face darkening with anger. "How — "

"Don't get your pantyhose in an uproar, Oberon," Susan said, fearlessly — or maybe stupidly — interrupting the tirade before it got started. "It happened a long time ago, when I was a kid; one summer vacation. About fifteen, skinny, nerdy — if there was a contest for 'least popular,' I'd have won it. *You* said you wanted me to call you 'Gidget,' " she finished, nodding at the pink-clad elf.

Dharinel stared at Susan with his mouth dropping open. *I guess that no one's ever talked back to him before,* Eric thought, holding back a grin. "Gidget?" he said. *"Gidget?"*

The elf blushed. "It seemed like a cute name at the time," she said apologetically. She turned to Susan, and stared at her. "Thirty summers ago, roughly?" she asked, frowning. "Would you have been . . . the math scholar? The one going to Yale? And you only wore black, right? You read nothing but math and fantasy, you watched no television except educational, you had a black cat, and wanted to be a witch so that you could curse the cheerleaders with terrible acne and bad hair for a weekend."

Susan's face lit up. "You remembered! I didn't think you would! What *is* your name, anyway?"

"Melisande," the girl replied. "I never use it with humans." She grinned. "I remember you as much for the fact that you simply wanted the pretty girls to experience what you were enduring as anything else.

Despite the fact that they constantly made fun of you, all you wanted was justice, not revenge. That was actually charmingly forgiving of you."

It was Susan's turn to blush.

"But how on earth did you remember *us?*" Melisande asked. "After your magic summer, you mortals aren't supposed to recall a thing!"

Susan made a face. "A combination of luck and sheer stupidity," she said. "I started smoking in college, which was stupid, and I went to a fellow psych student to get him to hypnotize me to make me stop, which was even dumber. *He* was interested in previous-life regression, God help me." She shook her head. "Well, he didn't get Bridey Murphy, but I woke up without needing cancer-sticks, and remembering my fifteenth summer without the blurs around the important parts. It wouldn't have happened if he'd been more competent and ethical, and a little less eager to get a story about himself in *Rolling Stone* and usher in the Age of Aquarius."

Dharinel seemed a little more appeased, if a little puzzled by some of Susan's terminology. Melisande sighed with relief. "Part of the forgetting is to keep you from breaking your hearts over us," the young elven girl said. "You will grow up. We remain teenagers forever."

"I never thought about it that way. I just figured it was infatuation on my part, and whatever on his. Anyway," Susan continued, "I spent ten years thinking I'd hallucinated it all. Then I realized that it didn't matter. I'd had a wonderful summer, you gave me confidence that let me ignore the cheerleaders that fall, you taught me all about the differences between lust and love, and love and sex."

"A not inconsiderable set of lessons," Elizabet observed from the staircase.

Susan nodded. "When I finally got to Yale, what I

learned from you elves even kept me from doing anything horribly stupid. I didn't start drugs, I didn't buy
into the Hari Krishnas or the Moonies. I did two minor,
stupid things: I started smoking, then I went to an idiot
to find a way to quit." She shrugged. "So there it is.
Now I know you are real. And it still doesn't make any
difference. I still had that summer. And I'm enough of
a scientist to know that there are plenty of things in the
universe that are weirder and harder to explain than
elves and magic."

" 'There are more things in heaven and earth,
Horatio,' " Elizabet murmured.

"Exactly." Susan spread her hands. "There it is,
friends. Now that we have the question of my sanity
settled, is there anything we can do to stop Blair from
creating Nevada beachfront property out of Northern
California?"

"None of us are scientifically trained," Beth
reminded them, as Eric nodded vigorously. "Susan, is
there any way of you getting in there and sabotaging
that stuff? Or maybe coaching us and getting some of
us in?"

"Same as a snowball in hell," the scientist said frankly.
"After the little war you had in there? There isn't going to
be a cockroach in there without an I.D. badge, and they'll
be running every one of them through the scanner to
make sure the badges and stats match."

The elves looked baffled; Beth explained to the con-
cepts of "I.D. badges," "computer records," and the
types of objects their magic could not duplicate to
them, while Eric thought of another question. "Susan,
is there any way you can tell from out here if Blair's
turned that thing on? And when he does — how much
time do we have?"

She closed her eyes and sucked on her lower lip for a
moment, thinking. "I couldn't tell from outside the lab
without a lot of really specialized equipment," she said.

"I really couldn't. As for how much time we have, that's theoretical. I mean, we only just proved we can trigger micro-quakes — but — "

"But?" he prompted. Stray bits of PBS science programs ran through his brain. Something about simulations. . . . "Come on, you have to have run some computer modeling on this before you started!"

"We did," she hesitated. "Theoretical. Purely theoretical, and we really didn't want anyone to *think* about the possibility of using Poseidon as a weapon. Instead of using the array at the point where the fault-creep is hanging up, on a line on either side of that place, you use it at the greatest area of stress, and just increase that stress until it *has* to break loose." She began spouting techno-babble at him; he stayed patient for a while, and finally she calmed down and returned to speech ordinary mortals could under-stand. "The computer says — well, it would take some time to set up it, but then you could kick the machines to trigger a quake in maybe an hour, maybe less. Maybe not less, because it'll take some time to build up that kind of stress. Not much more, though. At least, that's what the computer says." She shrugged. "You know what they say about computers: garbage in, garbage out. We were right on when it came to the micro-quake and stress reduction stuff. I would say, since the major-quake stuff is based on the same model, it would be just as accurate. But I won't swear to it."

"Uh-huh." He rubbed his eyes. "I assume they're going to have to do something different with the equip-ment — I mean, this isn't a Godzilla movie where everything's in a van. How long do you think it'd take them to get everything set up?"

That took her by surprise. "To trigger the quake? They'd have to move the sound probes, reposition them. Get clearances from landowners and permits — well, maybe not that — "

Eric smiled thinly. "Yeah, they can probably bluff for at least twenty-four hours, provided they don't have to set one up in the barrio. Or someplace where it's likely to get stripped for parts two minutes after it hits the ground."

Susan grimaced. "Yeah. Wish they did; our problems would take care of themselves. They'll have to recalibrate. Figure he can get an unlimited number of goons to go do the setup, where I had to make do with me, Frank, and one lab kid — so it'll take him — a day. Maybe less." She suddenly straightened. "Wait a minute — that's how we'd know they're going to start!"

"If they move the equipment!" Eric was elated, and the elves all turned to see what had gotten him so excited.

He explained quickly, and as soon as Susan finished drawing a rough map of where the probes were, Melisande left to recruit a team of Low Court "kids" who would keep watch on the probes. Dharinel cautioned her against interfering with the probes or the new placements.

"We do not know what the creature may have protecting these instruments," the warrior said, gravely. "They are probably at least partially steel, which means that you would not be able to affect them magically. My guess would be — were *I* he, and did I know that Susan might have gone renegade — that he will have a human at each of them."

Melisande tossed her pink hair scornfully. "And what can a human do to us?" she asked.

"Little," Dharinel replied, giving her a look. "But the creature may well be able to armor its agents against your magic and illusions, and their *steel-jacketed bullets* can do much."

Melisande blanched.

As well she might. Steel — Cold Iron in any form — had disastrous effects on elven physiology. Even a fragment of a bullet might well kill one, though the marksman managed only to wound.

Storming the gates is going to be right out.

Pretty obvious that Dharinel — who had apparently been appointed their war-leader by default — had already dismissed that idea out of hand. He might prefer to stay Underhill, but he wasn't stuck back in the Middle Ages like some of the Underhill crowd. He knew modern ways, and modern weapons, and he did not underestimate humans.

Okay, they'd have some notion of when Blair was going to rev up the engines. That would buy them time to do something. What, he had no idea. They probably couldn't cut the power to the probes. They probably couldn't subvert the guards. No way they'd be able to get inside the labs. Now if there was just something that they could do about the energy the probes would be putting out. . . .

Wait a minute. It's energy. Elves play around with energy a lot. I've seen 'em change electricity into magic power — oh, they don't do it well but they can! And I've seen Kory hold a lightbulb in his hands and make it work just for kicks. Can we feed that energy back on itself, or maybe — maybe turn it into something else?

Maybe ordinary humans couldn't — but Bardic magic seemed to have a lot to do with energy manipulation, just like the elves, might be able to work a conversion of one kind of energy to another.

"Who's the best mage here?" he asked aloud. Every pair of elven eyes looked from him to Dharinel.

Dharinel seemed less than pleased to be singled out.

Great. Figures. The one elf here who hates my guts. Could be worse, I guess. Could be Perenor.

Dharinel looked at him warily, but nodded his head. "I am," he said simply. "I can work with you, Bard. This is more important than my animosity."

Thanks, Laughing Boy. He gestured, and Dharinel followed him into the kitchen. Eric gestured at the chairs, and Dharinel assumed a seat as if it were a throne.

Welcome, Your Highness, to my humble kitchen.

He dug into the fridge and poured them both big glasses of Gatorade, then got out the pretzels. Elves, he had learned, loved pretzels. Maybe it was the salt.

Dharinel took one, gingerly, and raised an eyebrow in unspoken question.

"Relax, my lord," Eric said wearily. "I don't have any assumptions, and at this point, I have no pride. I'm a half-taught bonehead, and you're going to have to cram tensor physics into me in less than a day."

"Ah." Dharinel glanced out the window at the setting sun, then bit his pretzel in half. And managed something amazingly like a smile. "I believe it is going to be a long night."

Hey, this might work. This just might work. He relaxed minutely. "Yes, my lord — but maybe it isn't going to be as long as I thought."

• CHAPTER THIRTEEN

The Boys of Ballysadare

Melisande hugged the ground, ignoring the damp of fog and the dew soaking her clothing. She needed no spells of deception, no magic at all, to disguise herself; only ability. She held herself so utterly still that birds had winged in to feed within reach of her hand. It had been a long, long time since Melisande had used her skills as a warrior, but old habits were easy to take up again.

Gone were the pink hair, the Spandex bodysuit. Those, oddly enough, *were* the garb of a kind of warrior, but not the kind she was now. She had surveyed the ground of her chosen lookout point, above the green, flat lawns of Dublin Labs, and had created her camouflage accordingly.

Her hair was now a dull yellow-brown, blending with the weeds about her. Her clothing was of the same mottled coloration: gray, yellow, and brown. Her skin was hidden under gloves and mask of thin silk that blended with the rest; she had considered paint, and rejected it as too itchy and too likely to wipe off, had considered changing her skin, but rejected *that* as terribly conspicuous if she had to walk among humans. It was easy to hide the ears and the eyes; it would be a great deal harder to hide camo-colored skin.

She had cast spells of confusion to fool the eye of the humans who might be on guard against intruders, but

Beth, Susan, and Bard Eric had all spoken of machinery that might watch — machines that could detect scent as a hound, or the heat of a body as a snake.

So she had dealt with those, as well; her body was the same temperature as the ground she lay on, and her scent was that of a cat's. She only hoped that there were no other subtle machines to befool.

Below her was one of the probes Susan Sheffield said must be moved. There were a dozen more of them, all told. A dozen and one, to be precise. Somehow Melisande found that number appropriate.

Not evil, she reminded herself. *In fact, Susan meant for them to serve a good purpose. It is the one who uses them that is evil.*

There were elven watchers over all of them, although Susan was not sure which of the "array" would be repositioned. Melisande thought that this one was likely; for one thing, it was on Lab property, and there would be no attention paid when someone came to move it. For another — she had a hunch. Elven hunches were not to be taken lightly.

How long until the Nightflyer creature decided that Susan Sheffield was not to return? And then how long would it be before it decided to act on its own? There was no way of knowing. Melisande had decided that she would wait, no matter how long it took — but she had some doubts about the patience of the others. Some of them, anyway.

Light-minded. Now they are afeared, but when the fear wears off, so will their interest. Too many distractions. It is hard for some of them to believe in the FarSeeing, when there have been so few things in the human world that could ever affect us.

So she had taken up this first outpost herself, to be sure that at least one watcher would remain in place.

There were other things that troubled her. Before she left the Bard's home, there had been some discussion of *how* the Blair-human — before he became a

Nightflyer's host — had found Beth, Eric, and the human healers. Melisande was not terribly interested, until Susan had speculated on more machines, and that had caught Dharinel's attention for fair. The two of them had conferenced, with Dharinel becoming more animated than Melisande had ever seen him before. They came at last to the conclusion that there must be machines that could see the thoughts that moved from mind to mind, the energies of the healer — and, yes, most probably the powers of magic.

The very thought of that made Melisande shudder. Machines that had the same ability to See as the Gifted! Worse, machines that could do so for the benefit of humans who were otherwise blind to magic and all that it meant.

That meant, that in addition to everything else, Dharinel and the others must needs construct the tightest shieldings they had ever created for each of the watchers — and for the humans as well. The healers, Eric, and Beth were shielded so tightly that they no longer existed to Melisande's inner Eye — and on the chance that there might be some subtle telltale on Susan, she had been shielded as well. It would do them little good to discover that the Blair-creature could track them and know where they were, or if it would actually *want* to find the elves. It would accomplish nothing if, with all their careful planning, the Blair-creature found and took Bard Eric.

The younger healer, Kayla, had gone out into the city to try to collect other humans with the Gifts. These, Dharinel had determined, would be needed for later work.

It was a complicated plan they had made; it relied on the abilities of humans and elves, on humans and elves working together. Melisande only hoped that it was not too complicated to succeed.

Their plans were further complicated by their

inability to speak mind-to-mind through the shields, which must remain in place until the last minute. So when a man came for this probe, Melisande would have to leave her watchpost, go to the BART station, and take the humans' transportation to their headquarters. She could not even ride her elvensteed-motorcycle. Dharinel had ruled that the elvensteeds, being creatures of purest magic, had too much potential for being easily detected.

Wait — there was something moving below.

Melisande checked her shields and peered through the foggy gray of early morning. Was it a grounds-keeper? Sexless in its muddy brown coverall, it — no, he — towed a trash barrel upon wheels behind him. . . .

Then the snout of a high-powered rifle poking out of the open top of the barrel told her that this was no gardener. And as he moved across the grass towards the probe, she smiled in satisfaction.

When he reached it, and began to load it into his barrel, she inched backwards to slither down the side of the hill.

Six rings. Seven. Eight. "Damn," Elizabet swore quietly, hanging up the phone. The house seemed terribly quiet with Eric and most of the elves gone. Occasional car noises filtered up from the street, and Elizabet tried not to listen too closely for the sound of one stopping outside. The elves had pledged that they were safe. She had to believe that.

"No answer?" Kayla asked with a grimace. She had accepted the elves' assurance with no question. Elizabet wished she had her apprentice's faith.

"No answer." Elizabet stared off into the distance, her lips compressed into a tight line. *No answer — but most of them were at the conference. Most of them were already paranoid — and what happened there must have simply proven to them that their worst fears were a reality.* "Not that I blame them. After what happened to us, I wouldn't be answering my phone either."

Kayla drew a neat line through the last name on the list. "Yeah. Answer the phone and there could be a car outside your door five minutes later. Teach, we got a problem," she said. "We've got three — count 'em, three — psis contacted so far. The rest, everybody from the conference, changed their numbers in the last day and got unlisted ones, aren't answering, or just plain disappeared. Now what? Where are we gonna find anybody on this short a notice?"

Elizabet shook her head, feeling suddenly tired. *I can't feel tired. I don't have time to feel tired.* "I don't know," she said frankly. "I'm fresh out of ideas."

Kayla blinked, then licked her lips. "I got one," she offered. She had that look about her that told Elizabet she was probably not going to like the idea, that this was something that a child shouldn't be doing. On the other hand — they were rapidly running out of choices.

Elizabet spread her hands. "I'm open to any suggestion at this point." *Just make this one a reasonable one. Something that might work.*

"Well — " Kayla took a deep breath. "You know I'm pretty street-smart. And you know I know how to find people when I want to."

In fact, Kayla's ability to find people was quite uncanny. She knew somehow when people who were pretending to be out were at home; she even knew when people who were out could be expected back, usually coming within ten minutes of their actual return. It wasn't precognition as Elizabet recognized it; it certainly wasn't anything like clairvoyance, for there was no vision involved. Just a "hunch" — one that had served Kayla well when she had been pilfering apartments for food and small amounts of cash. It was astonishing how few people locked their windows even in a city the size of Los Angeles.

"You're street-smart in L.A.," Elizabet reminded her. "This is San Francisco; you don't know the territory." *And I don't want you out on the street; you're a child, and children are terribly easy to snatch when the abductor is an adult and looks official. Flash some kind of badge, say the child is a truant or a runaway. . . .*

"Okay, I don't know this area," Kayla admitted, "but Sandy — Melisande, I mean — she does. She's got the entire BART schedule in her head. And her Grove's way up on one of the hills, so she can even go into Oakland, Berkeley — basically wherever BART can take her. So we had this idea. I know what the real high-psis around here look like, at least the ones that showed up at the conference. And I kind of picked up on things like, where they work, what their neighborhoods are like, so I could probably track them down if they're still around. And they probably remember me. So —"

"You and Melisande want to go hunting, is that it?" At Kayla's eager nod, Elizabet sighed. "A pair of teenagers."

Kayla's face fell. "What's wrong with that? We can take care of ourselves!"

"But who would believe you?" Elizabet asked gently. "Honey, if I didn't have the same Gifts, I probably wouldn't — "

"They'll believe me," said a low, tired voice from the doorway.

They both looked up to see Beth leaning against the doorframe. "Not only that," the singer continued, "but I probably know some of them myself. As far as that goes, I would bet that I know some high-psis that didn't go to your conference for one reason or another, and we could go track them down."

Kayla looked their patient over with a critical eye. "Are you sure you're up to this?" she asked, as Elizabet opened her mouth to protest, then shut it again.

Beth nodded, then smiled thinly. "Even if I wasn't,

we don't have much choice, do we?" she pointed out.
"It's either that, or those of us who can, run for the
East. I imagine we could get into safe territory before
the quake hit, even on motorbikes."

"Run out while we still have a chance to stop this
thing? Leaving the people and elves who can't escape
to face those — things?" Kayla snarled. "I don't think
so."

"The visions all depend on Eric being there," Beth
pointed out. "They all show him *here,* as the instigator.
At least, the ones we know about do. . . . "

"But they're getting worse, not better." Kayla shook
her head. "That's what Sandy says. The elves haven't
told us much detail about theirs; maybe they don't
show Eric. The only details we know came from Eric;
and me and Elizabet have been putting him too far
under to dream when he sleeps, so he's not getting
them anymore. Which means, I bet, that it wouldn't
matter if Eric was here or not. Hell, he's done his gig.
They don't need him; I bet they've got some other way
of coming over without him calling them. If they did
need him, you can bet that bastard Blair would be on
him like flies on — "

"Kayla," Elizabet said warningly.

"Yeah, well, he would." Kayla frowned. "So I don't
think we got a choice. I think we gotta stop this if we
can. And the only way we know of is Eric's plan."

"I don't think we have a choice either," Beth
admitted. "I just wanted to hear somebody else say it."
She pulled her hands out of her pockets; one of them
held a bit of shiny covered elastic. She put her hair into
a tail and nodded at the older healer. "So, am I suffi-
cient chaperone for the two delinquents? Think I can
keep them out of trouble?"

"You'll do," Elizabet admitted tiredly. Kayla bounced
up out of her chair and stopped only when Elizabet
held up a restraining hand. "We have three for the

circle — plus you, Beth, and me. Eric won't be in the circle; he can't be, since he's the channel. The elves will be working their own magics. That means we *have* to have no less than seven more. I'd personally like more than that, in case we have some last minute cancellations."

One corner of Beth's mouth twitched, as if she was trying not to smile. "The classical thirteen? I thought you didn't subscribe to traditional ways."

"I don't," Elizabet snapped, "but out of the six we have so far, three of us *do*. Belief is a powerful weapon."

Beth reacted to Elizabet's unusual burst of temper by straightening and looking a little livelier. *Like a tired cop that just heard the Chief growl,* Elizabet thought. *As if she figures if I have enough left to snarl with, she should, too. Good — that was the reaction I hoped to get.*

Or maybe it was the reminder of how powerful belief *was*. Belief, after all, had helped them make it through the last one. . . .

Belief, and the unlikely combination of Eric and a plan.

The Bard is growing up, I think. Nowhere near so feckless these days.

"In that case," Beth replied, "let's see if we can't find you a few more believers." She nodded at Kayla. "Come on, kid. Let's go collect Sandy and hit the road."

Elizabet dropped her hand, and Kayla bounded to Beth's side.

Kayla let Beth take over; it didn't matter who played leader, and Beth knew San Fran better than Kayla, though not as well as Sandy. The two of them headed out the back way into the garden, Beth in the lead, figuring to look for Melisande there first. Anytime Kayla didn't know where to look for one of the elves, but knew the elf in question was somewhere around, she always checked the garden right off.

They didn't have to look far; she was sitting in one of the little bowers, with her knees tucked up under her chin, watching — something. She sat so quietly she could have been a garden gnome — if anyone made them with pink hair. She had changed back to her pink punk look as soon as she got back to the gathering.

Come to think of it, somewhere someone probably does. Only they're in cutesy peasant costumes, not pink Spandex.

When they got a little nearer, they saw what it was that Melisande stared at so intently. An early rose, the same color as her hair and Spandex tights and mini-skirt. Small, but perfect, with dew on its velvet petals, straight out of a honey-sweet greeting card.

"I always loved roses," she said, sadly and softly, as they neared. "They won't grow Underhill — did you know that? They won't grow without true sun." There was something about her; something resigned and wistful. . . .

That was when it hit Kayla: Sandy expected to die. In fact, now that she thought about it, at least half the elves gathered here had the same attitude Sandy did. Now that the probes had been moved, they expected to die; all of the Low Court elves and many of their High Court cousins. Of the High Court elves, only Kory and Dharinel seemed reasonably confident that this save could be pulled off.

I bet they figure we can't hold up our end. Huh. We did it before, we can do it again. You bet.

"Yeah, well, it'll still be here in a couple of days," she said. "From the look of it, you'll have a whole bush full of flowers you can admire. Right now, you'n me'n Beth have got some tracking to do. Beth figures she knows where some of the witches around here live."

"Not all witches," Beth corrected. "Or at least, that's what they'll tell you. They run the spectrum from ultra-Christian to the absolute opposite. But they're all psychic and they're strong, and I'm pretty sure once they hear what we're up against, they'll be willing to work together. At least, I hope so. There's a lot of rivalry and a couple of feuds we'll have to deal with."

Kayla heard an unspoken undercurrent and asked, sharply, "What's the catch?"

Beth shook her head and sighed. "The catch, me dear young child, is that most of these people range from — ah — eccentric, to pure, unadulterated out-there. I'm hoping they're enough in touch with the planet to believe they can't vibrate their way out of this one without help. But — honey, these people are the nuts and flakes in the bowl of granola."

"Great," Kayla replied as flippantly as she could manage, while Sandy got to her feet. "In that case, it'll be just like a family reunion. Everybody got change for the BART?"

Beth rubbed her temples and tried not to snap. Behind her, Kayla and Sandy stood in respectful silence.

"But the Universe is a friendly place, dear," Sister Ruth chided gently. "You simply haven't *communicated* properly with these entities. I'm sure that once you talk to them, they'll understand that they mustn't hurt anyone when they come over to Our Side."

Right. And Ted Bundy is a real sweetheart, once you get to know him. Ruthie, you'd sign Charlie Manson's parole petition. But Beth didn't allow a shadow of her real feelings to show on her face — or get past her defenses. Sister Ruth had an erratic, but unfortunately accurate, ability to read people — and this was not the time to let her read what Beth thought of her "the Universe is a friendly place" drivel.

"Once we have the time, we'll do that — " she promised glibly. "In fact, I don't see any reason why we can't put you in charge of the project. You're so *good* at communicating with the non-human spirit-entities."

Sister Ruth beamed with pride, but Beth continued before she could say anything and get off on her own Cosmic Muffin tangent. She did not need the guided tour to the spirit-world to get in the way of the real business. "Right now, though — unless we can stop this quake before it starts, we *won't* have the time. In fact," she continued grimly, "the visions of the future that we've been granted show most of us dead. Including me. The entities aren't the real problem, Ruth, the quake is. According to the seer I've consulted, it's the quake that kills most of the people."

Sister Ruth frowned slightly, and Beth knew she'd inadvertently tripped another button. *Oh gods. Karma. Karma and predestination.* She hurried on, keeping Ruth from getting off on the "no one dies until it is time" kick. *How do I get out of this one? Ah — I know.*

"Sister Ruth, please remember, this *isn't* a natural quake. It's being created, by those military men over in Dublin Labs." She paused to let that sink in. "I know. I was there; I saw the machine. It's no more natural than if one of them dropped a bomb on the city. These people in Dublin Labs have no compunction about cutting everyone's karma short."

Yeah, and you signed on every petition to close them down since the sixties, whether or not you knew what it was about.

Sister Ruth hesitated a moment. "Dublin Labs? Oh dear. Oh my . . . they do horrible things in there. And I know that what we ignorantly call Good and Evil are just parts of the Cosmic Balance — and I'm sure that there may be a place even for people like *that* in the Balance — but they do *horrid* things in there, cutting up poor little bunnies and white mice. Making those awful nuclear bombs and lasers. Taking over our minds with Rays. And there is such a thing as Free Will . . . one can choose to be Wrong Minded. . . ."

"I'm sure that's exactly what they've done," Beth said firmly. "Really, Sister Ruth, it's your duty to help us stop them so that they learn the lesson that not all their machines and power can prevail against the Cosmic Balance. It's the kind of lesson they really need to learn."

Dear gods, I hope I'm making all the right noises, she thought frantically. *She's about a dozen bricks short of a full load, but she's really powerful — one reason why nothing's ever actually hurt her. And we need her.*

"We need you, Sister Ruth," she pleaded. "I can't tell you how much. You'll have to work with a few people you may not agree with — but do you know, I think your wonderful example in this hour of crisis may be just what they need to see the Light. Jeffrey Norman, for instance — you just might be the one to show him the Cosmic Way with your shining leadership."

The simultaneous appeal to vanity, responsibility, and the opportunity to show up some of the people she despised most in the psychic community was too much for Sister Ruth to resist. She agreed to come, with much simpering and disavowal of her own powers.

Second verse, same song.

New setting though; instead of ruffles and flowered cotton, she and her crew were surrounded by red velvet and black leather. Instead of potted plants and birdcages full of budgies, there was a microcomputer and a sleek, hi-tech stereo. Instead of genteel, gentle middle-class, the place reeked of money.

Instead of an overweight myopic woman in a flowered caftan, they made their pitch to a goateed, middle-aged cynic in leather jeans. Black, of course. Like his sofa and chairs.

"Look, Jeff, you've got a choice," Beth said rudely. "You can help us — or you can watch everything you own go down in a pile of rubble."

Although Jeff — a self-proclaimed Satanist — sat back on his leather sofa with his hands laced casually behind his head, not all the control he *thought* he had over himself kept his body from tensing up. Nor did it keep him from glancing at some of the more expensive appointments of his living-room out of the corner of his eye.

"How long did you say we have?" he asked cautiously, and Beth could almost see the little wheels turning in his head, as he tried to calculate how much stuff he could load into a trailer before the zero hour.

"Under forty-eight hours at this point," she said honestly. "I don't know if you've ever tried to rent a trailer or a truck on short notice, but it isn't easy. The things are usually booked pretty well in advance. You could probably waste about twenty-four of those hours just trying to find one."

Now she could tell that he was trying to figure how big a bribe it would take to rent a truck out from under someone.

"Besides," she continued, "you've got a lot sunk into this condo. I know you think your insurance will pay for it — " she leaned forward, intently " — but let me clue you in on a little fact of life. Insurance companies are in the biz to make money, not lose it. And the last couple years have been real bad for insurance companies. Lots of disasters." Now it was *her* turn to lean back, and spread her hands wide. "We're talking a Richter nine or even ten quake here. With a disaster of that magnitude, the city is gonna be flat. Every vision we've seen has shown major damage to every building in sight. From the looks of things, you wouldn't even be able to rescue more than a couple of suitcases worth of clothing. I'll tell you right now — *that insurance company of yours will declare bankruptcy before they pay out.* They all will. They can't *afford* losses like that. Maybe the Feds will bail them out — but after all the Savings and Loan bailouts and the hurricanes and tornadoes and floods, I wouldn't count on getting more than ten cents on the dollar. And that's a fact, Jack."

She watched his face pale for a moment, watched a
tic pulse in his cheek as he calculated odds. He had *sold*
insurance at one point in his life. He sometimes joked
that this was how he had become a Satanist in the first
place. From selling insurance to selling your soul
wasn't that big a step. . . .

*Actually he became a Satanist partially because it suits his
cynical, hedonistic attitude, and partially because it's a good
way to part fools from their cash. As witness this condo.*

He didn't like the numbers his own calculations were
coming up with; Beth read that in the narrowing of his
eyes. Finally he leaned forward, took an oversized deck
of cards from the handcarved ebony box on the teak-
wood table between them, and called upon his court of
last resort. As he shuffled them, his hands trembled a
little.

"I hate to admit it, but I couldn't figure why all my
readings kept telling people to get out of town this
week," he said, half to himself.

*But he is high-psi. I'll give him that. His clients may be fools,
but he does give them what they overpay for.*

Like most psychics, Jeff was a little *too* good; he
couldn't read for himself, for what he wanted to see
would skew the reading off the true. And he was too
proud to go to someone else for a reading. Which was
probably why he'd missed seeing the quake for himself.

He stopped shuffling, evened up the pack, and laid
out the cards; the Tower of Destruction occupied a
prominent place. Swords were everywhere, most
reversed — including the Princess. It was the single
most negative reading Beth had ever seen with any
Tarot deck, much less the Crowley.

*So even if he runs — which is what I bet he was asking —
he's screwed to the wall.*

"Shit." He picked up the cards of the Crowley deck
carefully, and put in back in its little ebony shrine. Only
then did he look back up at her.

"All right," he said with resignation. "When and where? And what do you want me to bring?"

The sun set over the Bay, dull red in a cloudy sky, leaving them still on the hunt; one short of a full thirteen, with no spares or backups. Beth trudged wearily down into the BART station, with Kayla and Sandy trailing behind.

She stood staring at the map for a while, her eyes fixed on the YOU ARE HERE spot without really seeing it. Behind her, elf and human fidgeted restlessly in the way of teenage young.

Was I ever that young? She thought back to endless, sullen hours of playing the same tapes over and over at ear-shattering volume while native diggers cast quizzical glances at her while they followed her parents' direction. Or squirming in stiff wooden seats while one or the other read papers to an audience of fossils stiffer than the seats, when all *she* wanted was a chance to get out of there and Shop in Civilization.

Yeah, I guess I was.

"Okay, guys," she said finally. "I've got an idea. It's a long-shot, but there's two groups meeting tonight over at UC that tend to attract high-psis. Some of our missing persons probably belong to one or the other. One advantage is that both groups bring bodies in from off-campus. The other is that the devotees of both tend to be fanatic about their hobbies."

"What is the disadvantage?" Melisande asked. "We know you by now. You never state an advantage without there being a disadvantage."

Beth shrugged. "Only the usual with hobbyists. They tend to take their hobby a little too seriously. That's why they meet on the same night; the *real* fanatics on both sides don't want their members to 'waste their time' with the rival group's activities."

Melisande sighed. "Like Jeff and Sister Ruth."

"Exactly." Now that she'd decided to take the plunge into the wilds of Berserkely, Beth wanted to get it over with and get out of there. "Are you game?"

"Lead on, McDuff," Kayla replied, gesturing grandly. The train to the campus area pulled up, just as she straightened. "See? The gods are smiling upon us."

"I sure hope so," Beth muttered, and ran for the train.

"See anyone you recognize?" Beth asked Kayla, as the young healer took a slightly more aggressive stance, and Melisande tried to shrink behind both of them.

There were fifty-odd people in the room, and most of them wore expressions of faint hostility. They also wore creative variations on medieval and Rennaissance clothing.

Except for the half-dozen Costuming Nazis, who wore completely *authentic* clothing, and expressions of complete hostility.

"They probably figure we're from the Women's Lib meeting down the hall," Kayla observed, absently. "Uh—yeah. The guy in the green and black tights with the great ass, the woman that looks like a Rose Parade float, and the chick with the pregnant guitar. They were all at the conference."

"Sandy?" Beth asked. The elf peeked out from behind her shoulder. "The young man in the particolored hose, the woman in the Elizabethan farthingale, and the girl with the lute."

"They're all strongly Gifted," the elf assured her. "And imperfectly shielded." She squinted a little. "Unless I'm greatly mistaken, the woman and the young man are related. And I *think* I see a Celtic knotwork embroidery pattern on the woman's gown that used to be used as an identifying agent among the devotees of the Old Religion about twenty or twenty-five years ago."

"Oh really?" Beth's eyes narrowed, but she couldn't make out anything special amid all the decoration on the gown. "If you're right, we might have hit paydirt." She turned her attention back to the speaker on the dais. "I think they're going to break for refreshments in a bit. We'll move in then. Sandy, you try for the lute-girl; Kayla, you take the guy and I'll take the Architectural Monument."

They waited, patiently, enduring the glares from the mortally offended, until the Seneschal finally ran out of wind. When people began leaving their seats, Kayla and Beth headed for the woman and the young man, while Melisande took a lateral to intercept the musician before she could join the others who were gathering in a corner.

"Hi," Beth said cautiously, as she stepped in front of the Farthingale, forcing the woman to stop. "You don't know me — but you do know a friend of mine. Her name is Elizabet — "

"And she's the teacher of that charming and obstinate little child who's trying to back my son into a corner," the woman said, with a faint smile. "Since you don't have that nasty 'desperately mundane' look of those goons that were lurking about the conference, I assume you must be all right. Or has Elizabet sent you to warn me about them?"

"Uh — sort of." Out of the corner of her eye, Beth watched the lute-girl shaking her head violently at whatever Melisande had told her. Her face was white, and her hands clutched the neck of the lute like a life-line. "Listen, this is awfully complicated, and well — "

"I know just the place." The woman waved at her son, who nodded at Kayla and gestured at her to preceed him with full High Court grace.

Wonder if there's a touch of elven blood in there somewhere?
All three of them followed the woman out into the hall, to a little alcove with a pair of loveseats. The

Farthingale needed one all by herself; the son took up a seat on the arm of the sofa, and Kayla and Beth took the other seat.

"By the way, I'm Marge Bailey. Which was *not* the name I used for the conference, if you're interested." The woman smiled again, this time wryly. "Call me paranoid if you like, but I've always had a suspicion that some day some government goons would show up at one of these things and start taking names and addresses. So I only use the SCA post office box, and one of my old persona names."

Beth grimaced. "Just off hand, I'd say that this time your caution was entirely appropriate. . . . "

Fifteen minutes later, Marge and her son Craig were pale with shock, and Beth was dry-mouthed and talked out. She nodded to Kayla, who took over.

"We've got a plan," she said. "We think we can head this thing off. But we need — "

"A circle," Marge interrupted, leaning forward, her eyes afire with intensity. "A circle. The kind the witches of England gathered in to thwart the Armada."

"Wow!" Kayla went round-eyed. "I didn't know that! Yeah, that's exactly what — "

"When and where?" Craig said. "We'll be there; Dad'll come, and maybe we can get a couple of others." He took a deep breath. "We knew something wasn't right; we've been getting signs for weeks. But none of us are real good at prediction. That's why we went to the conference in the first place; we figured if there was anyone who'd know what was up, he'd show up there."

Beth felt a great weight lift from her shoulders. This was her thirteenth body — and one, maybe two spares. "Mount Tam — if you've been up there, you know the place. As soon after sunset as you can manage."

Marge nodded. "No problem. Did you plan on checking the Paper-gamer's Club meeting for some more recruits?"

This time it was Beth's turn to be surprised. "Uh, yes. Why?"

Marge chuckled. "Because my husband's in there. Ask someone to find Chuck Bailey for you; he'll round up the couple of gamers with — ah — esoteric talents. That should save you some time."

Beth didn't know quite what to say. "Marge — thank you. I think you just bought us our chance at making this work."

Marge shook her head. "Well, I grew up reading old J.R.R. and the Norse sagas — I always wanted to be Galadriel, the Ringbearer or another Beowulf. You know what they say about being careful what you ask for." She recovered some of her color, and managed a weak chuckle. "I suspect you've had a time convincing some of the others to get involved."

Beth nodded. "I'm still not sure why you agreed so easily."

This time Marge Bailey laughed out loud. "My dear Beth, it's really quite simple. I may be crazy, but there's one thing that I'm not."

"What's that?" Kayla asked.

"Stupid." Marge rose majestically. "I'd better get back before the others think you've recruited me for your biker gang. And we will see you tomorrow night."

"With the proverbial bells on," Craig added, as a dejected Melisande approached from the door of the meeting room. "Listen, I know Mom. This is going to work. If she can make the Kingdom Seneschal back down and *apologize* for screwing up the demo we had for the science fiction fans at ConDiego, that earthquake hasn't got a chance."

● CHAPTER FOURTEEN

The Light in the Window

Eric's head was spinning from everything that had happened, and all the concentrated magic lore that Dhariel had rammed between his ears. He leaned against the cold glass in the window seat, wishing he could wake up, pretend that it was just a nightmare, that all of this would go away and never trouble his thoughts again.

It didn't matter to him that the elves thought his actions were justified. It was the look of horror in Dr. Sheffield's eyes that kept coming back to haunt him, that look that said one word:

Murderer.

So he'd sat quietly through the remainder of the war conference, as an amazingly recovered Beth and the others left on their various errands. No one had noticed as he slipped away from the gathering of elves in the living-room, continuing a discussion of whether or not the humans should carry firearms, or if the magical firepower would be enough.

The war plan seemed straight-forward enough: gather the elves and the human magical/psychic talent of the Bay Area to use in case the earthquake device was triggered prematurely, to try and redirect the energy wave. Meanwhile, an elven hit squad would deal with Blair himself and destroy the machine and the other equipment in Dr. Susan's lab, so it couldn't be used again, at least not until they were *certain* that Blair was no longer a threat.

A great plan. Except that he remembered the security levels of that laboratory complex, and could guess what it'd be like with increased paranoia about a break-out. Translation of that formula: someone, or more than likely several someones, in that elven assault team were going to die.

He couldn't deal with that thought. There were too many deaths in his memory and on his conscience: the elven warriors lying still and lifeless in Griffith Park, Dr. Sheffield's colleagues.

Death follows me like a watchdog.

Maybe it didn't have to be that way. He thought about alternatives. Like running away. They could still do it — gather their friends and run.

But then something else intruded. Not a memory, but a vision.

San Francisco in ruins, the Nightflyers gliding noiselessly through the streets, drifting over the corpses lying on the cracked sidewalks . . .

No. He couldn't leave, not now. But maybe he could arrange things so that no one else was in danger. *I started this whole mess; I can finish it. Just me, alone.*

"Eric?"

He looked up to see Kayla standing in the doorway. She walked in and sat down on the edge of the waterbed. "Back already?" he asked.

She stretched like a cat, and yawned. "Look at the clock, Bard. It's after midnight. Everyone's downstairs, still making war plans, but I wanted to do something other than that for a few minutes."

He glanced at the clock involuntarily, surprised at how much time had passed. It seemed like just a few minutes ago that the others had left on their various quests. "Did you have much luck?"

"Oh, yeah. We'll have a United Wiccan Liberation

Front to go up on Mount Tam tomorrow, no problem."
She yawned again. "Wish I could understand all this
Wiccan witchcraft stuff. Doesn't make any sense to
me . . . what good is magic that you can't see?"

He blinked at that. "What do you mean, that you
can't see?"

She gave him a tired but wicked grin, and held out
her hands. Faint traceries of blue light appeared on her
hands, brightening and moving in flickering patterns
over her skin. "Elizabet taught me how to work without
showing off, as she put it." The fine blue lines faded
away as suddenly as they appeared. "But this Wiccan
stuff, you just kinda pray and hope something happens. At least, that's how it seems to me."

"Me, too." Eric thought about his own magic, that
quiet pool of — something — that he drew upon with
his music. "But it seems to work."

"Sometimes. I've seen Elizabet cuss a mean streak
'cause it didn't, though." She grinned and sprawled out
on the waterbed. "I prefer the kind of magic that I can
do. I know it'll work, every time." Her face clouded.
"Well, almost every time," she said in a low tone.

The girl's calm seemed nearly supernatural to Eric.
How does the kid manage it? he wondered. *All I can think
about is how many people are probably going to get killed
tomorrow, and she seems so calm. Maybe she doesn't know
enough to be afraid.* "Are you scared of what's going to
happen tomorrow?" Eric asked.

The kid shrugged. "Yeah. A little. I hope it'll be quick
and easy, but I know it probably won't turn out that
way. But that's my job, to make sure everyone gets out
okay." She gave him an odd look. "Hey, Bard, don't you
want to be in on the war conference downstairs? They
could probably use your input."

He shook his head. "They've got half the army of
Middle Earth down there, they don't need me."

"What's eating you, Bard?"

He glanced up to meet her wry dark eyes. "Is it that obvious?"

"Only to someone standing within five miles of you. Up close, it's even more obvious."

He looked out at the street, at the cold glow of the streetlights. "What do you think it is, kid? Do you think I'm used to killing people? Fourteen people died in those labs the other night, and a lot more could die, and it's all because of me, because of what I did. Knowing that doesn't make me feel like dancing in the park, y'know?"

"I know. I was there, remember?" Kayla's voice was quiet. "It was scary, Eric. I didn't know what you were going to do, but I knew this much — you weren't in control. That's why those — *things* — went on a killing rampage through the building."

Cold settled around his heart. "Are you scared of me, Kayla?"

She didn't answer for a long moment. "I don't know. Maybe." A flash of a grin, her teeth bright against the dimness in the room. "All I can say for certain, Eric, is that life is never boring when you're around."

"Thanks," he said grimly. "Welcome to another war zone, kid. Sorry, I didn't intend to screw up your San Francisco vacation this way."

"Hey, I already saw a war before that mess in Griffith Park, thank you very much." There was an odd catch in her voice . . . Eric saw something strange in her face, a shadow of an old pain.

"I never heard about that." It occurred to Eric how little he knew about this girl, other than the fact that she was Elizabet's apprentice.

She spoke quietly. "It was in L.A. I was running wild on the streets — this was before Elizabet adopted me. Things got a little hot between two street gangs, and I was caught in the middle — see, they both wanted me, and I didn't want any part of either of them. So I played 'em against each other. A lot of people died in that one, too, Bard. And you could say it was my fault, sure." She clenched her hands into fists, staring down at them, then looked up at him, her eyes bright. "I think it's a curse we have to deal with, Eric. We're different, unusual . . . you have to learn how to deal with it."

"How do you deal with it?"

She grinned. "I try not to hurt people, unless I want to. I try not to do anything that's unethical, or will put someone else into danger. I just try very hard."

Not put anyone else in danger. . . .

"What would you say," he asked, choosing his words carefully, "if I said I had a solution to this situation that didn't involve a lot of people risking their lives in a major assault on the Dublin Labs?"

"I'd say I'd like to hear more about it," Kayla answered cautiously.

"I think it might be possible for me to slip myself and maybe one other person into the labs, undetected. Then we could go down to the level with that earthquake gizmo, take a couple sledgehammers to the machinery, and get out of there again." *Well, getting out would probably be a lot more difficult, but . . .*

"It's a better idea than taking fifteen people in there, guns blazing. I can handle the heavy magic, you can make sure . . ." *Make sure that I don't kill anyone else by accident . . .* "Make sure that my back is covered, and that no civilians get hurt this time."

"That's very true." She gave him a sidelong glance. "You keep surprising me, Bard. I never know what to expect with you." Her voice took on a more businesslike tone. "I'm guessing that you don't want the others to know about this, since they'd definitely try to stop you."

He blushed. "Well, yes."

"It sure beats watching Elizabet go back into that place," the kid said, apparently thinking out loud. "I

don't want her to go back there, ever. Not after . . . "
Her voice wavered a little. "Not after what those bastards did to Bethany Kentraine. I don't want to risk that
happening to Elizabet."

He licked dry lips and considered the other half of
the unlikely pairing. "You two go really far back, don't
you?"

Kayla gave him a little half-smile. "She saved my life,
and then gave me a real life, off the streets. And a future. I'm not going to let some monster outtake from
the movie *Aliens* play with her mind, no way." She
rubbed her hands together. "So, Bard, what's the plan?
Go there ahead of the crowd tomorrow, beat the rush?"

"Yeah, we'd have to. Probably leave here in the middle
of the morning, so we don't have to fight the traffic, too."

"Good plan, good plan." Kayla stretched again, and
stood up. "I probably should go get some sleep, if we're
going to do this tomorrow for sure. G'night, Bard."

One moment an ancient, the next moment a kid.
"Good night, Kayla."

The kid left the room. Eric turned back to the window and the view of the street beyond. *It could work,* he
thought. *It could work, and I wouldn't have to watch Beth
and Kory die, like in my nightmare.*

He much preferred risking only his own life, not
others. Though taking a seventeen-year-old kid along
was an idea that still made him twitch . . . he needed
her, though. If only to make sure that he didn't go nuts
and kill off most of the city.

He could feel them in the back corners of his mind, a
shadow of drifting blackness. The faint whispering, the
voices calling to him . . .

:Do you hear us, Bard?:

:Go to hell,: he thought at them. *:Get lost. Get out of my
brain. Take a hike.:* He mentally pushed them away, with
about as much success as someone trying to push a

shadow with their hands. The whispering drew closer,
echoing in his mind. He shoved at them again, feeling
the creatures drift through his mental hands again.

Then, annoyed, he closed his eyes and called light,
surrounding and filling himself with incandescent il-
lumination. The world seemed to explode with light,
searing the inside of his eyelids. It was too bright to see,
but still he increased the light, filling his thoughts with
it, pouring it into every corner of his mind. "Chew on
that, scum," he whispered to himself, hoping it would
work. If it didn't, he'd probably have to get used to
having this evil Greek Chorus lurking in his brain —
an awful thought, that. He crossed his fingers and held
onto that image of pure light within his mind.

The whispering Nightflyers scattered with a strange
skittering noise, vanishing off . . . somewhere, he didn't
know where. But they were gone, which was a relief.
He grinned, feeling a little more confident for the first
time in days.

Still smiling, he headed downstairs to join the others.

Kayla rolled over on the sofa bed, pulling the blanket
tighter over her to ward off the chill of the attic room.
Sleep was a great idea, but somehow it didn't seem to
be in the cards, at least not for tonight. Too many
thoughts, plans, running through her mind . . . too
many memories.

Hey, I already saw a war. . . .

No magic in that war, not like this — no elves in
bright armor, no Wiccans, no cheerful Bard Eric with a
simmering magical presence that she could sense from
miles away. None of that magical stuff, just a darkened
room in Los Angeles with half a dozen dying boys lying
on the torn mattresses and the bare floor. . . .

I don't want to think about this, I don't . . .

The smell of blood as she worked, trying to save one
boy's life, then another . . . the colors of pain and terror,

knowing that if she failed, she'd probably die as well . . . Carlos standing in the doorway, watching her with that terrifying cold gaze of his, watching as she tried to work harder and faster, as everything blurred around her and she couldn't stop, couldn't escape from the pain, feeling her own life fading away with each passing moment. . . .

Don't think about it, don't torture yourself. It's over, you survived, it won't happen again.

Unless she lost control again. What if they went into the Labs tomorrow and all hell broke loose? She wasn't worried about catching a bullet herself — there were ways to avoid that, if you knew the bullet was coming — but she envisioned a hallway of wounded people, herself moving from person to person, caught up again in that nightmare of not being able to stop, not being able to disengage, to pull herself back and keep a little life energy for herself, watching her own life drain away into the bodies of those she healed.

She thought about warning Eric, telling him that this could happen. That she didn't know any way of stopping it, once it started, unless someone else intervened. The first time, the intervention had been because Ramon didn't know not to touch her when she was working, and that had cast her out of the endless cycle, kept her from killing herself. Next time, she might not be so lucky.

And she had been lucky, so far. Just the fact that Elizabet had found her, and had helped her escape from Carlos, that had been pure luck. If Elizabet hadn't been in the neighborhood, close enough to sense Kayla's near brush with death, she would never have returned to try and track down the "little powerhouse" she'd detected.

In another lifetime, without that luck, Kayla probably would've stayed with Carlos and his gang, stayed until one day when Carlos couldn't protect her anymore and someone else had tried to "acquire" her instead. And that she probably wouldn't have survived. Not with Carlos having made it very clear that he'd rather kill her than lose her.

But that's over with, over and done. I don't have to worry about Carlos, not anymore. Now we have some other minor problems to deal with. . . .

Eric wasn't talking about it, but she knew something was wrong. He wasn't quite as . . . obvious . . . about his problems as Bethany, but there was something going on there, under the surface. She'd considered trying to "read" him without letting him detect it, and decided it was too risky. After a stunt like that, he'd never trust her again, and with good reason. It had taken Elizabet several months, but she'd finally convinced Kayla that listening in on people's thoughts without their knowledge was unethical. Tacky, like peeping through someone's window blinds.

So she hadn't taken the direct approach of just looking to see what was bothering the Bard. But she could tell it was something. There was that way that he'd look away, as if listening to something that no one else could hear. Very strange, and rather disturbing.

Still, he's my best chance for solving this situation without Elizabet getting killed. I don't think he's going to completely "lose it," at least not in the next few days. After that, though, all bets are off.

Beth was the one that Kayla didn't want to trust right now. She knew how fragile that "patch" was, the only thing that was keeping Bethany Kentraine from a long downward slide into insanity. What that bastard Blair had done — Kayla's fingers tightened into a fist, remembering — was inhuman. To deliberately try to break another person's mind . . .

They'd stop him. They would. He wouldn't be allowed to do that to another human being, ever. Whatever was animating his body, Nightflyer or otherwise, Eric would get rid of it. She wasn't too certain how that would happen, but she did have confidence in Eric on that count.

She just hoped that Elizabet would understand. Sure, this was dangerous, what they were planning to do, but it was something that had to be done. And Eric was right — better two people, alone, than a whole army trying to infiltrate that security complex. A neat, clean surgical operation.

But Elizabet would be very . . . angry . . . when she found out that they'd gone off on their own. Kayla reconsidered; maybe this wasn't such a good idea, after all. . . .

What the hell. She'd survived life on the street, and Carlos, and a street war in Los Angeles . . . she'd survive this, just fine.

She smiled, clutching that thought to her like the warm blankets, and drifted off to sleep.

Korendil, Champion of Elfhame Sun-Descending, Knight of Elfhame Mist-Hold, sat in the living-room of his San Francisco home and tried to pay attention to the conversation around him, without much luck. His thoughts were elsewhere, not on the war council that he had called and that he should be concentrating upon.

"Kory, what do you think about the main entrance? Should we try to draw the guards out with a distraction, or just have Eric go in and do some kind of mass hallucination on them? Kory?"

He shook himself out of his reverie, and nodded at Beth. "A distraction is best, milady," he said.

Distractions were all he could think of now. Once, he'd known exactly what his life should be, the life of a near-immortal elven warrior, but then he'd been distracted — distracted by a lovely dark-haired woman named Beth, and a handsome young man with all the powers of an ancient Bard. Because of them, his life had changed, and he had changed, into someone that he would not have recognized many years ago.

They were mortal. That thought could never leave him a moment's peace now. Dharinel had asked him that, in a quiet moment tonight when they were alone in the kitchen, refilling their glasses with dark red wine. "Why do you care so much for these humans?"

Kory had only smiled, knowing there was no answer he could give to the elven lord that the other would understand.

He was bound to them, by choice and by love. He could not imagine living without Beth's warm laugh, or the slow smile that often lighted Eric's face.

And how will I live without them, a scant hundred years from now?

That was the thought that terrified him, that he would have to watch them grow old, as humans do. It was a thought that he had not shared with either of them, not knowing what he could say.

There were answers, of course. He could ask them to join him Underhill, journeying across the veil between worlds into the elven realms where time moved slowly, if at all. But somehow, he didn't think they would accept that offer. Life in Faerie was a quiet and unchanging existence, nothing like the unpredictable life in the human world. He wasn't certain that he, himself, could return Underhill without longing for the human realms. That was why so many of his kind had chosen to live here, among the mortals. Beth had once described his inability to sit still as being "stir crazy" — somehow, he suspected that phrase also described how he would feel after several years of life in Faerie.

Until these last two days, the thought of his friends' mortality had not haunted him so. But seeing Beth so ill, with a human malady unknown to elvenkind, had brought home the differences between himself and his friends. Without warning, without explanation, they could be taken from him, simply because of their nature: they were human.

Then again, all of us could die tomorrow, fighting this demon-creature that wishes to destroy this entire city.

Worry about this in another ten years, Korendil, he told himself.

For tomorrow, you concentrate on surviving a battle.

"Korendil, do you have any opinion on that?"

He looked up, realizing that everyone was watching him, waiting for a reply, and shrugged. "Decide as you see fit," he said, and stood. "I will be back shortly."

Outside the house, standing in the garden, he breathed in the night air, letting the moonlight wash over him. Through the open door, he could hear the arguments over strategy and tactics continuing.

Beth yawned again, and rubbed at her aching eyes. *Enough already.* "Guys, I can't keep my eyes open anymore; I'm going to call it a night. Susan, we've set up the other bed in the office for you, whenever you want to get some sleep."

Susan Sheffield also looked exhausted, but she only nodded. "Not just yet," she said. "I'm used to late nights at the office . . . but I probably ought to get some sleep soon."

"I'll probably be up in a little while," Eric said.

Beth headed wearily up the stairs. It had been a very strange, surreal evening — long discussions of magic and battle, the best methods for infiltrating the complex, and how to link with the Mount Tam witches. Throughout the evening, Eric had been strangely quiet, not contributing much to the discussion.

Probably still in shock over what's happened in the last few days.

She hoped he'd get over it, and quickly. Their plans depended on him, and his Bardic abilities. If he couldn't do the job . . .

She stripped off her shirt and jeans, and pulled on an old caftan, climbing into the large waterbed. The bed squished beneath her, rocking slightly, a gentle rhythm . . .

. . . *the floor tilting beneath her, everything vibrating and shaking as long cracks zigzagged down the walls, plaster falling onto her* . . .

Beth grabbed onto the edge of the bed for support, fingers whitening. She felt as though she was teetering on the edge of a dark chasm, hearing the screams of lost souls echoing up from below her. *That way lies madness.* She closed her eyes and concentrated on breathing slowly in through her nose, out through her mouth. The whirlwinds caught at her, trying to pull her down, but she held on tightly to the bed, refusing to let go.

After a long moment, the storm died away, leaving her alone again on the bed with only an echo of distant noise in her head.

She buried her face in her hands, as the tears silently leaked from her eyes. She wanted to scream from terror and frustration, and bit her lip instead.

She'd never thought this could happen to her. She'd always thought of herself as tough, independent, able to deal with anything. Except that it wasn't true — now she knew that it had never been true. Now she knew just how fragile her reality was, and what lurked out beyond the edges of sanity.

There was no way to understand this, to guess when she'd recover from it. Maybe she'd linger on this line between madness and waking for years. Maybe she'd never recover. That thought was the most terrifying of all — to continue this nightmare existence for the rest of her life. She remembered Ria Llewellyn's face after that terrible morning at Griffith Park, the awful blankness of a body without a mind, someone lost in the depths of insanity that now threatened her. She couldn't imagine herself that way, alive but not living. Trapped within her own mind, her own nightmares. It was inconceivable.

I'd rather die.

The more she thought about it, the more certain she became of that idea: better not to live, not this way. Just the thought of trying to sleep tonight, knowing what nightmares awaited her, was more than she could bear. She crossed to the bathroom door, taking two Tylenol-with-Codeine pills from the medicine cabinet. That would work as well as sleeping pills, at least for tonight. She slid back into bed, pulling the covers tightly around her.

The fear was like a fist around her heart; despite her exhaustion, she didn't want to close her eyes, even for a moment. She knew what waited for her in the darkness.

To live like this, for years . . . maybe forever . . .

Well, tomorrow we're heading into a major fight. A lot of things can happen in a fight. Maybe I won't have to worry about this anymore.

She didn't want to die. But she wasn't too certain that she really wanted to live, either. She could feel the tenuous wall between herself and the terrors coiled beneath her, and knew that they were waiting to drag her down, bury her alive. That wall was so thin and fragile, it could break at any moment.

She knew she didn't want to live this way.

Tomorrow, they would try to save the city. She and Eric and Kory and their friends, Elizabet and Kayla, the elves of Mist-Hold, the San Francisco witches. She had a responsibility to them to help them in any way she could, and she knew she wouldn't shirk that responsibility. Somehow she would hold herself together, until the Poseidon Project equipment was destroyed, and Warden Blair was no longer a danger to anyone, and San Francisco was safe.

But afterwards . . .

• CHAPTER FIFTEEN

Frosty Morning

The house was very quiet at 8 a.m., no sounds except for the faint noise of cars driving past, half a block away. Eric sat in the kitchen staring down into a mug of coffee that had been warm once, maybe an hour ago.

"You're up early," Dr. Sheffield said from behind him. He turned quickly. The lady scientist, wearing one of Beth's bathrobes, walked into the kitchen and sat down on one of the other chairs next to him.

"There's more coffee in the pot," Eric offered.

"Thanks." She reached across the table for a clean mug and the coffee pot. "Did you get much sleep?"

"No." He shook his head. "Too much to think about. All of this happened so fast — things used to be so easy for us. Uncomplicated. No problems, not in the last couple years. . . . "

"You mean, you don't usually go around summoning monsters and consorting with elves?"

He smiled. "Consorting with elves, sure. All the time. Summoning monsters, not if I can avoid it." The smile faded. "I didn't want to . . . to do what I did, at the Labs. But you know that, right?"

She didn't answer at first, swirling the coffee in her mug. "Friends of mine are dead or brain-dead because of you, mister. I can't say I could ever forgive you for that. But what Blair was doing, it was illegal and evil. Even if he hadn't gotten hold of my project, he probably would've graduated to some more extensive levels of cruelty eventually. I've read enough on psychopathic sadists to know that they never stop until they're arrested or dead. Fourteen people died that night at the Lab . . . yeah, and we don't know how many people 'disappeared' under Dr. Blair's tender care." She shook her head. "The man was already sick and dangerous, and the truth is that even without the Poseidon Project, if Blair continues unchecked, he'll beat that record of fourteen eventually if he hasn't already. Just a matter of time."

Eric's mouth opened; he closed it again.

"Besides, it's not like the Lab people don't know that they're at risk, always. Working at the Labs, you know you're a target. It's one of the first places a nuclear would hit, if we ever got into that kind of war, and it's a constant target for terrorists. Those scum probably think of all the plutonium in that complex and can't stop drooling." She took another long swallow from the mug. "And then there's the possibility that something could go wrong from the inside, that some Lab technician could press the wrong switch and the entire place could go up in smoke. Colonel Steve — my boss — he thought that what happened with the monsters could've been an internal accident, that all of us were hallucinating from a chemical accident or something like that. So you know you're a target when you work there, in more ways than one." She stared down into the mug. "It's just when it happened, when something did go wrong, somehow I wasn't expecting it. I mean, I was expecting some lunatic guys with automatic rifles, not an army of monsters."

"Sorry about that," Eric said sourly. "Next time, I'll leave the demon army at home and bring a squad of terrorists instead."

She gave him a sharp but steady look. "There won't be a next time, kid, because you and your army of

Tolkien fans are going to get it right the first time. That's why I'm still here, instead of taking off in the middle of the night and heading for Sheboygan until all of this is over. I'm going to make sure you do it right."

"We'll try." *She's a good lady, Susan Sheffield. She didn't deserve this. It's the least I can do to make sure that she doesn't get hurt.*

He looked up and around, wondering where Kayla was. She ought to get up soon; they'd need to head out as soon as the morning traffic was over. He set his coffee mug down, and refilled it from the pot.

The mug rattled once on the table, then again, more insistently. The windows began to vibrate, one window swinging open. He could feel the ground moving beneath him, gentle swells that felt like floating on the tides of the ocean, close enough to shore to feel the motion of the waves.

"Oh shit, is that . . . ?" Eric turned to Susan Sheffield.

The rattling noise ceased, as suddenly as it had begun.

Susan drank some coffee. Eric could see the unsteadiness of her hand as she lifted the mug. "Well, it could be natural. But—"

"But you don't think so."

She shook her head. "I'd say he's testing the engines, so to speak. Calibrating the probes. He's moving faster than I had expected . . . still, it'll take him a fair amount of time to calibrate the system, if he wants to do it right the first time. He has my notes and all my project files to work from, but Frank and I were the only ones who really lived with the system. He'll have to absorb a lot of information very quickly. And the physical calibration, even with the system computers to plot the resonance intersection points, that'll take time."

"How long?" Eric asked.

She was quiet for a few seconds, thinking about it, before she answered. "Definitely all day. Maybe by sometime tomorrow, if he works through the night. He might be able to do something tonight, but if he rushes too much, an improperly triggered earthquake could destroy the probes and he'd have to start over with the recalibration."

"Maybe we should've destroyed the probes ourselves, last night."

Susan shrugged. "Wouldn't have mattered that much. There's a roomful of them back at the Labs, though most of them still need some assembly work. We could've slowed him down a little, but not much. Maybe an hour or two. That's why I didn't suggest it at the time. What we need to do is stop Blair, not the project. In fact, I'm hoping we can do that without damaging the project equipment or laboratories — it'd sure be nice not to have to sacrifice most of my last two years' work tonight."

Kayla vaulted into the kitchen, still wearing a long flannel nightgown. It looked strange on her, now that Eric was so used to her leather clothing and studded jewelry. "Was that a real earthquake?" she asked.

"Just Warden Blair warming up the engines," Eric said. "Shouldn't you, like, get dressed or something?"

"Oh, yeah." She dived back through the doorway, and they could hear her feet pounding up the stairs.

"She's a good kid," Susan observed. "Why are you letting her get involved in this mess?"

Eric thought of Kayla after the battle in Griffith Park, soaked in blood up to her elbows, and tried to remember that this lady didn't know them, didn't know anything about them and what they'd already been through together. "She's very important. Kayla is a healer, a genuine 'lay on hands and fix what's broken' healer. If anyone gets hurt during this fight, it'll probably be Kayla who saves their lives."

"But she's just a kid!" Susan protested.

"She'll do fine. I'm more worried about the flaky

Wiccans that Beth dug out of the woodwork, to be honest. From what she was saying, some of those people need to consult a crystal ball before they can tie their shoelaces in the morning. I'm not so worried about the elves; they believe in the danger and know what they're fighting for." *But with luck, none of them will need to go anywhere near the labs. I started this mess, and I'll deal with it.* "But I don't need to tell you about elves, you know enough about them already."

"I'd rather not talk about that," she said.

That was something of a surprise. "Why not? I thought you had a good experience with the Misthold elves that summer."

"I did." She looked up to meet his gaze. "But then it ended, and they left me." She stood up abruptly. "Well, I'm going to shower and get dressed. I'm not certain what kind of clothes one is supposed to wear to Armageddon, but I'll see if I can borrow something from your friend Beth."

She set her mug down in the sink before leaving the room. Eric contemplated pouring another cup of coffee, and wondered if adding a shot of whiskey to it would help clear the blurriness from his mind. *Probably not,* he decided.

He'd never been a morning person, ever. Morning was that awful thing that happened every day before noon, something to avoid if possible, endure if not. But today he had a schedule to keep, if he wanted to keep his friends out of danger as well as the rest of San Francisco.

Maybe a little more caffeine would help. . . .

"Hey, pour me one of those," Kayla said, sliding onto the chair recently vacated by Susan Sheffield.

"It'll stunt your growth, kid," Eric said, pouring her the last cup of coffee in the pot.

"Hell, I'm tall enough already. So, are you ready? Did you eat breakfast?"

"I never eat breakfast," he said grimly. "Breakfast is for people who wake up before lunch."

"Look, Bard, you have to take care of yourself. You're about to go burn a lot of magical energy, you need something to replace it." Kayla hopped off the chair and began rummaging through the refrigerator. "How does scrambled eggs and toast sound?"

"Awful."

"I can add some cheese and salsa, if you want."

"That's worse. Kayla, make whatever you want for breakfast. I'll stick with coffee, thanks."

"Better to watch your nutrition. That's what Elizabet always tells me. Well, it's your funeral, Bard." There was an awkward silence between them. "I didn't mean it quite that way, Eric," Kayla said after a moment. "I'll cook up some eggs, and then we can get out of here."

"Right. I'll get my things together."

He headed upstairs, quietly opening the bedroom door. Beth and Kory were still asleep. He took his flute case from the top of the dresser, and slipped it into his gig-bag. His leather wallet was lying on the window seat; he checked to make sure that he had his BART card in the pocket for the subway fare, and change for the bus, enough for Kayla and himself. There was a ten-dollar bill with the BART card — *maybe Kayla and I can stop for lunch at Gordo's Burritos in Berkeley after we save the world*, he thought with a wry smile.

On the other hand, Kayla knew how to drive. Maybe they should take Beth's elven steed.

A last look at the waterbed: Kory, sleeping with his arm flung out wide, as relaxed in sleep as he always was when awake. Beth, frowning slightly in her sleep. He knelt and kissed her gently, careful not to wake her. *I might never see them again.* The thought was like a physical pain. He hurried downstairs to where Kayla was waiting, already wearing her black leather jacket and boots.

"Listen, Eric," she said, a little hesitantly. "There's something I need to tell you . . . I don't know how to say this, exactly, but . . . you're kinda visible. I can see it, and I know the elves can, too. I'd bet the bad guys could see you that way as well, so I thought you might want to do something about it."

"I don't understand," he said.

"It's a little difficult to explain . . . you kinda . . . glow, a little. Well . . . more than a little. You glow a lot, to be honest. When I close my eyes, I can still see you."

This was a bad time for a joke. Or maybe it wasn't a joke. "Are you serious?"

She nodded vigorously. "Scout's honor, Bard. You look like a neon light at five hundred feet."

He thought about that for a minute. "Okay. Let me try something." He closed his eyes and reached inside, to that still pool of power within him. With an odd mental twist, he switched it off, like a light switch, or like opening the floodgates and letting it all pour out instantly.

The wooden floor was pressed against his cheek. That was the first conscious thought that registered, that and the fact that Kayla's hands were bright with a pale blue light. He sat up slowly, waves of dizziness washing over him.

"Don't *do* that, Eric!" The threads of light faded from Kayla's hands. "Jesus, you scared me! You stopped your heart. Are you okay now?"

He nodded, not quite trusting himself to speak. *I can just see the headlines in the newspapers — "Bard Commits Suicide Out of Sheer Stupidity."* He took a deep breath. "Let me try that again."

This time, he moved more carefully into that pool of light, and the light slowly dimmed away, leaving a pool of shadows instead. He opened his eyes again, relieved to see that he was still alive. "Did that work?" he asked.

Kayla closed her eyes. "Yes," she said after a moment. "Looks good, Bard." She helped him to his feet, then hesitated. "Oh, almost forgot." She darted into the kitchen, reappearing a few seconds later. "I left them a note," she explained. "I've told them that we've gone out shopping for supplies, and told them to wait for us. Maybe we can be finished with this before they realize where we've gone."

"Yeah, sure." *You're being very optimistic about this, Kayla,* he thought. *I'd guess that you're as scared as I am, but you're even better at not showing the fear. If you can be this calm once we're inside the Labs, maybe we'll survive this after all.* "All right," he said. "Let's go."

Kory rolled over in bed, then sat up abruptly. Something was wrong, very wrong. . . .

It took him several seconds to figure it out. Nothing was wrong with him, and there were no enemies in sight, nothing more unusual than the sounds of traffic outside the window. Beth was still asleep, curled up in a ball next to him. Eric was . . .

Eric was missing.

Not just missing, but completely gone. Usually he could just think about Eric and know where he was. The touch of Bardic magic was unmistakable. Even when he had been captive in the tunnels of the Dublin Labs, it had only taken a small effort to reach out and find Eric, to touch him across all the distance of the city and the Bay.

Now he couldn't sense anything. No Bardic magic, no Eric — He cast out his thoughts in a widening ring, searching . . .

Nothing.

Kory fought against the cold terror that wrapped itself around his heart. "Don't panic, don't panic," he whispered to himself, and shook Beth awake.

"Wha — Kory?" She blinked, propping herself up on one elbow. "Is something wrong?"

"Do you know where Eric is?"

"He's not asleep . . . ?" She glanced at the alarm clock. "It's ten a.m. and Eric's already out of bed? Amazing!"

"He's gone, Beth. I can't find him anywhere."

She sat up. "You mean, you can't find him magically? Are you sure?"

He nodded. "He is not in the city, as far as I can tell. I should know where he is, but I cannot find him."

"Is he . . . ?" There was a question in her eyes that Kory did not want to answer.

"I — I do not think so. At least, I should feel that, as well. The death of a Bard . . . we would know it, I am certain of that. It would leave a mark upon the bones of the land." *Unless he was taken far away before they killed him, perhaps to the realm of those shadow-monsters. . . .*

"So either someone is hiding him from us, or Eric went AWOL." Beth was suddenly all business, pulling on her bathrobe and slippers. "If this is Eric Banyon's idea of a joke, I'm going to kill him. Can you tell where he was last, before he disappeared?"

"I don't know. *I don't know.*"

He concentrated, imagining the Bard's handsome features, remembering his laughter, the intense look on his face as he played an ancient Irish air. . . . "Downstairs," he said firmly. "In the hallway, very close to the front door. That's where Eric vanished."

"The front room? But that doesn't make any sense — If someone had come through the front door and attacked him, Eric should've made enough noise to awaken everyone in the house." She was out of bed and running downstairs before Kory could say anything else. He followed her a moment later, to find her standing near the front door, staring at the floor, then she looked up at the row of hooks where they always hung their jackets and coats. "No sign of a scuffle down here. And Eric took his leather jacket. If he'd been kidnapped, he wouldn't have done that."

Elizabet, sleepy-eyed, walked out from the kitchen. "Are they back yet?" she asked.

"What?" Kory asked.

"Kayla and Eric. They left a note saying that they were going to get some supplies. . . . Can't imagine what they're doing, unless Kayla wanted to get some extra first aid supplies. I thought they might be back by now."

Beth shook her head, a thoughtful frown on her face. "I think I've figured this out — they took off early, leaving a note so we wouldn't worry about them, and Eric makes sure that we can't track him magically . . . where do you think they are right now, Elizabet?"

The older woman smiled wryly, her white teeth very bright against her dark skin. "Kayla isn't someone who'd run away from a fight, so I know they didn't just run for the hills — I'd guess they're on their way across the Bay to the Dublin Labs right now, wouldn't you?"

"That's what I think, too." Rage smoldered in her eyes. "Damn it, Eric Banyon, you are such a twit! How could he do this?"

"Perhaps because he did not wish any of us to risk our lives," Kory said. Beth and Elizabet both turned to look at him. "I had thought about doing something similar," he confessed, "but decided that I would probably not be able to succeed on my own."

"And Eric, on the other hand, thinks he can do anything!" Beth clenched her hands into fists. "Okay, okay. Here's what we do. I'll call the psychic team, get them to head over to Mount Tam and start ASAP. The rest of us, and the elven assault team, will head over to the Labs and save Eric from his own stupidity. I can't believe he dragged Kayla into this, too!"

"That doesn't surprise me," Elizabet said. "You don't know Kayla quite as well as I do. By the way, has anyone seen Susan this morning?"

*   *   *

Maybe this isn't the best idea I've had in a long time, Susan thought. *But I'm not going to be a bystander anymore. This is my project that some insane nut is trying to pervert into a killing machine, and maybe I can stop this without anyone getting killed — crazy human witches, elves or whatever other refugees from fantasy they can drag in.*

It was that thought that had sparked her flight from the house on Broderick Street: the image of Melisande, lying dead with several .45 auto bullets in her, her blood soaking the white linoleum floors of the Dublin Labs. *Not if I have anything to say about it.*

As she expected, the traffic driving east along the Bay Bridge wasn't too bad at this hour of morning. In the other direction, she could still see the "parking lot" of cars, inching their way into the city. It was a beautiful morning, with the last of the fog already burned away by the bright sunshine. She navigated the freeway interchange through Oakland, glancing involuntarily at the cleared area off to the right that had once been the double-decker Nimitz Freeway. *This is what I'm going to prevent,* she vowed silently. *That's why I fought to do the Poseidon Project, so that this would never happen again. Now I'm going to stop the inhuman bastard who wants to use my project for destruction.*

It was a simple plan, what she was going to do. If she could get to Colonel Steve without being intercepted by Blair or any of his people, she knew she could convince him. Steve was ethical, no matter what Blair was. No amount of double-talking would get Blair out of this. Just the physical evidence, the fact that Blair was moving the probes and recalibrating the equipment to trigger a major quake — five minutes in the lab, explaining what was going on to the colonel, and all of this would be over. Lab security would arrest Blair, she'd deactivate the machinery, and that would be the end of it.

The only tricky part was getting to Steve without alerting Blair. But she had a plan for that, too. . . .

With luck this would work, because she had no intention of trusting that flaky dark-haired boy and his neurotic girlfriend. The elves she trusted, of course, but she couldn't understand the overwhelming belief they had in their "Bard." *He screwed things up royally before, didn't he?* No, what she was doing was risky, but safer than the other options. And she wouldn't have to watch Sandy die.

She turned on the radio, and punched the button to bring up the local talk radio channel. The station announcer was talking about the morning's earthquake, and another very minor one that had hit ten minutes ago — *right while I was driving across the Bridge,* she thought. *Terrific.* But the announcer assured everyone that there was nothing to worry about, the seismologists at Cal Tech had said that the faults were just releasing a little pressure, there was no chance of a major quake.

She smiled humorlessly at that, and drove a little faster.

A half hour later, she braked to a stop at the guard gate at the Labs, flashing her I.D. to the security officer. She parked in the underground lot, leaving the car doors unlocked and the keys in the ignition. She knew she didn't have to worry about car thieves, not in this complex. And there was a high possibility she might want to leave in a hurry.

Her first stop was the cafeteria on the second floor. There was a small dining room off the main area, which had a telephone in it. She strolled past the security officers, staying away from the elevators that descended into the underground laboratories. At this hour, the hallways were mostly deserted. Still, she breathed a sigh of relief when she walked through the cafeteria doors.

The cafeteria was empty. She guessed that all the personnel were in the kitchen, preparing for the lunch crowd. A few seconds later, she was standing next to the telephone. She dialed Steve's extension and listened to the ringing tone. *Come on, Steve, pick up your phone!*

A click, then she heard his voice. "Colonel O'Neill, Poseidon Project."

"Steve, this is me. Are you alone?"

"Susan, where are you? Are you all right?" His voice sounded concerned.

"I'm okay. Listen, we have to talk, right now. Where's Warden Blair? Is he in the lab?"

"No, he's organizing the cleanup on Level Thirteen. Where have you been, Susan? Security said you never went home, you've been missing for twenty-four hours . . ."

"I'll explain later. Meet me in my lab, in five minutes. And please, don't tell Blair or any of his people, all right?"

She waited, wondering how that security-- overconscious mind was taking what she'd just said.

"Okay. I'll be there ASAP, Susan."

She hung up the phone, and hurried to the closest stairs. Ten minutes later, she was in her lab.

For a moment, as she stepped through the doorway, it felt as though all of the events of the last two days had been only a nightmare. Maybe, if she wished for it hard enough, Frank and Dave would walk back in the door, ready to help her set up the next test run. But no, there was the oscilloscope she'd thrown at the monster, broken and dented; someone had placed it back upon the worktable.

No time for funk, not now. She moved quickly, making sure that the computer workstation was up and running, then loaded the Poseidon simulation program. She set it to run a simulation based on current test run parameters, and waited impatiently as the numbers scrolled past on the screen. The screen cleared, then began to build the three-dimensional fractal landscape of the Bay Area, pinpointing the exact trigger point of the quake and the widening circles of area of effect and potential energy release levels.

"Son of a bitch!"

Until now, I wasn't certain. It could've just been an evil fantasy, a delusion that Warden Blair wanted to destroy the city.

Now it's laid out in front of me in full-color graphics . . .

As she'd guessed from the elven scouts' reports, the Poseidon device was aimed at the San Andreas fault, directly beneath Hollister. And the potential energy readings were off the scales, somewhere beyond 10.0 on the Richter.

He'll wipe the entire Bay Area off the map. Hell, the effects would destroy the Labs as well! How did he plan on surviving it?

The answer came to her a moment later, in a memory of the shadow-monsters drifting through the hallways of the Labs. Shadow-monsters that wouldn't care if the complex crumpled in on itself, burying level upon level in rumbling death. She remembered the alien intelligence behind Blair's eyes. *He looks human, but he isn't.*

"Susan?"

She turned quickly, to see Colonel Steve walking toward her. "Steve, thank God! Listen, we probably don't have much time . . . Blair is planning to use the project as a weapon, with San Francisco as his first test case. I have proof of this — he's moved the probes off our test run coordinates and set them to trigger a major quake. Let me show you the computer simulation . . . it displays exactly where he was going to trigger the quake."

He smiled. "It's okay, Susan. I know."

Shock froze her mind and her body — but her mouth kept going.

"But you haven't arrested Blair yet?" Surely this was just a sting. Surely Steve had something planned.

He didn't answer, only standing there, looking at her. There was something strange about Steve's face.

She hadn't seen it at first, but now it was visible to
her . . . lines of tension that hadn't been there before.
No, not just the lines in his face . . . it was in his eyes, a
cold blankness, an alien intelligence that was staring
back at her. . . .

If she'd seen this before she'd met the elves, the
musician, she'd have assumed she was the crazy one.
Not now,

*God, no. Not Steve. Please, this can't be happening, this
can't be real.* . . .

She had to get out of here, before this insanity consumed her as well. That was her one thought, that if
Blair could do — whatever it was that he'd done — to
Steve, it was only a matter of time until she was
changed into something like him: a walking and talking human being with an alien's thoughts peering out
from within her eyes. . . .

But Steve was between her and the door. And Steve
had a gun.

"This goes too fast," she whispered, sitting down on
one of the wooden lab stools with a thump.

*I am stuck. If he has Steve, and Steve has me — he has me.
It's over.* "So, Steve, what happens now?" she asked conversationally, looking up at him.

He seemed momentarily taken aback. "I — I don't
know," he said uncertainly. "I'm supposed to keep you
here, until Blair tells me what to do. I wish — I wish
you hadn't come back, Susan. For a little while, I
thought you were safe, safely far away from this."

"I could've been, if I'd had any brains." *What's going
on inside his head?* she wondered. "Steve, can't you just
let me walk out of here?"

"Can't — can't do that." He shook his head, as if to
clear it. "He won't let me." His hand twitched next to
the pistol holster on his hip.

"I see." Her glance fell upon the broken oscilloscope
on the table next to her. The thought occurred to her

that while the oscilloscope had been useless against a nightmare creature, it might be significantly more applicable against a human being. Especially if she swung it hard enough. "Steve, is that Blair out in the hall?"

Steve's glance swung toward the open door. "No, I can feel where he is, he's still on the thirteenth —"

The oscilloscope crashed into his chest. Steve made an odd choking sound, and stumbled backwards into another lab table. A split-second later, Susan was out the door and running down the corridor.

She heard Steve's voice from behind her, furious. "Susan! Stop or I'll shoot!"

He won't shoot me, she thought, *any more than I could've hit him in the head with the 'scope. I couldn't kill him, and I know he won't —*

The noise of the gun firing was very loud in the narrow corridor.

Something slammed into her back, a sudden pain like her body had been set on fire. The shock threw her forward against the wall; a second shock, a moment later, as she landed hard on the floor. Everything was very bright, very white . . . she tried to move, to get up and run, but somehow nothing seemed to be working right in her body anymore, everything was numb with pain and her legs just wouldn't move at all.

She heard footsteps approaching, and Steve's voice whispering, "I'm sorry, Susan . . ."

I can't forgive you, Steve, she wanted to whisper back to him, but the whiteness engulfed her before she could say a word.

● CHAPTER SIXTEEN

Soldier's Joy

"So, Eric, what's the plan?" Kayla asked, looking at the gate of the Dublin Laboratories, a hundred yards ahead of them.

He shook his head, frowning. "I'm still trying to figure it out. Give me a minute, okay?"

He'd been thinking about this during the motorcycle ride across the Bay, and still couldn't think of a good plan that included both of them surviving this experience. "All right, here's what we do. I'm going to cast a spell over both of us, so that we'll be nearly invisible. I'll do myself first, so you can tell me whether or not it's working. Then we'll just walk in there, take a crowbar to Dr. Sheffield's machine, and walk back out again."

Kayla tilted her head to one side. "Susan will hate you for that, Eric."

He snorted. "Well, tough for her. Better that than watching all of San Francisco slide into the ocean. And after that, we can take our time dealing with Warden Blair. I was thinking that we could follow him home later, and find out whether he's a man or — or a demon wearing someone's body like a set of clothing."

Kayla shivered. "I know this sounds crazy, but I hope he really is a Nightflyer. Then maybe you can just banish the Nightflyer, and we won't have to kill him. I don't want to kill anybody," she concluded, wistfully.

"I don't want to either, kid," Eric said seriously. He

brought his flute to his lips, playing an experimental scale. Next to them, the parked motorcycle made an odd sound, almost a horse's whinny. Kayla stepped back from it hastily.

"Don't worry," Eric said. "Those elven horse-bikes are mostly friendly. I think that one has an awful sense of humor, though." He played another scale, then tucked the flute under his arm, rubbing his hands together briskly.

"Is something wrong?" Kayla asked, concerned.

"It's just cold out here. My fingers are stiff." He lifted the flute again and played a run of arpeggios. "That's better." He began playing "Banysh Mysfortune," slowly at first, then building in speed and intensity, concentrating on the thought: *I'm invisible, I'm unseen, I'm the wisp of melody that drifts past, unnoticed*. After playing through the A,B, and C parts twice, he ended the tune and looked over at Kayla curiously. "So, did anything happen?"

She couldn't quite meet his eyes. "Oh, yeah. You're still there, but I can't look at you, not really. It's like my eyes keep sliding off of you, it's very hard to keep trying to look at you. I think it'll work."

"Good." He ran through the melody again, this time focusing his thoughts on Kayla. When he finished, it was exactly as she had described . . . he could see her, but she was very difficult to look at. *Not bad. Maybe I'm starting to get the hang of this whole magic business.* "Let's walk in, calmly and quietly," he said. "No hurry at all. Just stroll past the guards and into the building."

"I'm with you, Bard." She grinned at him. "How 'bout going for beer and pizza after this?"

"Aren't you a little young to drink?"

She shrugged. "Alcohol can't do anything for me. I just like the taste of beer. Don't you?"

He sighed, and they started down the road toward the gate. As he had hoped, the man at the gate barely

glanced at them. They received an identical lack of
response from the receptionist in the lobby, and walked
past what looked like a military SWAT team. . . .

A SWAT team!, Eric's mind screamed silently, but he
kept walking.

Dr. Susan's directions had been very specific: take
the stairs to the third level, walk down the corridor to
the stairway connecting to the lower levels, continue
down to the bottom level, turn left onto the main corridor, follow that to the end, turn right, then go into the
fourth door on the right.

The third level was deserted, not even a security
guard in sight. They continued down to the last level
and were halfway down the main corridor when Kayla
stopped him, her hand on his arm. "Something's
wrong," she whispered. "There's someone . . . oh shit,
it's Susan!" She vaulted into a run, and Eric ran after
her. He turned the corner a split-second after she had,
and stopped short at the sight of a tall man in a military
uniform, carrying a bloody and unconscious Dr. Susan
Sheffield.

Too many things happened at once: the man
dropped Susan onto the floor, reaching for the pistol
holstered at his side; Kayla screamed something
incoherent and leaped at him; Eric desperately
whistled a single shrill note — the noise of the magic
and gunshot blended together. The Bardic magic
caught the man and lifted him off his feet to slam
against the wall, as if hit by a giant fist. He landed in an
unconscious heap next to Susan.

Gunshot . . . he missed me, did he hit . . . ?

Kayla staggered backwards against him. He caught
her; his flute clattered on the floor. He saw the bullet
hole in her leather jacket, and felt the warmth of her
blood, dripping down her back and onto his arm. She
coughed suddenly, bright red blood running down her
chin.

"Oh my God, kid . . ."

"Bastard . . . got a lung . . . " Kayla whispered, so faint that he could barely hear her. He could hear a strange whistling noise as she breathed. "Set me down next to Susan . . . need to be close enough to touch her . . . "

"No! Kayla, heal yourself first!"

"I've got . . . a few seconds . . . she doesn't . . . do it, Eric!"

He carefully set her down next to Susan's unconscious body. She rested her hand on Susan's shoulder, closing her eyes. Eric felt the magic in the air, as blue lines coiled and twisted over Kayla's outstretched hand. He held her other hand, her blood slick against his palm, watching her face furrowed in concentration.

Suddenly, the blue light faded.

Eric reached desperately with his own magical senses. Susan was still alive; he could see the magical light that was her life, growing brighter and brighter. But Kayla . . . he couldn't find her at first, even though he knew he was still holding her hand. She had poured all her energy into saving Susan, leaving none for herself. . . .

Wait a minute!

He caught a pale thread, held onto it. Fed it with his own magic, until Kayla moved against him, struggling feebly. Then he poured everything he could into her, giving her the power she needed to heal herself. The world dimmed around him, and he knew he was dangerously close to pouring all of his own life force into Kayla, exactly what she had done to Susan.

Kayla's hand tightened around his own. He opened his eyes and looked at her, to see a faint smile on her face. "We . . . we aren't doing so great today, are we, Bard?" she whispered.

"Yeah, I know," he whispered back.

"You're doing worse than you think," a man's voice said from behind him. Eric turned quickly, to see three

drawn pistols aimed at him. Though he had never met
Warden Blair, he recognized that cold smile from
Beth's memories.

"Oh, hell," Eric said, wondering how fast he could
call his Bardic magic. Before he could even pucker his
lips to whistle, a pistol barrel caught him on the side of
the face, and the world exploded into darkness.

He awakened to an aching headache, and a feeling
like his arms were being pulled out of their sockets.
When he tried to move, he realized why: his arms were
handcuffed behind him. He opened his eyes, wondering why he was still alive.

Kayla was lying on the floor near him, also handcuffed. And Susan, on the other side of the room,
apparently still unconscious. They were in a room that
Eric remembered from Susan's descriptions: the
laboratory that contained the Poseidon computers.
Two business-suited young men stood near the door,
watching him intently. He saw the handguns stuck into
their waistbands, and decided against trying to leap
at them with his hands cuffed behind his back. Probably the world's stupidest idea. Then again, coming
here with just Kayla now seemed like the world's
stupidest idea, too.

He whispered Kayla's name, and was rewarded by
seeing her eyes open, then slowly focus on him. She
was very pale, blood still smeared across her face.
"Eric? You okay?"

"Yeah, I think so. Just an awful headache, and everything's a little blurry. You?"

"I'm okay. Susan . . . " He saw tears begin to roll
down her cheeks, mixing with the drying blood. "That
bastard shot Susan in the spine. I saved her life,
but even if we make it out of here, she'll be paralyzed."

"Keep quiet, both of you," one of their guards said
roughly.

Okay, so we will. He fought against the exhaustion that threatened to overwhelm him, and whispered to her in that silent speech that Kory had taught him.

:Kayla, can you hear me?:

She twitched visibly, then nodded.

:How long was I out?: he asked.

A moment later, he heard her voice answer silently to him. *:Maybe an hour, hour and a half. I don't know. I've been mostly out of it until just a few minutes ago . . . I feel weak as a kitten right now . . . .:* A pause, then she continued. *:You saved my life, Eric. I could feel everything slipping away, it was like I was drowning, sliding under the surface, and then you pulled me back.:*

:Hey, no problem,: he answered. *:Let's concentrate on getting out of here, now. Susan needs a hospital, and you don't look so great yourself. Is there anything else I need to know before I bust us out of here?:*

She nodded slightly. *:Blair was in here a few minutes ago, doing something with the computers. He left with that military guy, the one who shot me. I pretended like I was out cold. When they left, I looked through the door . . . I don't think there are any other guards except for these two guys.:*

:Good. I'll see what I can do to these guys, then we'll trash the place and leave.: Eric sat up, looking closely at the two men near the door. A simple Irish melody to make them sleepy, like "My Darling Asleep" — that might do the trick —

He held back another wave of exhaustion that threatened to drag him under, and whistled the first couple measures, watching the two men closely to see if there was any effect. If they were Nightflyer-possessed, like Warden Blair, his magic might not have any effect on them.

One of the men yawned. Eric continued the melody, not pausing until both men were slumped against the wall, one of them snoring loudly.

He stood up unsteadily, realizing for the first time how

much he usually used his hands for balance, and headed to the two men. Fumbling in their pockets with his hands handcuffed behind him was awkward, but he found what he was hoping for—the handcuff key. He managed to unlock his own cuffs, then unfastened Kayla's and Susan's. Susan didn't move at all when he removed the cuffs; she looked awful, very pale and breathing shallowly. As Kayla sat up and rubbed her wrists, Eric crossed to the computer console and cursed quietly.

"What's wrong?" Kayla asked, moving to stand behind him.

"I think Blair already triggered the quake, when he was in here before. It says that the energy level is rising several percent points a second. We can stop it from getting worse, but the fault is already getting ready to blow. Damn!" Eric looked around for something handy, and picked up a metal box, some kind of weird machinery with a broken green glass screen, that was lying on the floor. As he was about to swing it into the computer console, he heard Susan Sheffield's voice. "Eric, wait . . . "

He turned to see her trying to sit up, and giving up a moment later to lie helplessly on the floor. "Help me up," she said. "I'll stop the program."

Eric and Kayla exchanged a glance, then together they lifted her. Kayla winced and Eric saw the blood drain from her face, but she didn't say anything about her own pain. Together, they moved Susan to the computer console, holding her up so she could use the keyboard. She typed several commands quickly, watching the screen intently, then nodded. "Okay. It's done."

They lowered her back to the floor; she lay there for a moment before speaking, pain fighting with terror on her face. "It reached sixty-five percent before I crashed the program," she said weakly. "That's a very bad earthquake, I don't know exactly how bad. The resonance will take thirty minutes to build, maybe a few minutes more than that, depending on how well he aimed the probes, and then it'll release the faultline." She pointed at a small cardboard box on one of the shelves. "Eric, get that for me."

"Susan, are you . . . ?"

"I'm okay. Just do this, quickly."

He took it down from the shelf and opened the box. Inside was a small electronic device with a crude switch built into it, something he didn't recognize, and a computer disk.

"Put the disk in that computer and type GOODBYE, please. Now the electromagnet — walk over to that wall that has the tape backups and switch it on. If you move it next to every box of tape, that'll erase everything." She managed a smile as Eric followed her instructions. "Welcome to the wonderful world of computer destruction, kids. That disk had a specialized worm virus on it that'll keep the main computers down for hours, and it'll destroy all the pertinent data about my project. And you're wiping clean all of our data backups. Blair won't be able to do anything with the system for quite a while." She frowned. "I programmed that virus in case the military decided to play games with the project. I never thought I'd ever actually use it."

"Good planning, though," Kayla murmured.

Susan nodded, closing her eyes. Kayla knelt painfully next to her, placing one hand on her shoulder. After a moment, she looked up at Eric.

"We can't move her again. I don't know how bad the neurological damage is, but moving her again could kill her."

"Can't you — " He gestured helplessly. "Can't you just heal the damage?"

Kayla shook her head. "All I do is convince the cells to heal themselves faster. Nerve cells won't regenerate that way."

"You — you'd better get out of here," Susan whispered. "The quake's coming — you don't have much time — leave me here, just go —"

"Susan, we can't!" Kayla protested.

"Please — don't die because of me —"

"Come on, Kayla." Eric took her by the arm, moving toward the door. "She's right. We can't do anything for her, not now." He opened the door, and stopped short.

A familiar-looking man in a military uniform, with a familiar-looking .45 automatic handgun in his hand, stared back at him.

Eric shut the door.

Thinking quickly, he grabbed the broken machine on the floor, turning with it just as the man kicked the door open. Eric didn't hesitate. Ten pounds of high-tech metal crashed into the man's face. The gun dropped to the floor; Kayla retrieved it before the man could recover. She held it aimed at his chest as he straightened slowly, wiping the blood from his nose.

"Okay, slimeball," Kayla said, clicking the safety off the pistol. "Start talking."

He only stared at her blankly.

Eric hoped the man couldn't see what he so clearly could — Kayla's bravado was skin-deep. She could barely hold onto the gun, and he wasn't certain whether she could fire it, either. *If he makes a break for it, she'd better shoot him,* Eric thought, *'cause I'm sure as hell not going to be able to wrestle this guy down to the ground. And I don't think she'll be able to shoot him.* He felt the bruise swelling on the side of his face, and distantly wondered whether he had a concussion. Then he decided it didn't matter, not with the world about to crash down around them sometime in the next half hour.

No . . . the next twenty-five minutes, now.

The man was still standing, not speaking.

Eric saw it first, before Kayla did. "He has Nightflyer

eyes," he said aloud, wondering what they could do with the man now.

"Please — don't kill him — " Susan's voice was weaker. "He was a friend of mine, once."

Eric thought about it, how he would summon a Nightflyer *out* of someone's body, instead of from — from wherever it was that Nightflyers came from.

"Whatever you're going to do, Eric," Kayla said, not wavering the aim of the pistol, "get moving with it. The clock is ticking, remember?"

"Right." He saw where someone had kicked his flute underneath one of the computers, and picked it up quickly. He began playing the first notes of the solo from "Danse Macabre," focusing on what lurked behind the man's pale blue eyes.

Something materialized between them — a thin shadow, smaller and less opaque than any of the other Nightflyers he had seen. *A baby Nightflyer,* he realized with a start. Without missing a beat, he slid into the A part from "Banysh Mysfortune," and the Nightflyer faded from view.

The man blinked, then stared at Eric. His pale blue eyes suddenly filled with tears. He walked past Kayla, completely ignoring the pistol in her hands, and knelt next to Susan. "Susan, I'm sorry, oh God, I'm so sorry . . . "

Kayla glanced at Eric, the pistol still clenched in her hand, obviously uncertain what to do. Eric gave her an "Okay" handsign. "He's okay now. I'm sure of it."

Susan's voice was very thin, strained. "Steve, you have to get out of here. This whole place could collapse in a few minutes . . . "

"Then I'm taking you with me." His voice was firm. For a moment, Eric saw what kind of man Steve used to be, before his own nightmare of the Nightflyers had begun.

"No, you can't move her, she's — " Kayla began.

"I've decided I don't want to die down here," Susan whispered, closing her eyes. "Take me out into the sunlight, Steve."

"We'll have to go out by one of the emergency exits," Steve said. "There's a major firefight going on in the upper levels — some crazy people dressed in medieval armor shooting it out with security."

"That sounds like the rest of our team," Kayla said. "Where did you say they were right now?"

"Upstairs, level three. But you can't — " He glanced down at the .45 automatic in Kayla's hand. "Then again, maybe you can," he said.

"Get Susan out of here," Eric said. "She needs immediate medical attention. Spine injury."

The military man looked around the laboratory, then took a metal cart covered with research material, shoving the papers and books onto the floor, and then with Eric's help carefully lifted Susan onto it. "Good luck," he said to Eric and Kayla.

Susan whispered a goodbye as they left the room.

"Good luck is right," Kayla said, turning to Eric. "What in the hell are we going to do against an army of security officers? How much time do we have left, anyhow?"

"God knows. Maybe twenty minutes." He thought about it quickly. "If we can get to the others, there might be some kind of magic we can do to stop the quake. I don't know. But we'll need an army to get to them. And I know where we can get one."

"Eric — " Kayla's eyes widened in sudden understanding and horror. "No way. You're not going to do that again."

"It's the only solution I can think of."

"Eric, if you lose control of them again, we're all dead!"

He met her eyes squarely. "Kayla, I already have enough deaths on my conscience. I won't make any mistakes this time. I promise."

Kayla still looked very uncertain, but she nodded.

"All right. I won't stop you." She stepped back from him, clicking the safety on the pistol and shoving it into her waistband.

He brought the flute to his lips, and began to play the classic melody that he now privately thought of as the "Yo, Nightflyers, want to come hang out over here?" tune. "Danse Macabre."

He felt it starting around him, the whispers of sound, the cold wind touching the back of his neck.

The shadows on the floor lengthened, darkening and rising to surround him. This time, he held onto them tightly, knowing what would happen if he lost control now. They whirled around him, fast-moving shapes that circled and laughed silently.

He held them with the music, weaving an image of what would happen to them if they disobeyed him — dissolution, oblivion. The Nightflyers silently wailed with anger and fear, but the deadly whirlwind of shadows slowed to drift quietly around him.

"Forward, march," Eric muttered, catching his breath for a moment. His shadow troops floated behind him as he and Kayla started down the corridor toward the stairway.

The anti-terrorist team commander, Captain Brown, tried once again to convince the scientist to go back upstairs, where it was safe, and get out of the area of fire. Warden Blair shook his head, not explaining his real reason for wanting to be so close to the gunfight.

When they die, my children will feast on their death-agonies, he/it thought. There was so much potential here, and all of the futurepaths wove together at this point, screaming "Breakthrough, Breakthrough!" to his alien senses. In the next few minutes, all futurepaths would join into a single one, with no more chance of failure. And his children would sweep out over the city, glorying in the life-energies that were theirs for the taking.

He blinked suddenly, sensing something different. There were others of his kind, very close. He did not understand it — he had not brought them across the veil between worlds, and he knew there were no others of his kind here, except for his first child that now possessed Colonel O'Neill. That had been the easiest solution to the problem of Colonel O'Neill, since direct control by Blair had been very tiring, and dangerous as well.

Ah, that was it, he decided. Though it was risky to reproduce so young, his child must have used the life force of the music-maker and the other human to create others.

One of the other officers reported in to his captain, taking the same time to reload his assault rifle. "They're still holed up behind the barricade down the hall, sir. We have them covered from both sides, but so far we haven't managed to advance. No change in status."

"Tear gas?" the captain asked.

"Didn't seem to have any effect the first time, sir. We can try it again, if you want."

The captain shook his head. "No, keep working closer down the hallway. Get close enough to spray the area, and that'll be it. We don't need to risk any of our people trying to take these lunatic terrorists alive."

"Can I go closer to see the action?" Blair asked, trying not to sound too eager.

"No, sir, you cannot. You're already too close to our operations, and you really should leave the area." The captain looked up suddenly, down the hallway behind them. "What in the hell is that?"

Nightflyers, drifting toward them. Blair gloried in the sight, knowing that the moment was at hand.

Except...

Except there were two humans walking with his kindred, and one of them was the music-maker. Alive, and playing music that he could feel, even at this distance. He was *controlling* the Nightflyers, bending them to his will, and Blair could feel the tenuous strains of that music touching the edges of his mind, trying to force him to submit.

He made a snap decision, and ran in the other direction, leaving the humans to deal with the problem for him. From the end of the hallway, he could hear the music-maker's voice:

"Hi. You have three seconds to get the hell out of our way, or else."

And the sound of a human's scream of pain, though Blair could sense no death-agony. Only unconscious, not dead. Then he was among the other human soldiers, trapped between them and the elven warriors behind the barricade, and realized that he had nowhere else to run.

"So far, so good," Eric murmured, leaving two of his demon army to guard the disarmed captain and his unconscious soldier. Kayla knelt next to the sprawled soldier's body, one hand on his wrist, then looked up. "He's okay, Eric."

"All right, let's go." He gave the captain a serious look. "Don't try to run, okay? If you stay put, my demons will disappear and let you go, after I've rescued my friends. Understand?"

"I'm not stupid," the captain said flatly.

Eric and Kayla half-ran down the hallway, the Nightflyers following behind them. *This is going easier than I thought,* Eric decided. *If we can disarm the rest of the soldiers like that, maybe we will survive all of this . . . at least until the Big One shakes loose from the faultline. Minutes. All we have is minutes.*

• CHAPTER SEVENTEEN

Anima Urbis: Mount Tam

Lord Dharinel, Magus Major and one-time War-leader of the elven court of Mist-Hold, did not believe in giving up.

However, at the moment, he did not see many alternatives.

They were trapped in this rabbit warren of concrete and Cold Iron, caught between two opposing forces who were armed with the best human weaponry the elvenlord had ever seen. After the initial startled clash, where the elven swords had done quite well at close range against the human guns — one rifle, sliced cleanly in half, was still on the floor near his feet — the humans had withdrawn to use their ranged weapons more efficiently. Dharinel had cast magical wards against the gunfire for as long as he had the strength, while young Korendil organized the others into building a barricade out of office equipment that was heavy enough to withstand bullets.

Now they were trapped within it, as the humans hesitated to approach within range of the swords, and the elves could not venture out beyond it, out of fear of the superior firepower. Their own ranged weapons, the bows, were all but useless in these cramped hallways. They required exposing too much of the bearer — and shots clattered uselessly off the walls and ceiling as often as not.

Dharinel fumed, impatient to end this stalemate. He strode to where Korendil crouched near the open edge of the barricade, ignoring the dizziness that made his steps unsteady — an aftereffect of too much magical channeling. "What shall we do now, young knight?" he asked tersely.

Korendil looked up, his eyes bright. "An excellent question, my lord. Perhaps if one of us charged them, to draw them out into the open . . . "

"I would not wager good odds for that first warrior's survival," Dharinel said thoughtfully. "No, we are not ready for a move that desperate yet. Korendil, go attend your human friends. I will watch for any further attacks of poisoned smoke, and deflect them from us."

"My lord." Korendil bowed slightly, and went to where the two human women were seated near the wall, very close to each other.

That was something Dharinel still could not understand — he enjoyed living in the human world, for many reasons, but he could not understand how Korendil had woven his life so thoroughly with humans. Humans were so . . . fragile. Such as the human woman with pale skin and dark red hair, who even now shuddered and cried from the effects of some incomprehensible human illness. Claustrophobia, that was the word that the dark-skinned woman had said, but the word meant nothing to him.

Still, it was Korendil's life, and however he wished to spend his time was his business. Though Dharinel privately wondered how much time any of them had left now, with the bullets singing overhead every few seconds.

He turned back to watch their enemies, around a corner of the barricade, and his eyes widened.

The human guards were walking around the corner, hands raised in the air. He recognized that as a common gesture of surrender from all the movies young Arvin had shown him. Behind them was a roiling mass of darkness, moving toward them.

What . . . It was herding them. None of them wanted to touch it. It wasn't more poisoned smoke, for it moved with purpose.

Then he saw the individual shapes within the darkness, and he realized in surprised horror that it was an army of shadow-demons.

And beside them, playing music, a faint Irish melody that he now heard over the clattering of arms, was the Bard.

"The Bard!" Dharinel shouted elatedly, then was momentarily annoyed at himself for that display of unseemly emotion. The other elven warriors gathered around the barricade, and Korendil and the two human women joined them, peering around the pile of overturned desks and cabinets.

"The Bard, the Bard!"

The Bard saw them and smiled, though he continued to concentrate on playing the melody. The dark-haired human child walked beside him for a moment, then dashed past, heading toward the others at the barricade. The older human woman caught up the child in a hug, pausing only to wipe tears from her eyes.

Dharinel also saw someone else, and it was a sight that heated his blood with quick anger. Warden Blair, described to him by the human scientist and seen in the memories of young Korendil, walking with the other captured human guards. Warden Blair, the man who was responsible for all of this.

Warden Blair, who alone of his contemporary humans had captured and held an elf — and who might come to realize what he had done. Warden Blair, the most dangerous human to elves to walk the waking earth.

With a start, Dharinel realized that Blair was the target of the Bard's melody-magic, that Eric was using his music to keep the Nightflyer-possessed human under his control.

Not bad, the elven lord thought grudgingly. *Perhaps this Bard is all that Korendil has said he could be, not merely a powerful child gifted with too much magic for his own good. He seems to have overcome this situation easily enough.*

Perhaps one of the captured human guards had that same thought at the same moment. Because, before the Bard could react, the human guard broke from the ranks of captured soldiers and leaped at him. Startled, the Bard turned too quickly, and the guard's closed fist connected with a large darkened bruise on the Bard's temple.

The Bard fell like a poleaxed horse. A moment later, his flute clattered to the floor, rolling to a stop several feet away.

A stunned silence descended upon the corridor. Dharinel saw the guard blink in surprise at his unexpected success, then turn toward the shadow-demons, as if suddenly realizing that the Bard had been the only one preventing the monsters from harming him.

The demons surged forward, and that guard was the first casualty, caught for a brief moment with his mouth open in a silent scream as the monsters descended upon him.

Dharinel brought up magical wards an instant later, though he knew that he could only hold them for a few minutes. Fighting against a single demon, he might give himself even odds in that kind of battle — against a horde of them, he knew they had no chance. And what of the others? Some of them had only the thinnest of defenses. Had the crisis foretold in all the visions begun?

The demons rose slowly, leaving nothing behind from their first victim, ignoring Warden Blair and the other guards to drift toward the unconscious Bard.

Of course, Dharinel thought, even as he fought to

bring up a ward over the Bard's body as well. *The Bard, the only one who can control and banish them, he will be their main target. Only then will they turn to feed upon us*

The Bard braced himself with one hand, painfully levering himself up to glare at the demons.

No wards, no shieldings. Nothing between him and the horde.

"Get lost," the young man said hoarsely, and Dharinel felt the rush of magic pouring from the human. His jaw dropped in disbelief, and he did not even try to close his mouth.

Like standing in the full desert sun — or beneath a pounding waterfall — now his shields were shunting some of that incredible power away, rather than warding against the demons. He noticed out of the corner of his eye that some of the lesser mages had ducked down behind the barricade to avoid being overwhelmed by the profligate strength of the young human's magic.

The Bard hadn't used the crutch of music this time, only focusing his will upon the creatures; his will, and the power that he now controlled, Dharinel sensed, with a sure if heavy-handed touch.

Silently, the mass of demons faded from view.

The young man slumped back against the floor, not moving.

Dharinel let out a breath he hadn't realized he was holding. The other human soldiers, as if recognizing how narrowly they had just escaped death, looked at one another, saw no officers among them, and took off running in the other direction, quickly disappearing around the corner.

Warden Blair stood alone, glancing from the unconscious body of the Bard to the elven warriors behind the barricade.

Korendil was the first over the barricade, vaulting over an overturned desk with a sword in hand.

Blair moved quickly, and even as Korendil ran

toward him, placed one hand on the Bard's unconscious body. Korendil skidded to a halt, sensing that
there was more here than met the eye, and poised,
sword ready, but posture betraying uncertainty.

"Harm me," a voice hissed from the human's mouth,
a voice that had the lifeless tones of the demon within it,
no longer even pretending to be human, "and I will eat
his soul before I die."

Can't we ever do something like this according to plan?
Beth Kentraine asked herself, still not quite understanding how they'd gotten themselves into *this*
situation.

She was still unsteady on her feet, shaking from the
claustrophobia attack. Elizabet had managed to stave
off part of it, but just walking down the hallways of this
place had brought back all of the living nightmares.
Just remembering that the decompression chamber
was here, several floors below her. . . .

I'm not going to lose it now. I'm not.

She heard the shouts of "The Bard!" and fought her
way to her feet — saw Eric leading an army of the
shadow-things, and let out a cry of her own. She staggered to the barrier, but by the time she got to the
barricade the situation had changed.

The thing in Blair's body — she didn't know how she
recognized that he wasn't the same scum she had faced,
but she knew it with complete certainty — held Eric's
life beneath his hand. Kory faced him, sword in hand,
but too far away to strike before the thing killed Eric. If
anyone else moved, she had no doubt that the creature
would strike.

Stalemate.

Suddenly she knew what she could do, what *only* she
could do. She was the only one with the contacts, the
training, and most importantly, the knowledge. She
was the only one that Blair would not see as a threat,

because he had already reduced her to nothing. And she greatly doubted that he would understand what she was doing.

The demon within Warden Blair was going to kill Eric in another few seconds, unless she did something, unless she . . .

. . . reached out to the impromptu coven of witches and psychics, reaching for the mind and heart of the woman she related to best: Marge Bailey, who had been made impromptu leader of the circle on Mount Tam.

They were singing and holding hands, those crazy thirteen people — Marge and Chuck and their son, Jeff and Sister Ruth, a wild long-haired singer who was into more political and religious fringe groups than Beth could count, seven more who Beth only knew as casual acquaintances but who had come through when they were needed. Even Jeff, who was pouring everything he had into this — even Sister Ruth, who was calling up a tower of light and fire. And Beth heard a faint echo of the words, something about Mount Tam, and all of this like being back in Viet Nam, with the battle coming soon . . .

. . . reached further, to the circle of power that they had been building for the last hour, and caught hold of it. The magical energy coiled down to her, making her skin tingle.

Unbelievable. Intoxicating. Riding the whirlwind, roping the lightning.

She wanted to laugh, half-drunk with the power of it, but fought for a last measure of self-control. *This must be how Eric feels, when he's controlling that unwieldy but ridiculously powerful Bardic talent of his.* She struggled with it; after a moment it seemed to recognize her and came tamely to her hand, the wild stallion willing to bear her because it pleased him.

She pushed her way past the elves, walking slowly toward Warden Blair. Permitting him to see what a tasty little chocolate eclair of Power she was — but not permitting him to see the trap behind the bait.

"Beth!" Kory called, and she glanced back at him.

He looks terrified. I bet he's afraid that I'm trying to commit suicide.

Am I?

Good question. Wish I knew the answer.

Something cold pressed against the back of Eric's neck, a touch of ice. The cold sensation dragged him up from a tangled web of pain and exhaustion, as effective as a sharp slap in the face.

Oh, please, I don't want anybody else to hit me in the face again today, he thought blearily. *I can still taste blood from the last time . . . can't I just go back to sleep now?*

He took a deep breath, about to open his eyes . . . and froze, all senses gone to red-alert.

There was a Nightflyer right next to him. An uncontrolled, full-grown, very hungry — he could sense that without even opening his eyes — and very deadly Nightflyer, not even six inches away from him.

He knew he was closer to death than he had ever been in his life. In fact, he *should* have been dead, but the thing wasn't doing anything, other than keeping one hand (*hand?*) on the back of his neck. That was what he had felt — a human hand with a Nightflyer on the other end, going through that hand to touch . . . something of his. *The source of my magic? My soul?* Whatever it was, it made him want to scream, that icy touch that cut through him to his most private self. *Warden Blair,* he realized a split-second later.

Warden Blair, and whatever is inside of him.

Calmly, calmly, he thought. *Don't want the thing to sense that I'm awake, or that I'm going to blast it into Eternity if I get half a chance. . . .*

Oh bravado.

The problem was that if he gathered any of his

Bardic magic, that *thing* would know it in the same instant, and probably kill him a second later. He knew how fast it could strike, having seen too many Nightflyer killings in his own memory and through Beth's. Maybe it was only fate, justice, that this be how he died — after having caused so many other deaths, to be served up as the Blue Plate Special to a hungry alien monster.

"Hungry, are you?" someone said, not far away from him. Eric nearly replied, *No, it's the beastie that's hungry, not me!* when he recognized Beth's voice, strained and tired.

He opened his eyes without even thinking about it.

Beth stood a few feet away, holding out her hands to Warden Blair, aglow with power. Behind her, he saw the pale faces of the elven assault team, Kory in the forefront.

"Come here, you slimy son of a bitch," Beth coaxed, a wild look in her eyes. "Don't you want me? I know you do. Here I am, I'm all yours, come and get me. Yummy, yummy, little monster."

Eric blinked, trying to reconcile the Beth standing in front of him with the Beth that he knew so well. She glittered to his magical senses, inhumanly bright with life energy, more than he'd ever seen in a single person before.

There was no doubt that the Nightflyer/Blair was drawn to that, as irresistibly as a moth to the flame. The monster yearned towards her, most of his attention off Eric.

Too bad his hand wasn't.

"You thought you'd bury us, didn't you?" Beth continued. "Bury us down in the dark with the monsters, with the walls screaming and the air too thick to breathe? Everything's burning, and all my life is on fire because of you. You're crazy, did you know that? You're as crazy as the human you took; you're infected with him, reduced to *his* level, just a bastard, just a . . . "

Blair's hand left Eric's neck. He straightened and took a step toward Beth as she spoke, and another.

"No, Bethy, don't!" Eric shouted, calling up his own power and knowing that Blair would strike before he could.

Just before Blair touched her, Beth swung her fist and connected hard on the man's jaw.

Eric Saw it then, what she'd been hiding behind her glittery, enticing surface: the instantaneous flow of magical energy from Beth, combined with the power gathered by the coven on Mount Tam, slamming down with a rushing magical roar like a triumphant orchestral chord.

Blair staggered back, silhouetted in lightless black, only a dark shape of a man with the tall cloak-like wings of a Nightflyer.

Held for one timeless instant, a moth against an arclight. A hungry moth, that had met something it couldn't eat. The Nightflyer tried to separate from Blair to save itself. Too late.

That blackened figure suddenly shattered into a thousand shards, clattering metallically on the floor around Beth with an odd musical ring.

Of Blair, there was nothing left, nothing at all.

The black pieces that had been the Nightflyer dissolved an instant later, a hundred thin trickles of dark smoke that rose slowly and faded away.

"Bastard," Beth concluded, rubbing the knuckles of her hand. "Damn, that hurt. You'd think I could've remembered how to hit somebody from all those Shotokan Karate lessons." She looked down at Eric. "Hey, Eric, you okay?"

He found his voice. "Oh yeah, sure. How 'bout you?"

"I'm . . . I'm fine . . . " She staggered, nearly falling; Kory was beside her a half-second later. She gave him a wan smile as he held her for a few seconds until she could stand unaided. "We're still alive. What a concept."

Together, they helped Eric stand up — both Eric and Beth leaning on Kory, the only one of the three of them who seemed able to stand on his own two feet without assistance. Eric leaned into their embrace, too wiped out to do anything more than hold onto them, as the elves gathered around them, silent and respectful.

We aren't done yet. Shit.

"Uh . . . " He tried to gather his thoughts, which was a remarkably difficult task at the moment. "Listen, guys, we have to get out of here . . . Blair set up the quake before we could stop him, it's going to hit any second now."

He saw panic in the human eyes, calculation in the elven, as they tried to figure out how much of the original vision might still come to pass.

"We have to stop it," Kayla said. "Dr. Susan said it'd be a major quake, very bad. She thought it could collapse this complex; what would it do to the rest of the city?"

"We can't stop an earthquake," Beth said shaking her head. "Do you know how much energy is released in a quake? It makes an atomic weapon look like a bottle bomb. We can't stop that. Nothing can stop that!"

"Not — not stop it," Eric said, wishing that his eyes would allow him to focus on his friends. Beth was still a vague blur, and looking at the elves was even worse. "Deflect it. Send part of it south, L.A. can handle a small quake. Send the rest of it out to sea, where there's nothing for a few thousand miles; a tsunami probably wouldn't hit the Orient or Hawaii from here. I hope."

"Even if it did they'd have hours of warning," Kayla said. "Plenty of time to evacuate."

"It's worth a try." Elizabet looked around at the elves, then back at Eric. "What can we do to help?"

"The Bard can gather all the energy we can give," Dharinel said firmly. "Ours, and the circle's."

Beth closed her eyes for a moment. "They're still

going strong," she said. "I don't think they even noticed when I took out Blair."

"I believe in his abilities now," Dharinel said, with a nod towards Eric. "Perhaps our power, with the human witches, will be enough."

Oh God, is it up to me again?

He picked up his flute and sat down unsteadily, Beth and Kory next to him. He closed his eyes, gathering his thoughts, trying to think how in the hell he was going to do this. Not without music, that was for sure.

Next time, I just want to call in the U.S. Cavalry. Or figure out a solution and send it FedEx to Washington D.C. I hurt too much to do this. . . .

Like a distant echo, he heard the Mount Tam group singing. The melody was unfamiliar to him, but powerful, and he followed their lead, breaking away after several measures into an improvised counter-melody. He felt the magic brightening around him, and let his mind drift down, following the near-musical resonances of the Poseidon device to where the resonances gathered and built upon each other, far below the city of Hollister, many miles away.

He quailed when he saw what he faced. It was impossible. He saw the weight of the forces at play, far beneath the surface, and knew that there was no way their group could affect those vast pressures. It was completely impossible. In another few seconds, the pressure would build to the breaking point and smash the entire Bay Area with a rippling wave of destruction. . . .

And he Saw the devastation that would bring; no Nightflyers this time, but whole neighborhoods flattened, people dead and dying. High-rise buildings breaking out in fires, trapping those who had survived inside the swaying structures. The face of Warden Blair, laughing. The man *and* the monster.

No! This is my city, my home. I'm not going to let that bastard win!

He reached out, in a way that he'd never thought to try before, to touch the others in the building around him, not just the elves and his friends, but the few remaining guards and personnel that hadn't been evacuated. Carefully, not wanting to hurt them, he drew power from them as well, then reached out further, drawing in as many of the people of the city of Dublin as he could reach —

More, farther, the people of the cities along the East Bay, across the Bay to San Francisco, south to San Jose. People, people, the huge sprawling, brawling megacomplex of people, as diverse as any place on the face of the earth.

The city. The city itself was alive, had a soul, the soul of millions of people that lived in it and loved it and wouldn't live anywhere else. And that soul had power as well. The power was deeper, more akin to the force building within the fault — and perhaps it would touch that force in a way nothing else could.

He cast the power down as quickly as he drew it, forcing the energies in the faultline to dissipate harmlessly outward, gently releasing the pressure from the merging continental plates. It was a fragile balancing act —

And a deadly one; it frightened him, knowing that if he faltered and held onto any of it for more than an instant, it would destroy him, a giant hand swatting a fruit-fly. Too much, too quickly . . . he felt caught in a vise, trapped between the pressures of the faultline and the searing magic that he channeled, suspended between the live wires of a million volts of electricity. There was no way to know whether this would work — to pause for a moment, even to check the faultline, would overset him, and he would lose his balance and his life.

Something . . . shifted . . . in the fault, and he felt it in his own bones — the rising wave of energy, the earthquake arcing out in all directions from the epicenter — he cast away the last of the magic that he was channeling, and yelled, "Hang on! Here it comes!"

The floor rippled underneath him, then vibrated sharply. He felt the rumbling turning his insides to water as the floor rolled beneath him, like a boat on stormy seas. He held onto Kory and Beth and waited for his nightmare to become reality, for the walls to crack and tumble down like the houses of San Francisco in his dream.

Suddenly, it was over. The hallway trembled one last time with a faint aftershock, then everything was quiet and calm again.

It's . . . it's over? Eric asked himself, looking around. The elves and humans were staring at each other in disbelief.

"That — that was it?" Elizabet asked in an unbelieving tone. "That's *all*?"

"I guess so," Eric said, surprise in his voice.

"It worked." Kayla grinned at him, and shot her fist ceilingward. "Yes! It worked! We did it! Yeah! Way to go, Eric!"

"Th-thanks," he said. It was hard to breathe for some weird reason, and every muscle in his body seemed to be twitching. He thought about standing up and decided against it, just as everything tilted around him.

"Eric?" Kayla's voice sounded very far away. "Eric, you okay?"

"Fine," he tried to answer, but for some reason his voice didn't seem to be working right, either.

"What is wrong with him?" he heard Korendil ask in alarm.

Eric felt the magic in Kayla's hands, though he couldn't seem to focus his eyes well enough to see the pale blue light that he knew was flickering over her hands. Kayla's voice sounded closer, stronger. "Yeah. There's just a hell of a lot of energy running through this guy, and it kind of overloaded his nervous system.

At least, that's what it feels like — touching him felt like sticking my hand in an electrical socket."

What an image. Eric thought of the commercial possibilities: Bard-O-Matic Fluorescent Light, just add magic. Barderator, take him on your camping trip and bring all your appliances. Compu-Bard, plug in your computer and use him as the backup power source.

Maybe he'd do better just to lie there and not worry about it. He felt terrible, and lying on the floor did seem like the best idea, at least for the next few minutes. This "saving the world" business wasn't all it was cracked up to be, and certainly didn't seem to be a very survivable hobby.

He lay there, half-awake or half-asleep, the healing energy warm and calming. He could almost breathe easily again, which felt marvelous. Other than that, he hurt too much to move.

Next time, he decided, *we'll just call Chuck Norris and the Delta Force. Or maybe Arnie. Or better yet, the IRS.*

Kayla straightened at last, and Korendil breathed a sigh of relief. The Bard was barely conscious, but he was no longer shivering or so deathly pale. The young healer, on the other hand, looked tired and drawn, not much better than her patient. She stood up unsteadily, muttering some human curse under her breath. "Can we go home now?" she asked plaintively, and fainted.

Kory caught her easily, and the older healer was at his side a moment later, pressing fingertips to the young girl's wrist and checking beneath her closed eyelids a moment later. "Someday she'll learn," Elizabet murmured, then spoke louder. "She's all right, just exhausted."

"We'd best leave this place before other guards arrive," Dharinel said. He gestured at two of his warriors, one who lifted Eric easily, the other who took Kayla from Kory's arms. "Help your other friend,

Korendil," the elven mage said quietly, glancing at Beth.

Kory walked closer to Beth, who was standing very still, her eyes distant. "Milady Beth, please walk with me," he said, taking her hand. She did not answer, but followed beside him as the group began to retrace their steps out of this underground maze.

They had survived. That was the first and foremost thought in his mind, that though many had been wounded in the battle, either in body or in spirit — he glanced at Beth, who walked woodenly, eyes downcast — they had all survived, against all odds. Healing would come with time, at least for the physical damage. For the wounds of spirit, he had no way of understanding what would happen.

Beth had been hurt that way, as seriously as a sword cut to the vitals, and it was only now something that he was beginning to understand.

She had survived; how long until she could be healed?

● CHAPTER EIGHTEEN

The Pleasures of Home

Kory had thought he would never again feel as terrible as he had the day he had gone off to the bulldozed Fairesite to die. He learned differently in the next few moments.

No sooner did they reach the parking lot unmolested, than reaction set in.

Physically, while he was not wounded, he was as exhausted as it was possible to be and still remain on his feet. He had a headache from a blow one of the soldiers had dealt him on the head, combined with the unaccustomed exercise of feeding Eric with mage-energy. No, not a headache; the word was not adequate for what he was enduring. There was someone standing on top of his head with spiked shoes, while driving stakes into both eyesockets, as a third person pulled every muscle in his neck and shoulders tight and tied knots in them.

Emotionally, he was a wreck. There were the minor worries, of course, about what would happen to Susan, to Kayla. And he fretted about Eric, who looked as bad as Kory felt. He was sick with fear for Beth, who had not emerged from her silence in all the long walk to the parking lot.

And there was the old fear, driven home yet again by this series of brushes with death. *Humans. They are so fragile, so easily hurt. And they die so soon. I love them, and in a few short years they will leave me forever. . . .*

Elizabet took one look at them all, and ordered them into *her* car, turning to face the waiting elvensteeds with the kind of look Kory associated with training dogs.

"You two," she said sternly. "Go home. Go *directly* home. Invisibly. No excursions. No frightening the police. Got that?"

The bikes flickered their lights, and Kory got the impression of great disappointment. "Wait a moment," he said, and they canted their wheels in his direction with a sense of anticipation.

"The humans are still in circle up on Mount Tam," he pointed out. "Perhaps they could take Melisande and Arvin there to thank them, and let them know what has occurred? The countryside is a bit rough for conventional vehicles."

Elizabet nodded. "That's reasonable," she said. "And a good idea. The others should recognize Sandy, at least. Once she kills the ears and eyes. All right, go on, then."

Recognizing that the older healer had taken charge of the war-party, Lord Dharinel nodded to the two, who leapt onto the bikes and roared off into the darkness.

"With your permission, Lady Elizabet," he said, bowing, his voice only a *little* ironic, "the rest of my people and I will go home Underhill or to our Groves. We have rest and healing to accomplish."

So they did; while Kory was unwounded, that was not true of many of the others. None of the wounds were life-threatening, but many were serious, and while they had lost no one, the unspoken message was that it had been a very near thing.

Elizabet nodded, the irony in her gesture carefully gauged to exactly match that in Lord Dharinel's voice. "If we could help you, we would," she said. "As it is —"

"As it is you are fully as weary as we, having paid your portion in full, unstinted measure," Dharinel replied. "We have somehow averted many tragedies this night, coming forth relatively unscathed. I come to the conclusion that there is value in working with mortals."

Elizabet's smile widened a little, making her look like a cat with a bowl of cream *and* a bowl of tuna in front of her — and a canary feather at one corner of her mouth. But, "Thank you, my lord," was all she wisely said.

Dharinel, just as wise, bowed again, and led his forces out into the darkness, over the grass hills, away from the roads. Elizabet turned her attention back to her captives.

"You three in the back," she ordered. "Kayla, you in the front. *Passenger* side." For once Kayla didn't object. She simply got in and leaned back against the seat with a sigh that spoke more of exhaustion than disappointment at being unable to drive.

Kory helped Eric in at one door, then got Beth installed in the middle of the bench seat. This was a newer car; mostly not of metal, and the bits of Cold Iron in the framework and engine were not enough to cause him discomfort.

He waited for one of the other four to say something after Elizabet took her place in the driver's seat, but no one did. There was a bit of a stir back at the building they'd just left, but it never got as far as the parking lot. Finally, after they got past the gate guard without incident, he leaned back and closed his eyes, with no further distractions to keep him from his troubles.

Beth stared at the patch of road between Elizabet's and Kayla's shoulders, and flexed mental muscles to see if they still hurt.

They did.

She *hadn't* gone into screaming hysterics when the quake hit; that in itself was something of a miracle. She wasn't certain that she believed it even now. She still walked that tightrope between sanity and the abyss; it wouldn't take much to shove her over. Not much at all, actually.

A room with no ventilation, a little commuter plane. An elevator.

A closet.

She'd never been weak. Eric and Kory always counted on *her* to be the strong one. How could she still face them like this, knowing that if they needed her, she might be falling apart?

In a state of numbed pain, she climbed the stairs to the house, then up to their room. She didn't even remember getting out of the car. She flung herself down on the waterbed and stared up at the high ceiling. After a while Kory and Eric came and sat on the rails beside her.

So, she wasn't so strong anymore, and now they knew it. What if they decided to arrange things so that they *wouldn't* need to count on her?

That's what really hurts, doesn't it, Kentraine? The idea that they might be able to live just fine without you?

One short step to the abyss. How could she live like that for the rest of her life? How could she live her life within the limits of a phobia?

She wanted to cry, but the tears were all gone.

I can't live like this, she thought. *I can't —*

Then don't, said the little voice in her head that always prodded her when she started thinking something really stupid. Like now. *Don't live like that. You aren't the only one in the world with claustrophobia, you know. Other people have gotten help.*

Yes, but — she wailed silently, her eyes closed against the two faces bent over hers in concern and fear. *But — But you're afraid to admit that you have weaknesses, Kentraine,* the little voice continued without remorse. *Why don't you ask those two to help you and see what happens?*

But what if they don't want to?

But what if they do? the voice answered, then fell silent.

She opened her eyes. They were still there, faces still twisted with fear, eyes bright —

"You know," she said, conversationally, a catch in her voice telling her that if she wasn't careful, she'd break down and weep after all, "you two look really funny when you're about to cry. Your faces get all red and your eyes get narrow and squinched up — "

She reached out while they were still trying to think of an answer to that and snagged their supporting arms, tumbling them into bed on either side of her.

"I've — got a problem," she said, pulling the words out of pain. "That claustrophobia thing. It's kind of a big problem, and I don't know how long it's gonna take to get over it. If I can."

"Then we work around it," Eric said promptly. "We'll see what we can do to make it better, and meanwhile we'll work around it. So if we can't take the BART some days, so what? We'll bike it, or walk. Stairs instead of elevators. Outdoor gigs. We'll manage."

"You say that now —" she began. Kory interrupted her.

"We say that for always," he replied firmly. "You do not abandon a part of you because it is sick. You help it to heal, as best it can. And if you limp, where's the harm? What," he concluded, mockingly, "did you think that all tales ended in wedding the perfect princess? What a bore if they did — "

"And what a bore to be perfect!" Eric finished.

She looked from one to the other, and finally, with a flood of relief, believed them.

"I love you two," she said, hugging them as tightly as she could. "Kiss me, you fools."

• CODA

The park was a good place to sit and read on a week-day during school hours. The only children around were toddlers. Not terribly noisy. Peaceful — and the closest she got to hiking, now.

"Nice lookin' rig you got there, li'l lady," drawled a pseudo-Texan voice.

Dr. Susan Sheffield looked up from the book she had been reading, and was blinded momentarily by the sun. When she could see again, she found she was surrounded by three people she hadn't thought she'd ever meet again.

"Thanks," she said, patting the side of the wheelchair. "I'm still trying to get used to the way people either try to pretend they aren't watching you, or try to pretend that Ahsera isn't here."

Eric smiled shyly. "I thought that might have been an elvensteed. I didn't think wheelchairs were supposed to hold mage-glow."

"Elvenpony, actually," she replied, relieved to be able to talk about it. Colonel Steve thought Ahsera was just a really high-tech chair — but then she never let him in the apartment, where the pony could raise or lower itself, or take any configuration at all to help her through her day. "Not as bright as an elvensteed — about the candlepower of a chimp, I think, without the tendency to get mad and throw feces."

"Are you getting around all right?" Beth asked. Susan took an appraising look of her own, and saw the scars of mental wounds still healing.

"As well as I can," she replied honestly. "What can I tell you? Some days I'm pretty bitter, but you know what George Burns says: living like this isn't so bad when you think about the alternative." She sighed. "And I have Ahsera here — who helps me get along pretty well in private. Colonel Steve pulled strings and got me a telecommute job at JPL. I work from my apartment."

"No more Poseidon?" Beth asked, with a shudder she could not repress.

"I sent the kernel to the Japanese," Susan said, still angry at how her vision had been perverted. "To someone I know and trust. He has a good team, and *they* don't think of earthquakes as weapons. They're going to have to go back to square one, but I think they might do better than we did. I've conferenced with some of their people, not specifically mentioning what happened here, but suggesting a terrorist scenario, and they're going to build a fail-safe into it, right from the start." She shrugged. "The package has been hedged around with so many conditions, it looks like a Hollywood contract. When they get a working model, it goes public *immediately*, and then to an international committee to watchdog it. Anybody with faults gets the probes, and the committee will make sure no faults ever build up enough stress for a quake. It's going to take them years to get where we were. And in between, quakes are still going to kill people. I can't help that. *That* is what I'm bitter about."

Eric sat down on his heels so that his face was level with hers. "So what would have been better?" he asked. "For you to have completed the project and then have *real* terrorists take it over and hold a whole *country* hostage? What would Poseidon have done in Turkey, with all those mud houses? Or one of the Slovokian republics? What if someone had taken it and used it on his *own* people — behave and do what I want, or you get a quake?"

"I'd thought about that," she admitted. "Fewer casualties the way it happened. . . . "

"But even one is too many." He straightened. "Just so you know I feel the same way."

"We did not wish to disturb you or cause you any pain," Korendil said carefully, "but Arvin said you might wish to speak with us now. Perhaps more than once."

She thought of all the elves, scatterbrained as they often seemed to be, who had rallied around her to keep her from going crazy these past few months. Arvin being the ringleader of them all —

He had *not* been the Prince Charming of her adolescent fantasy summer — in fact, when she saw him, she hardly recognized Lirylel anymore. Tastes changed . . . and he was still a teenager. But Arvin, now — intelligent, well-read, fun to be around —

— not a bad choice for a casual lover, good friend, occasional pupil. She wasn't ready for any kind of commitment of course, and if and when she made one, it was going to be with a *human*. But Arvin was a shoulder when she needed one, a cheerleader when she needed one, and he was quite inventive in the bedroom. By the time he got done experimenting, she'd have an entire repertoire ready for a steady customer. . . .

"Yeah," she said, finally. "I think I'd like to see you guys once in a while. If you wouldn't mind inviting me over to your place, that is. *Mine* doesn't have a hot tub."

Kory smiled, Beth sighed in relief, and Eric gave her the high-sign. "You're on," Eric said. "How about Saturday? We're hosting an elven full moon party. Ahsera would be right at home. We're having Greek carry-out." He lowered his voice, enticingly. "And homemade baklava."

It had been a *long* time since she'd had Greek food. The hospital hadn't allowed her anything but bland with lots of fiber.

"Is Arvin invited?" she asked.

"We invited him, but he said he didn't want to come without you," Beth replied, with a ghost of a grin. "I don't know what you're doing to him. His harem is down to less than a dozen."

Susan threw back her head and laughed, long and hard, earning startled glances from the nannies around her.

They probably think handicapped people shouldn't have any fun, she thought, but without bitterness this time.

"All right, I'll tell him tonight it's a date." She stretched a little. "Do I bring anything?"

"Retsina if you can find it," Beth said firmly. "Ouzo if you can't. Only a little — a little of that stuff goes a long way. Two bottles, max. We never get anywhere near liquor stores without a zillion instruments to carry."

Susan smiled. They hadn't patronized her by telling her "nothing," and hadn't insulted her by asking for something too simple. She'd have to go looking for Retsina, if only in the yellow pages, and either send someone out to pick it up for her, or get it herself.

"I'll take care of it," she promised, both herself and them. "Don't worry about it."

Eric grinned as the other two nodded. "I won't."

Somehow she got the feeling that they meant that the words applied to more than a simple bottle of wine.

For that matter, so did she.